Sleeping in SATAN'S DEN

Folk Stories and Scary Tales of Eastern Kentucky

Compiled by Kimberly Kozee, a Dreamer

Authorized manual of interpretation for
agents of Alpha Domini only
Lurlene Joy McCoy

Kim Kozee

First Edition

PAGE PUBLISHING
Conneaut Lake, PA

First originally published by Page Publishing 2023

ISBN 979-8-89157-262-1 (pbk)
ISBN 979-8-89157-295-9 (digital)

Printed in the United States of America

To Mr. Bill, who walked with
me up Spook Holler.
He wrestled his own sin when
the Giggle Hounds came.
Now he walks in righteousness with his
Savior on Heaven's Golden Shores.

No honor be to Satan,
Who doth plague my dreams.
All glory be to God,
Who chaseth away my screams?

—Aunt Tildy, 1847

Defile not yourselves in any of these things: for in all these the nations are defiled which I cast out before you: and the land is defiled: therefore I do visit the iniquity thereof upon it. And the land itself vomiteth out her inhabitants.

—Leviticus 18:24–25 (KJV)

Contents

Warning!

The book you hold in your hands contains both thrills and chills intended for entertainment purposes. While real people, places, and events, in some instances, are used as the bases for these stories, much of what you will read is fiction. Actual research and factual information from both religious and secular viewpoints are presented in the sections that follow each story. The notes of Lurlene Joy McCoy contain a compilation of both fictional presentation and situations and very real facts that can be found in textbooks, internet searches, and resources as indicated. Caution is STRONGLY ADVISED in pursuing a deeper look at some of the websites and resources mentioned as they can be HARMFUL TO THOSE WHO DO NOT HAVE A BALANCED UNDERSTANDING OF THE SUBJECT MATTER. Personal research for the supporting evidence required me to walk in some very dark places in an effort to provide an educated presentation with as little bias as possible. Do not take any one fact or statement to be reflective of my opinion or belief. As a follower of Christ, my loyalties lie with scriptural evidence. Being a sinner saved by grace, I am drawing upon previous experience with things of the supernatural from my journey to find God. I am not proud of my past; neither do I take pride in having overcome my past. But for God's calling upon my life to be a scholar and His revelation of the truth of His Word, I would be a far different person than I have become. While I could be really nice and give away all my secrets and the names of people, the locations, and the circumstances of events, I won't. Photographs, diagrams, and other accompanying illustrations are from personal files and will not be identified unless it is personally mine to give. Anything that is in public domain will be credited. This is to protect reputations and eliminate any fact-finding fodder an unscrupulous mind could use against the innocent. Not that anyone would do that! If you happen to be "in on" one or more of the truths presented in word or illustration, please *keep it to yourself unless you are adding to the fun!* History and heritage are important for understanding who we are and what we could become.

Life is a series of choices—some good, some bad, some utterly destructive. There is always a choice. The best choice is Jesus Christ as Lord and Savior. All other choices are temporary and carnal. "This, too, shall pass" is not in the Bible, but "It came to pass" is. Each passing led either to salvation through obedience to God or to destruction through disobedience. Hence, all stories are moral tales—whether they are described as fiction or nonfiction (and let's face it, there is a lot of fiction in nonfiction nowadays), yet a kernel of truth lies within each. Truth is *not* relevant. It is the same for all. It is unwavering. If it is twisted for individual relevancy, it is not truth. That is why we like chills and thrills. They test us. They scare us. We like to face death and walk away, wanting more. But what if, one day, you go back for more, only to find yourself…sleeping in Satan's Den?

—Kim Kozee, 2022

In the deeper magic of Narnia stirs truth that will take us to the brink of Mordor and reveal to us how Paradise Lost can be regained.

Deven and Marcus:

Our separate paths have converged for a time and are now diverging once more. You were privileged to become aware of AD as very few outsiders in the history of time have ever been. We are all soldiers in an endless war in which we must choose our champion. Only one has already won the war, but the other continues to battle uselessly. His goal is to take as many soldiers as possible down with him. There are those who have no clue they are in battle because they obey in blindness and declare it their right. Others intentionally seek out and choose their master with ulterior motives. The remainder are those who seek out truth but become caught up in the melee of confusion in which no one knows whom they are fighting for because the enemy has so completely camouflaged himself in the mirage of truth that it is indistinguishable without discernment. In your time with my sister, nieces, and myself, I pray you have begun to develop that discernment. Remember, God created the tools, but it is the devil who perverted them. Choose your weapons carefully. Fighting fire with fire may put out the flames, but it doesn't remove the fuel that could reignite the flame. It only takes a spark to get a fire going. Make sure your fire has the ultimate fuel to quench the deceptive spirit of the enemy you face. Perhaps our paths will merge again. Until then, remain armed and faithful.

—Lurlene Joy McCoy

Welcome to Satan's Den!

The place we go to in our dreams. A place of vulnerability. A place where we chase—or are chased by—our fears and concerns. When we wake up knowing we dreamed, but can't remember it, we shake it off and get a cup of coffee to get our day started. When the shadow of a dream remains, without any real recognition, just a nagging feeling, it takes a cup of coffee and a hot shower to wake us up and refocus on better things. When the dreams refuse to leave the shadow of your thoughts, or you wake up gasping for breath, it's harder to let go. It follows you throughout the day. The worst are when you wake up screaming, crying out for help, sweat pouring down your brow, or you fail to wake up at all because you are paralyzed in your fear. Most of the time, these dreams can be put off as a bit of Scrooge's bad beef or watching a horror film before going to bed. Sometimes, it is something much worse, something an antacid or comedy before bed can cure. Such are the stories of Satan's Den, a small town infested by poor choices and the evil that fed and bred humanity's basest desires. There is a very real name for this place, but it is best known as Satan's Den. Don't try to figure out where it is on a map. You may just discover your own hometown!

The New Generation

Power, like a desolating pestilence,
Pollutes whate'er it touches.

—Shelley, *Queen Mab, III*

Tragedy isn't new. Read your newspaper. Watch the televised news networks. Check social media. So often, tragedy comes in numbers—cost in lives, property destruction, level of depravity, or of special interest by fringe groups looking to make an outrage of violence into a political statement that may or may not change the future and prevent further tragedies of such a nature. Tragedy happens, even when we hear nothing about it. The quiet desperation of a suicidal individual is more likely to go unnoticed than the car crash that killed a local family or a mass shooting at a public event that made national news. International tragedies are often given more media play as a means of indoctrinating current political agenda than to infuriate humanity to be and make a change in their tiny worlds that could create a ripple effect of kindness and love that could end these senseless woundings. Alas, human freedom of will revolves around self and not others. Feeding our base desires for physical pleasure, intellectual stimulation, and power over ourselves to the exclusion of others blinds us to a Greater Power that washes away the pain of self-pursuit and bathes us in peace unending as we serve one another in the name of love.

On the outskirts of the town of Satan's Den, along the lonely road that comes from the faster-paced civilization of larger domains, with far larger concerns than an ancient hillside stripped of its fossil past and abandoned to die in peace, the curious traveler can see the remains of the Stevens Gas N Go, once a combination country grocery and filling station, the only convenience store locals could claim before the term *convenience store* was ever applied to those in-town gas stations and places to buy cigarettes, combinations that aren't all that convenient if prices were really taken into account. It was this last chance for gas "till you get to the city" or "best place for groceries and a bologna sandwich" that brought the curse that is Satan's Den into the twenty-first century and reminded the people that sometimes superstition is very real.

In fact, every attempt made to raze the ruins or to carry away a "souvenir" has ended only in tragedy or destruction of one sort or another. Equipment brought in to tear down the building or unearth the still full gas tanks below the rotting pavement either refuses to run or rusts into scrap overnight. Security guards set to watch over the site have lost their mind, gone missing, or committed suicide there. Items taken by thrill seekers are returned in the wake of a death or life-shattering event. Superstition has grown to cult status here but has failed to teach the lesson intended. So a new generation must learn the lesson anew.

It was a delightful spring morning when the rattletrap busload of newly graduated young adults pulled into the small, graveled parking area next to the paved gas pump area directly between the road and the two-story cinder block building nestled against a densely wooded hillside. Rowdy young people spilled through the ancient bus doors, alerting the host family that their expected guests had arrived. The driver was the last to exit and left the door open invitingly, knowing it would be a long time before the bus would be filled with weary partygoers ready to return to the high school where they had left their cars.

The proprietor set aside the notepad he had been writing on; the pencil slid easily behind his left ear. He crossed the floor to the simple screen door that served as the front entrance to the store. The door squeaked as it opened, and he set out to greet his son's guests. "Come on around back," he called. "Your supplies are ready. If you need anything else, just holler."

Behind the lonely gas station stood a wild tangle of trees; a single, subtle path split the unbroken underbrush. A mountain of party supplies melted as anxious young people loaded themselves down and followed Andy Stevens into the cool darkness of the unknown. Goose bumps rose as the warm morning sun was replaced by dark shade. Young men and women shivered as they bumped against one another and wise-cracked about geese dancing on their graves as their crazy old grandparents used to say.

The deep gloom of a never-ending path was suddenly split by the shimmering sun fighting with the treetops that suddenly gave way to a glorious glade of wildflowers surrounding an inviting pool of idyllic blue-green water. Gasps of surprise and wonder peppered the warm air.

"I told you it was a great place for a party." Andy Stevens grinned proudly. "It's a wonder that this place has remained a secret for so many years. I've lived here my whole life, and I didn't know it was here."

They wasted no time setting up a shaded area with card tables and picnic supplies. Coolers were placed in the shade to preserve the ice, cool their sodas, and protect the lunch meat and cheese from spoiling. Blankets and towels staked out prime locations, and clothing littered the grass as the water called to sunbathers and swimmers alike. Bodies scattered; a splash and giggle started the party as someone was thrown into the water unexpectedly. A radio operated by long-life batteries snapped on, volume leveled to heart-pounding, tree-shaking level.

New graduates from a government-imposed educational system to the freedom they perceived adulthood to be, they sought one last fling before going their separate ways, perhaps forever. The rickety bus that brought them to this small paradise belonged to Andy Stevens, purchased just for this day. Though never popular, Andy was well-liked enough, by experience or reputation, for this many of his classmates to have come at his invitation. The naturally shy young man felt flattered and hoped to get better acquainted with some of them before the end of their era.

Andy's father had agreed to provide refreshments free of charge for the small army as long as Andy agreed to work off the expense summers and holidays throughout college. Scholarships were paying his tuition.

Andy enjoyed his king-for-a-day status as even the most popular couple in school applauded his generosity. The only thing that would make his day complete would be to gain the attention and affection of the only woman he would ever love—Elizabeth Ann Suder, the shy and beautiful daughter of the Methodist minister. The object of his delight sat beneath a shade tree, watching the others. Sometimes she would lean forward and whisper something into Mandy Sowards's ear. Elizabeth and Mandy had been best friends since kindergarten. He had done all this for *her*.

The day grew stiflingly hot for early spring. Those not swimming took refuge in the shade, cold sodas in hand. Flies began gathering around filled-to-overflowing garbage bags and tasting abandoned sandwiches. Talk turned to plans for the future, with many attending colleges in the fall. A few couples were making wedding plans. Entering the workforce of the humble and lesser-skilled was the destiny of those who remained. Those who had chosen not to attend this party were already working, preparing for an obscure existence at the government's expense, or were just doomed to fade from existence in this small town.

The sun grew relentless as the afternoon faded and evening approached. Canned or bottled soda was replaced with smuggled alcohol, carried in by the daring few who had already walked the wild side and would likely become alcoholics early in life, if life did not otherwise intervene. Some of the alcohol had been purchased illegally in another town; some were homegrown and processed secretly by disreputable moonshiners in questionable stills. Bottles and jars were passed among knots of young people who were not otherwise imbibing beer. Those not partaking of the "adult beverages" satisfied themselves with lukewarm bottled water or sodas that had never met the melting ice. Someone turned the radio to a soft rock station, more conducive to possible romantic hookups, however brief. A few less-inhibited couples began to slow-dance or make out.

Without warning, the sultry air cooled. Andy decided it was time for excitement. With a primal scream, he ran out onto the sturdy diving board at the deepest end of the pond, gave a single powerful jump into the air, rebounded, and plunged headfirst into the darkening water. The light from a well-fed bonfire lit the water where Andy had gone under. Tiny bubbles rose to the surface, then ceased to exist. Everyone watched, waiting for him to resurface. Moments of anticipation ticked agonizingly by. The pond was still.

"Andy!" Elizabeth Ann gasped, now standing midway between her favored tree and the edge of the water.

The former captain of the football team rushed forward and dove into the water. A moment later, he resurfaced, Andy in tow. By the time they reached the grassy beach, Andy was gasping and sputtering murky water from his blue lips.

Slowly, everyone returned to trying to have fun before the night completely ended and real life began. A few brave souls even returned to the water, skirting the diving board. A full moon illuminated the clearing, preventing too many intimate spaces. The near tragedy was forgotten.

Elizabeth Ann watched the revelry from her blanket where she had pulled it into the moonlight. Mandy had paired off with Roger Skaggs. Most everyone had been in the water at some point, but Elizabeth Ann couldn't swim. She watched a group play some kind of dunking game near the diving board, with Andy being the chief dunker. She never would have believed Andy to be so outgoing if she hadn't seen it for herself. Andy had always been so quiet.

Midnight approached; the games and dancing continued. Food was left forgotten for insects and night creatures to feast on.

"Elizabeth Ann, come join us," a voice called from the water.

Elizabeth Ann searched the moonlit shadows to identify the speaker. Mandy waved at her from the water's edge. Elizabeth Ann waved back and shook her head no. Mandy knew she couldn't swim; why would her best friend be asking her to get into the water?

A group of the popular girls surrounded Elizabeth Ann. Peggy Marshall, recently abdicated head cheerleader, extended her hand to Elizabeth Ann. "Come on," she said. "It's your turn. Everyone else has already done it."

When Elizabeth Ann declined once more, two of the girls, both former cheerleaders, grabbed her by the arms and hauled her to her feet. As they began to drag her toward the water, she started to struggle, unsure of how far they would go in their game.

"Really, I can't swim," Elizabeth Ann protested. "I don't like water deeper than my ankles. I even shower rather than sit in a tub."

The girls continued in their determined task. Elizabeth Ann struggled harder. More of the girls took hold of her. Elizabeth Ann began to scream in panic and terror. The hands around her arms tightened their grip, leaving indentations from their matching French tip manicures.

"Wait!"

Everything seemed to stop. Even the radio lost all power. The night was dead silent.

Andy pushed his way through the crowd. Angry stares moved from Andy to Elizabeth Ann and back. Andy motioned to the cheerleaders holding Elizabeth Ann. They released her reluctantly and rather harshly, snarling as they jerked their hands away, adding deep scratches to the bruising indentations. Elizabeth Ann rubbed her arms where welts were rising and beginning to bleed heavily.

Andy gently ran icy fingers down Elizabeth Ann's cheeks, wiping away the tears of fear. Elizabeth Ann began shivering uncontrollably. Andy placed his arm around her shoulders and led her to the bonfire, where he sat her gently down on a log placed there for that very purpose. An anonymous hand thrust a blanket through the crowd. Andy took it and wrapped it tenderly around Elizabeth Ann's shoulders. Her T-shirt and modest shorts were wet from the water dripping from her assailants during their assault and ensuing struggle.

"No one," Andy addressed the crowd angrily and sternly, "is to touch her! *She* is mine!"

Grumbles rose from the crowd. Peggy Marshall roared in indignation, "Why should *she* remain uninitiated."

Andy stared unforgivingly into Peggy's eyes. Peggy stared back defiantly until the anger turned to fear, and she had to look away. Andy put his arm around Elizabeth Ann once more, protectively.

Elizabeth Ann shivered again, this time in fear of the young man beside her.

"Elizabeth Ann," Andy whispered, "I never intended to hurt you. I have always loved you from the first time I saw you in middle school."

Elizabeth Ann's eyes widened. She had no idea Andy felt that way. She had always liked him but never suspected this.

"Now," Andy continued, "I can have you as my own, and no one will ever hurt you. That is why you must remain uninitiated. I want you to come to me in your natural purity, desiring me as your own, by your own choice."

"Wh-wh-what?" stammered Elizabeth Ann.

Andy laughed a deep and brutal laugh. "These *people* are *mine* to command. It was promised to me. *We* have been chosen as the first acolytes to the god of the pond. *I* am *their* chief priest. As such, I am exercising my right to choose my own mate. I have chosen *you*, Elizabeth Ann Suder. Our children will be the children of our god!"

Elizabeth Ann stared speechlessly in horror. Andy stood with his hands raised in praise and adoration. She couldn't believe what she was hearing. The enraptured audience around her began to sway and chant, their eyes closed. Andy's back was to her.

With lightning flair, Elizabeth Ann jumped to her feet, the blanket falling to the ground around her, and bolted toward the path that would take her back to the Stevens' home and, hopefully, safety. She entered the encompassing darkness just as her would-be captors discovered she was gone. She dove deeper into the woods, praying she would not fall from the path or be ensnared by grasping branches. The voices of her pursuers echoed through the trees. Elizabeth Ann fled blindly in the direction she believed to be her haven, brushing past thorny bushes and skirting giant tree trunks that seemed to loom up before her. She prayed her sneakers would not come untied or snag on an unseen source.

After what seemed like hours, Elizabeth Ann broke free of the trees and into the narrow yard behind the gas station. She stumbled across the yard to the steps that would take her up to the family apartment above the Gas N Go. She gasped deeply for air as she dragged herself up the steps.

Mrs. Stevens answered the incessant pounding on the door. Gently, she led the hysterical young woman into the kitchen. Cradling Elizabeth Ann like a child, she cooed calming thoughts into Elizabeth Ann's ear. A cup of hot coffee was thrust into Elizabeth Ann's trembling hands by Mr. Stevens, who sat across from her at the small kitchen table, his smile meant to reassure her.

Elizabeth Ann began to babble about the danger she was in and the need to leave immediately. Mr. and Mrs. Stevens smiled condescendingly and continued to try to soothe her.

A click echoed as a door from another part of the apartment was opened. Shuffling footsteps announced the arrival of a small group of people, filing along the hallway. Elizabeth Ann froze as Peggy and her sycophants entered the room. Evil lingered in Peggy's eyes, and a maniacal grin appeared when she saw Elizabeth Ann.

"You *will* be one of us," she hissed and reached for Elizabeth Ann.

Elizabeth Ann screamed and threw the steaming hot cup of coffee at Peggy. Peggy screeched as hot coffee splattered over her, scalding the skin exposed by her very skimpy bikini. Elizabeth Ann darted past Peggy and down the hallway. She found the doorway that led down to the grocery below and threw herself to the mercy of the dark stairs.

Never having been in the little grocery, she fell over stacked shelves in her attempt to reach the moonlit door to the outside. The muddy sludge on her sneakers caused her to skid across the floor and into the deli counter. Regaining her feet, she staggered toward the door. Shouts and footsteps from upstairs alerted her to the approach of danger. She began fumbling with the ancient locks on the door. She managed to unlock the last one as the first of her pursuers descended the stairs. She flung open the door and tossed herself into the open air.

Where could she go? There was very little traffic on this road this time of night. She had come on the bus with the others and had no idea if the keys had been left on the bus or if she could even drive it if they had been. Running was out of the question. She looked around for some other solution. Spotting several gas cans next to the soda machine, she prayed they were full. Grabbing the closest one, she tossed it aside when it proved to be empty. The second can felt to be half full. Taking it, and the very full third can, she moved to the entryway. She shoved the full can over onto its side after removing the lid to allow the gasoline to pour freely across the threshold. She opened the second can and tossed it as far into the dark store as she could. She heard it bounce on the floor, followed by a *thunk* and the satisfying glurp of gasoline pushing its way out.

Now she realized her dilemma. How was she to light a fire without a match? She ran to the bus. Possibly someone had left a match or lighter on the bus. Some of them had been smoking, and not just tobacco. Finding none, she looked around her. Mr. Stevens's battered pickup truck was parked across the lot. She dashed from bus to truck, trying desperately to stay close to the ground.

A cigarette lighter lay on the dashboard, next to a pack of cigarettes. Elizabeth Ann reached through the open window and snatched the lighter. The first of her former friends and classmates stood in the doorway, watching her. They parted as Andy moved forward. His smile seemed so sane and rational. Elizabeth Ann hesitated where she stood.

"Elizabeth Ann," Andy cried. "I love you! Come back to me. You have nothing to fear from me or these others. I will protect you."

"No!" screamed Elizabeth Ann. "You're all crazy! I want no part of this! Get back, or I will set that gasoline on fire!"

Andy motioned his followers back into the darkness. He stepped out into the dim light of the security light. Elizabeth Ann stood terrified next to the pickup. Andy stepped closer to her. Elizabeth Ann prayed under her breath, "Lord Jesus, help me!"

"Elizabeth Ann," the familiar little-boy voice cried, "help me! I don't know what is happening to me. This *thing* is inside my head, and it won't leave!"

Elizabeth Ann began to cry. Was it really Andy, or was it the *Thing* trying to fool her?

Andy stepped closer, his arms held open, his eyes pleading. "Come to me. Only you can help me."

Elizabeth Ann took an uncertain step toward Andy. He certainly *seemed* sincere. Another step took her closer. She felt drawn to him. Her steps continued, closer and closer. Andy continued pleading with her hypnotically. She began to feel she was losing control.

Just as she drew close enough to embrace him, she suddenly jerked to the side and dropped to the ground. Sitting on the pavement, she brought the lighter to life. Leaning forward, she just managed to reach a puddle of gasoline in the doorway. Instantly, a fire exploded in screams of agony from the people inside.

"No!" screamed Andy. "You've ruined everything!" He dashed into the flames as if to pull his companions from the fire.

A passing car swerved into the parking lot just as Andy disappeared into the flames. The driver leaped from the car and dragged a distraught Elizabeth Ann to safety. A passenger in the car used her cell phone to call for help on the spotty signal notorious on this strip of road. In moments, it seemed, the little parking lot was filled with flashing lights, fire trucks, police cruisers, and a single ambulance. Elizabeth Ann and her rescuers had been evacuated from the scene in case the gas pumps themselves became involved. There would be questions to answer later.

The next morning dawned to a smoldering scene of contained fire being allowed to burn itself out, while firefighters kept it at bay from the real danger of an underground explosion. Only a miracle had prevented that very thing so far. Elizabeth Ann had been questioned and sent to the closest hospital for treatment. There were no clear explanations as the driver and his wife had only seen the young man run into the building and had pulled Elizabeth Ann from harm's way. Mysteriously, the fire that destroyed the Stevens Gas N Go had set off on a narrow path through the woods, destroying nothing around it until it reached a strange clearing that appeared out of nowhere. Here, the fire had consumed all life and left only a murky sludge at the base of a singed diving board.

The town eventually recovered. The clearing became known as the Devil's Drink. People who knew better avoided that spot. Elizabeth Ann never returned to Satan's Den.

Oh! As to the lesson to be learned, there are three ways we are tempted into evil: the lust of the mind, the lust of the body, and the lust of the spirit, also called the pride of life. Poor Andy lusted for the attention of Elizabeth Ann, whom he was too shy to speak to. When he was offered the power to get her, in his mind, he genuinely believed he could have her simply by giving in to the spirit that discovered his weakness. As a result, Andy gave in to the worship of this evil that hungered only for souls and cared nothing for humanity. The lesson here is when lust stirs your soul, mind, and body, only Jesus can prevent forest fires.

Numbers 16:23–33 (NKJV)

> So the Lord spoke to Moses saying. "Speak to the congregation, saying 'get away from the tents of Korah, Dathan, and Abiram.'"
>
> Then Moses rose and went to Dathan and Abiram and the elders of Israel followed him. And he spoke to the congregation, saying, "Depart now from the tents of these wicked men! Touch nothing of theirs lest you be consumed in all their sins." So, they got away from around the tents of Korah, Dathan, and Abiram; and Dathan and Abiram came out and stood at the door of their tents, with their wives, their sons, and their little children.
>
> And Moses said, "By this you shall know that the Lord has sent me to do all these works, for I have not done them of my own will. If these men die naturally like all men, or if they are visited by the common fate of all men, then the Lord has not sent me. But if the Lord creates a new thing, and the earth opens its mouth and

> swallows them up with all that belongs to them, and they go down alive into the pit, then you will understand that these men have rejected the LORD."
>
> Now it came to pass, as he finished speaking all these words, that the ground split apart under them and the earth swallowed them up, with their households and all the men with Korah, with all their goods. So, they, and all with them went down alive into the pit; the earth closed over them, and they perished from among the assembly.

Leviticus 4:24

For the Lord your God is a consuming fire, a jealous God.

- Jealousy here does not mean envy, as is most often the modern translation. God is not envious of something that He created. That kind of jealousy exists only in the minds of those who choose their own desires over those of God. God is *jealous for us.* It's right there at the end of the word—*jealous*. It represents God's desire for us to choose Him over the things of this word that we deceive ourselves into believing are greater than God. These things become our gods, our false idols. They detract us from the truth of God's love for us. When we remain unrepentant, despite God's warning, God *will* remove those things in your life that can never love you the way He does. If you continue to remain unrepentant, like Korah, Dathan, and Abiram, God will take everything you have from you, even your life. This is not a lack of love; it is because of love. We don't always know God's plan for us; that is why we need faith and trust in Him. Is it worth an all-consuming fire to cleanse your life of idle idols? If God is seen as the loving Father who wants what's best for His children? Yes, it is.

Notes by Lurlene Joy McCoy

On the surface, this account is pretty cut-and-dried. It is a common message—comply or die. Conform or die. Go with the flow or be drowned. Any way it's put, death is the only way to avoid the discomfort of selling your soul in order to be free.

Plot proof: A young man plans a party for his classmates, and it goes terribly wrong simply because one girl refuses to party like a rock star.

Breaking it down, however, raises some critical questions that should be addressed.

Q. Did Andy Stevens know what was going to happen, so he transported his classmates by bus to keep them from escaping?

A. Initially, it appears that he did not know what was happening as he had to be rescued from an apparent near-death experience in the water. He even stated that he had lived on the property his entire life and had not known the pond was there until just weeks earlier. While shy, he possessed enough charisma to convince even the most popular of his classmates to attend this party, along with most of the class itself. Popularity had never been his prior to this time. Why now? His parents also seemed to be aware of the ulterior motive for the party as they not only supplied the refreshments at what would have been great cost to them as small business owners, verging on bankruptcy at the whim of the cost of running a business, but they also remained awake and prepared throughout the night. Elizabeth Ann was welcomed with words of comfort, a hot cup of coffee, and gentle hugs, though she was hysterical—not the greeting you would have expected from concerned parents awakened by a desperate pounding at the door.

Q. Wouldn't Andy have preferred a more submissive mate, someone "initiated" to understand and accept his new authority better?

A. Normally, yes. The girl would be "initiated," "indoctrinated," "brainwashed" into submission, allegedly to her own credit. Instead, Andy admired Elizabeth Ann for her spiritual purity, which he translated into earthly beauty and desirability. She appeared vulnerable and timid. His position of authority should have drawn her to him to find strength in him. It didn't. Peggy Marshall, however, was drawn by the power she could wield as consort to the chief, so she tried to undermine Andy's plans for Elizabeth Ann. Neither motive was of concern to anyone but themselves. Elizabeth Ann was merely a pawn. If Andy had developed a real relationship with Elizabeth Ann years before, this story could have ended differently. Then again, Elizabeth Ann could have discovered this obsessive quality for ownership in Andy and turned away from him. Did he truly desire to "own" Elizabeth Ann, or was it that he desired a real relationship of mutual love and respect that was twisted and perverted by the god of the pond? Only God knows. Would Elizabeth Ann have "come around" and accepted Andy as her "chief priest and mate"? With enough deprivation and torture, it is possible. Think Stockholm syndrome here. Praise God that question did not have to be explored.

Q. Who or what was behind this madness?

A. I would automatically respond, "the Prince of this Earth" (Ephesians 2:1–3). Otherwise, this is debatable, depending on your own understanding of and beliefs about the universe, God, and the supernatural. In the Middle and Far East, you will find references to elemental beings and beings that can control the earth's elements. Genies, for example, like dragons, are often associated with the element of fire. They can use fire against their enemies readily but are not made of fire themselves. The Golem of Prague, in Jewish tradition, was made of clay, an earth material, but was brought to life by inscribing the word *truth* upon it, and its existence ended by changing the Hebrew word for *truth* into *death*. A true elemental is made up of the element itself and can shapeshift into any appearance yet remain fully that element. In this case, a water elemental, or undine, could have made its way to this location via underground water routes, finding that particular location vulnerable and receptive of its presence. It set about creating an attractive environment that would draw in the perfect prey for establishing its "kingdom." Andy and his family fit the bill. When Andy stumbled on this restructured clearing, he likely was confused as it had not previously existed in this way. It may not have even been a clearing but simply a break where two hills converged. Its power of persuasion and temptation combined with human curiosity and confusion led Andy and his family to investigate and believe in a false miracle. Availability led to the choice of Andy as the young and potentially virile "chief priest." It fed and fueled his desire to be with Elizabeth Ann. It made promises that would give Andy not only what he thought he singularly desired but what would give him the power to keep and control what he wanted without the interference of others. Andy's own insecurity was given fodder for domination of others to get the security he desired from others. This set off the disastrous decline of a single generation, resulting in this great tragedy.

Q. Elizabeth Ann set fire to the Gas N Go, knowing her classmates were inside. That explains the burned-out ruins. But how did the fire travel from the building to the clearing without setting off a massive wildfire in the process?

A. Again, this could be debated with scientific speculation and superstitious theory at one another's throats, though I believe it was the hand of God that drew that very controlled path from inferno to idolatrous altar so that only what had been contaminated by the demonic elemental and the elemental itself was destroyed and what was left cleansed. Like the righteous fire from heaven rained upon Sodom and Gomorrah, the fire destroyed the source of sin and those affected by it, leaving a cleansed location, free to be recreated naturally, according to the laws established by God. The spirit of disobedience, however, remains to haunt those who wish to either rekindle it or to test its power by attempting to alter what has been wrought.

Q. What about Elizabeth Ann? Was she ever charged with arson and/or murder?

A. All records I have been able to locate and access indicate that Elizabeth Ann was taken to the hospital for treatment for burns she received while igniting the fire as well as the wounds of her fight and flight. While there, she was evaluated for psychological impact and PTSD due to panic and fits of hysteria. Those findings were used to deter all charges filed against her by concerned and angry families as she was not competent to stand trial and respond to those accusations. Her own trauma was far too great. All those who accused her of being "a cold-hearted killer who premeditated the arson in order to get revenge on the classmates she was so clearly jealous of" were forced to live with the dissatisfaction of "lack of justice." With only the story being told firsthand by Elizabeth Ann and hearsay of those close to the situation, there were no grounds for prosecution, only the persecution of social media, local gossip, personal opinion, and those who played both sides as a means of keeping the embers hot as long as possible for the entertainment of small minds. Elizabeth Ann's family left town quietly, without a forwarding address, to alleviate the stigma attached to them in general and to their faith system in particular. Though the land was cleansed of an evil presence at the Gas N Go, the evil remained in the lives of those who failed to heed the harbinger and embraced the enemy. Barring a trial, Elizabeth Ann was placed in a long-term mental health treatment facility for therapeutic assistance and preparation for returning to life outside the facility, if possible. Her fear of water has escalated into serious hygienic issues as well as daily living interferences as she cannot participate in any activity requiring water—washing clothing or dishes, food preparation, etc.—that could enable her to be placed in a recovery home with supervision. She cannot eat any food that is thin or watery in nature, like soup. Consuming any beverage that has the appearance of water or has water as a base sets off a psychotic break that has led to serious issues of hydration and weight loss on her already slender frame. At the opposite end of the spectrum, she has developed a severe phobia of fire, lapsing into catatonia or violent acting out at the mere suggestion or perception of smoke around her. She insists on daily fire drills and demands her room be equipped with a fire-escape ladder, though she is on a first-floor unit, and her window cannot be opened. When in these distraught states, she may require isolation and sedation with a care technician always monitoring her. Oddly, she has not given up her personal religious beliefs and spends her calmer moments in prayer and Bible study, giving God thanks for protecting her and bringing her through the fiery trial of refinement.

Topic: Elementals

Source: Wikipedia

Summary

- Mythic beings described in occult and alchemical works from around the time of the European Renaissance and particularly elaborated in the sixteenth-century works of Paracelsus.
  - Four categories of elementals
    - Gnomes
    - Undines
    - Sylphs
    - Salamanders
  - Correspond to the four Empedoclean elements of antiquity
    - Earth
    - Water
    - Air
    - Fire
- Paracelsian concept of elementals extend from several much older traditions in mythology and religion.
  - Folklore
  - Animism
  - Anthropomorphism
- "Pygmy" from Greek mythology.

- Earth, water, air, and fire classed as fundamental building blocks of nature.
- System prevailed in Classical world was highly influential in medieval nature philosophy.
- "Homunculous," a Paracelsian idea with roots earlier in alchemical, scientific, and folklore traditions.
- Paracelsus
    - Sixteenth-century book *A Book of Nymphs, Sylphs, Pygmies, and Salamanders, and on the Other Spirits*
    - Identified mythological beings as belonging to one of the four elements
    - Wrote the book to "describe the creatures that are outside the cognizance of the light of nature, how they are to be understood, what marvelous works God has created."
    - (There is more bliss in describing these "divine objects" than in describing fencing, court etiquette, chivalry, and other worldly pursuits.)
    - Archetypal beings.
      Gnome, being of earth
      Undine, being of water
      Sylph, being of air
      Salamander, being of fire
- Concept of elementals seems to have been conceived by Paracelsus in the sixteenth century—did not use the term *elemental* or German equivalent.
- Regarded them as beings between creatures and spirits, generally being invisible to mankind but having physical and commonly humanoid bodies, as well as eating, sleeping, and wearing clothes like humans.
- Gave common names for the elemental types, as well as correct names, which he seemed to have considered somewhat more proper, "recht namen."
- Also referred to them by purely German terms, which are roughly equivalent to "water people," "mountain people," and so on, using all the different forms interchangeably.

Correct Name (Translated)	Alternate Name (Latin)	Element in Which It Lives
Nymph	Undina (undine)	water
Sylph Sylvestris	(wild man)	air
Pygmy Gnomus	(gnome)	earth
Salamander	Vulcanus	fire

- Tractatus II, *Nymphs* (book)—referred to elementals collectively as Sagani
- Undines are similar to humans in size.
- Sylphs are rougher, coarser, longer, and stronger.
- Gnomes are short.
- Salamanders are long, narrow, and lean.
- Elementals are said to be able to move through their own elements as human beings move through air: gnomes can move through rocks, walls, and soil; sylphs move through air like humans, burn in fire, drown in water, get stuck in earth
- Paracelsus states that each one stays healthy in its particular "chaos" but dies in the others.
- Paracelsus conceived human beings to be composed of three parts:
    - An elemental body
    - A sidereal spirit
    - Immortal divine soul
- Elementals lack souls, but marriage with a human being, the elemental and its offspring could gain a soul.
- Heinrich Cornelius Agrippa, *De Occulta Philosophia* (1531–33)
    - Identified four classes of spirits corresponding to the four elements but did not name them—"In like manner they distribute these into more orders, so as some are fiery, some are watery, some aerial, some terrestrial"; gave an extensive list of various mythological beings of this type without clarifying which belongs to which elemental class

- 1670, French satire of occult philosophia, *Comte de Gabalis*
  - Particularly focused on the idea of elemental marriage as discussed by Paracelsus
  - "Count of Kabbalah" explains that members of his order (to which Paracelsus is said to belong) refrain from marriage to human beings in order to retain their freedom to bestow souls upon elementals. *Comte de Gabalis* used the terms *sylphide* and *gnomide* to refer to female sylphs and gnomes (often *sylphid* and *gnomid* in English translations.
  - Male nymphs (the term used instead of the Paracelsian "undine") are said to be rare, while female salamanders are rarely seen.
- Rosicrucians claimed to be able to see such elemental spirits.
  - To be admitted to their society, it was necessary for the eyes to be purged with the Panacea, or "universal medicine," a legendary alchemical substance with miraculous curative power.
  - Glass globes would be prepared with one of the four elements and for one month exposed to beams of sunlight; with these steps, the initiated would see innumerable beings immediately.
  - Elementals were said to be longer lived than man but ceased to exist upon death.
  - If elementals were to be wed to a mortal, they would become immortal.
  - If elementals married an immortal, the immortal being would gain the mortality of the elemental.
- Comparison with Jainism
  - In Jainism, there is a superficially similar concept within its general cosmology, the ekindriya jiva, "one-sensed beings" with bodies (kaya) that are composed of a single element, albeit with a five-element system (earth, water, air, fire, and plant), but these beings are actual physical objects and phenomena such as rocks,

rain, fires, and so on, which are endowed with souls (jiva). In the Paracelsian concept, elementals are much like human beings except for lacking souls. This is quite the opposite from the Jain conception which rather than positing soulless elementals is positing that physical objects have some type of soul and that what are commonly considered inanimate objects have this particular type of soul.

- Twentieth century
  - Wiccans and others study and practice rituals to invoke elementals.
- Elementals became popular characters in Romantic literature after Paracelsus.
- By the seventeenth century, elemental spirits after the Paracelsian concept appeared in works by John Dryden and in the *Comte de Gabalis*. Alexander Pope cited *Comte de Gabalis* as his source for elemental lore in his 1712 poem "The Rape of the Lock":

> The Sprites of fiery Termagants in Flame
> Mount up, and take a salamander's name.
> Soft yielding minds to Water glide away,
> And sip with Nymphs, their elemental Tea.
> The graver Prude sinks downward to a Gnome,
> In search of mischief still on earth to roam.
> The Light Coquettes in Sylphs aloft repair,
> And sport and flutter in the fields of Air.
>
> —Canto 1

- Fouque's wildly popular 1811 novella *Undine* is only one of the most influential literary examples.
- Another is the DC Comics superhero team the Elementals, composed of the characters Gnome, Sylph, Salamander, and Undine.

- Elementals related to the four classical elements appeared in the fiction of Michael Moorcock, notably in his 1972 novel *Elric of Melniboné*, and a variant appeared in the 1970s *Dungeons and Dragons* role-playing game. The concept has since been expanded on in numerous other fantasy, computer, and trading card games.

Topic: Numerology, Particularly the Number 4

Source: *Numbers & Roots of Numbers in the Bible*
Author: Taichuan Tongs

Summary

- The number 4 represents all creation, especially angels who were created earlier than men.
- As created beings, including humanity, there is always something hidden and ready to make trouble inside—the ego—which makes obedience to God difficult.
- Unless the grace of God intervenes, no one is able to break free of the vicious circle of disobedience.
- Characteristic feature of fallen angels is that they once walked from a path of obedience to a path of sin and rebellion against God because of ignorance, making it difficult for them to repent, causing them to fall deeper into sin and disobedience, meaning there is no repentance unto death.
- The rebellious nature of these fallen angels who rebelled in heaven and tried to establish another kingdom has been passed on to mankind, causing humanity to fall into a vicious, self-centered cycle apart from God.
- Enter you in at the strait gate: for wide is the gate, and broad is the way, that leads to destruction, and many there be which go in there at: Because strait is the gate, and narrow is the way, which leads to life, and few there be that finds it. (Matthew 7:13–14, KJV)

Research: Numerology, Especially the Number 4

Source: *The A-to-Z Guide to Bible Signs & Symbols*
Authors: Neil Wilson and Nancy Ryken Taylor

- The number 4 and groups of four connect with a sense of place in the horizontal world
    - Four directions: east, west, north, south
- Old Testament descriptions develop in sets of four.
- In New Testament, Zacchaeus promised to "pay four times as much as I owe to those I have cheated in any way" (Luke 19:8, KJV)
- Four gospels
- Four as a literary technique: (Isaiah 58:6–10)
    - Provides a strong sense of direction covering every facet of life—symbolize or imply these specifics, plus everything in between

This is the kind of fasting I have chosen:
Loosen the chains of wickedness,
Untie the straps of the yoke,
Let the oppressed go free,
And break every yoke.

Share your food with the hungry,
Take the poor and homeless into your house,
And cover them with clothes
when you see them naked,
Don't refuse to help your relatives.

Then your light will break
through like the dawn,
And you will heal quickly,
Your righteousness will go ahead of you,
And the Glory of the Lord will
guard you from behind.
Then, you will call, and the Lord will answer,

You will cry for help, and he
will say, "Here I am!"
Get rid of that yoke.
Don't point your finger and say wicked things.

If you give some of your own food
to feed those who are hungry
And to satisfy the needs of
those who are humble,
Then your light will rise in the dark,
And your darkness will become as
bright as the noonday sun.

- Four in Apocalyptic Prophecies (primarily Ezekiel, Daniel, and Revelation)—collections of four convey a sense of completeness, whether it has to do with God's judgment (John's vision in Revelation 6:1–7 and the four winds of heaven (Daniel 7:2) or God's saving plan to "every tribe, language, people, and nation" (Rev. 5:9; 7:9; 10:11; 11:9; 13:7; 14:6)—a ringing endorsement of God's heart for the whole world
- John's vision of the throne room in heaven describes four living creatures (one like a lion, one like a bull, one like a human, one like an eagle), which see everything and can't stop glorifying God. This parallels the vision of Ezekiel in Ezekiel 1:5–8.
- Four as a term of geographical completeness
    - John's vision of New Jerusalem in Revelation 21:2 describes a massive cube (vv. 16–17)
    - God's instructions for the structure of the tabernacle in the wilderness was filled with fours (Exodus 25–39)
        - Four golden rings on the Ark of the Covenant for the carrying poles
        - Four bronze carrying rings on the square altar for burned offerings

    - "Four posts set in four bronze bases" that supported the screen of the outside entrance of the tabernacle
- Four represents a sort of signature of the Designer.

"Apples," Sighed Her

It is a wise devil that feeds into a person's
confidence in self. The devil is willing
to give much credit to self as long as
he accomplishes his objective.

—*The Dangers of a Shallow Faith,* A. W. Tozer

The town of Satan's Den has many legends that ebb, flow, and intertwine with one another in a majestic tapestry of history. It is a tight-knit, superstitious little town, much as outsiders would expect from such "hillbillies" as they have been stereotyped. Tourists come, hoping to experience some mystical or terrifying event, but leave quickly when they realize the tight-lipped townsfolk refuse to exploit themselves for their entertainment. The diligent visitor might accidentally encounter one of the more colorful townspeople who are willing to tell the tales of Satan's Den. Such a lucky individual is touched by the magic of the storytelling in such a way that his, or her, life is changed.

The town of Satan's Den grew up along a dark, winding game trail deep in the wooded hills that spawned the first evil before time can remember. Satan's Den—the deeper you go, the older the evil. The tragedy at the Stevens Gas N Go was only on the fringe of the full scope of what power lies deeper within Satan's Den.

In the early 1960s, a farmer happened to be passing through the town with a load of young fruit trees and other supplies. His truck broke down at the foot of a pitted narrow road that climbed up a steep hill where it quickly disappeared as it curved back on itself. The grass and weeds led him to believe the road to be abandoned and unused for a long while. The remaining ruts could have been made by a wagon from a not-so-long-gone era. He hoped he would be able to get his old '47 Ford running as no help would be found here. He didn't know how far he would have to walk to get help if the repair was beyond his ability. He was on this road simply because he had made a wrong turn somewhere along the line. No signs had been seen to tell him where he was or was going. He was lost. As he looked around him, seeing no way to move his truck to a shady spot, he caught the hint of movement from the trees along that lonesome road. Looking more closely, he spotted a girl descending through the trees.

"Good morning, miss," he said as he took off his hat and nodded his head. "I wasn't aware that anyone lived nearby."

The girl looked at him strangely with her overly large and sunken brown eyes as she stopped near the foot of the trail. She could have been fourteen, give or take, for the haunting of her gaunt frame, dressed in boy's clothing. Her stringy brown hair hung in an uneven bob. A little girl of about six, clad in a dirty, ragged dress that was too big for her, peeked out from behind the older girl. Two other children—boys?—peered at the farmer from where they hid among the trees in the dense woods.

"My truck has broke down," stated the farmer.

When no one responded, he nervously began tinkering with the engine of his truck.

After a while, the eldest girl spoke. "Them's mighty fine apples ye got there, mister," she said, eyeing a bushel of red apples the farmer had bought at the orchard where he purchased the fruit trees.

The farmer eyed the gaunt-looking children. They looked like they hadn't eaten in days. Nodding his head at the children, he said, "You kids help yerselves. I don't need all them apples. Reckon they'd just start spoilin' afore I get 'em home anyways."

The children didn't move; they just stood and stared at the farmer. Finally, the farmer went to the back of the truck and picked out eight of the best apples from the basket. The children wouldn't come down to him, so he climbed up the road a little way. The two little boys disappeared behind a dense bush in fear. The little girl hid further behind the older girl, who hugged the smaller one closer and eyed the farmer suspiciously.

The farmer held out an apple to the girl. She still didn't move. He stopped and placed them on the ground at the girl's feet before heading back to the old truck. He peeked back over his shoulder. The apples were gone. *Deposited in pockets and tucked in shirts, no doubt,* he thought with a chuckle.

He watched the children from the corner of his eye as he continued working under the hood. After a while, the children sat down, and he could hear the crunching and slurping of apples as the children ate. Without being obvious, the farmer tilted his head just enough to see beneath the brim of his cap. Juice ran down their thin chins as they bit and chewed furiously. The farmer grinned and shook his head. "Probably haven't et in a week, poor things," he wondered beneath his breath.

When he had tinkered a while longer under the scrutinization of the children, the farmer slammed the hood and tried the engine. The motor roared to life. The children's eyes widened in wonder and fear. The farmer shut the engine off.

Man and children stared at one another for several minutes. The farmer felt uncomfortable with hollow eyes staring at him. He couldn't just abandon them beside the road. They seemed so pitiful. He didn't know what if it were his own young 'uns looking like that.

At last, he spoke. "Would you like some more apples…to take home? Maybe to yer folks?"

The staring eyes shifted longingly to the basket of apples. The farmer climbed from the cab of the truck and filled his arms with apples. Following his previous path, he climbed the hill, placed the apples on the ground, and returned to the truck. Once again, the apples had disappeared by the time he turned around.

"You must really like them apples," the farmer said, growing more uncomfortable and longing to leave. Four weary heads nodded yes.

"We don't got no trees to et from 'round here," said the oldest girl.

The farmer thought for a long time. At last, making up his mind, he asked, "Would you like to have your own apple tree to eat from?"

Four pairs of eyes lit up. The farmer grinned and chose a sapling from the truck bed. Shuffling through the supplies in one corner of the truck bed, he found a shovel. After assessing the hillside for the best place to plant the tree, he selected a small sunny clear spot just to the side of the overgrown path. It was almost as if the hillside itself had shifted to make room for the little tree. The children watched from a careful distance. Eight ears absorbed the farmer's narrative on the growth and care of apple trees.

When the job was done, the farmer returned to his truck and put away the shovel. A red bandanna handkerchief appeared to wipe the sweat from his face before disappearing back into his pocket. The children had gathered around the little tree and stood staring at it as if they could see it grow right before their very eyes.

Feeling good in spite of being tired, the farmer climbed back into his truck and started the engine. As he pulled away, he glanced once more to where the children were still watching the little tree. The eldest girl turned to watch him go. Her mouth moved as she spoke. The roar of the engine drowned out the words. The farmer thought she was saying, "You are the one." Puzzled, the farmer drove on.

He stopped to fill his tank with gas and get a bite to eat at the Stevens Gas N Go a few minutes later. He asked the very pregnant woman at the deli counter about the children he had seen. She wouldn't answer. The old man behind the cash register motioned for the farmer to follow him outside. Once there, he warned the farmer to forget he had ever seen those children. Curious, the farmer asked why.

"Them chil'ren have been dead nigh on thirty year. Died of pisenin' they say."

"Dead?" queried the farmer in confusion. "You must be mistaken. Them children was very much alive. I seen 'em breathin' and movin' about."

"Yep, that's them," continued the old man.

"How can that be? I gave them some apples and even helped them plant a saplin' of their own. They looked so hungry."

The old man nodded wisely and motioned for the farmer to have a seat in an old porch chair. "Got a story fer ye," he said.

The farmer sat, heavily, prepared for the worst.

"'Bout thirty year ago, a fambly of young 'uns lived up in that holler top o' that mountain. They was a poor bunch. Couldn't afford nothin'. Depended mostly on charity for what little they did have. The momma was dead, and the poppa not quite right. Them kids had to fend for themse'ves. One day, the whole fambly turned up dead. Seems they'd et some bad apples. They found the tree right up 'side the road leadin' up to their place. Seems the roots of that tree'd grown right down inta some kinda nat'rel pisen. Ever'one of them apples was bad."

"That can't be," protested the farmer. "I just planted a tree beside that road today. They was no other apple trees. I'd swear to that!"

"I knowed what I knowed." The old man nodded mysteriously. He got up from his chair and went back inside the block building.

Stunned and confused, the farmer sat, thinking for a long time. After a while, he got back into his truck, started it up, and pulled out into the road, back the way he had come.

He found the place where his truck had broken down. There was no sign of the children. In the place where he had planted the tiny fruit tree grew a twisted, gnarled apple tree, its fruit knotted and hard. The tree appeared vilely unwholesome. Astonished, the farmer fell to his knees, tearing at his hair in guilty despair.

"I *am* the one!" His shouts echoed from the mountaintops.

Genesis 3:6–7 (NKJV)

> So when the woman saw that the tree was good for food, that it was pleasant to the eyes, and a tree desirable to make one wise, she took of its fruit and ate. She also gave to her husband with her, and he ate. Then the eyes of both of them were opened, and they knew that they were naked; and they sewed fig leaves together and made themselves coverings.

Notes of Lurlene Joy McCoy

This appears to be a classic time twist account. With the resident evil present in Satan's Den, it would not be unusual to find pockets of poison of some sort. Sulfureous groundwater is the first to come to mind. Deposits of arsenic at toxic levels are more likely but have never been identified in this area. The apple tree in question has never been located, just as the Tree of the Knowledge of Good and Evil has been locked away from mankind in Eden (Genesis 3:22–24). The road in question has been lost to the overgrowth of neglected land that has remained untouched because it has been deemed useless for development or lumbering. Knowing it is near the ruins of the Gas N Go can begin the scavenger hunt, but no treasure has yet been found. Such is the nature of legend and lore, where fact blends with fiction to create its own version of truth. For those who believe, the Tree of the Knowledge of Good and Evil surely existed in that long-ago garden populated by the first creations and where the Creator walked among them. There, too, death occurred. It wasn't a physical death, as experienced by these children and their father, but a death in which two people who had known only goodness, love, and truth were deceived into believing they could become like the One who made them. They were instructed not to eat the fruit of that tree, or they would die (Genesis 2:15–17). Not knowing what death was, they were easily convinced that they wouldn't die (whatever that meant). Truth is, they did die that day. The obedience in love they had for their Creator was broken through disobedience, revealing their true humanity—a double nature called free will. It had always been within them; they just hadn't discovered it. They walked in love beside their Father. They chose it as a privilege, not a requirement. It brought them pleasure because it pleased Him. Free will introduced the concept of choice—serve Father in love and privilege or choose to serve self in search of pleasure in their own deeds at the expense of losing the relationship with Father who had given freely to His children.

Adam and Eve were led to sin by the deceiver. The children in this story died from no deception from the farmer, an innocent in his own right. Yet the farmer felt the cost of those children's lives was on himself.

Did he time-travel? The Bible describes visions of prophets who have been "taken up to heaven," and the apostle Philip was whisked hundreds of miles away from where he baptized an Ethiopian eunuch to a city where he was called to preach (Acts 8:39–40) as if transported from the deck of the enterprise to the colonized planet it orbited.

The structure of the universe is debated heavily; time flows, but does it curve back on itself, or is it a continuum with no end? Mobius, the German mathematician, described time as flowing in a circular pattern, with a half twist that ensured that the path never ends but retains an eternal shape. It can be recreated by cutting a long narrow strip of paper, giving the band a half twist and taping the ends together. Placing the tip of a pen or pencil on the paper and drawing a line across the central horizon of the strip will travel in a continuous mark that covers both sides of the paper strip until it returns to its origin. No matter how many circular loops are added to the initial twist, the results will always be the same. If additional half twists are added along the way, it is conceivably possible that they would interface at some point. Mayhaps that is what happened here.

Did this hapless farmer get caught in a "twist" of time, or was there some other force at work? The answer is beyond my training. Perhaps some of my colleagues with advanced degrees in physics can unravel this one.

The Demon Rock

Faith is not an organ of imagination, but rather an organ of knowledge. It enables us to see with the eye of faith what is really there. This faith does not project imaginary things, look at them and say, "There they are." There are no illusionary tricks to produce something that does not exist. Through the eye of faith, we can see the reality of things.

—A. W. Tozer

The Ohio River borders Satan's Den, where it helped carve the majestic hills from the mountains to her east and south. Plains flow from the foothills to initiate the Midwest plains that are so fertile. The Big and Little Sandy Rivers deposit their contributions, while carrying away parts of ancient stone to be redistributed elsewhere. Three states currently converge where these waters congregate. What was once a vast unknown territory known as Virginia and the Ohio Valley separated the wilderness from the civilization of the earliest colonies by the massive Appalachian Range that nearly spans the north-south borders of the lower North American continent on the Atlantic side. Even the natives found living in this area were superstitious enough to not occupy this region for longer than a season. Studying the mythology of these peoples—Cherokee and Powhaten—wields wickedness, fear, and respect of the land and its other natural inhabitants. Little people, giants, Sasquatch, cryptids of unnatural creation, not to mention the many spirits who inhabited the land, water, and air created a culture of deep spirituality unmatched by the modern inhabitants who seem hell-bent on raping the land of its resources, leaving it barren, and the people destitute. Surviving in these mountains takes skill and strong belief in Someone Greater than yourself, especially when you meet up with one of these supernatural beings often passed off as a fairy tale.

Some old-timers still speak of the New Madrid earthquakes of 1811. Mostly told from memories of ancestors who had experienced it firsthand, or recalled from other recollections as handed down by inhabitants of the land, few actually understand the real impact the earthquakes had on the area of Satan's Den. The New Madrid fault line travels along the western edge of Kentucky, directly beneath the Mississippi River from New Madrid, Missouri, to Louisiana. Its rumblings stretch eastward to the Appalachians as well as westward into the Great Plains. Aftershocks were felt as far north as the Canadian border, as well into the southern part of what is now the state of Louisiana. The followers of Tecumseh interpreted the quake as a message to support their leader and his brother, the Prophet, who had predicted the earthquake shortly before its occurrence. The fault line itself still represents such a clear and present danger to the economic waterways, travel, and water distribution that the Federal Emergency Management Agency (FEMA) has distributed warnings about another devastating quake of 7.7 or greater magnitude.

Regardless of the New Madrid fault line present beneath us, Eastern Kentucky has treacherous mountain terrain of its own. Moraine deposits of passing glaciers can be seen along eroding hillsides populated by grazing cattle. Crumbling roadcuts reveal the seismic history where the land was blasted out and carved to create more direct passages from one place to another. Then there are those anomalous standing stones, sometimes singular, sometimes in clusters, all too large to be moved by even the largest of earth movers. Left where they are found, they are always incredible to see.

One such monolith cluster can be found in Satan's Den. It isn't really hidden, just hard to reach. It's an amazing place to play cowboys and Indians in the ready-built stage provided by time. Those who know better, though, warn against seeking them out.

Going back to a time when TV Westerns were popular and the good guys always wore white, a group of boys gathered in "Rock City" for a rousing game of chase and shoot, imitating their favorite heroes and villains. They dared one another to climb the massive monoliths, with little success. In particular, the largest of the standing stones had never been scaled.

One brave young man tackled the stone. He threw himself heartily at the challenge. Moss and poisonous plants were unable to deter him. Menacing crags and fissures only offered hand- and footholds for his nimble body. The boy was a natural talent when it came to rock climbing. He could climb where even angels dared not go.

His younger brother, Paul, and his cousin, Will, watched in awe as he made his way up the wall of stone. Three other boys, brothers, from a neighboring farm, stood nervously watching the escapade. They all knew the stories of the Haunted Rocks, but this boy still climbed on.

Just as his fingers reached the upper edge of the stone, a bone-chilling cold numbed his fingers. Using all the strength he had left, he pulled himself up onto the stone tabletop. The earth seemed to stand still in the cold. Early October felt more like the bitter days of February, minus the snow.

Wrapping his arms around himself in an attempt to warm himself, he stepped forward. The cold deepened. With each step he took, the temperature dropped considerably. Turning blue with cold and shivering with fright, the boy stopped just a step away from strange carvings gouged in the stone. Crude circles and odd shapes were entwined with moss and lichens. He knelt and began to tear at the confining growths with his numbed fingers.

A breeze began to blow as the boy worked. A faint chant rose with the force of the wind. The boy thought of his brother, cousin, and friends; were they feeling this cold? *They should see this,* he thought. *They'll never believe what I have seen. I can hear them calling me, but I won't answer. This is my secret to keep.*

The boy worked on. The chants grew louder, but still indistinct, joined now by rhythmic drumming. His body began to sway in response. He wondered where it came from. Listening carefully, he determined that it came from around him, the plateau of the rock, not from below.

The design came to light as he scraped with nearly bloody fingertips. It began to glow, ever so distinctly, then became brighter. The autumn day faded into darkest night. Spectral fires ignited in the woods around him and began an intricate dance of movement through the trees. His numb body began to warm.

The final bits of dirt and plant debris were removed, and the carving freed. The boy walked around it, trying to make sense of the ancient symbols from every angle, but was unsuccessful. He sat, staring at it. He knew there had been no Indians to live in this part of the country for a very long time before settlers arrived. It had been a sacred hunting ground, honored and protected, and highly believed to be inhabited by spirits. Burial mounds had been discovered nearby that led people to believe that any inhabitation by the Natives before the recorded time of our country, and for those who passed through in between were far too ancient to have much value in understanding why they left this fruitful place and led it to become sacred and a place to be feared. Perhaps these symbols were as old as those ancient people, or even older.

A mist began to rise around the boy, hiding the more familiar trees around him. It wrapped itself around the boy, hiding him from the sight of any who could have known where he was. Thus enshrouded, the boy began to dream.

Figures darkened by the night around, then dragged a much larger, much darker figure across a moonlit meadow by its arms. The darker figure gnashed its teeth and screamed an angry roar. Spears and sharpened sticks poked at the enraged creature and shouted curses upon it. A mob of angry figures surrounded the beast and limited its range of movement; otherwise, it would not have been able to be contained.

The huge figure was not only larger but capable of massive annihilation of its captors if it were to break free. Some supernatural or paranormal force had to have been in play in order for the mere mortals to control it in the manner they were. Sharpened sticks and stone spears would not have penetrated its hide otherwise. Perhaps they used a caustic substance that burned the creature with each poke or slash. Nonetheless, some unseen force assisted in wrestling the creature to the ground. Its roars of anger became rage as it struggled to break its bonds and gnash at its captors who dared too close to its mouth and head.

A costumed figure, all in yellow, from painted exposed skin to the skins it was wearing to the bright-yellow feathers secured in a halo around its head, entered the clearing, shaking a tortoiseshell rattle and chanting loudly. A second, smaller figure, clad solely in a loin cloth and painted red, followed the light into the clearing, drumming an anticipatory rhythm upon a small drum.

The two figures began an elaborate dance in which the light seemingly created the smaller red figure from the earth itself. The "man" danced delightedly around his Creator, and the Creator delighted in its creation. A lithe figure obscured in black feathers, furs, and paint slithered into the clearing and began mocking the small red man. It circled the man in ever closer mockery until it seemed to merge with the figure, and the two moved as one. The light tried to separate the two figures through chants and exaggerated spells but was unable to pull them apart. The drum rhythm had become increasingly chaotic as the dark had drawn closer. There was now no rhythm to be determined in the random beating and thrashing now being played upon it. The man threw its arms toward the sky and cried out to the heavens.

On cue, four white figures painted and barely clothed in white animal skins came forth and subdued the smaller figure, now liberally smeared with the darkness of the black demon now within him.

A faint bloody foam spilled from his mouth, his eyes wide and crazed. The Creator light drew a stone knife from his belt and stabbed at the air around the deranged figure. The creature tied to the stakes began screaming in agony. The defeated red-and-black figure fell to the ground, feigning death.

The light figure dipped his fingers into a paint pot drawn from a pouch at his waist and drew an intricate design on the chest and abdomen of the defeated figure. Abruptly, the staked creature bellowed in rage and pain as identical symbols mystically burned into the skin of its abdomen and chest. Steam rose from the creature as its very life force drained away into the earth. In the end, only ashes remained to show where it had been. The earth itself remained unblemished, except where the crude symbols had been burned into the very stone itself.

The dancers and the warriors backed fearfully from the place of the demon's passing. The earth began to shake; the very ground on which they were standing began to crack. They tried to flee, but the ground they stood on rose beneath them, separating them and trapping them. The earth gave a final rumbling belch and was silent.

Carefully, the remaining warriors and dancers lowered themselves to the ground. Nothing seemed disturbed except for the very rocks that had been pushed up. The demon had said his last…for now.

The symbol remained to mark its tomb, the tomb upon which the boy now sat. Shivering in the autumn air, the boy gathered his wits. Carefully, he lowered himself back to the ground where the other boys waited. They pried him with questions but received no answers. The boy refused to speak of his experience. Behind the boys, the ground seemed to shudder in laughter, and a stream of steam rose from the mysterious engraving.

Matthew 12:22–28 (NIV)

> Then one was brought to him who was demon-possessed, blind and mute; and he healed him, so that the blind and mute man both spoke and saw. And all the multitudes were amazed and said, "could this be the son of David?"
>
> Now when the Pharisees heard it they said, "This fellow does not cast out demons except by Beelzebub, the ruler of the demons."
>
> But Jesus knew their thoughts and said to them: "Every kingdom divided against itself is brought to desolation, and every city or house divided against itself will not stand. If Satan casts out Satan, he is divided against himself. How then will his kingdom stand? And if I cast out demons

> by Beelzebub, by whom do your sons cast them out? Therefore they shall be your judges. But if I cast out demons by the spirit of God, surely the kingdom of God has come upon you."

Why do we use Latin? Jesus spoke Hebrew and Aramaic. Latin hadn't become a classical language then. How can Latin be effective in casting out demons when the demons are older than Latin? Even Hebrew and Aramaic were infant languages to those demons. So if it isn't Latin that is the best language for an exorcism, shouldn't we just rely on the language of faith?

Glory Hallelujah.

Notes by Lurlene Joy McCoy

Here we meet our antagonist.

The Adena Indians (for lack of a better term) were prehistoric, and little is known about their culture.

Looking at Cherokee symbology, however, there are some prominent indicators that Adenas may have shared some of the same lore.

The dancer painted all in black to represent the creature they were imprisoning represents death. The creature must have been a horrible neighbor and brought much death to these people. Why else would they be so eager to banish it? If it is a fractal, a remnant of dust from the Big Bang of Creation itself, as I have proposed, this makes perfect sense and gives us a glimpse into the depth of knowledge and belief these people may have had.

The four dancers painted all in white represent peace and happiness, something denied under the tyranny of a fractal.

The tortoiseshell rattle was not just a musical instrument made from placing pebbles inside a tortoiseshell and jamming a stick into one end. The turtle represents Mother Earth. The Cherokee perceive our world as traveling through the cosmos on the back of an enormous turtle. The figure in yellow represents this Upper World where the Great Spirit dwells.

In more modern terminology, this event would be described as a classic battle between "the dark side" and "the light" (cue up your *Star Wars* soundtrack), with "the Force" being wielded by both sides, albeit with different agendas—good versus evil, the never-ending story.

The boy observed that whatever was pantomimed as being done to the dark dancer impacted the physical creature, and it responded accordingly. This is a magical transference, or sympathetic magic, where those who are acting out the marking of the ceremonial creature and its subsequent "death" within the rock are being enacted upon the real creature. Unseen, or spiritual, forces are represented by the white figures. We would call them warrior angels. The ceremonial dance itself demonstrated the "creation" of man, who was then stalked and engulfed by the dark presence. We would refer to that today as demonic possession. The man tried to rid himself of the darkness but could not. Only when he reached toward the heavens and cried out to the Great Spirit did relief come in the form of the white dancers. The man had to die in order to be freed from the darkness.

The vision ended with that man feigning death. In modern exorcisms, the goal is to drive the demon from the effected individual, leaving the person alive and free to continue living. Far too many people die during or as an aftereffect of the exorcism process. The true number cannot be calculated as the exorcisms are performed by cultural faith agents and not strictly by trained personnel. Even pagans have their own forms of exorcisms. Nonetheless, exorcisms are not regulated by government agencies and are not required to be reported. They only come to public attention when media attention and/or legal actions become public.

Jesus famously exorcised the demon Legion from a man, casting them into a large group of pigs, which then threw themselves into the sea and drowned. Later, Jesus said,

> When an unclean spirit goes out of a man, he goes through dry places, seeking rest; and finding none, he says, 'I will return to my house

> from which I came'. And when he comes, he finds it swept and put in order. Then he goes and takes with him seven other spirits more wicked than himself and they enter and dwell there, and the last state of that man is worse than the first. (Luke 11: 24–26, NKJV)

Possession is a spiritual issue. Demons can only enter where they are welcomed, consciously or unconsciously. You don't have to put out a FOR RENT TO DEMONS sign in order to attract demonic forces into your life. They are already present, simply looking for ways to sneak in. Simple neglect of spirituality of the proper nature can do it. Allowing negative emotions to accumulate, poor habits of partaking in unwholesome information from media, a lax moral compass, lack of proper spiritual development, and sometimes, just being in the wrong place at the wrong time, full possession occurs over time, is relatively rare, and is more often fatal.

When an exorcism is performed, the demon(s) is/are cast out, and the individual feels lighter, cleaner. If they don't take proper precautions to fill their mind and spirit with things that won't encourage the demon to return, that person is in great danger of being repossessed, possibly unto death.

Since this creature of darkness is imprisoned, it cannot directly harm or possess anyone. If that seal weakens and then breaks, all hell will break loose with it.

Author Patrick Meechan describes his personal experience of dealing with land that was cured following the signing of the Greenville Treaty of 1795. The treaty was made between the American government of that time and the Native Americans living in what is now much of the state of Ohio to our north and stretching into the area of Point Pleasant in what is now the state of West Virginia. Mr. Meehan's experience took place in Holmes County, Ohio, location of the second-largest Amish settlement in the world. His book *Nightmare in Holmes County* describes how the purchase of a plot of land in this beautiful location led to confrontations with his Amish neighbors who also practiced a form of old-world witchcraft common to their pagan Germanic ancestry, combined with the paganistic practices of the Native Americans with whom they have come in contact throughout the centuries here in America. This kind of witchcraft is known as powwow. He only later discovered the connection with the Greenville Treaty as he attempted to break the curse that had broken up his marriage and isolated him from most of those he had known before moving to that location. After reading this account, it is easy to understand how what this young man saw could very likely have been an attempt at breaking some much older curse that has befallen this land.

Topic: Judaculla Rock, North Carolina

Source: www.Appalachianhistory.net
Date: September 27, 2019

- Covered in depictions of animals and animal tracks, human figures, suns, and geometric figures
- One of the greatest archaeological mysteries in the United States
    - Largest in North Carolina
    - One of the largest in the Southeast
- Named for a Cherokee legend
- Sits in the Caney Fork Creek Valley in Jackson County, outside of Cullowhee, North Carolina
- 16' long × 11' wide
- Created by incising, pecking, and smoothing the stone
- Late nineteenth-century Cherokee groups were known to hold ceremonial assemblies around the rock.
- Additional outcrops of soapstone were used by Cherokees to sculpt pipes, beads, bowls, and nearby bannerstones.
- It is believed that Cherokees camped at, or near, the rock when they came to quarry soapstone.
- Recent excavations of areas surrounding Judaculla Rock may have once been a part of a larger grouping of soapstone creations.

- James Mooney, researcher at the Smithsonian Institution, recorded a Cherokee legend of Judaculla Rock in 1880s:
  - A being named Judaculla (called by the Cherokee sul-ka-lu or Tsu' Kalu (the Great Slant-Eyed Giant), greatest of all Cherokee mythical characters, a giant hunter who lived at the head of the Tuckasegee River in Jackson County
    - Very powerful and could control the wind, rain, thunder, and lightning
    - Known to drink down whole streams in a single gulp and stomp from mountain to mountain as one might over anthills
- According to Sequoyah's Cherokee translation of the Bible, the Philistine "Goliath" was renamed Judaculla.
    - One legend claims the markings are hunting laws that Judaculla ordered.
    - Another legend says that Judaculla jumped from his mountaintop farm and landed partially on the rock, while running a band of American Indians off his land.
- The seven-toed foot at the lower right-hand side of the boulder is said to depict Judaculla's footprint.
- The rock was once thought to depict a map of a 1750 Cherokee victory over Creeks at the battle of Taliwa in what is now Georgia, or perhaps a victory over another enemy, the Catawba
- Archaeologists have declared that the Judaculla Rock predates the Cherokee habitation of Western North Carolina, but its exact origin is unknown.
  - Currently dated from late Archaic Period, between 3000 and 1000 BCE, when evidence first appears of Native Americans forming mound societies
  - North Carolina Rock Art Survey organized a Judaculla Advisory Committee composed of site owner Jackson, North Carolina, members of the Eastern Band of the Cherokee Tribal Historic Preservation Office and

Tribal Elders, the Office of State Archaeology, professors from nearby Western Carolina University, and members of the surrounding community.

- Agreed to pursue a formal recording of the petroglyphs along with a condition assessment and conservation plan

Topic: Indian Head Rock

Source: https://www.en.wikipedia.org

Summary

This eight-ton sandstone boulder has been the subject of local lore since the 1800s when its presence became a center of curiosity during a period of low water level in the Ohio River between Portsmouth, Ohio, and South Shore, Kentucky.

Its name comes from the carving of a face that appears on the bottom of the boulder. The face appears to be human.

There is no existing lore from the native Shawnee to account for its carved features, though it is believed to be, at least in part, to contain petroglyphs. One accepted theory is that the rock may have been marked by John Book of Portsmouth, Ohio, who later fought at the Battle of Shiloh. Less likely theories include that it was used as a marker for a band of robbers to mark the location of their stash, and that a quarryman carved the face with a metal device. None of these have any substantiated proof.

What is known about it is its first historical reference by name in an 1848 volume written by Squier and Davis, *Ancient Monuments of the Mississippi Valley.*

Geologically, it originated as part of the "Quaternary Pleistocene and Recent Landslide deposits from the Kentucky hillside facing the city of Portsmouth." One description says it is "not of the riverbed at this point, but is a hard sandstone, and must have rolled from the top of the hill in remote ages. The face was probably made to commemorate the lowest water ever known in the Ohio River since white men settled upon it" (from an 1891 source). At that time, there was already "a multitude of…names and characters that were evidently quite ancient" carved into the rock.

The first known reference to the rock being used as a gauge of the Ohio River was noted November 10, 1839, when the mouth was noted to be 10 1/4 inches out of the water.

In September and October 1908, the access to the Indian Head Rock was noted to be exceptional. *The Portsmouth Daily Times* noted two specific dates of incredible access—Sunday, September 27, when over 1,000 people ventured out to the rock, and then Sunday, October 11, when 1,500 people visited the rock near the Kentucky Shore, opposite Bond Street in Portsmouth.

At least one hundred sets of initials are distinguishable in postcard-sized photos taken by amateur photographer J. E. Bradford of Portsmouth.

Later, the rock was deemed to be a hazard in the river, and there was a petition to have it removed.

Between 1875 and 1929, the US Army Corps of engineers built a series of dams along the Ohio River to improve navigation. One of these was Ohio River Locks and Dams Number 31, built 2.5 miles downstream of Portsmouth. It was completed in 1917 and permanently raised the level of the river, submerging the Indian Head Rock. Damage to Dam Number 31 in 1920 briefly lowered the river level, allowing the Indian Head Rock to be seen once more. Dam Number 31 was later demolished when Captain Anthony Meldahl Locks and Dam was built downstream.

Indian Head Rock remained submerged until it was retrieved by Steve Shaffer of Ironton, Ohio. There was a brief custody battle for the rock until 2010 when it was deemed to be an artifact of the state of Kentucky. It spent the next ten years hidden away in Greenup County, Kentucky, until it was placed on display at the city park in South Shore, Kentucky.

Henry Bannon et al. with Indian Head Rock, 1920. The city of Portsmouth is seen in the background.

Flee the Dark Image

When you meet temptation,
always turn to the right.
When you flee temptation, be sure you
don't leave a forwarding address.

—*Pocket Wisdom,* Robert C. Savage

We have within us temptations, which
if yielded to would destroy our soul.

—*Living as a Christian,* A. W. Tozer

A gnawing, hungry feeling
Causes your nerves to chill.
You feel yourself move forward,
As if against your will.

Giant red eyes
And gnashing sharp teeth
Appear before your frightened eyes.
You no longer feel the ground beneath.
You begin to run away.
The image pursues you.
You don't realize
What you must do.

Flee the dark image,
Before it knows you are there.

Flee thee the dark image
Before it's mark you bear.

The dark image pursues.
Don't let it catch you.
Flee the dark image.
There is salvation if you do.

1 Corinthians 10:14 (NIV)

Therefore, my beloved, flee from idolatry.

Notes by Lurlene Joy McCoy

This poem is about temptation and the consequences of giving in. Every moment of every day, we must make some sort of decision, mostly regarding the movement of our body to complete a task but could be life or death in nature if there is a crisis. We make approximately 35,000 conscious decisions daily.

We are taught rules for being polite, rules for interacting with others, appropriate and inappropriate vocabulary, and the list goes on. Every one of us is rebellious in heart and mind, even if we don't act on it. Some rush in where angels fear to tread simply for the thrill of being a troublemaker. Most of us, however, wear away at our morals, values, and learned rules in such a slow process that we can't figure out how stealing a penny from the change jar to get a bubblegum when you are three results in doing time for *Grand Theft Auto* in your twenties. Every temptation has a consequence—good, bad, or ugly, really, really ugly.

What we think about something and how we feel about it results in our behavior.

Every time we give in to a temptation, it becomes easier to give in to that or a similar one the next time, especially if we receive a perceived positive outcome from the first attempt. Note that an outcome can be perceived as positive simply because you didn't have a bad consequence. There is no connection with the behavior itself being good or bad, simply that the consequence was pleasurable in result. That is how rebellious thoughts and behaviors become corrupt behaviors. As long as there is a reinforcer that says it is okay for you to repeat a behavior because no one gets hurt (that is, no one is punishing you), that behavior must be okay. This runs true even if there are laws or rules which clearly state that those behaviors are unacceptable in that place and time. Therefore, the rules or teachings become obsolete and not applicable to you (in your way of thinking). You come to believe you are "above the law." When negative consequences or reinforcers are put in place to stop the poor choices and attempt to replace them with the expected rule compliance, there arises the sense of "fairness" and "justice" in which you should not have the same consequences as another for similar behavior because you are not accountable to the established law system.

Giving in to or fleeing from temptation always boils down to our thoughts and feelings about a circumstance and the laws applicable. Whether or not we accept those laws and the authority of those who enforce them will determine whether we yield to temptation or flee the urge to be disobedient. Desensitization through temptation is the devil's greatest weapon against us, and the most subtle. Any story in this volume or any other, real or fiction, hinges on our respect for law and those who enforce it. With God as our sole authority, we cannot go wrong. It is only when we try to replace God's authority with our own that we endanger our mortal souls. Even Adam and Eve were not protected from temptation. It is a lifelong battle. We must take our thoughts and feelings into captivity if we are to be "tempt proof."

Dr. David Jeremiah gives us five words to help us flee the darkness of temptation:

1. Fight.

   Battle the temptation; this is not the time for passivity (Ephesians 6:11; James 4:7; 1 Peter 5:8–9).

2. Follow.

   Follow the example of Jesus (James 4:7, 8; 1 Peter 2:21).

3. Flee.

   Do not remain in the presence of temptation (1 Corinthians 10:14; Genesis 39:12; Romans 13:14; 2 Timothy 2:22).

4. Fellowship.

   Isolation is the ideal environment for temptation. The community of believers is a safe harbor (1 Corinthians 15:33; Proverbs 13: 20; 2 Timothy 2: 22).

5. Feed.

   The Word of God is the Christian's daily bread (Psalm 119: 11; Matthew 4).

Keep your house clean and filled with righteousness.

Sweet Screams

Some men battle to the top;
others bottle to the bottom.

—*Pocket Wisdom,* Robert C. Savage

Satan's Den is a notoriously haunted place. Its demons have found their place in legend from the time the first humans experienced their treacherous temptations millennia ago. The land has a way of influencing the lives of people who choose to make their homes here. The strange goings-on are a part of everyday life in Satan's Den, and the people have learned to make the best of it. However, not all demons belong to the land or even the spiritual realm. Some are the creation of the human soul.

The heavy, dark fluid slid tantalizingly down his throat. His Adam's apple bobbed joyfully as his tongue guided the bitter nectar from his lips to the back of his throat.

"Ah." He gasped as he felt the stress begin to release from his muscles.

He closed his eyes, effectively blocking an insensitive world from sight. His mind whorled with fog. His feet felt as though they rested on fluffy, white clouds. His body draped over soft meadow grass. His head felt detached, free to roam at will.

He drank deeply from the bottle once more. Lights danced behind his closed eyes, mingling with the fog. He gasped his pleasure at the sensation of alcohol burning from his taste buds to his stomach. A few more drinks, and he would be in heaven.

His body and mind continued to relax. He felt himself sink deeper into the comfort of his malady. The bottle was half empty now. Soon, it would be gone.

The fog of his mind swirled faster. He began to feel giddy. He chuckled softly in the darkness. His arm cradled the now-empty bottle to his chest.

Shapes mixed with the fog. Memories danced tauntingly on the edges of consciousness. He brushed them aside. No time for that. The comforting emptiness was the respite he sought.

His stupor deepened as the alcohol became one with his bloodstream. Muscles relaxed; heartbeat slowed. Nerves lit up in panic, just before they went dead. The man slept.

Empty dreams flitted past like spring butterflies in flight, none staying longer than a moment before moving on to the next flower.

Darkness began to overshadow the pleasantness of the emptiness. Dark things began to creep into his mind. He saw their faces. He tried to hide from their gaunt, skeletal stares. There was nowhere to hide.

On they came, whispering curses, making accusations, grabbing the air in hopes of grabbing him. He cringed and tried to make himself smaller, to make himself invisible. On they came.

The first reached him, touched him. He began to sweat. Dark thoughts flooded his mind as this dark creature transmitted its pain to his consciousness.

As the next creature approached, he tried to run, but the thing got hold of him and held him in place. The pain increased as this creature added its memories to those of the first.

One by one, the creatures touched him, blinding him with flashing memories, fleeting thoughts, pounding accusations. How could one man have caused so much pain to so many people? He began to scream.

He opened his eyes to find himself in the same lonely bed. The room was dark, the sun set. Empty sounds roared from around him. Where was everybody?

His brain sent signals. Slowly the fog parted to allow reason to pass through. His family was gone…moved away. He could have gone with them, but he had preferred this lonely existence in an empty house with only a bottle for company.

Tears sprang from his eyes as he searched for an unopened bottle. He had to forget his pain.

As he put his hands on a new best friend, he stopped. Memories of gaunt, skeletal figures drifted into being.

This time, his screams echoed from empty walls.

Proverbs 1:20–33 (NKJV)

Wisdom calls aloud outside;
She raises her voice in the open squares.
She cries out in the chief concourses,
At the openings of the gates in the city
She speaks her words:
"How long, you simple ones, will you love simplicity?
For scorners delight in their scorning,
And fools hate knowledge.
Turn at my rebuke;
Surely I will pour out my spirit on you.
I will make my words known to you.
Because I have called and you have refused.
I have stretched out my hand and no one regarded,
Because you have disdained all my counsel,
And would have none of my rebuke,
I also will laugh at your calamity;
I will mock when your terror comes,
When your terror comes like a storm,
And your destruction comes like a whirlwind,
When distress and anguish come upon you.

"Then they will call upon me, but I will not answer;
They will seek me diligently, but they will not find me.
Because they hated knowledge
And did not choose the fear of the lord,
They would have none of my counsel
And despised my every rebuke.
Therefore they shall eat the fruit of their own way.

And be filled to the full with their own fancies.
For the turning away of the simple will slay them,
And the complacency of fools will destroy them:
But whoever listens to me will dwell safely,
And will be secure without fear of evil."

Notes (from the *Jeremiah Study Bible, NKJV*, compiled and commentary by Dr. David Jeremiah)

Throughout the book of Proverbs, wisdom and folly are personified as women, calling on all who listen to embrace them. Wisdom goes where people are, in the open squares…in the chief concourses, at the openings of the gates in the city. Personified, she calls aloud… raises her voice…cries out…speaks in the public places of the city. She speaks to three types of sinners: simple ones, scorners, and fools.

Fools make a habit of continually rejecting wisdom; in return, they receive the fruit of their own way. The New Testament sequel is that "whatever a man sows, that he will also reap" (Galatians 6: 7). The final step of rebellion (complacency) is destruction. What a fearful price to pay for rejecting wisdom's gracious appeal.

Notes by Lurlene Joy McCoy

Temptation is the gradual corruption of morals and values in a linear pattern. Addiction is circular and spirals inwardly until the dog not only catches its own tail but then devours itself until all that is left is the mouth, gasping for more.

Temptation can lead to a corroded character but is never irredeemable as long as the individual is prepared to make a conscious decision to stop—think—and turn away until the temptation passes or is overcome by something better, more conducive to contentment and acceptance of self-control as a means to ending self-destructive behavior.

Addiction occurs when, instead of taking responsibility for behavior and the resulting consequences for personal choices, an individual seeks a "quick fix" or "easy out," for at least a little while by substituting a self-prescribed remedy—drugs, alcohol, sex, food, extreme risk, etc.—as a means of covering up their lack of ability to cope and make choices that will have a better outcome, including seeking the help of someone trained in helping others, not just friends. Temptation corrodes character. Addiction destroys lives. Even cigarette smoking or other tobacco use can destroy lives. Most see addiction as self-destructive, but there are far too many victims of the individual's habits that are directly affected. Families fall apart, and people lose their jobs and homes. Crime rates increase as the individual seeks to fuel their addiction at any cost. Health care costs rise in attempts to rescue and rehabilitate these broken lives. A simple change in thought patterns and conscious choices won't work. It's no longer a matter of a corrupt attitude; it is a matter of reviving an unhealthy lifestyle that has become identified with destructive habits and has adapted to the less-than-good-for-you nutrient substitutes. The brain has altered its physical functioning as well as its cognitive processing. It has gone into primitive survival mode and is on constant alert for perceived danger or opportunities to fuel itself with the much-required new substances. It is a mind-body connection that requires a lifestyle change. Habits are hard to break but can be accomplished with diligence. Addiction becomes a soul issue as the body loses its natural desires and the mind perverts its responses to unhealthy stimuli. Negative thinking and yielding to temptation fuel further corruption of morals and values, eating away at the soul's desire to balance the id of the body and the ego of the mind.

The body is meant to return to the soil when it is no longer of use. The spirit is tethered to that body as long as it lives, giving it a life force and energy to pursue the delights of living. However, it is the soul that connects us to our Creator. It is that part that is essentially us. There are no two souls alike. It is this eternal portion that continues on into eternity after life has ceased in our body, and our spirit has been set free once more. The spirit can be broken. It can be corrupted. It can also be healed and cleansed. The soul will either call us to the Creator or pull us away into eternal separation from God. The body is along for the ride. What happens with the soul (mind) and the spirit lasts. The body responds only to what the spirit and soul subject it to. The body is a temple, a place for God to dwell, if we allow Him to. The Holy Spirit teaches and tempers our mortal souls so that righteousness can prevail in our lives.

Anything that interferes with the spirit and soul will corrupt the body. Addictions require healing in the soul before healing of the body can take place. The healing of the spirit is a lifelong process that never ends but overcomes in the end, with Jesus Christ as authority in the individual's life.

TOPIC: Thought Chart

SOURCE: Spiritual Warfare Manual (www.pdf4PRO.com)
AUTHOR: Peter Date

Thoughts = HOLY SPIRIT
Evil Spirits

Evil Suggestions Must Be Stopped Here

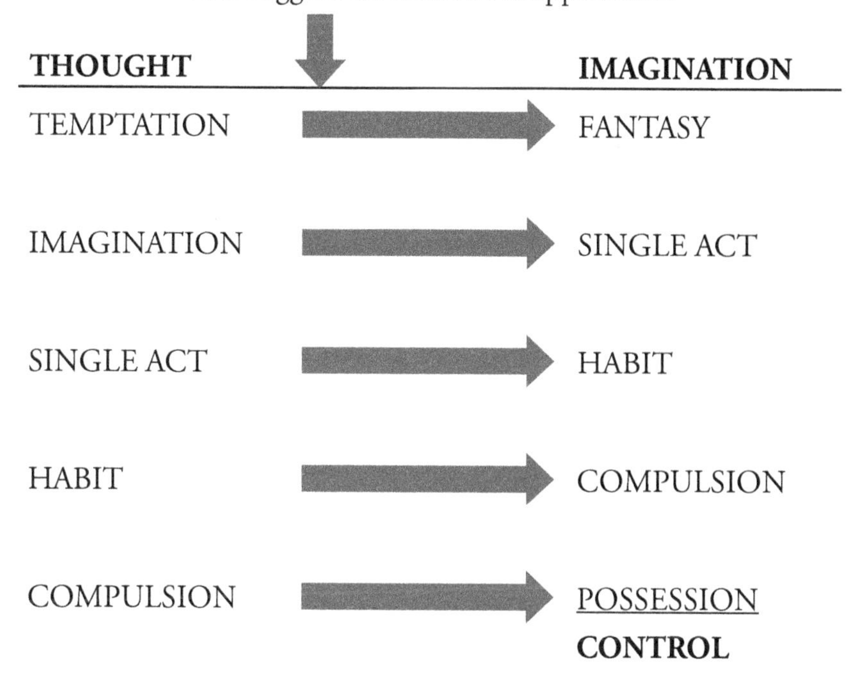

Summary:

- Temptation begins a thought process that forces an assessment of validity. (Is it true, or is it a lie?)
- If determined to be deceptive, turning away from temptation reinforces and strengthens good character.
- If unable to distinguish between truth and deception, or deception appears to yield a more desirable (even if false) outcome, the temptation gains power over the thought process and prevents moral authority from being absolute, and corruption begins.
- The imagined outcome leads to the single act of giving in to the temptation.
- Each time the individual is faced with a similar temptation, it is easier to imagine a more desirable outcome, leading to the development of a habit that slowly corrodes the innate morality of an individual based on upbringing and instruction.
- The habits become so ingrained that the individual develops a compulsion to achieve that desired outcome at an increasingly risky level.
- Eventually, compulsions take over the thought process, and the individual no longer has control over how the desired outcome is achieved. They are obsessed with achievement, while full possession of the temptation source (demonic suggestion) has taken possession of the thought process itself. The person has become the temptation, no longer able to discern morality or systems of law (psychological as well as social).

Desensitization begins in the mind. The battle is won or lost in the mind. Therefore, it is in the mind where the decision to flee temptation or yield to it must take place. Only the individual can make the decision.

Topic: Seven Deadly Sins
Source: www.learnreligions.com
Author: Scott P. Richert
Date: March 28, 2017

- The seven deadly sins are identified as follows:
  - Lust
  - Gluttony
  - Greed (avarice, covetousness)
  - Sloth
  - Pride
  - Envy
  - Wrath
- All are sources of temptation for individuals, dependent upon their personal desires (thoughts and feelings).
- Pride: a sense of one's self-worth out of proportion to reality; normally counted as first of seven deadly sins because it can and often does lead to the commission of sin order to feed one's pride; taken to an extreme, can even result in rebellion against God, through belief that one owes all that he has to his own efforts and not at all to God's grace. Lucifer's fall from heaven was the result of his pride, and Adam and Eve committed sin in the garden after Lucifer himself appealed to their pride.
- Covetousness: the strong desire for possessions, especially for possessions that belong to another, as in the ninth commandment ("Thou shalt not covet thy neighbor's wife") and the tenth commandment ("Thou shalt not covet thy neighbor's goods"); while greed and avarice are sometimes used as synonyms, they both normally refer to an overwhelming desire for things that one could legitimately possess.
- Lust: a desire for sexual pleasure that is out of proportion to the good of sexual union or is directed at someone with whom one has no right to sexual union—that is, someone other than one's spouse. It is possible to have lust toward

one's spouse if one's desire for him or her is selfish rather than aimed at the deepening of the marital union.

- Anger: the excessive desire to take revenge; "righteous anger" refers to a proper response to injustice or wrongdoing; anger, as one of the deadly sins, may begin with a legitimate grievance but escalates until it is out of proportion to the wrong done.
- Gluttony: excessive desire, not for food and drink, but for the pleasure obtained by eating and drinking; most often associated with overeating, drunkenness is also a consequence of gluttony.
- Envy: sadness at the good fortune of another, whether in possessions, success, virtues, or talents; sadness arises from the sense that the other person does not deserve the good fortune, but you do, and especially because of a sense that the other person's good fortune has somehow deprived you of similar good fortune.
- Sloth: a laziness or sluggishness when facing the effort necessary to perform a task; sinful when one lets a necessary task go undone (or when one does it badly) because one is unwilling to make the necessary effort.

Children of the Apocalypse

A good deed done for earthy gain is an
evil deed at bottom. Motive impacts
moral quality, and without a holy
motive there cannot be a holy act.

—*The Alliance Weekly/Witness,* A.W. Tozer

Each new day brings new challenges to the citizens of Satan's Den. Mundane activities have a way of turning into soul-wrenching adventures that test the power of faith. Everyone treads lightly on unfamiliar ground. Caution is the buzzword. Keep your eyes open and your heart pure.*

**Taken from the journal of a young woman not native to Satan's Den. Her job had drawn her to the area, as her friends had also been drawn. They became unwitting pawns in the spiritual warfare of Satan's Den.*

"There's something definitely weird about this place," I stated as I glanced around the naked living room. In one corner sat a small stack of books, the only memories that someone had once lived there.

"I know what you mean," said Ellie, picking up a book from the pile and examining it.

"Well, I find it very strange that the former owners literally disappeared, belongings and all, leaving only a mysterious message on an answering machine in an obscure realty office." Martin is Ellie's husband, and as confused as the rest of us.

My husband knelt, leaning over the stack of books, perusing their titles, and laughing at what he found. "These are all kid's books," he said. "Most of them quite old. Why would they have been left behind when everything else was obviously taken?"

I shrugged my shoulders. Martin and Ellie exchanged unreadable glances.

We were there to look at the house as potential buyers. Martin and Ellie already had a contract on another house pending but had found this one, much larger and in a better neighborhood, for a much lower price. We had come along in case they decided to pass; we were looking to purchase our first home as well.

Putting the books back in their short stack, we started on through the house. There was no realtor to pressure us or give us details. We had been told where to find the keys and invited to tour to our content. The dining room, though empty, seemed filled with anticipation, as though it expected a laughing crowd to burst through the door any moment and occupy a heavily laden table. I could smell the food. It felt good but eerie.

Our tour led to the stairs. Midway up, we seemed to simultaneously stop, engulfed in an unearthly chill. Exchanging glances, we had all felt it, I knew, whatever it was. I had flashes of children running and laughing—nothing definite, just sensations. I couldn't be sure if anyone else felt it.

At the top of the stairs was a window. Ellie and I stopped to admire the view, a large lot extending a half-acre or more. The winter-worn grass was just beginning to replenish its green carpeting. A faint brown spiral spun dizzily where a flower garden must have once flourished. I had a sudden vision of Victorian splendor—children at play, iron benches scattered about, a glorious garden in full bloom. The vision of beauty shifted unexpectedly to bleak, darkened winter. Tiny, neglected, unmarked graves crisscrossed the spiral path. Winter black leaves blew restlessly across the yard. I shuddered and stepped away from the window.

I turned and entered the nearest bedroom, wrapping my arms around myself to drive away the chills and rubbing at the bumps rising from my skin. Whispers seemed to echo everywhere in this room. It was, I felt, a child's room. Josh and Martin were talking loudly in a far corner of the room. The whispers continued to assault me, vying for my attention. I turned to Ellie. I could tell she, too, was affected by the ambience of this place. I wondered if she heard the whispers.

The whispers became louder, more insistent. One came clearer than the rest. A girl was speaking to me, drawing me back to the window in the hallway. Gently, she talked to me, told me her need. She told me she and the others had been longing for and seeking out one such as I. She explained that many children had died in this place—illness, injury, and murder—and that they sought only the chance to live again the brief years they once lived. She explained that we would be the vessels to give them life. They would live the same number of days as originally bestowed upon them, giving us the pleasure of parenthood and them the blessing of a happier life.

They sought no other obligation from us. They sought no retribution on those that had harmed them. Their only plea was for life. I questioned the voice regarding the safety of my two-year-old son. She assured me no harm would come to him. He would be a part of their family just as they became a part of ours. They promised to quietly fade away at the end of their life span, be it infancy, mid-adolescence, or somewhere in between. The voices were silenced as their peace was said.

I realized the voice had been addressing both Ellie and me as potential buyers. I could easily understand why this place was so cheap. Would anyone be able to withstand the temptation and fear presented by these presences? A childless couple would be easy prey, as would a couple facing fertility issues and miscarriages. Parents who knew the heartbreak of losing a child would fall for the chance at being guaranteed parents. Here was an opportunity for a pregnancy and delivery of who knew how many children, without heartache, all of whom would grow to a certain age and then fade away back to wherever they came from, leaving a satisfied family with fulfilled compassion.

Ellie and I didn't speak; we didn't have to. Our expressions spoke volumes. Quietly, we turned, walked back down the stairs and out the front door. Josh and Martin followed, puzzled. None of us spoke as we drove away, not once looking back.

None of us have ever discussed our experiences; I don't think any of us could. How would we explain it to one another as we each experienced it separately?

I don't know if the house ever sold. I don't go by there anymore. I often wonder about those children. Who were they if they had ever really existed at all? Had they really died horribly as they claimed? Could I have been the vessel of life, and hope, they so desperately needed for their redemption? Or were they foul spirits only preying upon the hapless souls who fell into their fetid traps? I never did find out about the previous owners. I always felt I could hear their muffled cries from the depths of that deadened spiral, where they were being tormented by demonic children eternally. May their souls find peace.

2 Timothy 3:14–17

> But if you must continue in the things which you have learned and been assured of, knowing from whom you have learned them, and from childhood you have known the holy scriptures, which are able to make you wise for salvation through faith which is in christ jesus.

Notes of Lurlene Joy McCoy

This is a story of demonic deception and predation. I have no information regarding the location of this particular house or property and have been unsuccessful in connecting any deaths of this number and nature to any one place.

The narrator mentioned she had a two-year-old son whom the spirits had promised not to harm. She also mentioned that this sort of temptation would be difficult to resist for compassionate parent-want-to-bes. Was she speaking of her own experience or that of her friend Ellie? These spirits had a very specific target type in mind. Whether they were attached to the house or the land isn't clear, though the vision of the spiral graves indicate it could possibly be the latter; it was a dangerous place for the desperate and weak of will.

Manifestation is the first stage of demonic possession. This house was infested with demons who manifested themselves as the voices of children. Children are a common form for demonic manifestation where compassion of the victims can be manipulated through their apparent innocence and playfulness, mistakenly taken to be harmless and, therefore, not a threat. It is only as their true nature begins to influence the victim that the true danger is realized, far too frequently, too late for the victim to fight back.

Demons are usually invited into a place or an individual in some manner, whether being too open to things of the paranormal, dabbling in the occult, performing dangerous rituals, or just simply being a magnet for a particular demon who then "hitches a ride" with the chosen individual.

The demons reveal their presence in subtle ways that are, at first, nearly imperceptible, then escalate more overtly until their presence is evident to their target, family members, friends, and others who come in contact with the target. This may include audible noises and/or voices; visual stimuli such as moving objects, shadows, or apparitions; physical contact from a feeling of discomfort to agonizing pain; medical conditions that worsen despite treatment or identifiable cause; accidents or unexplained injuries; and blatant attacks by unseen forces that lead to serious injury or fatality. Mental fatigue from persistent and increasingly tormenting mental conditions may result in suicidal and/or homicidal ideations or actions.

The demons described here manifested as children's voices pleading for compassion and a chance at being loved, a tactic that would play upon a woman's heartstrings. Judging by the journal entry, this young woman had some knowledge and/or experience with things not of this world. She only questioned the motive of the voices after she had escaped the house and their defined boundaries. Would she have fallen for their pleas if she had not already had a child of her own? What about Ellie? It's hard to say without speaking to either woman personally.

The journal was found in a dresser drawer by a man who had purchased it at a thrift store sidewalk sale. He had found it wedged into the back of the drawer when he began to work on it, to restore it to its original condition after years of being painted over. The only names in the journal were those involved in the events recorded; no indication of ownership has been found. He brought the journal to me, thinking I might be interested in purchasing it. While otherwise interesting but of no concern to me, I nearly turned him away. When he showed me this entry, I knew I had to investigate. I bought the journal. I asked the man what he knew about the dresser. He told me the name of the thrift store where he had purchased it. When I contacted the owner, she could only tell me it had come in an odd lot of items purchased from an abandoned storage locker. No other information has been found. Dead end, no pun intended.

Topic: Satan's Plan against Us

Source: Life Application Study Bible, King James Version, Zondervan Publishing

The Five Ds

Doubt—makes you question God's Word and His Goodness
Discouragement—makes you look at your problems rather than at God
Diversion—makes the wrong things seem attractive so that you want them more
Defeat—makes you feel like a failure so that you don't even try
Delay—makes you put off doing something so that it never gets done

Satan's Work in the World (Revelation 12–13)

His hatred for Christ (12:13–15)—"And when the dragon saw that he was cast unto the earth, he persecuted the woman which brought forth the man **child.** And to the woman were given two wings of a great eagle, that she might fly into the wilderness, into her place, where she is nourished for a time, and times, and half a time, from the face of the serpent. And the serpent cast out of his mouth water as a flood after the woman, that he might cause her to be carried away of the flood."

His hatred for God's people (12:17)—"And the dragon was wroth with the woman and went to make war with the remnant of her seed, which keep the commandments of God, and have the testimony of Jesus Christ."

His power and authority (13:2)—"And the beast which I saw was like unto a leopard, and his feet were as the feet of a bear, and his mouth as the mouth of a lion: and the dragon gave him his power and his seat, and great authority."

His popularity among unbelievers (13:3–4)—"And I saw one of his heads as if it were wounded unto death; and his deadly wound was healed: and all the world wondered after the beast. And they worshipped the dragon which gave power unto the beast: and the beast, saying, Who is like unto the beast? Who is able to make war with him?"

His blasphemy against God (13:6)—"And he opened his mouth in blasphemy against God, to blaspheme his name, and his tabernacle, and them that dwell in heaven."

His war against believers (13:7)—"And it was given unto him to make war with the saints, and to overcome them: and the earth shall worship him, whose names are not written in the book of life of the Lamb slain from the foundation of the world."

His ability to deceive (13:14)—"And deceiveth them that dwell on the earth by the means of those miracles which he had power to do in the sight of the beast; saying to them that dwell on the earth, that they should make an image to the beast, which had the wound by a sword, and did live."

God's Armor for Us (Ephesians 6:10–20)

Piece of Armor	Use	Application
Belt Truth		Satan fights with lies, and sometimes his lies sound like truth; but only believers have God's truth, which can defeat Satan's lies.
Breastplate Righteousness		Satan often attacks our heart—the seat of our emotions, self-worth, and trust. God's righteousness is the breastplate that protects our heart and ensures his approval. He approves of us because he loves us and sent his Son to die for us.
Shoes Readiness to Spread the Good News		Satan wants us to think that telling others the Good News is a worthless and hopeless task—the size of the task is too big, and negative responses are too much to handle. But the shoes God gives us are the motivation to continue to proclaim the true peace that is available in God—news everyone needs to hear.
Shield Faith		What we see are Satan's attacks in the form of insults, setbacks, and temptations. But the shield of faith protects us from Satan's fiery arrows. With God's perspective, we can see beyond our circumstances and know that ultimate victory is ours.

Helmet Salvation	Satan wants to make us doubt God, Jesus, and our salvation. The helmet protects our mind from doubting God's saving work for us.
Sword Word of God	The sword is the only weapon of offense in this list of armor. There are times when we need to take the offensive against Satan. When we are tempted, we need to trust in the truth of God's Word.
	Prayer is another weapon we can use against the enemy. While not listed directly as a piece of the armor, it is crucial for prayer to be a part of the believer's armor if we were to be truly effective in battling the enemy. We cannot have an impact against him if we aren't in constant prayer.

Topic: Twelve Points Regarding the True Identity of Ghosts

Author: Rev. Mark A. Hunnemann
Source: http://spiritualrealities.org

Summary

Ghosts are said to be the trapped souls of deceased human beings.

We can all choose the authority of autonomous reason or God's Word as our authority on this topic.

According to God's Word, all of what is perceived as being "ghosts" or "apparitions" are really demonic spirits mimicking human behavior in order to deceive us.

1. Deuteronomy 18:9–14, God commands us to not attempt to speak to the dead, which was a popular occult practice in Canaan. This practice is tied directly to idolatry, which is forbidden to God's people, as idolatry was demonic in nature.
2. 2 Corinthians 11: 14 warns that Satan can assume the appearance of an angel of light in an attempt to deceive humanity into believing he is a messenger of God. While he was once an angel in God's kingdom, he became an angel of darkness when he was ejected from heaven after attempting to overthrow God. Because of their very nature, these fallen angels can take on the appearance of children, elderly women, a favorite uncle, a benevolent spirit guide, and many other convincing forms that are designed to set an individual at ease before revealing their true destructive nature.
3. When biblically challenged, demonic entities will reveal their true nature.
4. Hebrews 9:27, along with other passages of the scripture, makes it clear that death of the physical body releases our souls to their final destination for eternity—heaven or hell.
5. Jesus's death on the cross defeated Satan, death, and the grave, as His resurrection shows. Hebrews 2:14–15 and Revelation 1:18 attest to this, thereby contradicting the belief that an unsuspecting or traumatic death can trap the soul.
6. The Judeo-Christian faith has taught that "ghosts" are demonic spirits for over 3,500 years, in contrast with paganistic "New Age" teachings to the contrary.
7. Based on current data available, "ghosts" lack true human aspects.

8. Although using the scientific method, paranormal specialists cannot explain why only some traumatic deaths appear to result in hauntings, while the majority do not.
9. Colossians 1:16–17 indicates that Jesus was not only present at the creation of the world and remains active in its sustainment, He walked on the earth among humanity, expelling *demons* from inflicted individuals. If ghosts of trapped humans existed, they would have sought freedom from their condition just as the sick, blind, deaf, and dumb sought healing for their conditions.
10. Human "ghosts" appear to undergo some character and personality changes in death. EVPs inevitably spout angry and blasphemous language. If they were truly deceased humans and were "in the know" about the hereafter, there should be more information about the hereafter and its nature—heaven and hell—yet there is no mention of the glories of the afterlife. God's grace is absent in their ravings. Demons despise grace.
11. The spirit world as we perceive it is merely a "holding cell" for Satan and his demons as they await their permanent exile to the lake of fire. We are "playing in Satan's sandbox" when we become involved in paranormal activity.
12. Any form of communicating with the "dead"—spirit boards, trances, automatic writing, etc.—is an invitation to make their demonic presence known, thereby giving them a foothold to enter an individual's life.

Looking for the Land of the Lotus Eaters

If we could forget our troubles as
easily as we forget our blessings,
how different things would be.

—Robert C. Savage, *Pocket Wisdom*

Many have tried to escape the horrors that engulf the soul in Satan's Den, but few have ever managed. Those few that are able to leave are haunted by it eternally. Woe to those who enter it unwillingly, as evidenced by this item found recently in a journal written by a distraught woman a number of years ago when she was admitted to the county's psychiatric ward ....

November 20, 1994(?)

Memory is a fragile and quite fickle mistress. It is odd what we choose to recall and what we choose to forget, or so I am told. Odder yet that we should choose to retain the memories that we would most like to forget and to forget those we would like to cherish. Contemplation of such complexities only serves to deepen the mystery I find myself enshrouded in.

I don't remember the year or even why we were traveling—three young farmgirls, best friends, alone on unfamiliar roads, but we were. Taking a picnic beside a pleasant roadside stream, we somehow missed seeing an unknown bandit or gang of bandits rob us of everything but the near-broken-down wagon we had been traveling in.

Devastated, we allowed ourselves to be taken in by people from a nearby settlement. Time passed. We, each of us, found ourselves attached to three different households: two of us by marriage, one by other arrangements. We all seemed to have forgotten where we had come from and where we had been going on that long-forgotten day. All that mattered was our present, miserable existences.

Claudia had married a wealthy citizen who considered her a pretty object that could provide him with an heir. She was given everything she could wish for or want. The finest fashions were hers but brought no happiness. Even her son, who took after his father, neglected her for other pursuits.

Nancy was unfortunate in her relationship as well. Her man refused to marry her, in spite of the children she had given him. Nancy was abused and battered by this drunken, low-class bum. It was later discovered he had been involved with the theft of our belongings. Nancy didn't love this hideous excuse for a man, but he was all the support she had.

I counted myself lucky to be married to the better man of the three. Though I did not love him, and he knew this, he was nonetheless attentive to me. He didn't pressure me about marital relations or social obligations. We lived more as companions than husband and wife. I felt no desire to become a part of the social culture a man of his financial stature belonged to. We were neither rich nor poor… nor happy.

At every opportunity, I met with my friends. We wept over one another's predicaments. None of us knew of an easy way out. Societal dictates required us to make the best of the life chosen for us by fate. Often, we wondered if our families were searching for us…if we even had families.

We were all, once, young, respectable, churchgoing girls. Now we were heathen, forsaken women trapped in a world not of our own making. Madame Memory had deprived us of what we most desired and entrapped us in a world where fear and despair reigned. We saw no truly happy people in our limited world. Everyone seemed to be in the same mindless stupor we found ourselves in.

Nancy was the first to crack. The increased drunken abusiveness of her man had finally pushed her over the edge, I suppose. Though she wouldn't discuss it, she began planning to escape. We were all drawn to her desire for freedom.

The plan came together one warm autumn afternoon. Nancy, Claudia, and I had tea together at Claudia's great house. Afterward, we all went to Nancy's. Nancy hid us about her sitting room. She wanted us to witness the behavior her man inflicted upon her. We were frightened—for Nancy as well as ourselves.

Just before her man was expected, Nancy thrust a sharpened knife into Claudia's hands and a small gun into mine, hissing that we were to protect ourselves if *he* were to discover our presence and attack us.

I was appalled by the scene played out before us that afternoon. Nancy greeted that beast softly, as though he were one of her small children. He returned her gentility with a gruff command. Nancy tried very carefully to maintain an innocent stature but occasionally glanced toward our hiding places to ensure our presence.

It wasn't long before that foul creature became suspicious and began questioning Nancy about where her "lover" was hidden. Nancy denied the presence of another man and all other beings as well. He became brutal at that moment. He knocked Nancy onto her bustle. She sat there on the floor as he began ripping the sitting room apart. I was afraid he would discover Claudia behind the makeshift china cabinet.

I must have gasped in fear, for he turned his rage in my direction. He yanked back the curtains from the alcove where I was hidden. Instinctively, I raised the gun and fired.

From the seated position I had fallen to as the man charged me, I realized the first shot would hit his hidden parts. I tried to rise and fire again at his chest.

The hammer hit upon the second chamber. As I heard the click of the empty chamber, I realized I had fired an empty gun upon an angry animal. In horror, I tossed the gun aside and looked toward my attacker.

He had grabbed his chest and was staggering, falling backward, as though he had, in fact, been shot. I saw no blood, except in his eyes. Nancy and Claudia stood screaming in terror.

I turned and fled from the house. I prayed Claudia and Nancy would follow.

I never knew if they were able to escape. I knew only the freedom of the wind as it tore at my clothing and snatched the hairpins from my hair.

As I overcame my fear and embraced the wind, I began to notice the scene around me. The town seemed to grow bigger and more complex with each step I took. Houses and buildings seemed to spring up before my exhausted eyes. Where horses had once ruled, new conveyances now stood—strange, multicolored things with hard-shelled tops, like giant turtles.

I slowed my pace to behold these wonders. The changes seemed to slow as well. Soon, I was walking, and all became clear. I was no longer where I had once been. Where I had gone and how I got there I did not know. Everything was familiar yet very strange. I felt overwhelmed by my experience. I collapsed tearfully on a soft, green lawn and prayed for a better future in this strangely familiar and frighteningly new world I had been magically transported to.

Only time would reveal its newest plans for me.

Isaiah 51:12–13, NKJV

> I, even I, am he who comforts you.
> Who are you that you should be afraid
> Of a man who will die.
> And the son of a man who will be made like grass?
> And forget the lord your maker,
> Who stretched out the heavens
> And laid the foundations of the earth'
> You have feared continually every day
> Because of the fury of the oppressor,
> When he has prepared to destroy
> And where is the fury of the oppressor.

Notes of Lurlene Joy McCoy

Here we are back to that troublesome time quotient. It brings along the concept of parallel dimensions and time travel. This unidentified woman (kept confidential by her doctors) seems to have many things happening all at once in her mind.

First, there appears to be some selective memory loss as the girls could only remember vague details of the picnic and robbery—nothing before that. She did not mention any physical harm they may have experienced at the time of the robbery, yet it would have been sufficiently traumatic that some harm would have to have naturally occurred as a result of the activity. The man, or men, would have been capable of harming or even killing these naive young girls, with violation being a likely scenario. The girls only remember the violence of the discovered robbery and the kindness of strangers to take them in.

Second, unhappiness is a theme present throughout the narrative and in all characters portrayed. Unhappiness and a desire to escape united these three best friends in that final violent act before the narrator fled.

She escaped. But to what? She was curious yet did not seem any happier about her escape.

Addictions begin with attempts at self-medicating unhappiness. Unhappiness seemed to be the addiction to being lost to all she knew. She fueled present unhappiness with a different form of unhappiness that led to a depressive cycle that presents as a temporal disconnect—she doesn't know past from present, real from imagined. Psychotherapy can lend a listening ear to reassemblage of this disconnect. Or it could serve to further confuse her.

If, however, she really did time travel, or cross-dimensional travel, her illness is irrelevant and irreversible.

Even churchgoing girls can be led down a disastrous path to destruction. Churchgoing is simply habit in a lifestyle designed to promote a form of righteousness, a social obligation that sets an individual apart from the "sinners" in their community who refuse to "step foot in a church filled with hypocrites."

The fracturing of the void during Creation left behind cosmic dust that has been throwing space-monkey wrenches into the works ever since, blinding the minds of humanity and distorting their understanding of free will.

As the woman said, "Only time will tell." Her story isn't yet finished. Perhaps her experience will open up new understandings for science to tinker with as they attempt to explain the universe and how it works in the future,

Time lapses, loops, and wrinkles appear in multiple records within these pages. While science struggles to explain the basic structure of the universe and the inner workings of time, with possible time travel and interdimensional journeys, James L. Rubart has attempted to put these into a spiritual perspective. In his Well Spring trilogy, he introduces us to five individuals who dare to go deeper into the many realms of the spirit world. They discover teleportation, soul walking, and more as they partake in spiritual warfare alongside angels, against the armies of the Enemy. The Song, the Leader, the Teacher, and the Temple have to face themselves and their own weaknesses if they are to survive. The Teacher happens to be a physics professor who has written a book on multiple dimensions and their structure and function in the universe. When he gets caught up in unexpected dimensional hopping, he has to address what he thought he knew with what the Holy Spirit reveals to him.

The Holy Spirit is their guide, but demons can also travel in these alternate realities and dimensions. It isn't always easy to determine friend from enemy, but they learn to trust one another, the Holy Spirit, and themselves in their life-or-death adventures.

When C. S. Lewis talks of the "deeper magic" within *Narnia*, I believe he may be referring to something similar to what James L. Rubart describes. While the children who visit Narnia are, at best, novice in things of the Spirit, they do "go deeper." Rubart expands this concept to take proficient Christian characters and instruct them in science-fiction-level dimensional travel outside of their own bodies that allows them to fulfill scriptures that may otherwise be obscure and easily forgotten, by using the power of God Himself to create and use weapons we can only begin to imagine. Faith is always an issue. Are they strong enough to win the battle when their own weaknesses are thrown at them by a clever deceiver?

So much to learn and ponder here.

Phantasee

God makes salvation conditional upon
a response to a message. That message is
the message of the cross—the message of
redemption of a dying and risen Lord,
and our faith in God's declaration of
intention, a thing that God declares He
plans to do, and will do, if we believe.

—A. W. Tozer, *Fellowship of the Burning Heart*

Determining fantasy from reality is often one of the most difficult tasks in Satan's Den. What one perceives isn't what really is in every case. Because these mountains have a way of bending and twisting reality, people have tried to bend and twist that very nature into a profit. One such brave soul came to town a wealthy man. How will he leave…if at all?

David Masters came to Satan's Den seeking to cash in on its reputation. With a doctorate in engineering, a wild imagination, and enough spending cash to choke a whole herd of elephants, David proposed to build a small amusement park in the heart of Satan's Den. It wouldn't be much more than an ordinary carnival but would feature an unforgettable tourist draw—*Phantasee*—a ghostly ride through mountains with roller-coaster actions through the very depths of the hell Satan's Den is known for.

Superstitious elders warned David Masters away from this dangerous and ludicrous plan, but the younger generation supported him in his efforts to bring Satan's Den into the twenty-second century where it most longed to be. The future would surely overshadow the past, making it obsolete. The young people—newly of voting age to early middle-aged dreamers—rallied around David Masters and were able to persuade the town council to permit a building plan to be submitted.

Six months of hard work brought forth a glorious architectural plan, a plan that did not alter Satan's Den's most famous mountain-top. In fact, it enhanced the very resources around it—natural and supernatural. The economics of the undertaking could result in phenomenal wealth for the local citizens. David Masters was not interested in the money, just the reputation which would come with the taming of the mountain itself. He was financially well off enough already but was lacking in ego and ego support.

Three years after its inception, *Hell's Garden* amusement park opened to the public. The name had brought heavy opposition from local churches but had been overthrown by majority votes and persuasive ad agencies. Test advertisements had brought positive press. Positive press was money in the bank and prestige at the Club.

Many teenagers and adults were employed. Most came from surrounding counties; the locals were unable to overcome their superstitions. It didn't stop them from lining up to see this newest technological eyesore. Among the locals who chose to set aside traditional fears were three young women, best friends, newly graduated from community college.

The three donned their uniforms proudly. Each was working a different part of the park but shared common breaks. They got together to share experiences for those brief moments of reprieve they were allowed. During one of these short breaks, they decided to check out *Phantasee* after their shift ended.

Promptly at four, the three met in front of the Devil's Grill for a quick dinner before their "ride into death and back." They ate hot dogs and french fries with their large sodas. They teased one another about their uniforms. Teri was lean and golden. Her athletic form suited her uniform well. Susan was naturally slender. Her uniform fit well but did not cling in the way Teri's did around certain parts of her body. Dawn was slightly overweight and self-conscious. She joked that her uniform had been meant for Teri but had somehow ended up on her. She tended to self-consciously rub her stomach area where she imagined mountainous rolls of fat created by a tight-fitting shirt. The three were very different in appearance but one in spirit.

Their giggles continued as they stood in line for *Phantasee.* It was the most popular ride in the park. People were discussing what they thought the ride would be like. Some of them recognized the uniforms and asked about the ride. The girls had no answers. Their training had included a no-discussion policy regarding park secrets. In fact, the subject of *Phantasee* had been forbidden. Only the individuals involved in its creation and David Masters were left to tell. All the others left town as soon as the coaster was up and running. No one knew who did the maintenance checks on the ride. The written reports just appeared on the right desk each morning before anyone came into the office. Preopening press had described *Phantasee* as "your dreams come true" and "a ride through your greatest nightmares." It was definitely high-tech. It was reportedly using an advanced design of some sort of virtual reality holographic system that could read your mind and make you think your greatest dream is coming true. This same technology was used belowground to bring out your darkest fears. Everyone believed this technology to be completely bogus and unrealistic. Science wasn't capable of this yet, was it?

As they reached the platform where they would board the train, their excitement grew. Two young men in front of them became more talkative. They had exchanged friendly conversations throughout their wait, but the talk became more openly flirtatious, especially toward Teri and Susan. Dawn felt like a spare tire. The two young men got into the seat just in front of Susan and Teri. Dawn sat alone in the third seat of the car. They were in the last of the three six-passenger cars in the train sporting a dual-faced image of a half angel-half demon figure. The train pulled out slowly. Jitters and giggles pervaded the entire train. Riders held their breath in anticipation.

The train slowly moved forward, almost relaxed, out of the station and into a wooded area. The wooded area opened into a narrow valley. Dawn looked eagerly to her right. She saw only a lush, green valley. To her left, she was taken aback. She saw a storybook castle nestled in the lush, green grass at the base of the mountain. On the lawn, beneath a single leafy tree, she saw a handsome young knight wooing a beautiful maiden. To her shock and delight, she realized the maiden was *her*. She could feel the passionate embrace of her lover. His kisses brushed protest from her lips. His words enflamed her heart and set fire to her cheeks. She melted inside as she began to respond to his gentle persuasions. She began to breathe heavily. No romance novel could match the passion she felt as she passed through this valley.

She was so enraptured by her dream (reality?) she almost didn't notice the change in the world around her. Her heart was beating quickly already, her face flushed with passion (embarrassment?). The sudden lurch of the train brought her abruptly back to the ride. Her pulse raced even quicker.

The train had passed into the woods once more. The air was chilly. It seemed darker than before and was getting darker by the moment. She found herself becoming frightened as the train began to pick up speed, though it was winding its way uphill. The woods seemed silent and still as they sped between trees, moving ever upward. The noise of the amusement park was gone, replaced by eerie silence.

"This is where we plunge suddenly into darkness," muttered one of the young men.

"Cool!" replied the other.

Dawn remained reserved. She wasn't sure she was ready for this. She closed her eyes, slid down in her seat, gripped the safety bar until her knuckles turned white, and began to pray. She had never been big on roller coasters before, and this one was so completely different from any other ever created before.

The train reached the peak and slid silently around a curve and…

fell…

into total darkness…

plunging at breakneck speed…

bottomless.

The train sped around curves. The rock walls oozed with blackened spring water. Images flashed as they sped by—emaciated, starving children, hideously deformed people, victims of violence, fiery car crashes. Any traumatic event known to mankind—natural, supernatural, manmade—imprinted themselves upon the minds of the viewers. Intense screams of thrill became desperate pleas for help as the tracks pulled them deeper into the heart of the mountain, jerking, spinning topsy-turvy through multiple loops and tight tunnels. At one point in the ride, the riders traveled upside down for several hundred feet before plunging unexpectedly into an inverted backward loop that seemed to go on for an eternity. The deeper they fell, the darker it became until it was so dark no one could see their hand in front of their faces. They felt enclosed and utterly alone in the pressing stone. The train slowed, then stopped, as if dead.

There was total impenetrable darkness. No one dared move or breathe. Speaking was out of the question. Some people were crying; their sobs seemed deadened by the very pressure of the earth around them. When the riders felt they would go mad with the stark nothingness, they were jerked back to life by the sudden forward movement of the train. More twists, turns, and images assaulted their already abused senses.

Their eyes dilated with sudden bright light as the tracks pulled them from the depths of hell and back to the reality of life on earth. The train came to a gentle stop at the station. Loud clicking alerted passengers that they were now free to exit the train cars.

Most of the passengers exited quickly, pasty-faced. One or two passengers stopped to vomit as their very souls adjusted to this new level of being. Dawn and several other passengers had to be coaxed from their seats by the staff assigned to the exit room, an empty warehouse-like space separate from the open loading area. The gently lit room had only one exit, marked ONLY ONE WAY in mysterious script.

Outside, the girls clung to one another. When they had calmed down, they quickly exited the park, without speaking of their experience. Each rationalized her own experience—"They used mirrors and holograms," "It wasn't real," "No one would believe me if I told them," "I must be crazy."

Their lives were touched by their brief four-minute experience. They finished the summer at Hell's Garden, then set off to universities at three different locations in the fall. Each chose a different school, far apart from one another. They were forever friends, forced to go different ways by their own personal convictions. Where their futures would lead, only time would tell. The only certainty they had was that they had been to hell and back, and that experience had caused them to mature beyond their years into young women who could make a change in their world—for good or bad, only their souls knew.

How long will *Phantasee* run? In Satan's Den, the ride never ends.

John 10:7–10, NKJV

> Then Jesus said to them again, "Most assuredly, I say to you, I am the door of the sheep. All who ever come before me are thieves and robbers, but the sheep did not hear them. I am the door. If anyone enters by me, he will be saved, and will go in and out and find pasture. The thief does not come except to steal, and to kill, and to destroy. I have come that they may have life, and that they may have it more abundantly."

Notes of Lurlene Joy McCoy

To put things in perspective, the pleasure trip at the beginning of the ride represents our deepest desires—love, money, power, prestige. These things may or may not be achievable in our lifetime. Circumstances could either catapult us to where we think we want to be or thwart us from achieving what we so desire. Here lies our temptation zone.

The darkness within the mountain is much more realistic. It shows us the world as it truly is—a black mess of pain and tragedy that befalls everyone to some degree. It is the stuff of true nightmares, not prophetic in nature, just an exposure of what lies beneath the scabs we have encrusted to hide our wounds.

If you have ever been in a cave with no light to guide you, you will understand the impact of absolute darkness when the ride comes to a sudden, unexpected stop, just as you were ready to escape the anguish you were feeling, stoking the fires of fear to a near wildfire within you. Hearing is the only sense you retain. The acoustics of the cave carry each sound, bouncing it around you until you feel them accumulate around you. Disorienting dizziness pulls your body around and around as you feel yourself spiraling into that eternal darkness, alone, eternally alone.

The sudden jerk of the car as it resumes its journey becomes a dual trial—will there be further darkness ahead, or will there at last be blessed light?

The overwhelming light at the end of the darkness is an assault on the senses, demanding response—fight or flight. Most don't hesitate to flee the exit chamber. A few spend time fighting the sensations within them, trying to reconcile what they can't unsee with what their world boldly presents through rose-colored glasses. Regardless of fight or flight, each person must endure the trial that results, often for the remainder of their lives.

There are the rare individuals who exit the ride laughing and rejoicing, tears of happiness running down their cheeks. They are not immune to the gravity of what they have experienced; neither are they so calloused as to find torment amusing. No, these are the ones who have found the ONE WAY hinted at in the sign at the exit.

They got into the line, looking like every other person there. They anticipated and supposed along with everyone else. The difference would have been revealed if it were possible to share their greatest desires with others. These individuals saw themselves in humble service to humanity. They were soldiers in the trenches, fighting against the dark ills of society by making themselves available to serve those in need. They wore the blood of social injustice like medals of valor as they fed small children with distended tummies, gave clothing and shelter to those who had none, visited prisoners in their cells, and bandaged those too shell-shocked to respond to their own wounds. They wept with those who wept and laughed with those who rejoiced. In the final moments, before they plunged into darkness, they saw themselves welcomed by loving arms into eternity.

In the darkness, they saw the torments others were experiencing. They wept for those who were lost in the darkness. They reached out to their neighbors and tried to tell them there was an escape. They knew they would never see the hell portrayed here or the one waiting in eternity, but they did not want to see anyone else condemned to this eternity either. They renewed their concern for humanity and vowed to never give up their efforts to lead others to the one way that leads to eternal rest, peace, and love.

These are the true fighters. They face death without fear. They will fight for you, even if you have never met. Victory is theirs, even if they die. While the rest of the world is content to hide behind their rose-colored glasses, these individuals see the world through lenses of eternal truth. They see a wall of solid darkness that engulfs each of us. It is our nature. We can hide in the darkness, but where light has been welcomed, the darkness is pierced. With many, it is the tiniest of pricks that causes the darkness to be disturbed and become disorienting. For others, who have not only welcomed the light but have also embraced it, there are more and larger pinholes where the light is penetrating the darkness and pushing it aside to reveal the truth within. A few rare, seasoned warriors will blind you with their light. The darkness has been dissipated into bits of dust, flitting through the light, trying to find its way back to that comfortable cocoon that had kept it hidden as it went about transforming and twisting the soul of the person it enshrouded. The darkness pounds at the light angrily as its work is undone and the person is transformed slowly into a being of light that can withstand any onslaught of the darkness.

Phantasee has always run through the lifetime of mankind. It will end only when mankind is no more. Heed well what you see and experience there; it will determine the one-way ticket for your eternity (John 14:6).

The idea of trial to determine eternal status is not exclusive to Christianity. Egyptians believed they would go through a series of trials ending with the weighing of their souls—their rights and wrongs—on a scale that would determine their destination in the afterlife. The Greco-Roman traditions outlined a series of eternities ranging from a place of peace to layers of increasing depravity for those who were unpleasant in life. Incan and Aztec traditions speak of a journey through a cave that connects our world with the underworld through a series of trials that determine the individuals' true character and their eternal destination. Even reincarnation is determined by an individual's behavior in their previous life, making it difficult to achieve Nirvana as long as any selfish evil remains in them.

Though all roads do not lead to heaven, much of the journey is always fraught with trials to condemn or strengthen us as we allow them to.

Could there be an elemental plane for the soul itself? Sometimes spirit is included as a fifth element—with air, water, fire, and earth. This brings up the concept of soul versus spirit. Are they one and the same or two separate entities, as described by some scholars?

We have all heard we are to take care of our mind, body, and soul.

Using just three concepts, we have identified humanity as being made up of three parts.

Our body was formed from the material of the earth, through Adam (Genesis 2:7), and to the earth we shall return in death and decay (Genesis 2:19). Therefore, our body is connected to the earth and is natural.

Our soul is described as being that supernatural and eternal part of us that connects us to God. It is God within us. We are His image-bearers—reflections of who He is (Genesis 1:27).

That leaves our spirits—the part of us that sets us apart from one another. What and how we think, feel, and respond to the world around us reveals our personality. Here is the seat of free will—our ability and privilege to choose between two opposing concepts, weighing for ourselves both sides before choosing one over the other, determining for ourselves what our beliefs are, and acting upon those beliefs. Genesis describes the spirit as having been breathed into Adam. It is our life force. It allows our natural selves (body) to interact with the part of ourselves that bears the mark of our Creator (soul). It bridges the natural with the supernatural. It is also our greatest weakness. The body will follow its natural course from life to death, at which point the soul is released to return to the supernatural realm. If our spirit has chosen a path of darkness, that soul, along with the spiritual body that houses it, will be condemned to eternal darkness. The spirit that has chosen the path of light will accompany its soul into eternal light.

The presence of a soul, the birthmark that is a reminder of God's presence, causes us to crave contact with and a connection to God. The physical body made in the likeness of God, however, acts in rebellion, being temporary and corruptible. The spirit is, therefore, a mediator between the natural body and the eternal soul.

Experience reveals what is acceptable and unacceptable in a given culture. This is defined as right and wrong. Prevailing opinion can alter these concepts. Therein lies the purpose of trials. We constantly experience and evaluate human behavior and how we feel about what we experience. Some behavior is never acceptable, while other behavior is dependent upon circumstances. There must be absolute rights and absolute wrongs to prevent confusion. The soul and the flesh are in contrary to each other. God established Law to establish boundaries of right and wrong. This is truth. Any variance from this truth is wrong. Free will provides us the opportunity to choose whether we honor these boundaries or break them.

This is why religion, in general, is so subjective. Cultural norms and mores vary and conflict with one another. Each group feels they are right and correct while the others are wrong and incorrect, leading to condemnation of other beliefs. The war on truth began when Adam and Eve were deceived by the serpent and ejected from Eden. That has not changed; there are simply more contenders in our modern world. The weapons remain the same, and the prize is truth.

Each person must come to terms with the presence of a Greater Power. They must seek their own understanding of their role in a universe dominated by someone or something greater than mankind. Each will be accountable for his or her choices regarding this supernatural power that IS. We can't all be correct, but how do we determine truth from false teaching? We have cold reasoning and rationalization (an absence of all that is natural) at one end of the spectrum and animalistic instinct (the pure natural) at the other. The answer lies somewhere in between. Let God lead through the teaching of the Holy Spirit, an extension of God Himself, to guide the process of recognizing where what is natural (and subjective through experience) meets reason and ration (which can be very subjective based upon belief alone). This is the realm of faith—the acceptance of what is not seen to influence what can be seen, even if it cannot be explained. It just IS. The Holy Spirit performs this function—an umbilicus from Father to child.

Then a day comes when the child must choose to cling to that umbilicus in a new birth of salvation, or sever that cord, condemning themselves to eternal separation from the One who gave them life. As long as we live, we can reconnect to that umbilicus by recognizing our need for our Creator. In this way, the spirit and soul are eternally connected.

Millennia of debates have not been able to prove or disprove the soul/spirit connection. It generally boils down to believe what you want as there is no agreeable answer.

The purpose of the mind and body remains the same, no matter the debate. The spirit is redefined as being supernatural and often interchangeable with the term *soul.* Either definition identifies it as being an immaterial life force that distinguishes between life and death as perceived by humanity. Once this life force leaves the physical body, there is no way to reanimate what is left behind. The material body begins to decay and returns to the earth. The electrical impulses produced by the brain are no longer present to communicate with the neural patterns that create movement and respond to stimuli. The soul/spirit, being immaterial, is then freed of physical constraint and incorruptible. They never cease to exist. Herein is the question of life after death.

The spirit life force is the mediator between the natural flesh that demands immediate satisfaction of selfish needs and the soul (the God part) that demands we put God and others before ourselves, to delay personal gratification and immediate satisfaction in a manner that creates relationship and community with others and God. We must have some level of self-care as well. Sometimes our needs require attention above those of others. That balance is learned as the soul and body compete for the attention of the soul—our emotions and thoughts are our guide here. If two hungry forces are at your door and you can only feed one, the one that is fed will dominate, though the other does not cease to exist. If the dominant force begins to fuel your emotions and thoughts in return, that force becomes your "god." On one end of the spectrum, natural instincts demand self as sole source of satisfaction, creating a lean and ever hungrier creature that is never satisfied. At the opposite end of the spectrum is the force of absolute altruism in which the individual loses him/herself in the process of self-denial and a striving to become self-righteous in a form of godliness that ultimately leads to isolation from "lesser beings." True altruism lies in knowing God, being obedient to His commandments to love Him and others fully, while retaining a sense of humble humanity in which God is provider and sustainer, worthy of worship, and recognizing we were created for a perfect relation with Him and through Him with others. Without that relationship, our efforts to discover the meaning of life would be moot. We are spiritually stillborn. That is the definition of the afterlife for those who choose to seek only the fleshly path of our baser nature or choose the lofty heights of reason and rationalization without recognition of the supernatural power that gives life here on earth and continues into the afterlife of eternity.

Regardless of where we fall on the spectrum, failure to recognize the "God part" within us leaves us to pursue endless and unsatisfying dreams while trapped in the darkness of our deepest emotions and thoughts as we struggle with the attempt to find happiness outside of ourselves and denial of our part in achieving or failing to achieve that happiness. As the riders of *Phantasee* far too frequently fail to recognize, all desire is darkness when it is based upon selfish dream. That is why the depths of hell are so terrifying—you are left alone, cut off from all others, realizing you are inadequate to do what only God can do. Your basest desires for food, sex, and power have left you in your own likeness. Intellectual pursuits, moneymaking ability, and prestige are now empty and fruitless. All those things have passed away with your corruptible flesh. While your soul/spirit never ceases to exist, their very nature is cut off from the life source of the Creator. It is corrupted beyond redemption—by your choice alone. While you still draw the breath of life on earth, seek out the love of life that made you. He will love you eternally, but there is a deadline for RSVPing your seat at His feet.

An unrepentant child cannot make amends once separated from estranged parents by death.

Topic: Ten Steps to Spiritual Renewal

Author: Dr. David Jeremiah
Source: The Jeremiah Study Bible, NKJV

Based on the last six chapters of the prophetic book of Nehemiah, Israel received instructions for reestablishing a national presence in Jerusalem through the renewal of a right relationship with God. While the nation of Israel was called to repentance, these same steps can be followed by individuals to rekindle their relationship with God as well.

1. Getting back to the Book (8:1–12). For modern readers, this is the Bible.
2. Getting serious about obedience (8:13–18). Obedience fuels the light that penetrates the darkness and pushes it aside until only our light shows to others. This is the premise behind "Let your light so shine before men, that they may see your good works and glorify your Father in heaven" (Matthew 5:16).
3. Getting concerned about sin (9: 1–37). We are all sinners. We can be saved from the sinner's hell by the blood and grace of Jesus Christ. When we find that grace, we should desire for others to discover it too. Sin is nothing to play with. It is always fatal and eternal.

4. Getting caught up in worship (9:1–37). A grace-filled sinner who has been cleansed by the blood of Jesus Christ can always find something to rejoice over and worship their Savior for.
5. Becoming accountable for conduct (9:38–10: 31). We are accountable for every thought, feeling, and behavior that originates within us. No one "makes" you behave in a certain way. You choose to respond according to your own thoughts and feelings, right or wrong. Face yourself first if you want to change the world. Everyone will be held accountable during the Great White Throne Judgment when the sheep will be separated from the goats. Be prepared to accept your responsibility. No one else will be there to blame.
6. Taking a pledge to give sacrificially (10:32–39). They say to give until it hurts. And it's not just money they mean. Put others first and sacrifice of your "me." Don't give all you have because that reverses your role from providing for others' needs to becoming the one in need. Do give generously, being willing to give up small (and large) luxuries to meet the needs of those who don't even have the basics—food, shelter, clothing, and unconditional love.
7. Offering themselves for service (11:1–36). "Spare change" isn't always available in our economically challenged world. Even our time can be precious. Which is better—to give blindly to a charity you know nothing about or to volunteer your services and resources to distribute food and clothing to homeless children? Which gives you a greater blessing? That is where you are called to serve.
8. Giving thanks for God's goodness (12:1–47). If God didn't love us, we would cease to exist. Every breath we take is a blessing. Here is a starting point. Thank God for every breath, then thank Him for all the other little and big things He has given you. You will not cease giving thanks as your blessings become endless.

9. Doing away with compromise (13:1–22). Every time we compromise with the world, our morals and values are weakened. It is not bigotry or hatred; it is simply a refusal to become something you don't want to be. It may be politically incorrect, but you will be stronger for it. So many apparently strong Christians suddenly "flip" positions to support what they formerly held to be against their morals and values simply because the issue hits too close to home. They allow their morals and values to crumble rather than standing firm in the crisis, then are unable to justify their new viewpoint scripturally when challenged. Know what you believe, why you believe it, and how to support it with God's Word. If you can't stand for truth, you will fall for lies.
10. Confronting sin (13:23–31). This begins with getting your own ducks in a row. You can't help a brother or sister confront their sin if you are hiding your own. It's more exposed than you think.

Steel Lust

Sex is the consolation you have
when you can't have love.

—Gabriel Garcia Marquez

I felt like an animal, and animals
don't know sin, do they?

—Jess C. Scott, *Wicked Lovely*

Greed, envy, sloth, pride and gluttony: these
are not vices anymore. No, these are marketing
tools. Lust is our way of life. Envy is just a nudge
towards another sale. Even in our relationships we
consume each other, each of us looking for what
we can get out of the other. Our appetites are often
satisfied at the expense of those around us. In a
dog-eat-dog world we lose part of our humanity.

—Jon Foreman

Satan's Den is a thriving place of business in spite of its reputation. Brave entrepreneurs come from outside to establish fast-food restaurants, shopping centers, an amusement park, and other moneymaking ventures on the outskirts of town. Reputation and superstition keep businesses from growing in the most haunted places, but sometimes those areas overlap into the so-called "safe" grounds, creating new legends. Such is the story of this legend.

She was the most beautiful woman Paul had ever seen. She was the type Paul had always dreamed of but had never been able to meet. That was why he was at the drive-in, alone, watching the girl of his dreams on the wide screen.

She moved with the grace of a gazelle and had such deep-blue-green eyes that Paul felt himself drowning every time she stared his way. He knew she was only an actress and that he could never have her, but he dreamed anyway.

He was awed by her ability to lure her lovers to their deaths in her arms. He felt he could gladly give his life for one of her kisses or the unimaginable beauty of death in her caressing fingers.

Paul groaned with pleasure each time the deadly angel embraced another victim and thrust the gleaming dagger between the man's lust-filled shoulders and into his stroke-beating heart. Paul could not believe his eyes as the angel turned toward him, her arms held open wide, as though to embrace him. He knew she was preparing to ensnare her next victim, yet he couldn't help but feel her passionate gaze was for him alone.

The hair on the back of his neck rose as the siren's eyes grew larger and filled the screen. As his eyes met hers, they became one. She seemed to glide from the screen and into the passenger seat of his car. His eyes never left hers as he shifted his body behind the steering wheel to be more receptive to hers. He felt her arms gently wrap themselves around him. He had never responded to a movie in this way before and was shocked at the reality. He closed his eyes, allowing himself to feel the full benefit of his imagination. It was then he felt the cold steel enter his body through his back. His screams were lost in the empty, abandoned drive-in.

Matthew 5:27–28, NKJV

> You have heard that it was said to those of old, "You shall not commit adultery," but I say to you that whoever looks at a woman to lust for her has committed adultery with her in his heart.

Notes of Lurlene Joy McCoy

Ah. Lust, the root of all sin.

It all began with Lucifer's desire to usurp the throne of God (Revelation 12:7–9; Daniel 10:13, 21; 12:1). He truly believed he could do the job of the One who created him better, the One who has always been and always will be. Lucifer had only the powers bestowed upon him at his creation—great beauty and intellect to be second-in-command to the Creator, a leader among his own kind. He willingly obeyed his Creator until that fateful moment he had a desire to be more than he already was. Rather than confessing his impure thoughts, he let them fester and grow until his desire became desperation to get what he wanted, nay, felt he deserved. Desperation and entitlement pushed him past his limits of self-restraint, and he rebelled, taking a third of the angels with him. His *death* came in the form of banishment to the newly formed earth, where he desired to become the lord of all that was there. Only Adam and Eve had the knowledge and potential for developing lust, so he watched and plotted against mankind. How delighted he must have been when he was able to instill lust into their otherwise pure minds and hearts. How he must have rejoiced at their downfall and exile from Eden that so greatly resembled his own fall from heaven. How he must have sneered in glee when the lust in Cain's heart led to rage that ended in the murder of his only brother. Sin begins in the mind and works its way outward to our behavior. It is always destructive if not stopped and defused.

Whether Paul was merely dreaming of his femme fatale, or he ran afoul of a nasty vengeful demon, perhaps Lilith herself, is anyone's guess. Satan's Den is tainted ground. It taints all whom it touches. Lust is fueled by taint and leads to unnatural behavior, like that of the man who preferred the company of his liquid placebo to the love and care of his family, and like Paul himself who found destruction in his willingness to sacrifice his life to the woman he could not have if only she would give him a kiss of recognition.

Be careful what you lust for. You just might get it…and more than you bargained for.

Topic: What Does the Bible Have to Say about Lust?

Source: www.gotquestions.org

Summary

- Defines lust as
    - (1) an intense or unrestrained sexual craving or (2) an overwhelming desire or craving
- Exodus 20:14, 17 describes adultery and covetousness as being against God's wishes.
- Matthew 5:28 links thoughts of an impure nature with the sin of adultery.
- Job 31:11–12 describes lust as a shameful sin and a crime that should be punished as it devastates and destroys.
- The focus of lust is on pleasing oneself and is often unwholesome as the actions taken to fulfill one's desires disregard the consequences that may result.
- Lust is about possession and greed.
- In contrast, the Christian life is about selflessness and is marked by holy living (Romans 6:19, 12:1–2; 1 Corinthians 1:2, 30; 6:19–20; Ephesians 1:4, 4:24; Colossians 3:12; 1 Thessalonians 4:3–8, 5:23; 2 Timothy 1:9; Hebrews 12:14; 1 Peter 1:15–16). The goal of each person who identifies with Christ in faith is to become more like Christ, putting off the old way of life, including the thoughts and actions that lead to sin.
- Lust of the flesh is a desire for things which God has forbidden. First John 2:15–16 identifies three types of lust that lead to greater sin: lust of the flesh, lust of the eyes, the pride of life.
    - Lust of the eyes occurs when what we see visually incites a desire that produces envy, covetousness, or sexually impure thoughts.
    - Pride of life is demonstrated in arrogance, self-promotion, and greed that has the purpose of establishing self as god.

    - Lust of the flesh can refer to flesh beings, such as animals, birds, and people (1 Corinthians 15:39), or the propensity to sin through our earthly nature, which is dominated by rebellion.
- First John 2:17 contrasts lust with the flesh (which is mortal and will pass away) with pleasing God (which is eternal).
- Matthew 7:21 states that a person who yields to the lust of the flesh, eyes, or pride of life will not inherit eternal life unless there is true repentance.

Topic: The Process of Temptation, Part 2 of 10, Casting Down Imaginations Series

Source: www.artlicursi.com
Author: Art Li Cursi

Summary

The book of James: four-step process leading to actualizing sin that begins in the mind.

1. A spontaneous "temptation" arises as a thought in the mind.
2. Being "tempted," we may be "drawn away," "enticed," due to the "lust" of the "sin in the flesh" (Romans 8:3).
3. When lust is conceived, it usually culminates in an act of sinning against what we know as truth. These thoughts are contrary to our true identity "in Christ."
4. Then with the act of sin, we bear the first consequence of "sinning," falling into the condemnation of the devil (as the accuser) (1 Timothy 3:6).
5. This brings "spiritual death." We feel hopelessly cut off and distant from God and those around us. This is all because we of ourselves chose to turn away from valuing our grace union with Christ in our spirit more than anything this earthly life has to offer.

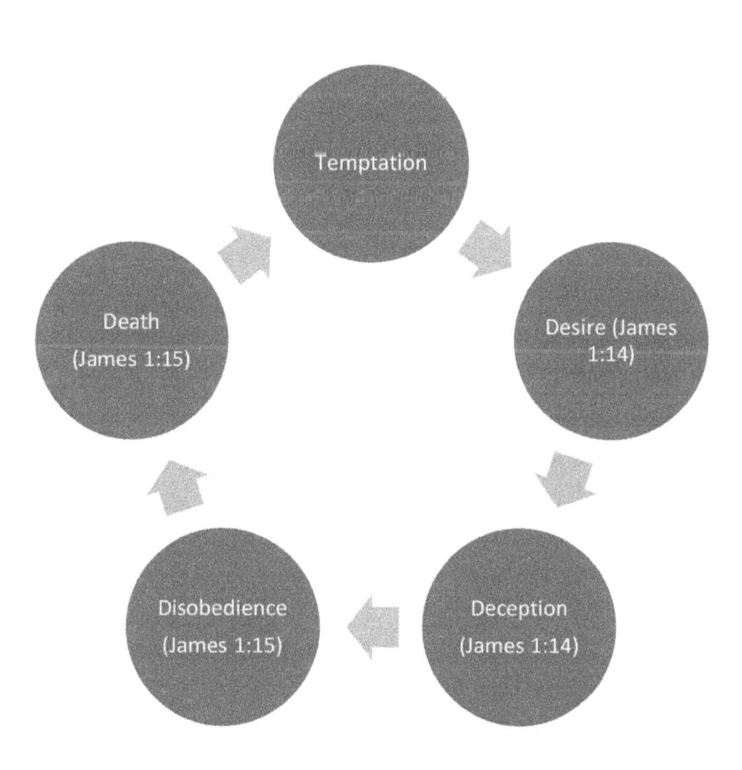
Temptation
Desire (James 1:14)
Deception (James 1:14)
Disobedience (James 1:15)
Death (James 1:15)

Curing the Ham
A Pig Tale of Terror

Pork over the bacon and nobody gets hurt!

—Anonymous

Not all evil begins in Satan's Den, though it often seems that way. There are gateways to hell everywhere; we just manage to avoid them much of the time. The late great writer Manly Wade Wellman wrote of such gateways in the Carolinas in his novels and short stories. He also wrote of the old gods that once ruled this world.

If one could speak with a survivor of such a gateway passage, skin would crawl, and hair would stand on end. A reporter for a local newspaper recently had just such a chance.

A woman was staying at the Inferno Motel, a place so named by local pranksters, and was desperately seeking someone to record her story before it was too late. This reporter was the only one willing to listen. What follows is a transcript of the tape he made during the interview.

"Did you hear that? You didn't hear a pig grunting and squealing? There it is again. Listen. Of course, you didn't hear it. I'm the only one who can hear it. It's me it's looking for. What…? No, I haven't lost my mind. There really is a pig after me."

"Ridiculous? Yes, it seems so…at first. But believe you me, I take it quite seriously."

"For many years now I have been able to outrun its horrible, gnashing teeth and bloodcurdling grunts. My running days are over it seems. Before this day is over, I will be pig slop."

"When did it begin?"

"Do you wish me to say, 'When I was a piglet'?"

"I *am* serious. This *isn't* my imagination."

"Okay, okay. I will try to explain it to you. I don't know if you can understand. Several years ago, I was traveling the back roads of a small mountain town in the Ozarks. No, I can't tell you *where*! It has all run together in my mind. So much has happened since then.

"I found this quaint general store. It sold old-fashioned things from fifty years ago and longer. I found the most unusual curiosities hidden beneath layers of dust. The most unusual of all was a piggy bank. It was as large as this table before you. I love pigs. They're so cute. I collect piggy banks. This one fascinated me.

"It was pink, with a wide red bow around its neck. A tiny porcine smile glimmered from its lips. Its painted eyes glimmered with a realistic glint. The coin slot was nearly big enough to put your whole hand into if you wished. The coins inside reflected the dim light of the store.

"The proprietress noticed my interest. She smiled. Almost too eager to talk. She told me the legend of the pig. It had been in the store for over a hundred years. People had put money in, but the pig never seemed to fill up. The pig must hold hundreds of thousands of dollars in old coins, some quite valuable.

"No one is sure where it came from. Or how it came to be there in that store. It just...was.

"I put my hand in my pocket. There I found some change left over from some former purchase, I suppose. I made a wish, then dropped each coin into the slot, hearing the tinny clink of coin against coin. Having made my wish, I walked to the door. The proprietress asked me why I wasn't taking the pig with me.

"I told her I'd only made a wish, not purchased it. A handful of coins, not even a dollar, really, couldn't have purchased such a prize. She said the pig was mine! I didn't believe her. It would never fit in my little car. I left.

"As I drove, I heard the occasional squeal and the grunt of a pig somewhere nearby. Not surprising for a tiny mountain community such as this. Pigs ran wild, along with the family dog. They all came home at dinnertime. I thought nothing of it.

"I spied two red, gleaming eyes in my rearview mirror. Too early in the day for lights, I thought. They came closer. Squeals and grunts amplified. I thought once more of my piggy prize, rejected in the dust.

"The day wore on. My body grew tired. The eyes and the sounds grew more intense. I could almost smell the piggy hide, mud-colored and odorous.

"Night fell, the nightmare continued to haunt. It drove me haphazardly through the mountains, seeking solace. At last, I found a well-lit town and slept in a well-lit motel room. Not a pig to be heard.

"The next morning, I breakfasted on eggs, but no bacon, sausage, or ham. The smell of pork turned my stomach. My head throbbed.

"On the road once more, I started to relax. Until…I saw them… in the rearview mirror…beady piggy eyes, a snuffling snout…gnashing piggy teeth… I heard its hooves pattering against the pavement.

"Sweat broke out on my brow as I drove faster…and faster…

"I have managed to stay just ahead of it for a while now. Sometimes months go by before I hear it coming for me once more. Then…I run.

"I had thought I had finally outrun it, until today.

"It is coming for me…too tired to run anymore. Before this day is over…I'll be gone."

Postscript

The morning after this interview was given, the reporter returned to the hotel to check on the woman. All he found was an empty room, permeated with a heavy smell of burned bacon and a handful of change on the nightstand.

James 2:26, NKJV

For as the body without the spirit is dead,
so faith without works is dead.

Matthew 25:31–40, NKJV

> When the Son of Man comes in his glory, and all the holy angels with him, then he will sit on the throne of his glory. All the nations will be gathered before him, and he will separate them one from another, as a shepherd separates the sheep from the goats. and he will set the sheep on his right hand, but the goats on the left. THEN THE KING WILL SAY TO THOSE ON HIS RIGHT HAND, "COME YOU BLESSED OF MY FATHER, INHERIT THE KINGDOM PTRPARED FOR YOU FROM THE FOUNDATION OF THE WORLD, FOR I WAS HUNGRY AND YOU GAVE ME FOOD; I Was THIRSTY AND YOU GAVE ME DRINK; I WAS A STRANGER AND YOU TOOK ME IN; I WAS NAKED AND YOU CLOTHED ME; I WAS SICK AND YOU VISITED ME, I WAS IN PRISON AND YOU CAME TO ME."
>
> Then the righteous will answer him, saying, "Lord when did we see you hungry and feed you, or thirsty and give you drink? When did we see you a stranger and take you in, or naked and clothe you? Or when did we see you sick or in prison and come to you?" and the king will answer and say unto them, "Assuredly, I say to you, inasmuch as you did it to one of the least of these my brethren, you did it to me."

Notes of Lurlene Joy McCoy

This one is much more difficult to analyze as it doesn't seem to fit into any one category.

It initially presents as a haunted object story, with thc attached spirit taking on the form of a demonic pig that hunted this poor woman down to her last gasp of willpower, but she did not have the object the spirit would have had to be attached to.

She heard the stories of the storekeeper, but there were so many gaps it was unclear of the purpose of the cheerful-looking bank to begin with. It was enormous and would have required a back-breaking effort to transfer it from the counter to the woman's car. And why this woman? She threw in some lose change on a whim, making a wish as she apparently believed the tradition to be.

It had taken a long time to fill that pig. Providing it had never been robbed, there were sure to be coins dating back to the Civil War and even earlier. There could have been a small fortune in rare coins, including those of pure gold or silver hidden in the depths of that rotund tummy. Imagine what anyone could do with that money—for good or evil. And she walked away from it as if it had been a nasty wad of gum she had scraped from the bottom of her shoe.

Could it have been guilt at walking away from opportunity or the slur of cultural traditions her refusal to go along with that brought the red-eyed squealer into her life?

In an attempt at understanding this event, I contacted my peers in the Ozarks region. Most had never heard of the pig story or the alleged event. But one, whom I promised not to name due to sensitivity of that person's position in the community, came through for me.

The piggy bank is apparently a sort of liar's Pandora box. It has taken on different forms throughout the millennia and has traversed the globe many times. In each incarnation, the object requires people to offer up some kind of sacrifice to it. In this case, it was coins. The last item placed into the object, to complete it, transfers ownership to that individual that made the sacrifice, which triggers the object's potential. The new owner is required to empty the object of the sacrifices and then decide what to do with those items.

Here is the rub, as Shakespeare would say. If a man knows he is being tested, he will be on his best behavior. However, if that test is being done without the knowledge of that man, he will continue his usual habits. Hence the name liar's Pandora box.

Pandora knew she was being tested. The box was a trap to tempt her. She gave in to her curiosity and opened the box, releasing all manner of ills into the world, managing to retain only hope inside the box. The evidence of her indiscretion was everywhere. She could not deny anything.

The liar's Pandora box operates differently, however. This box is usually opened and emptied in private. The owner makes an assessment of the contents and decides how best to utilize the contents. The person's morals and values system kick, in and plans are made. Once the individual takes action upon the contents, the true nature of the box appears.

Whatever the individual chooses to do with the contents is returned to him or her tenfold, with the same motive. So a kind and generous man who uses the contents for helping others and making his community a better place to live will be blessed with ten times the opportunity, enriching his own life as well as the lives of others.

A man who uses this new wealth for evil deeds will discover himself with ten times the consequences for the evil he caused. While others suffer for his evil, he is tormented by that same suffering, exponentially times ten.

Of course, there are many personality types all along the scale of good and evil, with each case dealt with justly. A man can lie about his actions, but he cannot outrun their consequences.

If this is what this woman encountered, it would explain so much. The apathy and disdain she demonstrated toward this unexpected and undeserved gift released a haunting spirit of apathy and disdain to give her a taste of her own medicine by separating her from her normal life and isolating her socially because no one would believe her.

What occurred that night, when the reporter had recorded the interview and left, is anyone's guess. Ironic, though, was the scent of badly burned bacon left behind.

Objects like the liar's Pandora box are neither cursed, blessed, nor haunted. They just are. We have no mythology or lore concerning them.

I guess the lesson here is, "God loves a cheerful giver, so donor beware."

Addendum

I have come across a possible explanation for the spirits found within the liar's Pandora box. A brief portion of our cosmic compendium has allowed itself to be translated. It seems that the process which created our universe produced the fractal dust that expelled from the void, introducing darkness to a kingdom of pure light. A tiny fragment of the void, like Pandora's hope, was placed in a cosmic vessel and set aside. This force, a null, acts as a scale that balances the universe so that neither light nor darkness can become dominant. It metes out justice as it perceives it, to maintain that balance. It is fully neutral and incorruptible in power. Its sole purpose is the balance of corruptible opposites within the cosmos. On earth, it acts as a sieve to filter mankind's true nature from its free will to expose the souls of those who encounter it for all to see. A corrupt person will receive the disdain of his fellow humanity as he is cast aside and exiled. A person filled with goodness will find himself embraced by society and lifted up as an example for all to follow. Those who fall between these cracks find varied status within their community, causing the rise of politics and discussions of relative truth versus absolute truth as humanity tries to emulate this null, the Sieve of Justice. Darkness and light lie within all of us, from conception.

From the very beginning, we were given boundaries—obey your Creator because He loves you and gives you all you need, unconditionally (Genesis 1:29).

When darkness overshadowed the love of obedience to the Creator, humanity fell.

Since that moment, humanity has cycled between obedience and depraved disobedience, with endless chaos between.

A single null is not responsible for the discipline of mere mortals. It knows nothing of us except that we need to be sifted in order to create balance.

The God of the Old Testament gave Moses and the people who would become the nation of Israel the Ten Commandments as their guide (Exodus 20:1–17). Their universal truths are found reflected in ancient civilizations and modern governments today, even if we don't agree on their origin.

That same God, in the New Testament, through Jesus Christ, summarized His expectations in just two broad commandments—love the Lord your God with all your mind, heart, and soul and to love your neighbor as yourself (Matthew 22:37–40). He includes our enemies as our neighbors (Romans 12:20; Matthew 5:43–44).

In America today, we are fond of saying, "Why can't we all just get along?"

If the null could speak, it would say, "Why not, indeed?"

Dr. Henry Morris gives us a hint of this Sieve of Justice in his discussion on the creation and purpose of the constellations in his book *THE BIBLICAL BASIS FOR MODERN SCIENCE*. He alludes to the biblical warnings against the pursuit of astrology, divination, and witchcraft as being perversions of the original intent of these celestial signs as indicators of seasons for mankind's use in overseeing and stewarding the earth as commissioned by God. It is then proposed that each of these signs are directly correlated with the gospel message as it unfolds in the pages of our modern Bible. He has summarized it as follows:

1. Virgo, the Virgin—promised seed of the woman
2. Libra, the Balance—scales of Divine Justice
3. Scorpio, the Scorpion—sting to be inflicted on the promised seed
4. Sagittarius, the Archer—corruption of the human race through demonism
5. Capricornus, the Goat-fish—utter wickedness of mankind
6. Aquarius, the Water Pourer—destruction of the primeval world by water
7. Pisces, the Fishes—emergence of the true people of God
8. Aries, the Ram—sacrifice of an innocent substitute for sins
9. Taurus, the Bull—resurrection of the slain ram as the mighty bull
10. Gemini, the Twins—the dual nature of the reigning king
11. Cancer, the Crab—ingathering of the redeemed from all ages
12. Leo, the Lion—destruction of the fleeing serpent by the great King

An examination of the scriptures reveals these truths:

1. Genesis 3:14–15 describes God's judgment upon the serpent, including the enmity between the serpent and the woman whom he had deceived., declaring that her seed would bruise his head and he would bruise the heel of the seed. Jesus Christ, the Son born to the Virgin Mary, fulfilled this promise of the seed. Satan, the serpent, then tempted Jesus in the wilderness and indwelled one loyal disciple to bring about the arrest, trial, and crucifixion of Jesus.
2. The serpent, Adam, and Eve were all cast out of the garden. After the slaying of Abel, Cain was exiled and sent to live far from his family of origin. Wickedness among humanity began to grow. In Genesis 6:5–8, God tires of the wickedness of His created image bearers and decides to destroy all He had made. If not for one man (Genesis 6:9), the world would have come to an end.
3. This wickedness arose in direct opposition to all that was good and of God. Since Satan had rebelled against God and been evicted from heaven, he corrupted humanity, which resulted, first, in their expulsion from the garden created for them and then continued as humanity gave up their directive to be stewards of the earth and, instead, became its destroyers under the twisted tutelage of the Father of Lies. When the cleansing flood failed to stop the spread of evil, God sent His only begotten Son as a sinless sacrifice to die in the place of the sins of those who chose to accept Him as their savior. Satan had "stung" Jesus by corrupting what had been created, turning the creation into an image of himself by convincing them they could become like a god by following him.

4–5. The Old Testament is filled with descriptions of demonic gods and the horrifying requirements of their worship, including the sacrifice of children. One such god was half human-half fish. Satan is often depicted as a goat-headed man.

6. God did destroy the world with a great flood. Only those people and animals within the ark were saved.
7. Wickedness prevailed in humanity even after the flood. In response, God called one man, Abram, to leave his pagan polytheistic country to become the father of a great nation that recognizes and honors only one God. Through this man and his wife, both of advanced age, the nation of Israel and the Hebrew race rose.
8. From the Hebrew race, God raised up a Messiah to not only reunite the people of Israel under the one true God but a Savior who would die for the Jews, as well as the Gentile nations who would then be adopted into the chosen children of God in the form of what we now call the Christian faith.
9. Christ not only gave His own life "like a lamb to the slaughter," but He rose from the grave as the lion of Judah. God is described as having the strength of a wild ox. In this description, the writers were referencing a creature of that geographical region that was considered untamable. It is an ox, as described, but is powerful and dangerous. It has remained undomesticated due to its fierce nature. Jesus rose as the conqueror over death itself. He is untamable.
10. Jesus is unique in that He is fully God yet walked among humanity as fully human. He reigns as the God who became man.
11. At some time in the swiftly approaching future, Christ will call all His children home. There will be a trumpet sounded, and the dead in Christ will rise from their graves and be gathered into the heavens. Those who are alive in Christ will follow. Those who are not "in Christ" will be judged accordingly. This Great White Throne Judgment will be the final reckoning of humanity, separating the sheep from the goats. The sheep will dwell eternally with their Shepherd, while the goats will be separated eternally from God and placed in a lake of fire.

12. Following this Judgment, God and Satan will face off in a battle to end all wars as we know them. These two vast armies will meet, and in the end, Satan will be defeated. The serpent will be chained and thrown into that lake of fire as well.

There, the Sieve of Justice will have its final say.

Ed and Lorraine Warren, founders of the New England Society for Psychic Research, have documented many cases in which the presence of a demon was marked by the grunting and squealing of pigs. Ed and Lorraine were part of the team that investigated the Lutz house, as documented in *The Amityville Horror*, by Jay Anson in 1977, and later made into a series of films. In that famous case, a "pig" named Jodi took on the persona of an imaginary friend before revealing its true demonic nature.

Topic: Haunted Objects and How to Break Attachments

Source: www.ghostlyactivities.com
Date: January 9, 2014
Author: Jacob Rice

Summary

- Haunted objects come in two general versions:
    - They absorb the energy of their previous owner.
    - They're cursed by a magical ritual.
- Most common possessed objects
    - Dolls
    - Jewelry
    - Antique headboards and beds
    - Paintings (especially self-portraits)
    - Mirrors
    - Clothing (especially gowns)
    - Chairs

- They either have a great deal of contact with their owner (i.e., jewelry), or they capture the image of their owner (i.e., mirrors).
- An untimely death can give energy to charge the object.
- Always ask about the object's history before buying.
- Ask a psychic, gifted with psychometry, to test objects for vibes, good or bad, before you bring them home.
- Objects may remain dormant until there's a change in their environment that activates the object.
- If you do have a haunted object, the following ghostly activities happen:
  1. Your possessions move on their own (not necessarily the haunted object).
  2. Apparitions and shadow people manifest.
  3. Nightmares become more frequent (three times per week or more)
  4. Bad luck happens around the home (minor injuries or plumbing/electrical problems).
  5. Illnesses become more frequent like colds, flu, and food poisoning.
- Timing varies but usually starts within the first two weeks or may manifest on the death anniversary of the previous owner.
- How to get rid of attachments to objects:
  - Five ways
    1. Spiritual cleansing of the object and home
    2. Cleanse the object with salt
    3. Return it to its original place
    4. Bury it in a graveyard
    5. Burn it (always works but should be a last resort)
- Seek out a paranormal specialist to burn it for you.
- Destroying an object can cause the evil attached to "jump" out and attach to you or someone else present.

Topic: Can an Object Become Haunted?

Source: Living Life in Full Spectrum
www.llifs.com

Date: November 6, 2017

Summary

- ✓ Residual energy of previous owners may remain with an object but is not classified as a haunting.
- ✓ The spirits of deceased could attach themselves to beloved objects and may lead to haunting behaviors when moved to another location or is in the presence of someone or something the spirit perceives as a threat to the object.
- ✓ Negative energy resulting from a traumatic event may attach to an object, perceived as being negative and feelings of discomfort but may not be demonic in nature.
- ✓ Destroying an object with negative energy can be dangerous; seek advice of a paranormal professional.
- ✓ How can we tell if an object is haunted?
- ✓ Do an investigation!
- ✓ Check EMF (electromagnetic field) readings.
- ✓ EVP (electronic voice phenomena) session
- ✓ Track activity in relation to presence or absence of item

I never recommend handling any suspect object in this way. The power behind these phenomena is far too great for mere humanity. Things of the unseen realm need to be dealt with by professionals who know what they are facing and have the necessary skills and faith to call upon the angel armies of the Lord God Almighty to see the battle through. While I have some training in this field, there are those who are called for this very purpose.

Revive Us Again

A revival can occur on one of three levels. It can occur on a personal level when an individual is revived. It can occur on a church level when the whole church comes under a new spiritual impetus. It can occur on a community level, when a church overflows, and the spiritual impetus in the church extends into the community.

—A. W. Tozer, *The Crucified Life*

We have changed the meaning of the world revival, and we need to upgrade our vocabulary. Revival is not just getting together for some religious hootenanny.

—A. W. Tozer, *Delighting in God*

A revival, among other things, is a sudden manifestation of God's presence. It is not the coming of the sun, but the sun breaking through the clouds.

—A. W. Tozer, *My Daily Pursuit*

A true revival means nothing less than a revolution, casting out the spirit of worldliness

and selfishness, and making God and his
love triumph in the heart and life.

—Andrew Murray

There can't be any large-scale revolution
until there's a personal revolution, on an
individual level. It's got to happen inside first.

—Jim Morrison

Not everything in Satan's Den is as dark as it seems. Occasionally, you find a little light to brighten your dark path. Such is the story of Aunt Tildy, Satan's Den's resident saint.

It was during the spring revival of 1847 that this vision of God was revealed. A traveling tent revival was traveling through town. Though not called Satan's Den at its inception, the nickname had been earned and its original name lost to history and those obscure maps that still show small-town America. The traveling preacher and his troupe of Bible-thumpers set up on a vacant field at the edge of town. He gave a long speech about "driving Satan from this land of God." People arrived in great numbers, hoping to remove the evil stigma that surrounded the superstitious burg and those who lived there.

With tensions rising between the North and the South, through years from war and conflict of territorial development in face of the Indians uprising, people were grasping for answers to questions no one dared to ask and peace of mind to soothe their restless hearts. The preacher had them eating out of his palm from the very first night. Evening after evening passed with people praying loudly and weeping in the arms of their neighbors. There were no denominations, no factions, no strangers. All were brethren and sisters in the eyes of the God.

Only one member of the town didn't relish in this act of faith. Aunt Tildy, oldest resident of the town, sat in the back row, watching the antics around her. She didn't sing the precious hymns she held so dear. She glared in scorn as the offering plate was passed and precious coins piled up before her. Tears never glazed her eyes, no matter how tender the plea or how touching the testimony. Aunt Tildy was usually the most spiritual individual in the county, coming from mysterious roots deeply embedded in the mountains themselves.

No one knew much about Aunt Tildy. No one could remember her being young. She was well known for her spiritual healing and outspoken ways regarding religious practice. It was rumored that she could perform miracles through unknown methods using herbs and prayer.

Raised in the old-world church tradition, she had strong convictions regarding what was proper behavior in church. She also had strong ties to the secrets of the land from her Shawnee ancestors. The combination of these traditions and convictions made Aunt Tildy a very formidable ally and an intimidating enemy.

Her matchmaking skills were unsurpassable. Young women came to her from miles around, seeking to know their future husbands and to obtain the charms needed to attract them.

Her knowledge of the old ways and means won her the reputation of a witch. Her faith and good works earned her the title of saint. One's opinion of this mystery woman was the object of many debates. The one indisputable point was the respect this woman had earned over the years.

No one had ever been surprised to see Aunt Tildy in that revival tent. Nor were they surprised to see her worn Bible in her lap. They were surprised, however, by her apparent disapproval of this particular tent revival. Countless preachers had come and gone over the years, leaving their mark in the lives of these people. Aunt Tildy had been one of their strongest supporters.

When the Reverend Willard Thomas Smith came to town with his troupe, everyone became excited. It seemed God had finally sent them the help they had prayed so long for. The evil would finally be driven from this land created by God to be used for the fruitfulness of mankind.

Aunt Tildy glared steadfastly into the eyes of Reverend Smith throughout each service. This didn't seem to bother the reverend the first night. With each successive night, however, the reverend became more and more visibly nervous. By the sixth night, Reverend Willard T. Smith was sweating and shaking visibly before he reached the pulpit for the welcoming hymn. He couldn't seem to concentrate, losing his place four times before closing his Bible and speaking from memory. More than one clean handkerchief was handed to him, along with a glass of water. Prayers could be seen whispered toward heaven.

The reverend finally cracked in the middle of a hellfire and brimstone sermon on the wages of sin. He stopped pacing the front of the tent. He stared back at Aunt Tildy, meeting her eyes for the first time in days. Determinedly, he strode up the aisle to where Aunt Tildy sat. He bent over, meeting her eye to eye, as close as he dared. "What do you want from me?" he whispered, barely moving his lips.

Aunt Tildy glared back, already perfect posture solidifying into a formidable wall. She drew in her breath and pursed her already thin lips into a barely perceptible line amid care-worn wrinkles.

All heads were turned toward the twosome. An air of expectancy brushed the already heady atmosphere. Everyone knew Aunt Tildy's reputation for outspoken honesty.

"Sir," she hissed, "it is not what I want from you but what *I* can do for *you*."

Reverend Willard Thomas Smith was taken aback by her statement. His eyes bulged from his ashen skull. Then anger reddened his face. He stood stiffly, pointing boldly into Aunt Tildy's face. His hand shook accusingly.

"This woman," he thundered, "has dared to defile the temple of God with her presence. Satan is here tonight, ladies and gentlemen." He dared a quick glance into the faces around him. Their shock and unbelief gave him courage to go on. Satan has chosen the guise of a bitter old woman to provoke and antagonize the *true believers* of God. *Here*, sweet citizens, lies the root of your problem. *Here* is the evil influence that has plagued your community for so long. *Rid yourselves of this evil creature immediately, and heavenly cleansing will bring spiritual prosperity to this land.*

Murmurs rippled through the crowd. Women cried. Children hid their faces in their mother's skirts. Men balled their fists in uncertain action. *Sweet Voices of Heaven*, the Reverend Smith's personal traveling choir, chanted hymns beneath their breath.

Aunt Tildy remained seated, though anger began to creep into her demeanor. White knuckles clutched the Bible in her lap.

Reverend Smith felt the tension mount. He chose his next words carefully so he wouldn't risk losing his control of these desperate people.

"The Good Book says, 'Thou shalt not suffer a witch to live.' I submit to you for judgment this wretched creature you see before you. This pawn of Lucifer is the reason this land is cursed. Her very birth brought a stain to this land. Her mother's labor pains were filled with hell itself to produce such demonic spawn. She consorts with demons to perform so-called miracles. She poisons your minds and bodies with her herbal remedies. Even her half-breed nature is the very mark of her parents' sin."

One man stepped forward tentatively. He gripped his hat tightly in his hands. "What would you have us do," he pleaded.

Reverend Willard T. Smith placed his hand comfortingly on the man's shoulder. "Friend," he said softly, tears in his eyes, "there is only one way to deal with the devil. You must fight fire with fire."

The man's eyes widened in surprise as he searched the preacher's face for confirmation of his understanding of those condemning words. Women gasped; tears flowed freely. One woman fainted. The man turned to his neighbors for reassurance. None would meet his eyes. In desperation, he turned to Aunt Tildy. She met his gaze, encouraging support glittering in her eyes. She trusted him to make the right choice. He turned back to the preacher, strengthened by his experience.

"You do what you feel you must, Reverend, but I take no part in the harming of this woman. She has done me and mine no harm."

Reverend Smith's heart fell with these words. Only a twitch of his mouth showed his reaction. He turned to a large man on his left, grasped the man's hand, and led him to the makeshift altar. "This man stands before you whole. A new creature in the eyes of God. He came to me two nights ago, confessing his part in the demonic rituals and witches' masses led by that woman. Why, he told me things that would make your hearts faint and your hair stand on their ends. Animal and human sacrifices made on a bloody stone altar by naked, frenzied men and women beneath a full moon. He himself has provided the babes for these rites. He has forsaken these ways for the love of God, and God has forgiven him."

He had their full attention. Shocked disbelief shattered any doubts his audience may have had. They were his to manipulate and mold with his holy hands. The fact that he had divulged the secret sins of another had not seemed to affect his audience. Instead, it had drawn them deeper under his spell.

One by one, men and women began to step forward in testimony. Each claimed Aunt Tildy had caused a cow to go dry or a crop to wither. The worst accusers went so far as to state the deaths of loved ones or livestock as the direct result of Aunt Tildy's ministrations. Many unexplained or misfortunate mishaps were blamed on the woman's occult practices. Some bold young men stepped forward to tell of witnessing the naked revelry around the bonfire after a sacrifice had been made. Each claimed they had happened to be in the woods by accident, hunting or going home from some late-night event. Young women nearby blushed to hear the details of the revelry. More than one hung their heads in embarrassment or shame. One clutched her gently rounded stomach in an attempt to disguise her own personal embarrassment.

The crowd began to come alive with each confession until nearly everyone was willing to stand up and defile their most beloved citizen. Those that held back wore confused expressions. Aunt Tildy sat poker-faced throughout, only her eyes showing the anger she felt.

When at last the accusations and testimonies came to an end, Reverend Willard Smith stood before his converted congregation. The smug look of victory awed his audience into silence. He climbed up onto the box that doubled as a packing crate and pulpit stage. He lifted his Bible up toward heaven.

"God has spoken," he chanted. "Testimonies have been given. I am convinced that the accused is guilty of consorting with Satan. She has bewitched the people into believing her to be such a good, kind, and oh-so-Christian soul. Yet she practices occult ceremonies and heals the sick. Where is her license? Where did she go to school? Her knowledge is of the devil, friends. This land is tainted by Satan's touch. If you give evil an inch, it will take a mile. The next thing you know, the devil is moving in next door to the church, holding hands with its daughters and corrupting its sons. Satan brings his own version of God's truth, blinding his followers' eyes with self-righteous contempt for what is truly right. When a community allows Satan this much control of its citizens, the land itself becomes corrupt, giving the illusion of peaceful prosperity while decaying evil destroys its very foundations. It only takes one soul to start the cycle to destruction, but it takes many souls coming together in prayer and redemption to cleanse the land. Won't you come forth today, sacrificing yourself for the greater good of all?"

People began to trickle forward singly and in pairs. The spellbound preacher continued his plea. More people came forward. Some of these concerned souls were deacons and Sunday school teachers in their own churches. A few were citizen of Satan's Den proper. A couple were from out of town. One or two were total strangers. The biggest surprise, however, was when Aunt Tildy herself worked her way to the front of the canvas room. Reverend Willard Thomas Smith gloated with the pride of having converted Lucifer to the workforce of God.

The crowd split as Aunt Tildy came forward, closing their ranks behind her as if to protect her or prevent her escape. She stopped in front of the makeshift altar and stared up at the gloating minister.

"God be praised!" shouted Reverend Smith; his hands and eyes were lifted toward heaven. A shout of praise went up from the people around him.

"Dear Father in heaven," he prayed, "cleanse this woman of the evil presence that has caused her to fall from the grace of your salvation. We lift up her soul to you before this altar so that she will be cleansed before her trial by fire and her soul enters its eternal state."

With this, Aunt Tildy was seized and dragged from the tent. She did not protest. Neither did she struggle. The Bible in her right hand never quavered or offered to fall. A bonfire had been set up during the service as if in anticipation of this very event. A tall post was set in its midst. Aunt Tildy was dragged to the post and tied to it with her hands, still clutching the Bible, behind her back. The Bible could not be pried from her hands, so it was left there to burn with its mistress. Torches were brought forth. The people surrounded the funeral pyre. Reverend Smith gave the signal. Four torches were lowered to the kindling at Aunt Tildy's feet.

Flames began licking the outer kindling. Aunt Tildy watched calmly. Women burst into hysterics and hid their faces. The fire crept slowly toward the center. Aunt Tildy's skirts began to smolder. Still, she made no comment. The skirts burst into flame, consuming aged fabric quickly. The smell of burning flesh was added to the odors of fear and irrationality.

The people watched as the flames consumed one of the most beloved women of their community. Men held back the urge to reach into the fire and draw Aunt Tildy from the fire. Women cried out for forgiveness. The sense of their greatest wrong came home to them in a flash. As one, they turned back toward the revival tent and moved toward the Reverend Willard Smith.

The accusations against the preacher came fast and furious. The maddened crowd was hot. They were looking for someone to blame their sins on. The reverend had been the instigator. It had been his convicting words that had led to this senseless murder. The reverend tried to hide behind a tent flap, desperately looking for his traveling companions. Mysteriously, they were nowhere to be found. Dear God, he had never intended for this to happen. Granted, he had been curious as to why this woman had come to torment him so. He was so sincere in his ministry, unlike those charlatans that took money from gullible people such as these. He had come here on an honest mission to comfort these people and hopefully remove the stigma of their own superstitious fears. Look where his faith had brought him.

He began praying fervently as the people he came to save turned on him and dragged him into the open. Someone called for a rope. A noose was thrown over a branch of a tree as the reverend's hands were lashed behind him. He was roughly thrown up onto the back of a horse and led beneath the tree. The noose slipped over his head and tightened.

"Say your prayers, Reverend," stated a large man in the front row. He raised his hand to slap the horse on the rear. The reverend began to babble and shake his head in protest, even as he lost control of his bodily functions.

"Stop!" The voice came from behind the lynch mob. Shocked expressions met the gaze of Aunt Tildy, whole and very much alive. The bonfire continued to burn emptily behind her.

"You know not what you do," she accused. "You have all been driven mad by your own fears and superstitions. This man came here in faith to help us, and you repay him in this way?"

"Reverend, I said I could help you, and I intend to. You came here hoping to walk through hell and leave a conquering hero. Welcome to hell. What you have witnessed here tonight is the same insane madness that has plagued our community as long as it has been here. The first settlers gave it a different name, one long forgotten now. They came in faith, seeking a better life in this wide expanse. They failed to heed the warnings of my Indian ancestors and must now pay the price, visited upon their children and their children's children. It is our fate to be doomed to relive our own history. No simple man can come here and release these people. Oh, you can release their sins in salvation and lift their hopes and temporarily waylay their fears. God has chosen this piece of earth as a window into hell. He has established it as a warning for those who fail to heed His cry. It is God and God alone who can release this land from its curse. My people were here long before your people, and the curse is even older than that."

The reverend was unable to respond. The people stood spellbound. The sight of the bonfire seemed to intensify into a golden aura around Aunt Tildy until she seemed to glow with the very same fire.

"This land is cursed," she continued, "but that does not mean the people must be that way. The love of God can keep us strong if we only follow Him. All my knowledge comes from Him. I glorify Him in *all* my deeds. Release the reverend. Allow him to go safely about his way. May he learn from this experience. The true faith lives in him."

"Thank you, sweet lady," the reverend stammered. "I don't know how to say I am sorry for what happened here tonight. I cannot explain it myself."

"It was something that needed to happen, Reverend. I knew it and accepted my part in it. Accept your part and prosper in His love."

The crowd released the reverend, apologizing to him as best they could. None would soon forget the madness of this night.

The next morning, a group of men went out to clear away the mess left behind. They were amazed to find a large pile of ashes where the bonfire had been. Lying peacefully on top of the soft bed of ashes was a petite skeleton. Clutched in its bony hands, unscathed, was Aunt Tildy's care-worn leather Bible.

No one speaks of that night, but it is rumored that Aunt Tildy still walks the hills of Satan's Den, protecting its people from harm.

John 8:7, NKJV

> So when they continued asking Him, he raised himself up and said to them, "He who is without sin among you, let him throw a stone at her first."

Matthew 10:16–23, NKJV

> Behold, I send you out as sheep in the midst of wolves. Therefore be wise as serpents and harmless as doves. But beware of men, for they will deliver you up to councils and scourge you in their synagogues. You will be brought before governors and kings for my sake, as a testimony to them and to the gentiles. But when they deliver you up, do not worry about how or what you should speak, for it will be given you in that hour what you should speak; for it is not you who speak, but the spirit of your father who speaks in you.

> Now brother will deliver up brother to death, and a father his child; and children will rise up against parents and cause them to be put to death. And you will be hated by all for my name's sake. But he who endures to the end will be saved. When they persecute you in this city, flee to another. For assuredly, I say to you, you will not have gone through the cities of Israel before the son of man comes.

Notes of Lurlene Joy McCoy

Oh, the joys of revival! Having been instructed in things of the spirit by God's most trusted angels, revival was an activity my family looked forward to.

When Papa put on his "preachin' pants"—an ancient pair of Levi's with the knees worn completely out—Glory and I knew it was time to put on our fire-retardant jackets in firefighter yellow because the townspeople were in for a blessing, whether they wanted it or not.

He started gently, by going door to door and having friendly conversations with everyone who would give him the time of day, which was almost everyone. Papa had no enemies, but there were those who didn't care much for his Jesus talk, and that was all Papa talked about, no matter the topic at hand—Jesus and baseball, Jesus and automobiles, Jesus and the newest dress fashions, Jesus and moonshine. He never judged anyone; he just dealt it as Jesus would. That scared some folks.

Everyone knew Papa was the great-grandson of the infamous Aunt Tildy and that his apple didn't fall far from her tree. He couldn't work herbs and create salves for healing. Aunt Tildy was long gone before he was born, and, they say, she could only pass it on to someone of the opposite sex, and no blood relation. If she had done so, no evidence existed any longer. But Papa's faith and his knowledge of the scripture were unparalleled, just as Aunt Tildy's had been.

Alpha Domini is made up of the descendants—blood and adopted—of the twelve apostles that were Jesus's inner circle. Paul was later included in that prestigious group. They were given privileged knowledge and understanding of what it meant to be a follower of Christ. Each generation passed that information to the next. As time passed and Christianity grew, more specialized training was required, and the children of the elect were taken up into that veil between heaven and earth where they could be given instruction by the angels themselves. Later, perfected, those who had passed from earthly life in Christ and possessed specific skills taught the children the things they would need to survive in the world they lived in. It was a kind of Sunday school with the angels. As they showed skill and ability, their gifts, the children were guided into specialty training that would assist them in their assigned missions. Aunt Tildy's father had been a member of AD, chose to marry a born-again Shawnee woman he had been witnessing to and had led to Christ. Several generations of his family had been upon the land, but he had the privilege of becoming the first missionary to the Shawnee and other tribes who passed through on their hunting expeditions. They were called ghost people because of their skin being fairer than the Natives. There were similar characteristics, but the differences kept the groups apart. A single warrior or, more frequently, a shaman was chosen to interact with the ghost people. They created a shared language, known only to them. Many beliefs were introduced into the tribal traditions as the Great Spirit revealed His presence through the spirits of the ghost people. The time had not yet come for these peoples to be brought to Christ, but the seeds were planted.

People wondered at the knowledge and understanding my family seemed to live by. They would have received no satisfying answer as AD is kept fully hidden from those not born into it or adopted in through marriage or the social adoption through legal avenues by AD families.

Anyway, Papa was a lot like Aunt Tildy. He was strong and quiet but not afraid to tell you how it was. Unlike the stoic Aunt Tildy, however, he had an easy smile and a sense of humor he wielded like a sword. Papa always began his visitations with easy chatter about common things to set the listener at ease. He never bragged but always lent a listening ear. If he agreed with you, he would smile and encourage you along your path. If he disagreed, he wouldn't say a word against you, but he would ask if you would like him to pray with you and what need did you have. Agreeable conversation ended with a prayer for blessings to come their way.

Glory and I went along with Papa as witnesses. He never set foot inside another's house but always talked out in the open for all to see that he was blameless of indecent behavior. We also sang when asked. We weren't the best singers, but we looked cute, like two bananas singing for others to bless their day.

When Papa had visited every home in town, he began going from business to business to "catch up" with the working men and the ladies who were taking care of their own business. Very few people got left out this way.

It could have taken Papa days to get in all his in-town visitation, but word spread, and those who could came to town looking for him. If they caught him at the pharmacy dinner counter, they'd pay for his meal or a cup of coffee just to talk to him. If they caught him on a street corner, a crowd would eventually gather, and Papa would begin to speak of Jesus, loud enough for everyone to hear. When the sidewalk could no longer hold the crowds, the gymnasium of the school would be opened and folding chairs put out for those who came.

And so revival began.

A good revival needs a true preacher, pure of heart, mind, and intent. The people, too, must come with sincerity to hear the Word of God and be willing to respond when God calls their name.

The word *revival* and what it means as it comes to mean in our modern culture seem to be at odds with each other.

As soon as a revival gets started, people begin counting heads and bragging about the number of people who attend their services. Others start counting "decisions" and baptisms so they can prove their church is alive and growing. There seems to be an unseen imbalance between what appears to be happening and the reality behind what is happening.

There are people who actually go from church to church or revival service to revival service and get "saved" over and over again. They've began to develop gills from being baptized so often. Their names are on more church rosters than they can count and attend none.

That's not how it works!

Salvation occurs when you humble yourself before God, admitting you have sinned against God through disobedience, and ask Jesus to forgive you and the Holy Spirit to indwell you as your guide for a changed life of righteousness.

If you have to keep going back to get it, you never had it to begin with.

Salvation can occur anywhere and at any time. There is no designated time or place.

Revival is a good time and place for the public profession of your faith.

Revival, however, is more than making that initial profession. It is an opportunity for weary believers to be revived. They need new inspiration. They need an injection of Jesus to recharge their spiritual batteries.

Revival is a well of Living Water, where those who already know its taste can refill their canteens for the next leg of their journey. It is also an oasis for those who are lost and wandering, a place for them to find what they have been seeking and partake of the life-giving water of Jesus.

It's not a competition to see which church can fill its pews the fullest.

It's not a time to air dirty laundry publicly and shame people into making a decision they may not be prepared for or even mean.

It's not a time to show off self-righteousness or go forth just to be seen.

It is a time of humbling yourself before God and allowing Him to cleanse you of worldly wear, clothe you in His righteousness, and strengthen you for the next thing He has planned for you.

Revival is self-care for the soul. That is what Papa always taught and what he always lived.

Topic: True Revival

Source: The Jeremiah Study Bible
Author: Dr. David Jeremiah

Ezra 9:3–10:14

Some people believe that revival involves little more than being swept along on the tide of emotion. But the book of Ezra shows us that restoration and renewal do not require a *feeling* so much as a *willing* and a *doing*. Revival hinges on a mentality that says, "Whatever it takes to maintain a relationship with God, I will do."

Ezra's experience with the people of Israel exhibits the three key elements of revival:

1. When Ezra hears that the Israelites are marrying people from idolatrous nations, his first response is godly sorrow, or true *remorse* (9:3).
2. His remorse moves him to *repentance* (9:5–9): he identifies himself with the people's sin, and without attempting to soften or diminish what the Israelites have done, he prays for the Lord's forgiveness.
3. Finally, Ezra's repentance leads to *restitution*. He seeks God's help (10:1), then plans an action to fix the problem (10:2–5), develops a punishment for failure (10:7–8), directs the people to promise to obey (10:9–12), and establishes a procedure to follow (10:13–14).

At heart, revival involves a favorable response to one question: are you willing to confront whatever must be confronted so that nothing stands between you and God? When you refuse, the adversary will remind you of your unresolved issues every time you are ready to do something for God, and your service may be hindered. But you can be restored at any time; you need only to make things right. Setting things right with God and with others—even when you've already received God's forgiveness—puts your heart at peace and instills His power in your life again.

Topic: Familiar Spirits *Can*, and *Do*, Plague Christians

Source: www.shoutingfromtherooftop.com

Summary

- God's people are influenced by Satan's attacks because they do not believe he can attack them (2 Corinthians 2:11; Matthew 10:16).
    - The physical reality of a spiritual landslide that has been going on since the beginning of time, which will not go away if we ignore it (Jude 17–23; James 1:27; Ephesians 6:10–18)
    - Lust not only affects the flesh, but it also affects the soul (1 Peter 2:11).
    - Christians are being misled to believe this influence of evil cannot happen (Isaiah 9:16).
    - The "voices" being heard by Christians do not always appear to be evil but may masquerade as angels or God Himself.
    - They may be deceived into believing they are seeing or hearing a loved one who has passed away.
    - "Unclean" items, including religious decor, can lead to evil visitations.
    - Participation in or viewing of events that do not have a spiritual connection to Christ may invoke evil visitations.
    - Generational sins or curses that are repeated or passed down through an object can invoke evil visitations (2 Corinthians 11:14).
    - Music and videos can influence evil activity.
    - Knowing God's Word and practicing it can alleviate fear (2 Timothy 1:7).
    - We can use what is of Christ (God's Word) to combat what is not of Christ; we should never create the image of something being "of Christ" (statue, picture, etc.) having equal power *as* Christ.

Topic: Christianity versus Paganism

Author: Reverend Mark Hunnemann
Date: Thursday, December 7, 2017
Source: www.eyeontheparanormal.blogspot.com

Summary

- There is a visceral yearning to know the meaning of life and universal morals.
- There are two basic worldviews:
  - Paganism—based on the ultimacy of creation; denies the duality of Creator and creation (duality)
  - Christianity— based on the ultimacy of the self-existent Creator
- Romans 1:18–25 calls this the "great exchange" of the knowledge of the true God for the lie of the worship of nature.
- Paganism perceives the world as self-creating (perpetually existing) and self-explanatory; made up of the same stuff—matter, spirit, or mixture; only one kind of existence, which is worshipped as divine (of ultimate importance); everything has the same worth, though there is apparent distinction and hierarchy; "homocosmology."
- Creation offers that the world is the free work of a personal, transcendent God, who creates ex nihilo (from nothing), was not constrained by or dependent on any preexisting conditions; there is God, and there is everything that is not God; God is triune (three parts in one)—Father, Son, and Holy Spirit; this worldview celebrates otherness, distinctiveness, worshipping as divine the distinct, personal triune Creator, who placed essential distinctions within the creation (male/female, right/wrong, humans/nonhumans); "heterocosmology," a worldview based on otherness and difference.
  - The triune God structured the fabric of the cosmos on the principle of distinctions within unity, reflecting the

very nature of the Trinity (One and Many); the interpersonal communication between the members of the Trinity gives meaning to human communication.

- With the many gods of paganism, there arises the question of, which gods do you choose? Personal preference, expectations, and definitions of a god give rise to the vast variety.
- Christianity offers a consistent and persistent insistence that the living God is the only God that is really there, has spoken to us true truth in human language through the Bible.
- Pagan texts do not agree with one another, lack historical details that are without contradiction or error, and are not supported by the archeological evidence. No such evidence has ever contradicted the biblical record.
- Prophecies within the biblical record are astronomical in their fulfillment—one in trillion thirteenth power.
- Evidence, paired with faith, strengthens the argument for Christianity, as paganism is more about faith (as a nurturing between the worshipper and the divine) than evidence by which that experience can be measured.
- Experience is a form of evidence. Pagans who accept their worldview are attacked spiritually by those gods or guides they followed unquestioningly when they begin to ask difficult and unanswerable questions. As long as they blindly follow, they are safe.
- The meaning of life can only be found in something, or Someone, greater than humanity and the natural order; otherwise, we are self-referential—trying to give ourselves meaning.
- In homocosmology, there is no qualitative difference between humans and animals, or humans and grass. How can one give meaning to the other if they are equal? All of nature is finite. Only Christianity gives finite creation an infinite starting point.
- Perhaps one will herald science as supportive of paganism, but Christianity is a necessary precursor for science; even

non-Christian "fathers of science" agree that paganism and its view of nature and reality could not have given rise to modern science.

- Pagans are adamant that objective, absolute truth does not exist, that right and wrong are human constructs. Where does this leave the pursuit of universal moral standards? Nature is full of cruelty—survival of the fittest rules. Without absolute morals, all that is left is sociological or statistical averages, or preference, that brings into question why some cultures have embraced pedophilia, cannibalism, and polygamy while others find these to be great evils. Have these cultures developed a greater self-realization or embraced the divine within?
- Morality is permanently defined for the Christian in the pages of the Bible. These reflect the character of the Triune God. Pagans eschew these guidelines completely.

The Thrice-Blessed Maiden

Faith translates the invisible world into
the visible; and so by the eye of the faith,
I can see what God has wrought.

—*A Disruptive Faith,* A. W. Tozer

Many moons ago, when the earth was young, before the white man came, a maiden was born. She was born with a spirit so strong and pure that the Spirit of All That Is Evil desired her. When she was but a baby on the cradleboard, the Spirit of All That Is Evil caused her to fall into the river. Her mother watched in terror as the cradleboard was washed downstream.

Her maternal prayers were heard by the spirit of the river, who sent a mighty warrior, an enormous rainbow trout, to rescue the maiden. The fish grasped the strap of the cradleboard and pulled her to the safety of her mother's arms.

The tribe was so grateful they held a ceremony in honor of the spirit of the river. The ceremony was so great the spirit of the river blessed the baby with the ability to swim like the trout and evade all enemies.

The Spirit of All That Is Evil hid in his dark kingdom for many years, planning how to make the maiden his own. When the maiden came of marriageable age, the Spirit of All That Is Evil took upon himself the guise of a warrior. The dark warrior courted the beautiful maiden with trinkets, ponies, furs, and precious stones. Still, she turned him away.

One day, the Spirit of All That Is Evil found the maiden alone in the forest. He grabbed her and tried to forcibly drag her to his kingdom. She cried out to the spirits of the forest and the earth to save her. The spirits sent brother wolf to save her. Brother wolf clawed and bit the dark warrior, driving the Spirit of All That Is Evil back to his domain.

The maiden's people were so grateful to the wolf and the spirits of the earth and the forest. They held a great feast to honor the spirits. The spirits of the earth and forest were so honored that they blessed the maiden with the ability to run swiftly and fight like the wolf.

The maiden came to be known as Twice-Blessed among her people.

Twice-Blessed grew older and became a wise woman of her people. She was sought out by maidens far and wide for advice and aid. The Spirit of All That Is Evil continued to plot against her.

It wasn't until Twice-Blessed was very old and near the end of her life that the Spirit of All That Is Evil got another chance. The Spirit of All That Is Evil took on the guise of the spirit of death and approached Twice-Blessed. The spirit of death is neither good nor evil but ushers the spirit into the afterlife for judgment.

Twice-Blessed's spirit recognized the Spirit of All That Is Evil and swam swiftly to hide within Twice-Blessed's body. When the Spirit of All That Is Evil failed to capture her soul in this way, it formed a net as if to catch the fish. The net swept upward from Twice-Blessed's feet. Her soul ran swiftly upward like a wolf. When it could no longer remain within Twice-Blessed's flesh, it fled into the air, calling upon the spirit of the air to help her.

The spirit of the air heard her and sent a great eagle to snatch her soul from the net and carry it to judgment where it was sent to a place of highest honor.

A shaman of the tribe saw what happened, and a ceremony to honor the eagle and the spirit of the air was held. The spirit of the air was so pleased it counseled with the spirits of the river, forest, and earth as to how they could bless these people once more. It was decided that once every generation, a maiden would be born, thrice-blessed with the ability to swim like a fish, run and fight like a wolf, and fly like an eagle.

And so it has been to this day.

Isaiah 40:31, NKJV

> But those who wait on the Lord shall renew their strength; they shall mount up with wings like eagles and, they shall run and not be weary, they shall walk and not faint.

There almost seems to be a sort of riddle going on here: what swims like a fish, runs and fights like a wolf, and flies like an eagle? This is no riddle. It is a very great reality to those who have cast their faith in God.

At salvation and commitment to follow Christ, we become "fishers of men" (Matthew 4:18–20). That means we were also once fish. As sinners, we swam in the Sea of Sin, hopelessly fleeing from every perceived danger and finding no refuge. Only when we became the fisherman did we find solace in rescue from our hopelessness and opportunity to rescue others from the same fate.

We are also prey to forces beyond our control—self, other members of humanity, and ultimately, the Evil One himself. We run willy-nilly, hiding in plain sight, ever the target. That doesn't change when we become children of God, but we do learn how to fight the predators that pursue us. We don the armor of God. We place our trust in the God of the battle. We pray. We resist the devil, and he must flee from us (James 4:7).

Finally, when we grow weary, we will be renewed. We will be strengthened and, like eagles, be lifted up (Isaiah 40:31).

Topic: Activating Grace

Author: Dr. David Jeremiah
Source: The Jeremiah Study Bible

James uses a series of Greek imperatives (commands) to communicate nine principles for approaching grace so that believers can withstand this world's tendency to pull us from God:

1. *Relinquish* control of your life (4:7).
2. *Resist* the devil (4:7).
3. *Restore* worship to a priority (4:8).
4. *Renounce* sinful actions (4:8).
5. *Reject* sinful attitudes (4:8).
6. *React* to sin with sorrow (4:9).
7. *Refrain* from a frivolous attitude toward evil (4:9).
8. *Respond* humbly to success (4:10).
9. *Refuse* to slander your fellow Christians (4:11–12).

The Legend of the Indian Wish Stone

When you need guidance, get close to
God and the nearer you are to him,
the clearer everything will appear.
Many people fervently pray, "Oh, God, guide
me", then they grab the steering wheel.

—Robert C. Savage, *Pocket Wisdom*

Without love, earth would not differ from
hell except for the difference of location. Let
us treasure what is left of love among the
sons of men. It is not perfect, but it makes
life bearable and even sweet here below.

—A. W. Tozer, *The Alliance Weekly/Witness*, 1950

Many years before Kentucky became a settlement of Virginia, the land was used as a hunting and burial ground by several tribes of Native Americans. While the ground was mutually shared by all the tribes, each tribe had its favored areas to camp in while hunting. If two tribes ever met on these grounds, disputes were settled peacefully, when possible, by blood when necessary.

It was during one of these infrequent meetings that the legend was born.

A Cherokee brave by the name of Raven Cloud had tracked a buck to the edge of a wild creek. As he drew his bow and prepared to let it go, he spotted a fair Shawnee maiden bathing in a deep hollow where two streams merged into one. He fell madly in love with her.

When Spring Dove, as the maiden was called, had finished bathing and was gathering her basket of berries to leave, she spotted Raven Cloud hiding among the bushes. She, too, fell in love.

As Spring Dove left the creek, she spotted a small, round, flat rock with a tiny hole worn through it by the water. She bent to pick it up. As she held it to her breast, she spoke a wish aloud. "To the man who finds this, I wish my heart to go." To seal her wish, she spit through the hole and tossed it, without looking, over her left shoulder.

A hawk flying overhead snatched the rock from the air and flew over where Raven Cloud was hiding. As the hawk flew past, Raven Cloud raised his arms. The startled hawk dropped the stone right into Raven Cloud's hands.

Raven Cloud strung the rock on a thong around his neck in honor of the beautiful maiden he had given his heart to that day.

The two met again the next day. Spring Dove came to the creek to gather berries. Raven Cloud was waiting for her. As he approached, the stone on the thong swung across his chest. Spring Dove knew it to be her heart. The two spent the day together, knowing they must soon part. They could never be husband and wife as long as their tribes did not get along.

The hunting was good. Raven Cloud and Spring Dove were able to sneak away and be together every day for more than a moon. They were each careful to return to their camps with enough meat or berries to satisfy their elders.

On the final hunt of the season, Raven Cloud was tracking a great, wise buck, experienced by years of evading hunters. He needed to bring in the biggest buck to gain the attention of the elders. If he brought in such a prize, perhaps he would be granted his choice of rewards. He knew the reward he desired most—Spring Dove.

He touched the stone where it lay on his chest. He kissed it for luck. As he aimed, the buck turned and looked him in the eye. The arrow flew straight and true. The big buck fell to the ground.

Raven Cloud presented his prize to the council of elders. They touted his bravery as a hunter and gave him his choice of rewards. Raven Cloud turned down each of the offered rewards, at risk of offending the council. Exasperated, the council asked Raven Cloud what he would have as his reward. Raven Cloud told them of the beautiful maiden he had met and how she had given him her "heart."

Impressed with his bravery, the elders requested a meeting with the father of Spring Dove. Though they were of differing tribes, they were willing to set aside their prejudices in the name of love. The Shawnee council was skeptical of Raven Cloud's story and questioned Spring Dove. Spring Dove told her story, supporting that of the one she loved. Unmoved, the council denied the marriage.

A quarrel arose between the two councils. For days, the two lovers were kept apart as their elders argued. One day, the argument came to blows. A Cherokee elder struck a Shawnee elder, causing him to fall unconscious. The Shawnee shaman was called to tend to the fallen elder. For two days and nights, the elder fought for his life. On the third day, he opened his eyes and spoke.

He told of the spirit of dream that had kept him near death. In that dream, a fox had come to him and called him foolish and unwise. He was told that the Great Spirit had made both the raven and the dove, the dark and the light. Though the two are very different, they are part of the Great Spirit's plan. Darkness passes into the light. Light passes into the darkness. In between the passings of light and dark lies a time of peace when all nature ceases activity and listens to the Creator. So be the coming of the Raven and the Dove together. The union of these natural enemies could only bring peace and prosperity to the Shawnee and the Cherokee, as destined by the Great Spirit.

Thus, a wish was made upon a simple stone with a small hole drilled by the rain united two young lovers and their warring tribes. Though the war went on, these two small groups met in peace, and the children of the Raven and the Dove knew a new and better prosperity than their ancestors had ever known.

Song of Solomon (Song of Songs) 8:6–7, NKJV

Set me as a seal upon your heart,
As a seal upon your arm;
For love is as strong as death,
Jealousy as cruel as the grave;
It's flames are flames of fire,
A most vehement flame.

Many waters cannot quench love,
Nor can the floods drown.
If a man would give for love
All the wealth of his house,
It would be utterly despised.

Love is the strongest force there is on earth. We are to love with our entire being—mind, soul, and body (Matthew 22:36–39). Love is the greatest of gifts—to receive or give (1 Corinthians 13:13). It is the preeminent gift that leads to all other virtues (Galatians 5:22). It lasts forever (1 Corinthians 13:8). Love is the birthmark of the children of God (John 13:34–35). God is love (1 John 4:8) and loved us so much He sent His only begotten Son to live among us (John 1:14), die for our sins (John 3:16), and then be resurrected to life to be our advocate (1 John 2:1). Jesus is our example of love (Ephesians 5:1–2). Love for one another makes for a happy home (Ephesians 5:25). Love conquers all (1 Peter 4:8). In the case of Raven Cloud and Spring Dove, their pure love for each other and their faith in a benevolent Great Spirit not only brought them together but united two groups of people, determined enemies, into a united force of peace. Indeed, we all can get along…if love is at the center.

The Lady in the Cave

The glory of God always comes
at the sacrifice of self.

—A. W. Tozer, *The Crucified Life*

Family ties cannot be hidden, though they would often like to be forgotten. Blood ties may often be ignored or simply not discussed, yet somehow, we know they exist. Therefore, we are both shocked yet not surprised when we discover our suspicions are, in reality, fact.

The young woman strolled thoughtfully along the creek bank; the others were well ahead of her. No one had noticed that she had fallen behind.

On a whim, the family had decided to have their annual reunion at "the old home place." They claimed they wanted great-uncles and great-aunts and distant cousins in their golden years to be allowed to share their memories before being lost to the annals of oral history and forgotten.

She had been interested in hearing these old stories of her family's past until she discovered that these elderly relatives had little real kinship claims with the forgotten family that surrounded them. These scions of tradition became lost and bewildered by the sea of unfamiliar faces, many of whom they had never met, only heard of through long-ago letters or forgotten phone calls. When they did recognize a face, they would call that person by the name of a more familiar relative and ask about family members as they were last remembered decades before. Finally, the younger generation grew weary of trying to communicate effectively with these bewildered kin and began to explore on their own.

Though distant and uninterested, one member of the family had owned this land for nearly a generation, making it a mystery as to what life had really been like there so long ago. Aunts, uncles, and parents could still identify some parts of the land by the stories they had been told or had vague memories of but, still, were open to conjecture, not fact. An air of mystery surrounded the place. Yet it seemed to affect only the one young woman.

As she strolled along the creek, she noted its shallow depths. The darker-blue-green water held mysteries that could not be solved in the clearer, more shallow surface water. Occasional shimmers of sun on scale revealed the presence of creek chubs and tiny minnows in the depths. She wondered what sustenance could be found in those depths.

The curious crew had crossed the creek over an unstable rope walking bridge to explore this side of history. A more modern fjord had been built by the current family to cross the gentle flow, weather conditions allowing. It would be easy to become trapped on either side of the rampage when high waters flowed. The young woman shuddered in thinking what life must have been like more than half a century before, closer to a full century if you count the many years her family had occupied this land before spreading out into the larger world.

Perhaps it was her frame of mind or maybe her kinship to the land. Either way, she was receptive if not prepared for what occurred during that simple stroll.

It was along a curve in the creek that her attention was drawn to what appeared to be the front of a tiny cabin apparently built into the side of a low hill across from where she stood. The cabin was nearly grown over by the flora of the creek bank. Only a door and one battered window could be seen. As the young woman stood on the bank and stared at the unexpected sight, a woman stepped from the darkness of the cabin, leaving the door open behind her. The woman was dressed in an ankle-length, long-sleeved dress of a bygone era; her long, dark hair hung loose to below her waist. She gestured for the young woman to cross the creek to the cabin. Without thinking, the young woman picked her way across the shallows, leaping from stone to stone. The older woman embraced the younger before leading her into the cabin. To describe the woman in the cabin as being older than the young woman was really not accurate as the two appeared to be nearly the same age. The woman in the cabin *felt* older—not just her clothing but also her bearing gave the air of maturity lacking in the younger woman.

The single room of the cabin was lit by tallow candles, revealing a rugged but sturdy table and two cane-bottomed chairs. The two women sat across from each other, contemplating each other and the meaning of this encounter. It was the elder of the two who broke the silence.

"Welcome, my great-great-granddaughter," she said cheerfully.

The young woman, dazed with this revelation, stated simply, "How…?"

"You do not know of me?" The question was more statement than inquiry. "Of course, you do not know of me. I have gone from memory, as from life. It makes no difference as you are here, now, and can rekindle my memory in future generations. I am Estelle, your great-great-grandfather's first wife and mother to his first four children." She paused to allow this to sink in.

"My great-great-grandfather had seven children, all by the same wife. Charlotte, I believe.

"That is what you have been led to believe. The truth was too sad to be passed on."

The young woman was unsure what to believe. This woman, Estelle, could not be her great-grandmother as she had been to the family cemetery only the week before and had placed flowers upon the graves of her great-grandparents. This woman was too young to be anyone's grandmother, let alone great-grandmother.

"You see me as I was in the last moments of my life, forever preserved in my youth." Estelle raised her hand and stroked the youthful cheek of her great-granddaughter. The younger woman was too enthralled to pull away from the woman's touch.

"'T'was too many years to count, though the years don't really matter. Your great-great-grandfather, John, and I were married. We bought this beautiful farm and began our family. Not so long after our fourth child was born, the eldest being nearly six, a terrible downpour took this area by surprise. The floodwaters rose, threatening our humble home. John ran in from the fields and called across to the house where I was with the children. We knowed the house wasn't going to last, and we would be lucky to save ourselves. I grabbed the two youngest children, neither of which was able to be walking, least not enough to cross the little footbridge in the rain. Leaving the two eldest in the safety of the house, I waded into the water of my front yard and passed them off to John at the footbridge. He took the two tiny ones and hid them in the back of the wagon he'd been using to haul seed to the fields.

"The water'd begun to fill the house by the time I got to the rag doll I'd made for my littlest, and only, girl. We reached the bridge, and John started across. The bridge swayed dangerously from his end. He didn't dare try to come any farther, so he held to it while I tried to cross. I pushed the eldest in front of me, picking up the other. John coaxed his eldest son from the far side of the bridge. The child bravely moved to his father, who then moved from the bridge to put him in the wagon so he could mind the other two.

"It was when he was turning around to help me that the bridge give way, taking me and the one boy with it. I can swim some, but not in floodwaters and with heavy, wet skirts. I kept my child above water, pushing him as close to his daddy as I could. John tried two or three times before he was able to get ahold of his son. Hugging the child with one arm, he reached for me.

"Our fingers touched for just a brief moment that felt like forever before I was pulled beneath the waters by something in the undertow.

"Back then, this creek was much narrower and shallower than it is now, especially when the waters ran wild. Our house was built between the creek and the hillside, away from the open fields we could farm. We had just enough room for our little home, a few out-buildings, and some chickens. Even the pigs were on the other side of the creek. John watched as our house washed away after me.

"Strangely, the rain stopped as John watched his world crumble around him.

"I don't know for sure how long it was, but John stayed with neighbors until the floodwaters stopped flowing. Every day, he would come and walk the creek banks, looking for anything that remained of his life.

"He found odds and ends where they washed up on the fields. These he carefully preserved, in hopes of putting his life back together. His greatest sorrow came when he found the headboard of our bed caught on some large rocks. The footboard he found further on, beat up, but whole, leaning against a tree.

"That must have been the last straw for him as he moved away, about thirty miles, and never come back this way. His older brother bought the place, but John never set foot on it again. The two youngest was too young to remember their Mama. The two oldest was different. Jacob, my second one, didn't speak for a long time after the flood. When he did, he didn't speak of anything about that time. The oldest, John Junior, your grandfather, got pneumonia and nearly died. They say he had to learn to walk and talk all over again. He was much like his younger brother when he got well.

"John found a young girl and married her before he moved off. They had three more children together, and no one never knowed he'd had another wife. Of course, the girl knowed, but she kept the secret. Those children growed up thinking she was their Mama. She treated them like they was her own. Thank the Lord for that.

"Time has passed on. My name forgotten. I didn't have no family to speak of when John married me. We never got too close to our neighbors, except for church. I was mourned for by neighbors. All felt sorry for John and the young'uns. They was ever so kind. But the secret of my passing became a sad tale told in parlors when hearts was kept in out of the rain. Even those stories stopped when the tale-tellers died or moved on. I've rested in peace all these years, knowin' my children were loved and cared for."

As Estelle ended her tale, she reached across the table and wiped the gleaming tears from her great-granddaughter's face. The young woman didn't hesitate to take the cold hand of her great-grandmother.

"Why are you telling me this now, if you are at peace?" the young woman asked.

Estelle pulled her hand away from the young woman and clasped her hands on the table before her. It was a while before she spoke.

"A day is coming soon when my sleep will be disturbed. It is up to you to see that I find peace once more."

Before the young woman could reply, the world around her grew black, and she could feel herself falling. When she could see once more, she was standing where she had been, looking across the creek at a weathered slope along the creek bank. She noticed for the first time that this hillock bordered a narrow field that ran between the creek and a hill, just enough space for a modest house and some outbuildings. It was barren of all but weeds growing waist-high from years of being left fallow.

The chatter of the cousins returning returned her attention to the reality of the circumstances. No one really spoke to her, having neither noticed her absence nor realizing she had rejoined them. It was as if she were surrounded by a fog.

When she crossed the rope bridge once more, she noticed how deep the creek was between the banks. Fishermen would have a difficult time finding a stable spot to set up camp. Repeated flooding had washed away the trees and brush, leaving bare limestone shelves forming rapids where the water was shallower. She shuddered as she crossed the bridge.

Over lunch, she made it a point to sit with a great-aunt and a uncle. She questioned them about family history, particularly family tragedies. She got the expected tales of stillborn babies, car accidents, and war stories. She tried to ask about John Sr. and the possibility of two wives. Neither the great-aunt, daughter of the alleged second wife, nor the eldest uncle believed John Sr. had ever had more than one wife. They seemed outraged that anyone would tell such an outlandish tale.

After lunch, she sought out other relatives and asked the same questions with similar results. Her husband tried to reason with her, thinking she was experiencing stress of some kind. He had to force her to go home before she ruined the reunion completely with her hysteria.

In the following weeks, she spent all her time seeking evidence that Estelle even existed. Her frustration mounted as she discovered few records existed of that time as people kept mostly to themselves in their own small communities, going out only to bigger towns for things they could not provide for themselves.

Her obsession grew, as did her husband's concern. They purchased a small lot from the family that owned the farm where her psychosis had begun. They were building a house there, in hopes her mental health would improve. She spent every day she could at the construction site, making sure the workers were following the house plan exactly. The house would be near the creek, the back porch overlooking the bend in the creek where her revelation had begun.

While sitting under a tree one evening after the workers had gone home, she was surprised to see a small furry animal climb up from the creek bank where it had been swimming. As it came near her, she saw it was a small black puppy. Mud and debris from the creek hid any other markings that could be used to identify the animal to its owner if it had one. She wrapped the wriggly creature in a blanket from the trunk of her car.

On her way home, she stopped to ask neighbors if the puppy belonged to them or if they knew to whom it might belong. No one recognized the hairy waif.

She cleaned the puppy in warm soapy water, discovering the curly tail and floppy ears of a mixed breed. A tiny star of white was the only break in the pure black coat. She named the puppy Star, in honor of her forgotten great-grandmother.

Her husband let her keep the puppy, hoping it would aid in healing her ever-increasing anxiety.

The puppy accompanied her everywhere she went. It played in a small area around her as she sat watching the house go up. It sat in her lap as she picked out wallpaper and paint samples, barking agreement whenever its mistress expressed an interest in a pattern or particular shade of paint. The house would reflect a definite turn-of-the-twentieth-century rustic look. A garage full of antiques waited to be moved into the new house.

Careful questioning of elderly family members resulted in locating some heirloom items for her home.

Hand-stitched quilts made by her grandmother would adorn her beds. Copies of old family photos in vintage frames would hang on the walls. Odds and ends would fill a curio cabinet. It seemed as though everyone was bending over backward to help her connect with her ancestry and give up the obsession of the missing Estelle.

It was a fateful day when the young woman and the ever-present Star passed by a neighbor's house on the way to her nearly completed home with a small load of items for decoration in the rooms that had already been completed. She was astonished at what she saw tossed haphazardly on a wood heap and turned her car around so as to go speak to her nearest neighbor. The object of her astonishment was an old bed, head- and footboards, strangely familiar and calling out to her.

The neighbor gladly gave her the bed parts. He had no use for them, other than as firewood. They had been found in the barn loft beneath ancient hay bales and wrapped in oilskin cloths. Though the years had been many, the oilskins had done their job well. The neighbor knew nothing of its origin as he had bought this farm only four years before and was just then getting around to cleaning out the hayloft of the barn. His priorities as a farmer had been more hobby than profit anyway.

The young woman leaned her prizes against one wall of the house while she examined them for authenticity and damage. Termites had surprisingly avoided this grand buffet of pure white oak. Patches of old mildew and mold could be seen where the floodwaters had swollen the wood as it was tossed about. Scratches and dents showed where they had encountered water-born debris and rocks. She had no doubt this had been John and Estelle's bed. If only she could prove it.

She managed to pull the two bed pieces into the front entryway of the house. She would find someone to redo the bed, make new sideboards for it, and replace the bed she now had in the master bedroom with this one. Her husband didn't have to know its story…yet.

The day came when her home was finished. She and her husband moved in with rapidly growing Star. The young woman seemed content, less excitable. She didn't bring up the issue of her "lost" great-great-grandmother. She went back to work after her "extended vacation" on doctor's orders. Life returned to normal. The crisis seemed to have passed.

In the process of restoration, a set of crudely engraved initials *JC + EBC* and a nearly faded date a century earlier had emerged. The person doing the restoration had carefully cleaned that spot and had preserved the information carefully. When he pointed out the more interesting flaws created by time to the young woman, he indicated an interest in the initials and commented on the story the bed could tell if it could speak. The young woman wanted to tell her story, but it was too fantastic to believe. Smiling knowingly, she had simply agreed with the man's assessment.

The young woman returned to the family cemetery to place new flowers upon the graves of those she loved but never knew. Star accompanied her. It was while she was at the cemetery that she felt a strong desire to do more detective work. She took drawing paper and charcoal pencils from the trunk of her car. Her artistic hobby had proven useful. She made charcoal rubbings of the weathered tombstones of her great-grandparents and the five children buried there. Two of the children had been buried elsewhere.

Later, she spread the rubbings out on her dining room table. She stared at them awkwardly for more than an hour, knowing there was something missing, but she could not identify what it was.

Star climbed up in her lap. The young woman, weary from effort, nuzzled her beloved pet. The little dog suddenly leaped from her lap to the table and began scrambling about. The young woman snatched the paper the puppy had grabbed for and was shaking angrily. Freed of its enemy, the puppy pushed another paper aside with her nose before sliding toward her mistress. The young woman lifted the puppy from the tabletop. It sneezed in disgust.

As she set the puppy on the floor, something caught her eye. The paper she had taken from the puppy had been placed next to the one the puppy had pushed toward her. The former belonged to her great-great-grandmother's second wife, and the latter belonged to the eldest son of John and Estelle. There was only fifteen years difference between the two!

While girls tended to marry young back then, it seemed difficult to believe a girl of that age would have married. She knew John's wife had been younger than him, but she had not considered he would have robbed the cradle with four children of his own. He needed a woman of some experience; he did not need another child to act as a mother to his kids! He needed someone who knew what raising children was all about and old enough to be in authority over them without question.

She decided to keep this information to herself for a while. She felt there was more information forthcoming but was unsure as to what form it would take.

The next morning dawned on a thunderstorm that darkened the skies as though night would never end. The wind ripped leaves from the trees. Water stood in the yard in ever-widening puddles. Through her kitchen window, she watched the creek begin to rise. She could easily understand how her great-great-grandmother must have felt as she watched the water washing away her home. Star refused to leave the porch to answer the call of nature, reminding her mistress of the fear Estelle must have felt when trying desperately to save her children.

The following day brought respite from rain and much healing sunshine. The floodwater began to recede. Star became more adventuresome. The little puppy would sit near the receding waters and sniff at the debris left behind. The young woman often accompanied her pet.

After a week of watching the water recede, the twosome ventured farther from home. The dried mud cracked beneath their feet, stirring up light dust. As they rounded a bend in the creek, Star suddenly dashed away from her mistress and galloped across the creek and up a shallow bank. The young woman called frantically to the puppy as she splashed carelessly across the creek. A piercing yip, followed by an echoing whine, accompanied the disappearance of the pup from view. Tearfully, the young woman searched the area where she had last seen Star. Following the panicked whines, she discovered the puppy in a sinkhole that had appeared after the floodwaters had eroded the final earth from the area.

On her knees, the young woman tried to reach down and pull her beloved friend from the muddy pit she had fallen into. The hole was too deep. She could not climb into the hole and out without trapping herself. She talked to the puppy in a calming voice, telling her to stay calm. She ran back to the house and grabbed a short ladder, praying all the while that the ladder would be long enough.

She could neither see nor hear the puppy when she returned to the hole. She spoke reassuringly, nonetheless, as she lowered herself into the muddy hole. Carefully, she stepped her way down into the darkness.

She had not thought to get a flashlight, hadn't dreamed of needing one. So she stumbled hazardously through the underground passage. The sunlight from above provided only enough light for her to see shadows of the limestone walls as they slanted downward in a gentle but muddy slope, indicating that the flood had reached this depth before it receded.

She stumbled as the sloping ground took a sudden upward plan. She called out for Star as she sat in the mud, tears streaming down her face. The answering barks drove her to her feet and onward into the shadows.

When something wet and furry brushed against her legs and sharp claws scratched at her already scuffed knees, she let out a scream. When Star responded with a concerned whine, the young woman dropped to her knees and clutched the wet animal to her. The puppy responded with repeated licks to her face.

Having retrieved her pet unharmed, she thought of returning to the ladder and the surface. Instead, Star jumped from her arms and disappeared deeper into the cave. The young woman could only follow. The path continued upward a short distance before ending in a small room. A strange luminescence lit the cavern. The low ceiling brushed against the young woman's head. Star ran to her feet, tugging at a sock for her to follow. The puppy pulled her forward to a low shelf in the back of the cave. The young woman moved forward in hope of sitting down on the shelf.

To her surprise, she found that the shelf was, in actuality, a hollowed-out space. To her even greater surprise, she found herself looking down upon the face of Estelle, her lost and forgotten great-great-grandmother, dark hair spread around her where she slept in perfect preservation.

The tiny cavern was excavated, and professionals gave their reports. With persuasion, DNA samples from known descendants of each of the children fathered by Great-Grandfather John were taken and compared with that taken from Estelle's perfectly preserved body. Family members were shaken by the news that the body was positively identified as the female ancestor of the descendants of John's four oldest children, but of no relation to the younger three. Eventually, records were uncovered in the courthouse where they had been registered as husband and wife. A wedding ring bearing their initials and wedding date engraved on the inside had been found on Estelle's delicate finger.

The experts presumed the flood that claimed Estelle's life had also opened the original egress into the cavern, depositing her body gently into the recess as it subsided. Other debris, stone, and earth had been deposited to block the entrance once more. Over the years, the creek had been rerouted both naturally and through the effort of landowners concerned about protecting their fields from floods.

Estelle was laid to rest in the family cemetery alongside her husband, and the family history was amended to correct the oversight. Just as the young woman had insisted so strongly that she had seen and spoken to her great-great-grandmother, the family took a new interest in their roots and genealogical history. The family reunion included a memorial tribute to the lost and forgotten Estelle. New stories were told. Relationships were reevaluated. Just as Estelle had predicted, her sleep had been disturbed, but the young woman had returned that peace to her and had rejuvenated a family who had grown distant.

Matthew 26:13, NKJV

> Assuredly, I say to you, wherever this gospel is preached in the world, what this woman has done will be told as a memorial to her.

Was this another "time slip," a dream, or some other impossible event? Only God knows. The only known factor is that the young woman made the claim of her visitation with this ancestress while at a family reunion in a place she had never visited before and hadn't known existed before someone came up with the idea of having the family reunion there. There had never been a hint of the tragedy passed down through the generations to fuel her imagination. Hysteria or hallucination could have explained the experience. It was not likely but possible. Stress can do some strange things to people. The woman's life demonstrated no such concern prior to this point, however. Did she speak to an actual spirit or have some kind of "out of body" experience? No way to tell. There was a definite message relayed that day. The finding of the head- and footboards could have been a mere coincidence as the initials JC could belong to any number of people from any era of the existence of the tree used in the construction of the bed. Without testing the bed in the condition in which it was found, before restoration, there is no proof of the bed having been in water, such as a flood, and no way to determine if the initials were carved before or after the tree was harvested and the boards made for the bed. There is always faith, as demonstrated by the young woman, that these events were factual. Evidence, however, gave credence to the rest of the story when the actual body was found, wearing a ring with initials that matched those on the headboard, including the date. Backed by courthouse records of the marriage registration, the facts were supported by the record and matched the faith. No doubt there were, and always will be, those who doubt the truth of the revised genealogy, but their doubt is due to a lack of faith, not lack of facts. They choose to deny fact to create their own truth.

This greatly parallels the core belief that separates Christianity from all other religions and belief systems—the resurrection of Christ. There are the biblical accounts in all four gospels that attest to the truth of the resurrection. The entire New Testament hinges on the truth of that event, including the end-of-time resurrection of those who have died in Christ (Matthew 24:30–31). The people who lived at the time of this earth-shattering event had difficulty accepting it. The Roman soldiers who were at the tomb at the time of the event attested to its truth but were paid to say it didn't happen but that the body had been stolen instead. (Matthew 28:11–15). This is a matter of looking at historical records as recorded by those who were in charge of chronicling such events for their kings. These same historians have recorded the significant number of witnesses who claimed they had seen and interacted with this resurrected person during the forty days before he reportedly ascended to heaven. He was seen eating and drinking with people. These extra-biblical records are used by non-Christians as their sources for disputing the truth of the Bible as these volumes are often critical of the man named Jesus. As skeptics, they would be the last to report these events as facts. They simply recorded what was occurring and how their government leaders responded. With the "discovery" of the existence of the Shroud of Turin and the controversy surrounding it, we have another source of evidence that appears to support the biblical account through *scientific assessment and evidence.* Those scientists who have conducted the tests on the shroud are in agreement that it contained a real corpse, bearing markings that are consistent with a man who had been seriously injured by beating, wore a crown of thorns that pierced his forehead, has a postmortem spear piercing, and demonstrates characteristics of blood shed both before death and after. They cannot explain, however, how the image came to be imprinted on the cloth. They suspect some sort of radiation caused it as it is similar to the process used in photography, only using organic material. Amazingly, the image is of a recently deceased, unwashed man. There are no signs of decomposition as would be seen if the image had been created by the process of natural decay. It is a matter of faith to believe that the image is that of Jesus Christ—through faith alone or with support of evidence. The denial of evidence that the shroud is real—not whom the image is of—denies science as truth. If you can't trust science, even when it is in error, you can't trust nature, even when it is inexplicable. What is left?

Topic: Petrified Man of Cumberland County, Tennessee

Source: The Granny Curse and Other Ghosts and Legends from East Tennessee
Author: Randy Russell and Janet Barnett

Summary

During the Civil War, potassium nitrate was mined from a local cave system and processed into gunpowder nearby. After the war, explorers in the cave system discovered the corpse of a man, about thirty-five years old, who appeared to have fallen asleep in gentle repose and died. Over time, the body had become petrified. After its discovery, it was buried in a local church cemetery. The people living in the community around the church became frightened by screams and other disturbing events around the cemetery. It became an unwritten law that no one speak of the petrified man. It came to be believed that although the unknown man had been given a proper funeral and burial, the spirits that had shared the cave with that man for so long were disturbed that they had not been invited to the funeral. The petrified man was unearthed and reburied in a secret location within the cave system. Only the gravedigger and minister were present to limit the disturbance of the new grave. The hauntings stopped upon the preaching of the funeral by a lone preacher to a cavern of spirits. The gravedigger stayed outside during the funeral, which lasted longer than an hour. Locals do give permission to curiosity seekers to visit the caves but do not discuss the petrified man or the circumstances surrounding his discovery, burial, and funeral arrangements.

Coming of Age

The things that are of earth belong
to sight, reason, and our senses. The
things that are of heaven belong to
faith, trust, and confidence in God.

—*The Crucified Life*, A. W. Tozer

Sometimes it is difficult to determine the exact nature of a haunting. This is even more true in Satan's Den. Granted, there are individuals with distinguished talents who are apparent magnets for the supernatural. Just as true, there are always certain places people avoid. In this next story, the faintly visible line between the natural and the supernatural becomes so blurred as to be indistinguishable for one young girl.

Several strange things happened the year she turned thirteen—prophetic dreams, hunches which proved true, the development of a direct link to her ancestress, Aunt Tildy.

Her family returned to Satan's Den the year she turned thirteen. They had escaped the superstition when she was only fourteen months old. Sabrina had been raised in the suburbs of Indianapolis, Indiana, protected from her past. Frequent summer visits had endeared Satan's Den to her heart. She loved the rambling hills and chilly creek that dominated the farm where her father had grown up. Therefore, she was thrilled at the prospect of returning to her favorite place to be.

They lived with her grandparents until they bought a single-wide trailer and set it up on a perfect five-acre lot at one end of the farm. She got her first horse shortly after that. These two elements—trailer and horse—would be the links to supernatural paths that crossed at that small lot.

The first event didn't seem significant at the time but later came back to her in a most unusual way. She was sitting at the breakfast table, sleepily regarding her bowl of oatmeal. It was a school day, and she was thinking about her schedule. She glanced up from her bowl, expecting to see her own reflection in the mirrored shelves across from her. Instead, her gaze was drawn to her left, to the cabinets of the kitchen's inner wall where it ran to a sharp right where the washer and dryer were before making a sharp left that led to the bedrooms in the back of the trailer.

The cabinets and walls seemed to melt to a soft haze. A small girl, approximately seven or eight, stepped into the kitchen from the laundry room alcove. Her long dark-brown hair had fallen around her face where she watched her feet as she walked. Her shoes were old-fashioned and an ugly, worn brown. Tan stockings covered her legs. Her arms were crossed against a light-brown pinafore over a darker-brown dress. The child looked up to meet Sabrina's eyes. She raised a hand to her mouth in surprise and gasped. Sabrina glimpsed chocolate-brown eyes as the child suddenly vanished before her eyes.

When she mentioned this to her mother, her mother mentioned the child fit the description of her mother as a child. The manner of dress, however, was much earlier. Jokingly, they named the child Tildy after Sabrina's great-grandmother.

The ghost child was never seen again in the ten years the family lived there.

The trailer was sold to Sabrina's cousin, who lived in it another three years before selling it to her ex-husband's nephew. It was moved from its original spot twice in that time.

Fifteen years after that original sighting, Sabrina received a phone call from her mother to tell her that her cousin had come by to visit and have lunch with them. During lunch, the cousin had brought up the trailer she had bought from Sabrina's parents. She went on to describe the little girl she had seen many times. After she sold it to her nephew, his family also reported seeing the same little girl.

Sabrina listened to the conversation in curiosity and listened intently. She stopped her mother to describe the little girl in detail before her mother could tell what cousin Katy had told them. Her mother was astonished.

Sabrina laughed at the apparent "guardian of the trailer." The child had not been discussed with anyone since Sabrina had seen her and her mother had made the comment of family resemblance. Though they had named her Tildy in response, the topic had never come up again, especially not to family. The fact that others had seen that girl and described her in the same way led credence to the fact she had apparently been an extra amenity that Sabrina's parents had not paid for and that the girl went wherever the trailer went. No one had ever been harmed or had reason to fear her presence. The trailer still stands but is now abandoned.

The second event involved Sabrina's horse. She had saved all her life to buy a palomino mare. That dream came true when she was thirteen. She and her "unicorn in disguise" rode all over that five-acre lot and down into the creek. After a time, it became mundane, and Sabrina began creating fantasies in her head while riding. Usually, these were the things of pure fairy tales, but one event proved them to be more real than she would have otherwise believed.

She rode for hours that day, enjoying the early summer temperatures. The shade of the overgrown creek lent a cool breeze to soften the deepening warmth of the open field. The warm sun made her feel drowsy. She allowed herself to relax and closed her eyes. Ginger strolled lazily wherever she wished. The swaying of the horse added to the enchantment.

When Ginger came to a sudden stop, Sabrina opened her eyes lazily and looked around. She was in the small barnyard beside the creek. This alone was unremarkable. What drew Sabrina's attention was the bottom across the creek from them. Where only hay had been growing moments before was now a late-autumn cornfield, its grains harvested, and the stalks broken over. Hidden among the brown crop, Sabrina could just make out the fieldstone foundation of a house. The uppermost layers of stone had been charred by fire as though the structure that had once stood there had burned down. To the right of the structure, Sabrina could faintly see a hand-dug well. Where the well sat, she saw the ghostly form of the walnut tree she knew to exist there in her time.

She blinked. As her eyes opened, the tree came back into solid focus. The hayfield had returned. There was no evidence of what she had seen at that waking moment.

She kept this vision to herself. No one would believe in a ghost house.

Three weeks later, she was sitting in the living room of her grandfather's house with her father. The two men were discussing the problems Sabrina's father was having with keeping enough water in his newly dug well. Sabrina grew bored with their conversation and tuned them out.

Withdrawn into her own imagination, she was unaware of what was being said until her grandfather's words drew her back to reality.

"...best well in the holler in its time I'm told," Papaw Newton was saying. "Wish I knew rightly where it was."

"I've heard about it too," her father said.

"What well?" asked Sabrina.

"It's an old story," her grandfather said with a mischievous smile and a twinkle in his eye. "You know that cemetery on the hill across from your house...there's a big tree near it with a little stone wall around it."

Sabrina nodded. She had wondered about that very tree for a long time.

"The family that used to own this farm way back before the Civil War, the Franklins, had slaves. They used to bury those slaves up there on that hill near their family cemetery. They just used field-stones to mark the graves, so no one knows who they all are. Well, after the Civil War, Old Man Franklin and one of the former slaves who had grown up together and were best friends, like brothers, moved into two cabins, across the creek from one another. Every day, one would cross the creek to visit the other'n. In winter, they'd move in together till spring come. As the end of their days come closer, they promised that the first to die, the one livin' would plant a tree on the chest of the one dead in memory. The old slave man died first.

Old Man Franklin did just as he promised and planted that tree you see on his friend's chest. It was just a little thing then. Then he built that rock wall you see around it so no one would forget his friend."

"Wow," said Sabrina. "What happened to the cabins?"

"I don't know, but they say the one had a hand-dug well that was purified by a big old limestone rock they kept over it. They say that water was the clearest, coldest, sweetest water around here."

Sabrina's dad spoke up, "If we could find that well, our water problems would be over."

Sabrina thought about telling them about her experience, but she knew they wouldn't believe her. She was just a kid.

Time passed, an alternative water source was found, and the well was generally forgotten except in the mind of one young woman.

Sabrina's father proved to be adept at finding water instinctively through walking around and examining the ground, not just on the farm but other places as well. He still searched for that elusive source, however.

In adulthood, Sabrina finally told her parents about her experience. They believed her. She and her father walked the bottom, seeking signs of the well's presence. The telltale tree was now gone, making the search more difficult.

Yet another secret is held captive in Satan's Den.

1 Corinthians 12:4–11, NKJV

There are diversities of gifts but the same spirit. There are differences of ministries but the same lord. And there are diversities of activities, but it is the same God who works all in all: for to one is given the word of wisdom through the spirit, to another the word of knowledge, through the same spirit, to another faith by the same spirit, to another gifts of healings by the same spirit, to another the working of miracles, to another prophecy, to another discerning of spirits, to another different kinds of tongues, to another the interpretation of tongues. But one and the same spirit works all these things, distributing to each one as he wills.

Notes of Lurlene Joy McCoy

Sabrina has since had many more mysterious encounters with the supernatural world, especially on the family farm. When her grandparents were no longer able to care for the farm, Sabrina's father purchased it from them. That is when the ghost trailer was sold.

That spot became a trailer court for a while. When that ended, the land grew lonely. At last, it was turned into a campground and meeting area for the new ministry that was the fulfillment of a long-time dream for Sabrina and her parents. For more than twenty years, the camp has operated, and the opportunities for ministry grew.

What not many people know, however, is that both Sabrina and her father had numerous dreams and visions of a church rising there. Sabrina's visions began years before her family moved onto that very spot. At that time, it was a hayfield her grandfather had fenced in. She had been walking with two of her cousins in the road across from the cemetery when she stopped to admire some daffodils growing at the side of the road. She picked one and stuck it to her nose. When she looked over in the field, just yards from the road, she saw an old-fashioned little country church. It was merely a haze in the sunlight. It could have been a vision of the past, for all she knew. It was quickly forgotten until a dream of a church where her parents still lived in that little trailer came to her. Again, she let it go. The vision/dream came even more frequently after that. Her father also began having dreams and visions of a church, but no idea where it would be. A number of years passed and then Sabrina's parents, still living on the family farm, but in a new double-wide closer to where the original house had been, were contacted by a small group of men looking for a place to build and start a church. They were looking to lease a piece of property from Sabrina's dad, whom they had known for a while. He offered them several spots, but none seemed satisfactory for one reason or another. Sabrina suggested the campground—at least one acre of it that had been primarily parking up to that point. They were sold. The land was donated, and the church was built. Now church and ministry, though separate, share the same space. People say God walks there.

As for the well, it still hasn't been found, but only because it hasn't been actively sought. One summer after her father passed away and Sabrina and her husband had moved in with her aging mother, Sabrina came across a series of cornerstones in the ground across the creek. The field had been used for growing corn for several years but was unused that season. Wear and tear on the road coming up from the creek had worn away the surface of these remaining stones. Sabrina recognized them as a part of the foundation she had seen years ago. From there, she could picture the location of the well. It felt good to be validated.

A friend she had grown up with on the holler had come back into her life and told her about the fifty or so cabins that lined the hill and creek bank from Sabrina's house to where her friend had lived. She said the cabins caught on fire one night, and they all burned. She had been told that much when she was a girl. In cleaning out one of the barns she had played in all her life, Sabrina discovered that what she had always thought to be part of an old log barn was, in reality, the only remaining cabin of that bygone era! The signs of fire became clear. The black paint on the rest of the barn was long worn away. History was coming to life in front of her!

Sabrina continues to seek ways to preserve not only her own heritage but also the pride and integrity of those who gave their lives to build it for her.

Snipe Hunt

To return evil for good is…devilish;
To return good for good is…neighborly;
To return good for evil is…godlike.

—Robert C. Savage, *Pocket Wisdom*

Life in Satan's Den is simple and often appears to be decades behind the rest of the state. It isn't really so, if you look in the right places. People have all the modern conveniences in their homes, and some have new cars, traded every year or so. With the coming of reliable internet, satellite dishes of earlier years rot where they were planted.

Old-fashioned values and habits are giving way to more modern acceptance of tattoos, piercings, and hair dyed blue, green, and pink. Sleepy little shops where all these can be purchased simultaneously opened in a strip mall on the outskirts of town.

The economy of the town itself tends to be depressed by its lonely location in the mountains. Money from the amusement park tends to be seasonal and primarily spent within the park itself. Tourists are forced to stay in hotels in surrounding communities as larger chains and self-respecting small operators won't waste time locating near Satan's Den. The Inferno Motel and a small café were all available locally.

Visitors do come, albeit infrequently. Most often, they are far-off distant relatives seeking family discovered during genealogical research. Locals know where the dead are buried, stories of ancestors long gone, and family secrets. Curious descendants long to connect with their roots and are thrilled to shake the living tree branches to find their places in the family structure.

One such visitor becomes the victim of the land when he is invited by a cousin to go on a snipe hunt. To the people of Eastern Kentucky, the snipe is an imaginary bird used to lure an unsuspecting innocent into a wild-goose chase. For those familiar with birds of the beaches, a snipe is a very real creature, running through the sand and feasting on tiny sea creatures washed up by the waves. Most people have never heard of such a bird.

Saul Miller sat on his front porch, comfortably barefoot and sipping a cold Pepsi. His father had taken up the King's Throne, a solid wooden cane-bottomed chair that had been used by the Miller patriarchs for generations. No one was allowed to sit in that chair otherwise. Pete Miller told family stories in between spitting tobacco juice into an empty plastic cup. Angie and Elton Milsap sat side by side on the porch swing, eyes and ears focused on Pete. He held out his cell phone to record the entire narration. A sullen teenager sat with his expensive tennis shoes dangling off the porch and brushing imaginary dirt from blue jeans that had cost nearly seventy-five dollars. The boy had bragged about that fact when he had seen Saul in his beat-up old Levi's.

Looking at the two boys, their obvious differences wouldn't have led you to conclude that they were very distant cousins. The only thing they seemed to have in common was their stylishly distressed jeans. Only a practiced eye would be able to detect that one boy wore jeans that had seen better days and had achieved their current condition through hard work and frequent washings, while the other boy had bought his jeans off the rack, already shredded. Country boy, city boy, just like the mice in that old story. Two different creatures trying to meet in the middle and find common ground.

Troy Milsap had made it quite clear he had come to this godforsaken place with his parents only because they had made him. He'd preferred to stay with his friend Steve and had even made the arrangements himself. When he proudly presented his parents with his plan, he was rudely shot down and commanded to pack. He *would* go to visit his long-lost cousins, even if it killed him. As a result, he had spent the last two days stuck in the boonies with people he didn't know and didn't care to get to know. He had been lonely and miserable the whole time. You can only gather so many eggs and watch so many cows get milked. He was stuck following around that kid, Saul, as he worked around the farm. This place was all work and no play. There wasn't even a basketball goal and ball to take up his time.

Saul had tried to draw Troy out of his sullen shell by showing him the farm and its occupants. Surely, a city boy would find all this interesting. After all, not many city folk met the creatures that provided them with their hamburger, steaks, and chicken tenders. Troy took no interest in the animals and their uses. He simply wrinkled his nose and pulled the collar of his shirt over his nose, while making rude remarks about the foul excretions littering the barnyard and stalls. He had gagged and puked three times the first day he was there. Saul didn't want any part of city life if it made you this soft.

Saul had taken Troy into town the day before. He had driven his daddy's ancient Dodge, even though he wasn't of age to get his license yet. Troy had found that mildly amusing and had wryly wished he could drive any time he liked. They had spent some time wandering around the General Hardware Feed and Seed. Saul talked excitedly about the new farm equipment he wanted to own someday and the best seed to use for the type of ground they had on their place. He told Troy about a pony he had once had and how he was saving up money to buy a horse of his own. Troy didn't know a bridle from a hay rake. He only got excited when they came to the four-wheeled utility vehicles on display. He asked the clerk in that area a thousand questions about speed, horsepower, rpms, traction, and gas mileage. The man patiently answered Troy's questions, recognizing the boy was a fish out of water, finding life-giving air in the dream of speed and danger found in the ATV lifestyles as perceived by those who have only seen it on television. The clerk loaded Troy with promotional brochures to take home and dream about.

When Saul had worn out his patience in listening to the city boy talk "country" about those loud four-wheeled mini-bulldozers that plowed through mud and dug ruts everywhere they needed traction, he offered to buy the city slicker some ice cream or a milkshake at the Chilly Cow. Troy reluctantly pulled himself away from the display. Saul waved at Mr. Glick, the store owner, as they exited. Mr. Glick grinned and winked at Saul, giving a little nod at Troy. Saul gave a curt nod back. He agreed with Mr. Glick.

Troy hadn't been impressed by the Chilly Cow. In fact, he'd compared it to the various fast-food and sit-down family restaurants in his hometown in Illinois. Saul was equally unimpressed with the crowds and drive-through windows. Food wasn't worth eating if it didn't take time to cook. Troy complained about artificial colors and flavors and preservatives, fat calories, and substituting plants for meat. Saul liked his food all-natural, just the way God grew it. He argued that no self-respecting man would stand for his food to be made up of things that weren't meant to be eaten and food that wasn't real. Countrymen earned their victuals through hard work and the sweat of their brow, and country women knew how to cook it up just right without having to dress it up to be something it ain't. They'd agreed to disagree.

Now they sat on Saul's front porch, each pretending the other didn't exist. Saul had plenty of things he could've been doing if his parents hadn't told him to keep his cousin company. Troy was likely dreaming about his video games. The kid held onto his cell phone like it was a life preserver and he was in water over his head. Saul kept it a secret that they had satellite TV and internet, just to watch Troy squirm. Cell phone signals were possible, though. Saul preferred using the computers at school and didn't care to have a computer at home. Cell phones were an expensive commodity that wasn't necessary where he lived.

Listening to the stories his dad had told so many times, Saul could tell them nearly as well: very boring. He had a new mystery book from the library he wanted to get started on. Reading for pleasure, and at a level well above his peers, would have shocked Troy, who expected all his mountain relatives to be illiterate rubes with crossed eyes and rotten teeth.

The sun was starting to set on the mountaintops across the valley. The blue skies of day were tinged with the pinks and purples of transition to a nightly hue. Streaks of rose gold shot through the darkening blues. A perfect summer night followed an otherwise perfect summer day. Saul thought about catching fireflies in a mason jar but dismissed it as too baby an activity for his sophisticated cousin. Flashlight tag might be an option, but it wasn't much fun when there were only two of you. Even moonlit hide-and-seek would be redundant. That left him with just one option: a snipe hunt. There would be a nearly full moon and lots of stars to guide the bored city slicker if—when—he got lost. Saul would even be merciful and leave him with a flashlight.

"Hey, Troy," Saul called out to the nearly comatose boy across from him. Troy turned his head in the direction of Saul but didn't make eye contact. He had heard Saul's voice and responded, but his eyes were glazed over and far away.

"I got an idea," said Saul as if he'd just eaten his mom's triple chocolate layer cake on his birthday.

The vacant stare flickered momentarily.

"Come with me," he directed with a nod toward the barn.

Troy shrugged and lowered his feet to the ground and stood waiting for further directions.

Saul set off purposefully toward the larger of the two barns. Troy, the stray dog looking only for something to hold off starvation, followed.

In a far corner of the barn, Saul rummaged through a pile of cast-out items until he found a moderately large feed sack made of thick layers of paper designed to accommodate the shifting contents without tearing. The mouth had been cut at an uneven angle and had gathered dirt and dust, which clouded around Saul when he shook it out, checking for insects or snakes that might have chosen that particular bag for a nest.

Troy sneezed and pulled the collar of his T-shirt over his mouth and nose. Saul could hear the boy breathing through his mouth, his T-shirt ruffling with each breath. He smiled to himself and gave the feed sack an extra shaking in the direction of his cousin. Troy's eyes were watering with the irritation. A muffled sneeze briefly pouched the T-shirt before deflating and resuming its in-out ruffle.

"Here," commanded Saul as he thrust the sack at Troy. Stunned by Saul's insistence, Troy took the sack. He held it between his thumb and forefinger away from his body.

Saul's next acquisition was a dusty flashlight he took from a shelf just inside the barn door. He flicked it on and shone it about himself, floor, walls, ceiling, before thrusting it out to Troy, handle first. Troy allowed the collar of his T-shirt to droop back down on his neck so he could take the flashlight. He turned the flashlight up toward his face, nearly blinding himself, before managing to turn it off.

"What are we going to do with these?" Troy asked with a hint of curiosity.

"Not me," replied Saul. "You. *You* are going on a snipe hunt."

"Snipe hunt?" Troy wrinkled his nose in distaste. "What's a snipe? And how do you hunt it with a flashlight and smelly old bag?"

"I'll tell you on the way. Come on." Saul was in charge now, his cousin in his complete power. For once, Saul felt superior to this know-it-all from Big City, Illinois. His smirk grew prouder as he led Troy up the hill behind the barn. Shadows were becoming deeper as the sun set. Being familiar with the terrain, he felt no need to make his way upward. Behind him, Troy fumbled and tripped through the hidden roots and crowding limbs and woody stems of the undergrowth.

Wherever the lay of the land allowed, Saul varied his path to twist and turn to disorient Troy further. When they finally reached the top of the ridge, Troy was gasping for breath and rubbing his arms where he had been scratched and whipped by the unfriendly flora. His fancy shoes were muddy, and his expensive jeans ripped in odd places. His hair was matted and sweaty. While Troy labored to catch his breath, Saul explained how a snipe hunt worked, omitting the real purpose of the game.

"You gotta really hunt for snipes," Saul began. "They's tricky critters. You gotta call 'em out by yellin' 'Snipe! Snipe!' Find ya a good stick and beat it against your sack. That's like its mating call. Don't turn your flashlight on. It scares 'em away. When ya hear one in the bushes, hold yer bag close to the ground with the opening toward the bush. Keep callin', and that snipe'll get right in that there sack real easy like. When he's in, choke up real high on the bag so's he can't get out. That's when you can turn yer flashlight on. All the other snipes'll just run away. You only need one snipe. They's so big a little goes a real long way. Ya got it?"

Troy was frowning. "I think so," he replied.

"Good," said Saul. "You go over that way and start calling for a snipe. I'll go this way and try to shoo one right to ya. Don't worry iffen you don't hear me. I know how to flush 'em out without callin' 'em."

Troy started off in the direction Saul pointed. He looked around for a good-size stick to beat his bag with. As he started deeper into the woods, he tripped and fell to the ground, hard. Grunting loudly, he rubbed his knees. Trying to save face, he used the tail of his shirt to wipe the grime from his face, taking particular care to wipe the emerging tears from his eyes. Saul pretended not to see and turned his back to the other boy. The smirk was now gone from his face. He felt a fleeting pang of pity for his cousin, paired with a gnawing sense of having gone too far. He swallowed the guilt and started back the way they had come.

Troy picked up the good-sized branch he had fallen over. He swung it in the air a couple of times to test its weight. He held out the thick paper feed bag in front of him and struck it tentatively. It made a hollow rustle. He hit it again, with greater power. He liked the way it sounded. He picked up the flashlight he had dropped when he fell. Trying to figure out how to carry the flashlight, stick, and bag without dropping any of the items was awkward. Finally, he tucked the flashlight into the waistband of his jeans, at his back, like he'd seen cops do in movies.

"Snipe?" he called. "Snipe. Snipe." Each call was punctuated by a thunk of stick on bag.

Trying to remain unseen, Saul began following Troy. Now and then, he would toss a pine cone or small stone in a random direction to draw Troy's attention to a nearby bush or brush pile. With each misdirection, Troy's confidence increased, and he was soon boldly calling out for a snipe. Smiling to himself, Saul decided to leave the city boy on his own. It was full night now, and Troy would become more easily disoriented. When he got home, he would let the adults in on the joke, and they would all get a laugh out of it. They'd wait until morning to go looking for Troy. The boy would be ready to admit that Saul wasn't as stupid as the city slicker thought he was. Snipe hunting was a rite of passage in the mountains. Every boy, and some girls, spent the night in the woods alone to prove their mettle. It was expected.

The waxing moon and bright stars did little to break through the thick darkness of the summer woods. The oppressive heat of day became an oppressive chill without the sun to provide heat. Nonetheless, Troy found himself sweating. He had been thumping that feed bag and calling for snipes for what felt like hours. He had begun to lose confidence in finding a snipe as he hadn't heard anything moving around for quite some time. He didn't know anything about summer nights in the mountains, but it seemed to be too quiet up on the ridge. The previous nights at the cabin of his newfound relatives had been filled with the cries of unseen tree frogs and a menagerie of unseen insects and a few strange animals. All that was absent here.

Fumbling for his cell phone in his back pocket, he nearly knocked the flashlight out of his waistband. He quickly rescued it and pulled his phone from his pocket. When he pressed the bar to bring up his screensaver, nothing happened. The screen remained blank. He had a full battery just after dinner. Now it appeared to have been drained of power. He cursed under his breath. These dumb hillbillies couldn't even get the internet or Wi-Fi out here. He stuffed the useless phone back into his pocket.

A soft rustle to his left caused him to remember the task he had been given. If he could really catch a snipe, he would have a great story to tell his friends when he got back home. The rustle came again, a little closer to him this time. He lifted his feed sack and thumped it with the stick. The satisfying rustle of the paper layers vibrating together encouraged Troy to step carefully toward the bush where he had heard the noise.

"Snipe," he called gently. "Snipe, snipe, snipe."

A noise from the bush took Troy by surprise. Could he have finally found a snipe? Saul hadn't told him what sound a snipe made, but the sound from the bush hadn't sounded like any animal he had heard of. It was sort of a snuffle-huff, like the creature was trying to stop a sneeze by blowing its nose.

"Snipe," Troy called again.

The forest was dead silent around him. Nothing moved.

Troy sighed loudly. It hadn't been a snipe after all, just his imagination.

Directly behind him, another snuffle-huff startled him. The snuffle-huff was followed by a low whistle-pop, as of gas being released by a good-sized creature. The scent of black licorice worked its way up from the ground around him and settled around his head, stinging his nose and causing tears to fill his eyes. He waved his hand in front of his face, but the odor refused to dissipate.

If this was what a snipe was like, he thought to himself, he wanted no part of it. He would leave the snipes to Saul and the other hillbillies. He looked around and tried to find his way back to where he had begun, but the darkness was too intent where the moon had been eclipsed by dense clouds and his eyes unaccustomed to such darkness. He had no idea where he was or which way to go. He stumbled blindly through the undergrowth, narrowly avoiding trees only because he struck them with his hands as he flailed his arms around him or was able to discern their darker forms looming out of the deep shadows as he veered near them. What was beneath his feet was of no concern as long as he was moving forward in any possible direction. The scent of black licorice became his shadow, never dissipating, no matter how far away from the original source he perceived himself to be.

The loud crack of a branch being broken, combined with the rustle of leaves and the disturbance of a large bush, caused him to freeze in his tracks. Whatever was in that bush was way too big to be a bird the size of a snipe. Hesitantly, he struck the feed sack with the stick he had managed to keep hold of. It sounded more like a thud than the rustle he had grown accustomed to.

"Snipe?" he squeaked, barely above a whisper.

There was no response from the bush. Troy exhaled deeply and resumed his forward trek. Looking up, he caught tiny glimpses of stars between the fullness of the tall trees around him. He wouldn't have known how to use the stars to get him back to the farm anyway. He'd never been a Boy Scout and had barely listened as his science teacher had droned through that chapter. He began to taste the fear knotted in his throat. It tasted of blood and vomit.

He remembered that some TV show he'd seen once recommended that you stay in one place if you thought you were lost in the woods. He collapsed to the floor of the woods. A sharp rock beneath his right buttock caused him to roll to his left side. The smell of damp earth and green leaves tickled his nostrils, mixing with the taste of fear. Without warning, his stomach gave up its contents.

When the gagging and wrenching had reached its end, Troy flipped over on his back. A sharp pain in his back reminded him of the flashlight. He arched his back and reached for the flashlight. It caught on the loop of his jeans, and he had to work it loose. Collapsing onto his back once more, he fumbled with the flashlight until he found the switch and turned it on. The narrow beam illuminated the lower branches of the tree he had landed under. That spot of life was the most beautiful thing he had ever seen. He closed his eyes and allowed himself to smile contentedly.

Lulled into a false sense of security, Troy slept.

The overbearing scent of black licorice brought gorge to the back of his throat, causing him to gasp deeply and sit up in an effort to take control of the nastiness in his throat. Bile burned as the hot liquid made its way back down to his empty stomach. He cough-gagged in response.

He pulled his cell phone out again and pushed the button to turn it on. Nothing. He had charged it that morning (yesterday morning?). It was a useless piece of metal out here in the wilderness.

Feeling a strong urge, he scrambled to his feet, retrieving the flashlight that had fallen when he stood. Though it really didn't matter, he sought out the most private location he could see.

Feeling relieved, he turned the flashlight on the area of forest he found himself in. He saw where he had been sick earlier. It was uncomfortably close to where he had been sleeping. Leafy plants, bushes, and trees of all ages and stages of growth seemingly imprisoned him. There was no sign of a path into or exiting from the area. With the lingering smell of black licorice, he wasn't pleased about staying in that area. Finding the place that seemed to give him the least resistance, Troy headed off into the darkness, with only his flashlight as a guide.

The narrow beam and tight circle made the dark shadows even darker. The absence of all sound, except his own footsteps and heavy breathing, was unnerving. He wished he had a GPS or at least a cell phone that worked. Of course, either of those would be useless as he had no idea how to enter the coordinates or the address of the Millers' farm. His dad would know, but Dad wasn't there.

Ahead of him, he caught the twinkle of a light. He stopped walking in order to see if the light was real. He'd seen too many movies and read too many books about people being led astray by mystery lights, never to be seen again. He needed to be certain. He didn't want to be a casualty of just such a phenomenon. The light continued to burn. It held steady. Hope was at hand! Troy didn't think it was Saul's porch light he saw. He hadn't traveled that far downhill, or downhill at all, really. He couldn't be certain, though.

Encouraged, Troy moved toward the light, his hasty steps creating a near-deafening ruckus. Mysteriously, the more he walked toward the light, the farther away it seemed to be. It was now flickering in and out of the trees in a game of catch me if you can. He persistently chased the elusive glimmer in hope of finding a house with a working phone and some way of finding out the number for the Millers.

Just as he began to tire of the game and give up entirely the hope of easy rescue, the light chose to stay in place, calling to his desperate need for civilization. The slight odor of black licorice reached his nose. He didn't like licorice for many reasons, but the smell was first and foremost. He wrinkled his nose in disgust but pushed ahead anyway.

The thick tree line suddenly broke to reveal a sort of clearing, spotted with less leafy trees that were squatter than those in the surrounding woods. Huge rocks rose from the ground as if they had been planted there and grown to their immense size. The scent of black licorice became stronger. Troy thought there must be some plant or tree that gave off that horrid smell. He really didn't know. It was just a thought. It would explain why he sometimes smelled it and sometimes didn't.

Intrigued, Troy stepped closer to the behemoth stone that lured him with its siren song. He had no idea such colossal rocks grew in nature. Where he was from, all the rocks were small; it took a fistful to make a good impression. Not that he really had much experience with rocks. He'd mostly seen them in people's flower gardens and such. The movies he liked best took place in cities, with car chases and explosions, or really ugly dead people killing living people for their brains.

He reached out to touch the stone, not sure what to expect. He was surprised by the warmth beneath his hand. Though it looked rough with protrusions and indentations, it felt smooth, like skin. It even pulsed beneath his hand, as if a giant heartbeat from somewhere within the stone.

"Awesome!" he cried, with a pleased grin. Excited now, he moved closer to the granite being and placed an ear against its surface. A strong rhythm beat into his ear. Gradually, he felt his own heart fall into exact rhythm with it. He felt one with the rock; he closed his eyes to the dream he had fallen into.

There was peace, perfect peace.

Troy was so enraptured by the absolute peace he was feeling that he didn't notice the dark mist emanating from the rock. It surrounded him and grew thicker, nearly solid. The enthralled boy felt nothing as the mist drew him into the rock until he had been completely absorbed, leaving only the flashlight to illumine a small circle at the base of the stone to indicate he had ever existed.

The stench of black licorice permeated the air as a loud snuffle-huff, accompanying an odd resounding belch, shook the area around the deadly monolith.

"Snipe," a deep, distorted voice said with delighted pleasure.

Snipe

Job 2:1–2. NKJV

> Again there was a day when the sons of God came to present themselves before the Lord, and Satan came also to present himself before the Lord. AND THE LORD SAID TO SATAN, "From where do you come?" Satan answered the Lord and said, "From going to and fro on the earth, and from walking back and forth on it."

1 Peter 5:8, NKJV

> Be sober, be vigilant; because your adversary the Devil walks about like a roaring lion, seeking whom he may devour.

Notes of Lurlene Joy McCoy

Snipe hunts were once the most fun people in rural areas could have with newcomers and guests from outside their own communities.

A snipe hunt can be the act of hunting wild snipe, if you happen to live where these birds happen to live. Otherwise, it is a type of practical joke in which an unwitting victim is sent in pursuit of something that doesn't exist, or a foolish or hopeless search for something unattainable, a wild-goose chase. Wikipedia (not the most reliable source) explains that in the US, snipe hunting is recorded as early as the 1840s. It was the most common hazing ritual for boys in summer camps in the early twentieth century. It has also been associated with the Boy Scouts and other such groups.

I don't believe Saul Miller meant for any harm to come to his city cousin through this terrible prank. No doubt, he intended to seek out his cousin when the families became concerned by his absence in the unfamiliar wilderness around them. Troy would have been found. His parents would welcome him home happily. Saul would get a wink and promise of appropriate punishment from his father. And it would become the stuff of legends for coming generations to be heard told, much exaggerated, at their father's or grandfather's knees.

Troy was never found. After brutal and extensive searches by law enforcement and volunteers, only a flashlight was recovered. Troy's family abruptly cut off all relationships with their new family and returned to their empty home in the city to wonder and mourn their loss.

Saul's family refuses to talk about the event, but the superstitious whisper about the sacrifice made to the devil that night.

If there have been any more snipe hunts in Satan's Den, they have all been far enough away from where our antagonist gathers strength for breaking out of his stony prison to roam his kingdom once more.

My research, along with the instruction I received as a child, opens new questions for me.

It is agreed that there is good, headed by God, and evil, spearheaded by Satan. Studies of the Holy Bible, as well as the religious texts and mythologies of the peoples that have developed civilizations in the area known as the Holy Land and ancient manuscripts that were rejected as part of the modern canon, it is clear that there is a most-definite hierarchy in heaven and on earth. God is Creator of all. Period. It is implied by resources currently available that He created a council, the sons of God, who are above the angels. Some members of this council and, subsequently, a number of angels were evicted from the courts of heaven when the Rebellion occurred. Lucifer and his angelic followers became the demonic forces most of us perceive to be evil. Those who were called the sons of God are the troublemakers of the book of Genesis, who brought contrary thinking to humanity after the fall, including breeding with them and creating giants. These creatures were allegedly eliminated with the flood survived only by Noah and his family, along with the animals bound in the ark with them. Many scholars refer to these beings as watchers. Could these fractals be lesser watchers or their half-human descendants? Could these creatures also be the fodder for the imaginings of H. P. Lovecraft and Cthulhu? It is interesting to note that the giant Judacalla was called Sul-ka-lu or Tsu' Kale by the Native Americans in that area of North Carolina. Even the names are similar. Could they be one and the same creature, an overlord watcher of the East Coast of North America?

Topic: Major False Gods of the Old Testament

Author: Jack Zavada
Source: www.learnreligions.com

Deuteronomy 32:17

They sacrificed to demons, which are not God, gods they had not known.

1. Ashtoreth (plural), or Astarte
    a. Goddess of the Canaanites
    b. Connected with fertility and maternity
    c. Worship strong at Sidon
    d. Sometimes called a consort or companion of Baal
    e. King Solomon's foreign wives drew him into Ashtoreth worship, which led to his downfall.
2. Baal (Bel)
    a. Supreme god among the Canaanites, worshipped in many forms, but often as a sun god or storm god.
    b. Fertility god who supposedly made the earth bear crops and women bear children.
    c. Rites of worship included cult prostitution and sometimes human sacrifice.
    d. Elijah the prophet challenged the prophets of Baal at Mount Carmel.
    e. Book of Judges indicates Baal worship was a constant temptation to Israelites.
    f. Baal worship was widespread, but regional homage varied.
    g. All worship of Baal infuriated God the Father, who punished Israel for their unfaithfulness.

3. Chemosh (the subduer)
    a. National god of the Moabites and was also worshipped by the Ammonites.
    b. Rites were said to be cruel and may have involved human sacrifice.
    c. Solomon erected an altar to Chemosh south of the Mount of Olives, outside Jerusalem, on the hill of corruption (2 Kings 23:13).

        Interesting choice of location. Solomon's wives brought in multiple false gods. Solomon pandered to their desires and allowed his faith and dependence on the God of his father, David, to be eroded away.
4. Dagon
    a) God of the Philistines
    b) The body of a fish and a human head and hands as indicated by his remaining statues. Modern influence on the belief in merfolk?
    c) God of water and grain.
    d) Temple of Dagon is where the Hebrew judge Samson met his death.
    e) 1 Samuel 5:1–5, Philistines captured the Ark of the Covenant, placed it in the temple of Dagon; when worshippers came the next morning, found Dagon face down on the floor before the ark, statue was reerected but discovered the next morning on the floor before the ark, its head and hands broken off.
    f) Later, King Saul's armor was placed into Dagon's temple, and Saul's severed head hung up there.
5. Egyptian gods
    a. More than forty identified, although none are mentioned in the Bible
        i. Included the following:
            1. Re—creator sun god
            2. Isis—goddess of magic
            3. Osiris—god of the afterlife
            4. Thoth—god of wisdom and the moon
            5. Horus—god of the sun

b. During their 400+ years of captivity in Egypt, the Hebrew did not appear to be tempted to worship as the Egyptians did.

Could it be that these were truly false gods and impotent of real power? Demonic forces provided a semblance of life and reality, manifesting their power through these aliases? Then again, these entities were often described as being giants in comparison to humanity. Watchers or their offspring?

c. Ten plagues of God = ten specific Egyptian gods humiliated

Equates power Jesus had over the demons in New Testament and then passed on to His apostles.

6. Golden calf
   a. Occurs twice in the Bible
      i. Foot of Mount Sinai, fashioned by Aaron
      ii. Rein of King Jeroboam (1 Kings 12:26–30)
   b. Physical representations of Yahweh, judged by Him as sin since no images were to be made of Him

      Archaeologists have discovered small golden calves used in home altar worship, indicating the trend may have persisted despite God's judgment.
7. Marduk
   a. God of the Babylonians
   b. Associated with fertility and vegetation (see Baal and Dagon for a parallel)
   c. Had fifty names, including Bel(!), resulting in confusion about Mesopotamian gods and hierarchy
   d. Also worshipped by Assyrians and Persians
8. Milcom (see research on Moloch, Appendix B)
   a. National god of the Ammonites
   b. Associated with divination, seeking knowledge of the future through occult means, strongly forbidden by God
   c. Child sacrifice is sometimes connected with Milcom.

d. Among the false gods worshipped by Solomon at the close of his reign

False gods mentioned by name in

- ❖ Leviticus
- ❖ Numbers
- ❖ Judges
- ❖ 1 Samuel
- ❖ 1, 2 Kings
- ❖ 1, 2 Chronicles
- ❖ Isaiah
- ❖ Hosea
- ❖ Zephaniah
- ❖ Acts
- ❖ Romans

Topic: Sons of God

Author: Douglas Van Dorn

Source: *The Unseen Realm, Q&A Companion*

- ✓ God's heavenly sons are called the sons of God, and His earthly sons are called humankind.
  - ○ Genesis 6:2, "The sons of God saw that the daughters of man were attractive. And they took as their wives any they chose."
  - ○ Job 1:6, "Now there was a day when the sons of God came to present themselves before the Lord."
  - ○ Job 37 "[Where were you] when the morning stars sang together, and all the sons of God shouted for joy?"
  - ○ Deuteronomy 32:8, "When the Most High gave to the nations their inheritance, when he divided mankind, he fixed the borders of the peoples according to the number of the sons of God."
  - ○ Psalm 29:1, "Ascribe to the Lord, O heavenly beings, ascribe to the Lord glory and strength."

    - "Heavenly beings" is *bney 'elim* in Hebrew. 'Elim is the plural of *'El. Bney 'elim* is literally "sons of God(s)." The same phrase occurs in Psalm 89:6.
  - Psalm 82:6, "I said, 'You are gods, sons of the Most High. All of you.'"
  - Psalm 89:6, "For who in the skies can be compared to the Lord? Who among the heavenly beings is like the Lord?"
  - Exodus 4:22 (NASB), "Israel is My son, my first-born."
  - Hosea 11:1, "When Israel was a child, I loved him, and out of Egypt I called my son."
  - Luke 3:38, "[Jesus,] the son of Enosh, the son of Seth, the son of Adam, the son of God."
  - Acts 17:29, "Being then God's offspring, we ought not to think that the divine being is like gold or silver or stone."
  - Romans 8:14, "For all who are led by the Spirit of God are sons of God."
  - Galatians 3:26, "For in Christ Jesus you are all sons of God, through faith."

✓ All disembodied spirit beings are *'elohim.* "Angel" is a designation of function (i.e., messengers) but may or may not be sons of God. Sons of God represent a rank of hierarchy, denoting administrative tasks of greater significance (territorial rulership, decision-making status in the divine council).

✓ Other terms used to describe the heavenly sons of God
  - Watchers—Daniel 4:13, 17
  - Hosts of heaven—1 Kings 22:19–21
  - Divine council—Psalm 82:1, 6
  - Rulers or princes—Ephesians 2:1–2; 1 Corinthians 2:7–8; Daniel 10:13
  - Cosmic powers or authorities—Ephesians 3:10, 6:12; Romans 8:38–39
  - Lords—1 Corinthians 8:5
  - Thrones or dominions—Colossians 1:16
  - Archangels—1 Thessalonians 4:16; Jude 9
  - Glorious ones—2 Peter 2:10–11

Topic: The Watchers

Author: Howard Schwartz
Source: *Tree of Souls, The Mythology of Judaism*

Summary

Two angels, Shemazai and Azazel, opposed God by questioning why mankind seemed to be so important to God and were exiled to earth. It is believed there were likely two hundred angels expelled at that time. These were the ones who never slept, the Watchers. As a result of their fall, they became flesh and lost much of their powers. They initially taught mankind in the ways of righteousness but were distracted by the beauty of the human female offspring. Being lustful, they bred with these women and produced offspring that was half immortal (demigods).

The instruction of mankind involved charms and enchantments, incantations and the cutting of roots, astrology and the knowledge of signs, as well as metalworking to make weapons, and how women could make themselves desirable to men. They also chose to sin with both men and women, as well as beasts, becoming corrupt and corrupting the earth.

The four archangels of heaven—Michael, Uriel, Raphael, and Gabriel—went to God regarding these fallen ones. God had them bound until the day of judgment.

The offspring of human women and these Watchers were not bound, however. Being giants, they consumed large amounts of food. The stench of the decaying flesh of their feasts is said to have been the prompting of God to destroy the earth with a flood.

Other scholars believe the devouring of these giants was beyond the norm of flesh and vegetation, possibly consuming the earth itself. It is also believed that these giants were killed by the flood, but their immortal spirits remain, becoming the evil spirits, above and beyond the demonic force that follows Satan. If this is so, then there is, in fact, a third hierarchy of beings—the Watchers and their Destroyers. This affirms my theory that God is Creator, and the ultimate Good, with Satan and his rebellious angels as the agents of evil with the purpose of causing mankind to fall from God's grace and be separated from Him, and the third hierarchy of those who once ruled in God's divine council, but now have the purpose of total destruction of what God created. The seven deadly sins are possibly lesser Watchers, the children of the council now imprisoned. They are also possibly the "princes" of regions of the world. In this manner, our local fractal may indeed be a lesser Watcher somehow captured by those long-ago braves and trapped in the Demon Rock. That would explain the power it has over the land itself, with help from the demonic forces of Satan to influence humanity from the inside (mind) by whispering of greater secrets to be found in the pursuit and/or worship of these lesser gods as they once ruled in ancient times. Of course, modern thinking and technology eschews the primitive rites and ceremonies but still influences the "higher order" thinking of modern man through neurological stimulation—sounds, tastes, smells, emotions—that create a chaos of the mind and are more easily influenced by demonic forces. The slow indoctrination of once-hidden and secretive ideas and techniques are now called science and act as psycho-tech influences that can induce despair, depression, suicidal ideation, a craving for occult answers, increased violence, and a general breakdown of society from the mind outwardly. Author J. A. Bouma explores this in his novel of spiritual warfare in our modern techno-world, *The Darkest Valley.* It is truly terrifying.

Corruption's End

Man's perception of God began to leave
his mind and he adopted the agenda of
Satan: "I will be like the Most High".
Since that time, man has tried to rise to
God, only to fall into a downward spiral
that eventually ends in the pit of hell.

—*Delighting in God,* A. W. Tozer

As seen by the incident with Aunt Tildy and Reverend Willard Thomas Smith, the forces of heaven are often at work trying to stop and overcome the evil that has congregated in this small town. Corruption is everywhere, and only the prayers of the faithful keep them at bay.

In every generation, there is born at least one individual who is closer to the spiritual forces of the average person. Aunt Tildy was one. Tamra Brown was another.

There is something about a wedding. You can't really put your finger on it. Some people are overjoyed by impending nuptials and go out of their way to help in any possible manner. Others become insanely jealous and try to sabotage all plans. Those dear, sweet bystanders who remain calm and rational are all that keep the chaos in check.

It is the usual habit of the minister to take the young couple aside and counsel them on the seriousness of marriage. It is most unusual, however, for the minister to plan and dictate the service itself.

Enter Stacey and Robert, a blushing, newly engaged couple who had been a part of the church since childhood. For some reason, the minister, who shall remain nameless to protect his surviving family, decided that ceremony plans should be made publicly, for the church to "yea" or "nay." The congregation was taken aback. This had never been done before. This should be between the couple and their families, not up for debate. Needless to say, certain factors were thrilled to be allowed to control what happened in their congregational lives. Mostly, everyone was in shock.

Thus began the public trial of a young couple falsely accused of whatever crime seemed appropriate to the naysayers of the congregation.

Stacey and Robert sat in their left front pew, where they had sat together for years: first as friends, then as a couple. Stacey was visibly nervous; Robert quiet and pale. Stacey began describing the ceremony she would like to have. Robert held her hand as she gave her speech. The ceremony would be traditional, it would seem, with a few alterations that would express their shared faith in a benevolent, loving God. They asked simply for a dedication of their salvation to a Christian marriage, followed by a shared communion as husband and wife, acknowledging God as their head.

The minister became angry and declared that the sanctuary was not a place for food. Even young children were denied a cracker snack and juice. The church shared in communion once a year, under the guidance of a specifically chosen visiting minister. Under those circumstances, only food would be allowed in the sanctuary.

The young couple was stunned. No one spoke. The silence was filled with the shocked electricity of the silent congregation.

"I think it is quite a beautiful and honorable gesture," Tamra heard herself speak. "The wedding ceremonies of many accepted faiths include a sharing of wine or other form of communion as a symbol of their faith."

The minister's face darkened at Tamra's apparent heresy. His eyes slitted shut as he replied in an icy tone, "That may be so in those *false faiths*, but in *my* church, I declare that such is unlawful."

A gasp issued from the congregation at this show of dictatorial power. There had been concerns for some time from more-learned factors within the church as to the sometimes-controversial interpretations of the minister's sermons. Now even his most avid supporters seemed surprised.

No one spoke. The prospective bride began to cry. Robert held her tightly, his eyes turning icy cold.

After a pause to allow them to overcome some of their shock, someone suggested that they discuss more trivial matters, such as the wedding court.

Stacey, tears still flowing in her eyes, sniffled and wiped her nose on a fistful of Kleenex thoughtfully passed to her by a generous, kind soul. She glanced around the room carefully and began to name bridesmaids, twelve in all. To her great surprise, Tamra was named.

Stacey hardly knew Tamra. They had both grown up in this church, but Tamra was so much older, by ten years. Tamra discovered later that she had been chosen for her brave words to the minister.

A week later, the chosen wedding party and miscellaneous women met again to discuss what the bride and bridesmaids would be wearing. None of them were certain as to the appropriateness of the minister to control such matters, but they were also uncertain of how to deal with it.

The bride began to describe the dresses to be worn by the bridesmaids. She had studied some fashion design and had created a dress based on some of the best features of dresses of the Middle Ages and eighteenth century. The minister approved of the floor-length gown but frowned at the design of the underdress worn beneath the main garment. He questioned her choice.

"Sir," she faltered, "these were called potty dresses by the women who wore them during the Middle Ages."

"This is most indecent and won't be allowed in my church!" thundered the minister.

"Excuse me," Tamra said.

His stormy face turned to confront her. She met his eyes with a glare of her own as she continued.

"Potty dresses are a kind of shift, or slip, that allows a woman freedom to answer the call of nature without soiling the overdress. They are quite decent and very dignified."

Stacey fingered a garment bag she had flung over the pew beside her. Tamra could see what she had in mind but was too intimidated to act on. Quickly, she acted in Stacey's stead. Standing up, she crossed the aisle to where the bag laid. She snatched it up and moved to the double doors at the rear of the sanctuary.

"Let me demonstrate," she stated, leaving no room for argument. She exited to the lady's restroom and slipped out of her dress. She donned the sleeveless bodice and thigh-length pantaloons before donning the knee-length potty dress. She checked to see that the simple bows spaced down the length of the skirt were tied snugly, and the fabric properly overlapped for decency. Confident that she was modest, she threw the overdress over her arm and returned to the sanctuary.

She was met by the nervous chattering such an exhibition would naturally result in. It ceased as she entered like a queen into her courtroom. She felt their eyes examine every inch of the sky-blue sleeveless dress with the modest neckline and line of bows. Its full skirt swirled and swished as she walked. The linen it was made of glimmered as the soft lights caressed it. It was impressive, she knew.

When the murmurs resumed, it was a casual fashion discussion. Awed women noted the fashionably appropriate cut and the neckline more modest than most women wore today. Only a few of the older women were disgusted by her brazen display of skin. The other eleven bridesmaids tittered in excitement at the preview of their dresses.

Boldly, she walked to the altar and stood before her critic. Her eyes met his. Her back stiffened proudly.

"As you can see," she stated, "this dress was made for decency and practicality in the use of a chamber pot. The overdress"—she held it up for all to see—"is delicate and easily stained. Practicality on the part of the designer made it a fashion must."

Women nodded in agreement and whispered of its usefulness with today's odd fashions. The minister only continued to glare in disapproval.

For further demonstration, Tamra slipped the overdress on like a jacket and fastened its tiny buttons, discreetly hidden among lacey white folds and soft-baby-blue satin skirt. Murmurs about the dress swept the gathered crowd. Stacey had been the designer and seamstress of this masterpiece. After a moment, the minister spoke.

"I must discuss this with the president of the Women's Circle," he said flatly.

Tamra's heart pounded even stronger as the president of the Women's Circle stood, and with pinched face, strode knowingly to the minister's private office.

Some began to pray, others to predict the outcome and debate the facts. Stacey and Robert withdrew to one corner of the church. Tamra could see Robert comforting Stacey, and then they, too, began to pray. Sensing a strong need to sit before she collapsed, Tamra sat in the front pew. She bowed her head and tried to pray. She began by closing out all distracting noise and concentrated on her prayer. She didn't know how this would end, but she wanted to be spiritually prepared.

As she prayed, she felt almost as if her spirit was lifted from her body and allowed freedom to float and embrace Jesus personally. Instead, to her wonder, her senses became more acute. She was aware of the sounds and smells within the church, even the parts she could not see. She could smell the dust gathered beneath heavy furniture in the minister's office. The smell of candle wax was now stale from a candlelight vigil. The mingled perfumes of the gathered women chased the fainter scent of men's cologne. She could detect the individual voices as they prayed or debated. At that moment, she knew who was for and who was against. She was shocked by the petty jealousies of those who believed *they* should have been chosen in her place as bridesmaid. She was soothed by the prayers and arguments which supported Stacey's cause.

On the edges of these voices, Tamra could hear the gruff voice of the minister berating the Women's Circle president. Apparently, she wasn't the staunch old biddy the congregation believed her to be. She supported Stacey's position vehemently. The minister seemed surprised that she should disagree with him. She had ever been one of the strongest supporters of his efforts. She felt his anger rise as his voice lowered to a dangerous whisper. He called her an unrepeatable name. Tamra knew the woman was in danger, but she could not respond.

Tamra's prayer came faster as she sought God's guidance. She found herself on her feet, alerting everyone in the sanctuary to the murderous intentions in the next room.

As a group, they broke into the office and found the minister's hands wrapped around the poor woman's neck. Her face was pale and turning purple as her breath was cut off. The minister dropped his hands and turned to his unexpected audience. He cursed and pushed his way through the group. The president's daughter rushed to her mother's side and yelled for someone to call an ambulance.

The next few moments were a blur. Tamra found herself in the graveled parking lot of the little country church, surrounded by most of the other gathered church members. Somehow, Tamra had removed the overdress and stood wearing only the potty dress. They seemed to grow taller, the minister and Tamra, as they stood in the center of attention. Anticipation caused the crowd to shudder. Tamra heard people talking, crying, praying. She offered up her own prayers that God's will be done.

They danced at Stacey and Robert's wedding reception. The young minister who had performed the ceremony chatted happily with several of the eligible bridesmaids. The president of the Women's Circle sat surrounded by her cronies and recounted her version of her near murder. She smirked happily at the attention she received. Bright-blue dresses passed like butterflies through the crowd. Tamra had been selected matron of honor for the occasion. Stacey hugged her and kissed her cheek before being swept away by Robert to their awaiting car. Tamra knew she was grateful but couldn't express herself.

Tamra tried to tell Stacey she had done nothing. It was difficult to tell what had really happened. Who would believe that as she stood face-to-face with the minister, a dark angel had swept down and snatched the screaming soul of the minister from his body, and flown away? They had only seen him grab his chest and scream a final scream as he collapsed, dead, at Tamra's feet.

2 Timothy3:1–5, NKJV

> But know this, that in the last days perilous times will come. For men will be lovers of themselves. Lovers of money, boasters, proud, blasphemers, disobedient to parents, unthankful, unholy, unloving, unforgiving, slanderers, without self-control, brutal, despisers of good, traitors, headstrong, haughty, lovers of pleasure rather than lovers of God, having a form of godliness, but denying its power. And from such people turn away!

Notes of Lurlene Joy McCoy

Satan's plan, much like buying real estate, has three criteria—deception, deception, deception.

Lucifer lost his high position in heaven because he wanted to be like God, though his powers were far from omnipotent, after his ejection from heaven, along with one-third of the angels, who had chosen rebellion based on Lucifer's ungodly desires. In that fall, they became the dark, twisted evil characters we know from God's Word and experience.

Everything Satan does is the direct opposite of God's desire for us. Demons use the scripture (out of context or twisted in truth) to justify our selfish desires and block us from the grace of God. They mimic the triune nature of God, appear as agents of light, and even appeal to the unguarded as Jesus or even God Himself. They can be so convincing that even true believers can be deceived if they are not knowledgeable of the scripture and the very character of God Himself as we are being transformed into His image as we walk closer with Him.

Anyone with eyes and ears can see Christianity at its worst all around them. For the unbelievers, it pushes them far away from the One who can set them free. For the immature believer, it could lead to arrested development of their spirit and cut them off from the blessings of God.

This unnamed minister is reflective of the wolf that has donned sheep's clothing and destroys the reputation of Christ through dishonest and deceptive means from within the fold itself. If the pastor, the shepherd of his flock, is himself a wolf, how many will be degraded and brought down before his tyranny is discovered and ended? Innocent people, though guilty in their sin, are told that Christ died for all, so all are saved, no need for a personal relationship involving repentance. Abominations declared by God are being reclassified as okay and natural, allowing wolves to rise up in power to deceive even more sheep.

Don't fear God. God is love. Fear for yourself and those who are enslaved by such wolves. Study your Bible, and learn what you can about the enemy's plans and strategies. *Actively* fight against the wolves in your life. Don't just keep them at bay. Destroy them! (I don't infer physical murder or character assassination here but the act of building a spiritual fortress around yourself that can effectively ward off the wolves and leave them nothing to prey upon. Only God can give that kind of strength!)

Tamra is one of those people who has built a fortress around herself that allows God to work in and through her and gives her spiritual eyes to see and spiritual ears to hear. She also has a willing spirit and great courage in knowing her King fought for her.

How does a sheep become a wolf?

Simple. We are born sinners into a sinful world that fuels wolf-eat-wolf mentalities. Without the intervention of the Holy Spirit and a willing heart, even the most sheeplike person grows into a wolf. A good moral person who does to others is still just a gentle wolf harboring a yen for Little Red Riding Hood deep within.

Anything we do that is not godly is open for attack. It all begins as simple lies from the enemy.

At first, we can combat the lie and deny it belief.

As the lie persists, we weaken. We still deny the lie belief, but we hesitate.

More pressure from a lie, in its many forms, leads to denial of belief, but only after a period in which we first hesitate, then meditate on the lie and its apparent virtues.

Pressure builds. We continue to deny belief. Our hesitation grows longer, our meditations grow deeper (in the wrong direction), and we begin to self-medicate to try and overcome the lie's temptations. Self-medication is fed by new lies. "Try harder." "You know it's true." "Go ahead, no one will see you." Alcohol, drugs, eating disorders, obsessive behaviors are all forms of self-medication.

Self-medication makes it more difficult to deny the lie. You hesitate and mediate, yet it persists, and you begin to relate to the lie. The lie-filled meditation and self-medication only mask the truth from your heart and mind. You know it's still there, even though you think you can't see it any longer. Relating to a lie is the worst-possible-case scenario because relating to the lie leads to believing the lie.

That lie, reinforced by the enemy and your thoughts, is redirected to that lie continually. There is no "out of sight, out of mind." Self-control and self-confidence are degraded by a lack of self-discipline resulting from the constant rewards for self-abasement.

That sounds strange, but the more out of control we feel, we become more vulnerable until we live the vicious cycle as a lifestyle we cannot escape from and fear the consequences if we did.

This results in total self-effacement, opening you for further lies, degradations, and self-destruction.

These people may not appear to be unhappy, but if you could peer inside their souls, you would see unrepentant darkness.

Christ can cleanse the soul and heal the hurts. But if you allow the lies to persist, your house will fill with darkness once more. This time, however, there will be a tiny night light to remind you where the true light is found and aid you in ridding yourself of the darkness, one prayer at a time.

Far too many churches and church leaders are allowing cult-like teachings and behaviors to infiltrate their churches. If the battle within the church cannot be won by one person's efforts, seek God elsewhere. Vengeance is in God's hands, and our righteousness in Him grows with each battle we fight.

Begin by making Christ the focus of your life. Rid yourself of everything that is not about Him. Sheep know their shepherd's voice and will follow only Him. Listen well and don't fall for the imitator.

Topic: Twenty-Two Attributes of False Teachers (2 Peter 2:1–19)

Author: Dr. David Jeremiah
Source The Jeremiah Study Bible

1. They infiltrate the church (2:1).
2. They come in secret (2:1).
3. They deny the work of Jesus (2:1).
4. They blaspheme the truth (2:2).
5. They are greedy (2:3, 14).
6. They use words that sound remarkably close to the truth (2:3).
7. They follow the flesh (2:10).
8. They are presumptuous and self-willed (2:10).
9. They do not want to be under anyone's authority (2: 10, 11).
10. They exhibit peace on the outside but are like untamed beasts on the inside (2:12).
11. They speak more evil than good (2:12).
12. They are ignorant (2:12).
13. They love to deceive others (2:13).
14. They are full of adultery (2: 14).
15. They cannot cease from sinning (2:14).
16. They prey on unstable new believers (2:14).
17. They intentionally speak lies (2:15).
18. They are out for monetary gain (2:15).
19. They talk a lot but say nothing (2:16–18).
20. They make grandiose promises but never deliver (2:17).
21. They use alluring thoughts to provoke attention from their audience (2:18).
22. They make promises they cannot deliver (2:19).

Topic: The Marks of the True Gospel and of False Gospels
Source: Life Application Study Bible

Marks of a false gospel

- ❖ Galatians 2:21 treats God's death as meaningless
- ❖ Galatians 3:12, people must obey the law in order to be saved.
- ❖ Galatians 4:10 tries to find favor with God by observing certain rituals
- ❖ Galatians 5:4 counts on keeping laws to erase sin

Marks of the true gospel

- ➢ Galatians 1:11–12, the source of the gospel is God.
- ➢ Galatians 2:20 knows that life is obtained through death: we trust in the God who loved us and died for us and that we might die to sin and live for Him
- ➢ Galatians 3:14 explains that all believers have the Holy Spirit through faith
- ➢ Galatians 3:21–22 declares that we cannot be saved by keeping laws; the only way of salvation is by faith in Christ, which is available to all.
- ➢ Galatians 3:26–28 says that all believers are one in Christ, so there is no basis for discrimination of any kind.
- ➢ Galatians 5:24–25 proclaims we are free from the grip of sin and the Holy Spirit's power fills and guides us.

One Small Step

Have you had a kindness shown?
Pass it on;
'Twas not given for thee alone,
Pass it on;
Let it travel down the years,
Let it wipe another's tears,
'Til in Heaven the deed appears—
Pass it on.

—Henry Burton, *Pass It On*

Little deeds of kindness, little words of love,
Help to make earth happy like the heaven above.

—Julia A. F. Carney, *Little Things*

If I can stop one heart from breaking,
I shall not live in vain;
If I can ease one life the aching,
Or cool one pain,
Or help one fainting robin
Unto his nest again,
I shall not live in vain.

—Emily Dickinson, *Poems I*

> Let me be a little kinder,
> Let me be a little blinder,
> To the faults of those around me.
>
> —Edgar A. Guest, *A Creed*

It began as a random act of kindness one snowy morning at 4:00 a.m. A mother, her son, and her son's best friend donned heavy clothing and armed themselves with snow shovels. Using boy power and the family's small tractor, snow blade attached, they cleared the half-mile of road leading to their home from the main road, then continued an extra two miles after the blacktop ended and gravel took over. Though school had been cancelled for the day, neighbors needed to get to work, doctor's appointments, and grocery stores. A cleared road would be a blessing as many had cars that were unreliable at best and definitely not roadworthy in the snow and ice of this snowy day. Only the three knew who had mysteriously cleared the road in the early morning darkness. Most were grateful for the act. Some were skeptical and cynical as life had taught them hard lessons.

In the weeks leading up to Christmas, the snow came and went. Sometimes the roads were cleared. Other times, small bags of groceries mysteriously appeared on porches of families with young children. Other neighbors found stacks of firewood on their porches to fuel the furnace that provided homey warmth.

Behind the scenes, the woman, her son, his friend, and members of their small community church had bonded together to help others. These secret angels never spoke of their deeds. In fact, some were unaware of the others. Some acted together in deliberate and planned acts of kindness.

Gifts from Santa appeared on Christmas morning for children in need. Boxes of food for a Christmas feast were left secretly on porches. Knitted hats, mittens, and scarves presented to members of the small community were sported happily by the recipients. There was no discretion of age, socioeconomic status, family size, or type or level of friendliness. Most everyone had begun to give back to their neighbors or pay it forward to someone else outside their community. Neighbors who had never spoken before or who had been estranged for many years became more open and friendly. Only the most isolated and suspicious held out.

As relationships began to forge and strengthen, people began to work together and barter services. Unsavory behaviors became more hidden by those who tried to remain aloof. Their self-imposed withdrawal only made them stand out that much more Some moved away. Some tried to blend in. The blenders discovered their secrets were not as secret as they thought. Embarrassment, resentfulness, and vengeance created pockets of ugliness. People rallied together to support one another in response to the violence and aggression. They continued to stand together as one against these challenges.

Children caught up in the confusion either followed their parents' examples or rebelled by seeking out their neighbors and the security of their homes. If Social Services became involved, the community shielded and protected the young they had adopted as their own, though unofficially. They sought resources that would not only serve the best interests of the children but also encouraged the parents and other relatives to seek out the services they needed to improve themselves and heal the pains they were running from.

In a perfect world, everyone would work for the good of the community. In reality, inequality continued. People were still unemployed, underemployed, and unable to fully provide for their families. Random acts of kindness erased the human inequalities of the psyche. People were learning to trust and to care about themselves and others. They became a tight-knit community of many differences but one goal.

One Easter weekend, the woman, her son, and three of his friends delivered small baskets of goodies to the families of children most in need. As they were returning from their predawn deliveries, they noticed the signs of other thoughtful acts. Bouquets of Easter lilies appeared on doorsteps. Food baskets sat next to unidentified packages. Handmade greeting cards from children were taped on doors. Home-canned fruit or baked goods were delivered to neighbors.

The churches overflowed with the presence of thankful neighbors, some of whom had never been to church before. Drug addicts and alcoholics set aside their demons to share in the delight of the love and support of friends, neighbors, and loving, accepting strangers. Some walked away, changed for the better. Others knew the guilt of their selfishness. Few went away, unaware of the truth around them.

By early afternoon, neighbors began gathering together to share in their bounty, great or small. Before long, the small groups became larger groups as neighbors drew together to sample new foods and share recipes. Barbecues sizzled, slow cookers steamed, and dish after dish of traditional family foods and nontraditional offerings filled ever-expanding lengths of tables.

Children played together in peaceful chaos. Puppies, kittens, and other spring babies were passed from snuggling arms to gentle strokes. Wildflowers were beginning to bloom. Vases and jars were filled with their colorful blossoms as gleeful children pulled or plucked them and presented them to every woman as a present.

Somewhere in all the activity, someone stated how very like the perfect Easter it was. Some women pointed out the Easter egg hunt taking place in one field of very young children toddling about. Others pointed out the petting zoo in the barnyard. Men discussed preparing their fields, planting crops, their jobs, and their desires for supporting their families with the improvement in the weather.

The conversation turned, at some point, to the morning services most had attended; sunrise services on hillsides or in small church sanctuaries had drawn those who had more understanding of the celebration. Traditional Easter morning services had attracted those who were unable to attend early morning services or were accustomed only to periodic attendance as required at Christmas, Easter, weddings, or funerals. Each had a different perspective on the meaning of Easter.

A group of children played in an old family cemetery in an adjoining field. A mixed group of boys and girls sat just outside of the opened gate. Two girls strolled purposefully toward an ancient grave, its headstone toppled irredeemably. A boy stood behind it, watching the girls approach. As they got closer, he smiled and pointed at the headstone. He said something, and one girl ran from the graveyard. The other girl stopped as she bumped into another boy. They spoke, and the girl crumbled to the ground as if hurt. The boy reached down to help her up. He spoke to her again, and she, too, ran from the cemetery. She stopped where the group of her peers were sitting. She spoke to them, gesturing wildly toward the cemetery where only one boy remained, standing guard innocently over the toppled tombstone. The group stood and followed the girl into the cemetery.

The playing continued as a group of curious adults approached to call the children to eat. To their surprise, they heard one girl call out, "It's my turn to be Jesus," as she hurried over to a grave and lay down on it. The other children gathered around to mourn. As they walked away from the "tomb," the girl "rose up" and hid behind a low monument. A second girl stood next to the headstone where "Jesus" had been. A boy and a girl approached the "tomb" and exclaimed excitedly as the "angel" proclaimed Jesus had risen. The girl ran off to tell the "disciples" at the gate. The boy pretending to be Mary Magdalene fell at Jesus's feet when she revealed herself.

The astonished adults watched as the Bible story they had heard that morning came to life before their very eyes. Those who had known Christ as Savior for a time were richly blessed. Others, who were coming to know Jesus, were given a clearer understanding of God's sacrifice on the cross and Jesus's redeeming resurrection. Still others had their eyes opened for the very first time.

As time continued to pass, the community grew closer together and began to spread their love to small communities around them. Several women in the community began the Vine, a support service that provided tutoring for children, adult education assistance, a listening ear, a helping hand, or other needed support. Men joined in helping neighbors with yardwork, fieldwork, and building projects.

A single act of kindness at 4:00 a.m. on a snowy morning grew into a thriving community of people who cared. One small step had changed the world.

Notes of Lurlene Joy McCoy

This is not a fluff piece intended to counter all the evil going on in Satan's Den. Neither is it a feel-good morality piece. It is simply an example of how one small slice of Satan's Den fought for, and won, the battle over the inherent evil present in the land.

After the devastating end to the unnamed minister, I felt it was important to contrast the evil that destroyed that man, his family, and some of his congregants, all of whom were affected in some way.

If, instead, that minister had embraced the true gospel as did this little community, it would have spread like wildfire to the other communities around it and then beyond, to the world at large.

The angel Gabriel told the young Mary, "For with God nothing will be impossible." Mary's cousin Elizabeth conceived John the Baptist at an age thought to be impossible, and Mary herself was a virgin whose child was conceived through the Holy Spirit (Luke 1:35–37).

When people allow the goodness within themselves pair up with the Holy Spirit, lives are changed.

Topic: Fifteen Key Instructions on How to Treat One Another

Author: Dr. David Jeremiah
Source: The Jeremiah Study Bible

1. Love one another.
    a. 1 John 3: 11, 23; 4:7, 11–12
    b. John 13:34–35; 15:12, 17
    c. Romans 13:8
    d. 1 Thessalonians 3:12; 4:9
    e. 1 Peter 1:22; 4:8
    f. 2 John 1:5
2. Be of the same mind/like-minded toward one another.
    a. Romans 12:16; 15:5
3. Do not judge one another.
    a. Romans 14:13
    b. Colossians 2:16
4. Admonish one another.
    a. Romans 15:14

5. Serve one another.
    a. Galatians 5:13
6. Bear with one another in love.
    a. Ephesians 4:2
    b. Colossians 3:13
7. Be kind to one another.
    a. Ephesians 4:32
8. Submit to one another in the fear of God.
    a. Ephesians 5:21
9. Forgive one another.
    a. Ephesians 4:32
    b. Colossians 3:13
10. Comfort one another with these words.
    a. 1 Thessalonians 4:18; 5:11
11. Exhort one another daily.
    a. Hebrews 3:13; 10:25
12. Do not speak evil of one another.
    a. James 4:11
13. Do not grumble against one another.
    a. James 5:9
14. Confess your trespasses to one another.
    a. James 5:16
15. Pray for one another.
    a. James 5:16

Christians are to love as follows:

1. Unconditionally. God calls His sons and daughters to love people as they are and to pray that he will do a work in their lives (Romans 5:7–8).
2. Sacrificially. We should not merely tell others of God's love but show them that God loves through our demonstrations of love.
3. Personally. The only Christ most people will ever see is the Christ they see in us (1 John 4:20–21).

Sins of the Father

The sins ye do by two and two ye
must pay for one by one.

—Kipling, *Tomlinson*

A loud moan, followed by a spine-tingling, ear-piercing scream, split the air like an axe cracking wood in two. She awakened abruptly, wondering what was wrong. It was then she realized that the hair-raising sounds had been her own. Awareness began flooding back to her as nurses and orderlies filled the doorway, then the small room around her narrow bed, the only furniture to be found in that cramped space.

She began to mumble incoherently, slowly raising her voice from a whisper to an aggressive scream as hands and arms tangled in her own, restraining her. A sharp prick in her arm, followed by a deep darkness, dragged her into a new hell of conscious memory but an inability to physically move or even escape.

She moved along a familiar road. It led to home, a place she hadn't been in as long as she could remember. She traveled at a steady pace, observing familiar sights, altered by the imagined passing of time. She knew she had a way to go before she reached her destination. She would tire long before she got there. Children riding bicycles appeared in the road beside her and in the yards of the houses on either side of the roughly paved road—tiny tots on tricycles, beginners with training wheels. Experienced riders on all varieties of bicycles circled around her, laughing like vultures, waiting for their prey to die.

She thought about asking for a bicycle to borrow to get her home. Shuddering at the prospect of riding a "vulture cycle" of these grinning grotesques, she closed her eyes and continued to plod on.

When she dared to open her eyes again, the less familiar terrain had changed from summer cycling to fall follies. The same children appeared to be raking yards, piling leaves, and jumping into the musty earth fragrance of the dead foliage. They frolicked around her as if she didn't exist. She felt the pang of hidden memories pounding within her, fogging her vision. The childish laughter mocked her by echoing in the mist as her muscles pulled her straining body forward to where home awaited.

The mist became snow, gently falling around her. The laughter became infused with the giggles of snowball fights and sledding. She felt the chill of the winter air begin to frost her skin. The condensation of her breath was the only sign of life left in her body. For the first time, she realized she had made no real progress in her journey home. She needed some other form of transportation.

She remembered traveling in a car, enjoying the view from the front seat that came with being the oldest child. She had siblings? How many? She also realized she could not drive. Was she not old enough? Had she never learned how? How old was she? So many questions flooded her mind. They returned to her, empty of response.

A single memory of riding a pony as a young girl swirled quickly into existence before whirlpooling back into her subconscious. She remembered the thrill of riding and guiding the massive power of the animal beneath her. Her hair blew around behind her as she laughed at the danger of allowing her mighty steed to gallop freely around the meadow where he lived. Fantasy met reality in those glorious moments of innocence found only in young childhood.

A longing arose in her. If she had a horse, she was certain she could achieve her goal of returning home. As if reading her mind, a magnificent black horse raised its head from the sparse grass not yet covered by the snow and nickered at her. Miraculously, it was saddled and bridled as if in anticipation of her need. The horse easily jumped the fence and trotted toward her. It stopped just out of her reach and reared up on its hind legs. Towering over her, its front hooves pawed at the air intimidatingly. Wild eyes rolled with evil intent as it dropped once more to all four hooves. A menacing, mocking horse laugh chilled her to the bone. What had she asked for?

The midnight stallion began to circle her, taunting her, pushing her to resume her walk. What did this mean? Wasn't she meant to ride the horse? Why did it seem she was being ridden instead?

She tried to ignore the shadow that clip-clopped behind her as she resumed her walk. The rhythmic sound of hooves on the pavement began to lull her into an insecure stupor.

When she finally began to rise from the stupor, she found herself in unfamiliar territory. Both sides of the road were lined with overshadowing trees, forming a cave-like arch. She couldn't tell the time of day or determine if it was night. It was shadowland found during the briefest moment of darkest dark and merest light.

The horse was still following her. She stopped; it stopped. She turned to confront this maddening nemesis. Once more, the stallion reared up on its hind legs, front hooves menacing the air around it. Its eyes glowed with a fiery scowl, teeth bared in a fang-like grimace. Lightning flickered and struck all around it as the smell of brimstone filled the air. The outline of an invisible rider appeared with each flicker of lightning. The thunder pealed around the horse in evil laughter.

In her innermost being, she realized that here was the crux of her condition. She was rousing from comatose amnesia to a conscious and semi-functional amnesia, a greater torment to the human condition. Satan had brought this condition upon her; only God could free her. How she knew, she didn't understand. Her madness refused to release her fully.

When at last she roused to full mental consciousness, she was examined physically and mentally and deemed able to return home. Once there, she spent months secluded in her room, still decorated for a young girl, going through everything she found there. She took apart dressers and her desk, seeking hidden spaces where something, anything, could have been tucked away. She knocked on walls and floorboards seeking hollow spaces or loose boards. She ransacked her closet and tossed the contents around the room in search of answers. She took apart her twin bed looking for any place a secret could be hidden. She never found what she was looking for, but she continued to look anyway. Her obsession knew no end.

Despair began to arise in her. Her grandmother tried to tempt her to come and eat at the dining room table, but she preferred taking her meals in her room. That was partially out of habit, as she had been fed in her hospital room by nurses who patiently coaxed her to open her mouth, to chew, and to swallow, and partially from her obsession to find answers.

She had learned that she was hospitalized at the age of eight with a mental breakdown that initiated with violent screaming and flailing about the room, heedlessly knocking all items she found to the floor. She had adamantly denied anyone to touch her and had spent much time in a sedated state in order to care for her basic hygiene needs. Slowly, she slipped into a sedate catatonia, staring unseen when awake and trembling nonstop when asleep.

There had been no explanation for any of her behavior. Psychologists and psych neurologists had been consulted. Every test performed indicated a normally functional body with an apparent mental and/or emotional block that prevented her from interacting with her environment. She was diagnosed with post-traumatic induced catatonia of unknown origin and placed in a hospital for such patients. She became a ward of the state as her insurance had no money to pay for her care. She was alone in life as she was in her mind.

When she had awakened after nearly twenty years of absence from reality, she remained amnesiac regarding the circumstances that had led to the trauma that resulted in her hospitalization. The doctors released her in the hope that she would remember on her own or adjust to a more normal life without those memories. Her case would be followed by a psychiatric social worker appointed by the hospital. It was a visit from the social worker that led to the opening of the dreaded memories that would reveal the horrible truth of her condition.

She watched from the window of the small bedroom built on the side of the run-down trailer as the red car driven by the social worker turned down the gravel driveway. It was a long driveway as the trailer sat back off the road quite a distance. The car stopped beside her father's decrepit pickup truck. The woman got out of the car and started for the front door. She waved as she passed the window; a gentle smile reflected in her eyes. Dogs barked at her heels as she climbed the rickety wooden steps to the tiny front porch.

She heard her father's voice yell at the dogs to shut up. They were more bark than bite anyway. In the living room, the murmuring of a conference traveled through the thin walls. They were deliberately keeping their voices low so she couldn't hear them. Her chance to talk would come last, as usual.

She nervously began rereading the soiled and wrinkled children's books from her childhood. As her anxiety rose, she stopped reading and began stacking and restacking them on her tiny desk. At last, her grandmother came for her.

She shuffled in bare feet the distance from her room to the tidy but musty living room. She sat on the floor like a child would, her long hair hanging on either side of her face as she studied her bare feet.

The social worker leaned forward in the sheet-covered chair she sat in so as to attempt to make eye contact. When eye contact didn't come, she began her interview but received only mumbled responses in return. As the interview began to wind down, a sudden flash of light caused the disturbed young woman to shake her head violently and look up at her father. She scooted closer to her grandmother. The social worker made note of the behavior and attempted to get her to talk about it. The moment had passed, and she shook her head no. Shortly after that, she was allowed to return to her room. She returned to her vigil at the window, wondering at the brief memory flash she had experienced. It had been all light, but she remembered hearing her little girl self crying. No matter of concentration would bring forth anything else.

She watched as the social worker negotiated the gravel walkway and her admirers, the waggling, whining entourage that had welcomed her and was now begging for ear rubs and kind words. The woman stopped just short of her car, knelt, and began to pet the more assertive of the lovestruck hounds. She stopped only long enough to reach into her tote bag and pull out a ziplock bag of dog biscuits. She gave each open mouth a treat, watching as they lolled off to lay down and enjoy their luck. The wistful look reminded the young woman of her mother. Another flash of memory brought to mind a memory of her mother laughing, surrounded by a frisky litter of puppies clamoring for her attention.

Somehow, she knew that was the last memory she had of her mother. Her mother was mysteriously absent from her memory, as well as the family, shortly after that. There had been no explanation and no further mention of her existence. There never had been pictures of her. They cost too much.

She sat on the side of her too-small bed, treasuring the memory of her mother. Looking at herself in the mirror reflected the memory. She looked like her mother. She may even be the same age as the woman in her memory. Her mother had been beautiful. Did that mean she was beautiful? She was too crazy to be beautiful. Everyone said so.

She returned to the memory of her mother and the puppies. It was the only memory she had to hold on to. She couldn't be older than eight years old because that was when she was hospitalized. What had happened in those brief years before that? Flashes began flickering in her brain. None of it made sense, no substance to grasp hold of. She rolled onto her side and pulled her knees up in a fetal position. The flashes lulled her into an uneasy sleep.

Hours later, she awakened to the sound of a truck engine idling in the driveway. It had to be a big truck by the sound of its deep rumble. The deafening silence that swept the air as the engine was shut off caused her to sit up in bed in full alert.

Once more, she looked out the window. She saw a tall, slender young man scratching ears and talking to the dogs as if they were old friends. He looked familiar, but she couldn't place him. Her deep frown was replaced with a pleased smile when she heard his voice greet her grandmother. He was her younger brother. He had been two when she went to the hospital. She was still struggling to get to know him, just as he was struggling to get to know her. He was a vague memory to her. He had no memories of her. They were learning each other for the first time. It was a very awkward situation for them both. She shuffled quickly to the living room to greet him.

He spoke first, in a friendly voice. She replied shyly, before dropping down on the floor. Her brother sat in her father's chenille-covered chair and began talking to their grandmother. She loved to listen to these conversations. They made her feel like a part of the family.

Apparently, her brother had stopped by on his way from doing a backhoe job. He worked freelance and could set his own hours and pick his own jobs. It was better than being an odd jobs man like their father, who only worked when the government money ran out in the middle of the month.

He discussed some work that needed to be done around the house as well. There were junk parts scattered throughout the yard that needed to be buried before the neighbors complained again. Their father dragged in junk from his odd jobs, often in lieu of payment, with great expectations of doing something with it that would make them rich. All it ever did was rust and rot in the weeds that grew over it until it was forgotten once more. The visual junk was the neighbors' concern. Snakes loved to breed in the cool shade of the rusted cars. When there were too many to occupy one vehicle, or there was not enough food for the slithering siblings, the serpents spread out over ever-expanding territory, including that of their neighbors. Poisonous or not, the reptiles were unwelcome.

Her brother rose to evaluate the property for the best place to dig a new hole. He asked if she would like to walk with him. She happily agreed and ran to get her shoes. She enjoyed the company of her brother, though she was at a loss to understand why. Together, they inventoried the most offensive piles of rusting hulks. He marked areas where he knew previous heaps had been entombed. At the farthest distance from the rusting heap she called home, she tripped over a rock buried in the grass. Curiously, she examined the area around the rock while she rubbed her injured ankle. From where she sat, she saw other rocks lined up along the ground, forming right angles at equidistant spaces to form a large square. When she asked her brother about the rocks, he shrugged and said that it must have been some kind of outbuilding a long time ago. Anyway, it was gone now.

She thought about that while her brother continued to examine the ground for an area that would accommodate the amount of digging required to dispose of the junk they needed to get rid of. The foundation surrounding her was no more than twenty feet by twenty feet. Her eight-year-old mind reflected on the pony she remembered riding. Maybe this had been an old barn that fell down while she was in the hospital. That didn't feel right. Wouldn't she have remembered an old barn?

They returned to the house. Her brother said goodbye and promised to return the next morning to dig the hole and move some of the junk. She sat in silence with her grandmother for a while. When she had sufficiently gathered her courage, she asked her grandmother about the stones near the foot of the hill. Her grandmother grew angry and told her to stay away from that place; they didn't mean a thing.

She chose to eat her dinner in her room, as usual. She could hear her grandmother and her father talking in the kitchen. They sounded angry. *Daddy must have had trouble with the neighbors again,* she thought.

Later that night, the door to her room opened quietly. She roused from sleep but did not move. Someone entered the room and shut the door behind them. She smelled her father's sweat and sour breath as he knelt down beside her bed. She clenched her eyes tightly shut, though her back was to him and he couldn't see her. He began stroking her hair as a father would a young daughter.

"Oh god, what have I done?" he whispered. He began to weep quietly.

She didn't know how long he stayed there beside her bed, but she was relieved when he finally left. She could not remember him ever touching her or speaking to her in such a tender way. Why did it frighten her so? Why now? She finally allowed herself to return to sleep only when she was certain her father was in his own bed and snoring quietly.

She dreamed that night; for the first time she could remember. It was a string of sensory memories, sometimes visual, sometimes auditory, rarely sequential or coherent. What these snippets of sensory input meant led her to further exploration of her inner psyche and a renewed examination of the contents of her childhood.

She was clutching a worn teddy bear and flipping through a tattered, partially used coloring book when her brother arrived. She heard him unloading the backhoe in the driveway. Barefooted and still clutching the teddy bear, she went out to meet him. He let her ride with him to the chosen site. He showed her how to operate the controls that dug the earth from the ground, then moved it to the side. She even laughed in glee as the iron monster ran through its paces for her brother. She couldn't remember having seen such efficient grace in motion. The roar of the machinery and the vibrations of the earth set her feet in motion. She was dancing in the grass inside the square of stones where she found such comfort when the sickening sound of crushing wood and the hollow pop of a cavernous space opening up beneath the jaw of the backhoe's fanged bucket jolted her memory once more.

She stopped the frolicking dance that had held her entranced. Her brother shut down the roaring beast and dropped to the ground. Together, they approached the hole gaping from the surrounding earth.

Tar shingles still clung to the rotting remains of rotting beams. More building rubble could be seen lining the dark crater. Her brother knelt and began pulling at some of the loose rubble.

"It looks like the whole building was just pushed into this hole," he said. He eyed the buried ruins, then the foundation. "May be whatever once stood there."

She turned to look at the foundation. Her teddy bear stared up at the sky from the grass where it had fallen. Her eyelids began to quiver as the flashing lights in her brain began again, this time with a vengeance.

"More," she whispered. "Show me more."

Her brother climbed back onto the backhoe and started it up. She stepped backward as the bucket swung forward and down into the rubble. He widened the hole around the remains of the building until there was space to climb down into the man-made grotto.

She beat her brother into the decaying building. Broken furniture was crushed together haphazardly. She pushed items aside as she worked her way to the farthest corner of what had been a one-room house. She pulled aside a disfigured card table. Remnants of a checkered tablecloth still clung to its surface. A loud gasp and a squealing cry forced its way from her throat. Tears began to flow freely as she gasped for air. Her brother placed his arms around her gently and leaned to look over her shoulder to see what had caused her reaction. Bile rose in his throat when he saw the tiny skeleton, still wrapped in a receiving blanket, lying where it had tumbled when the house had been leveled. A broken crib mingled with broken dishes and a mangled folding chair.

Without realizing it, she began to ramble out her memories. She was seven, her younger brother only sixteen months old. The baby had been born at home. They couldn't afford a hospital. It was a girl—Emma Sue. She had cried loudly, without end. Her mother was on the couch where she had given birth. Grandma had put the baby in the crib and started to clean up the blood. She had watched the delivery. It scared her. She thought her grandmother was hurting her mother. Her baby brother stood in his playpen, crying, snot running down his chin. She was frozen in fear.

Her father came into the house. He saw the baby screaming in the corner. He saw the blood pulsing from his wife. Her eyelids fluttered open, meeting his eyes before closing for the last time. Grandmother saw the passing of her daughter-in-law and turned away, clutching bloody towels to her face as she started crying. Her father began raging at her mother, accusing her of killing his wife. He hit her over and over again. Then he switched his anger to his newborn daughter crying in the crib. He accused the squalling infant of killing his wife. He picked up the tiny bundle and began shaking the flailing child. When an ugly crack stopped the crying, her father stared at the limp figure in his hands. He tossed the now-dead infant back into the crib and began rubbing his hands through his dirty, greasy hair. As he paced the room, he cooly ordered his mother to take the children to the house.

She remembered being led outside by her grandmother as her little brother continued to cry in his grandmother's arms. Inside the trailer, Grandmother locked the children in the newly built room that eventually became the little bedroom she now occupied. Eventually, they cried themselves to sleep on the floor of the empty room.

When they woke up, the door was unlocked. They sought out their grandmother in the living room and climbed up on the fraying sofa beside her. Their father sat quietly in a sagging chair across the tiny living room. No one spoke.

Life went on as usual. The new room became her bedroom, decorated in secondhand furniture and thrift store linens. Her brother moved into the tiny bedroom with their grandmother so she could take care of his needs more easily. Their father moved into the largest of the bedrooms.

The day of her eighth birthday came. Grandmother made a cake. They sang "Happy Birthday." Her grandmother gave her a worn teddy bear that had been hers when she was a little girl. She said the bear had been her best friend, and now she wanted to give the bear to her only granddaughter. Her father gave her a new dress for school. He had to work extra jobs to get the money for it, but he felt he owed it to his little girl.

She wore the dress to school the next day. Her new friend, the teddy bear, accompanied her. She had grown quieter in the days since her mother and baby sister died, knowing instinctively that she shouldn't talk about it. Strangely, no one asked.

Weeks passed by. She attended school but did little work. Her teacher became concerned and asked her to stay in when the other children left for recess. The teacher tenderly expressed her concern, but the child remained unresponsive. It was only when the teacher suggested calling her mother to come and get her if she was sick that the violent screaming began. The classroom was a disaster area by the time an ambulance could be called and removed the child to a hospital for her own safety.

That was where her memories ended.

Now she turned to where an overturned sofa stared up with broken springs. Broken wood framing and decayed fabric entwined to make it nearly unrecognizable. She grabbed one end and began tearing at it in an effort to flip it over. Her brother began tearing at the other end. Between them, they tore enough of the wood, cloth, and metal to reveal a twisted skeleton, hair still clinging to the scalp. They both slid to the floor and held each other as they cried.

Blue lights of police cars and the red lights of an ambulance slowed to turn into the driveway. Her father stood on the front porch, waiting for his destiny. She stood hand in hand with her brother, bravely watching their father. Their grandmother waited inside.

Satan had ridden off on his dark horse. Now only God could judge those who remained.

Exodus 34:5–7, NKJV

> Now when the Lord descended in the cloud and stood with him there and proclaimed the name of the Lord. And the Lord passed before him and proclaimed, "the Lord, the Lord god, merciful and gracious, longsuffering, and abounding in goodness and truth, keeping mercy for thousands, forgiving iniquity and transgressions, AND SIN, BY NO MEANS CLEARING THE GUILTY, VISITING THE INIQUITY OF THE FATHERS UPON THE CHILDREN AND THE CHILDREN'S CHILDREN UNTIL THE THIRD AND FOURTH GENERATION."

Notes of Lurlene Joy McCoy

This one breaks my heart. I can remember when all this happened. The young woman recovered her lost memories but continues to struggle with growing up. Twenty years of being eight years old was much easier than facing life as a sudden adult. The grandmother has since passed away. The young woman lives with her brother, who has become a confirmed bachelor who refuses to date, for fear of recreating his sister's memories and reducing the delicate progress she has made back from the catatonic state she had lived in for so long. She receives therapy with a doctor who comes to their home, a rarity in our modern world. Her intense grief for her mother and baby sister, the blame of her grandmother for hiding the secret, and the lies told by her murderous father have so greatly damaged her she is unable to leave the house. She has learned to care for herself and do household tasks, including some cooking, but she remains an eight-year-old in so many ways. That teddy bear stays nearby for the moments she is unable to deal with her current reality. She wears her hair in braids, like a child. Her clothing fits her adult body but reflects a childlike innocence. Her brother brought in a caregiver that could help her learn basic reading and math skills for improved functionality. Progress is slow. The television is on a cartoon channel while she is awake. Though she doesn't focus well, she does laugh from time to time at the antics of the animated characters. This is the only time she demonstrates any joy. She is still shy with her brother and those who come to work with her. She will never experience what it is like to be a woman socially. Her father caused the trauma by his thoughtless act of anger, followed by pushing the house off its foundation and burying his guilt beneath the bloodstained soil.

Sadly, her father had not previously nor following the event been known to be a violent man. Shiftless, yes. Even kind and gentle. What triggered the anger and grief in the loss of his wife that led to the unintended murder of his newborn daughter has never been explained. While sitting in the county jail pending a review of his case and an examination of the law and statutes of limitations on manslaughter and abuse of a corpse, his anxiety level and rising blood pressure led to a stroke which took him to the critical care unit of the local hospital. He never regained consciousness and passed away six months later in a poorly run nursing home with the reputation of being the last place you go before the grave.

The girl has no knowledge of her father's passing.

Shamefully, how we live our lives scars our children, who create scars on their children, until only scarred skeletons remain locked away in the closet of the family tree.

Stress is a traitorous taskmaster. It alone can raise blood pressure and create anxiety and depression. Paired with fear and guilt, the individual becomes a ticking time bomb—physically, emotionally, socially, spiritually. Personality can be altered. There are explosive moments of uncontrolled emotionality. It is fully psychosomatic—what is happening in the mind influences what is happening in the body. Sin begins in the mind and becomes outward actions which then influence the mind's responses to the next event of similar temptation. It is a vicious cycle. The father had some hidden guilt—an unrepented sin—that was triggered by the tragic death of his wife and led to the accidental death of his newborn child. It could have stopped there. Proper legal action could have been taken. The father could have received help while paying for his crimes. The family would have suffered, but they would have survived. By covering up his sin through the intentional digging of a hole and the burying of the evidence, he locked away all responsibility for his actions. By not talking about it, it never happened. When his oldest child had to be taken from her home and hospitalized because of what she had witnessed, he had another opportunity to confess his sin but refused. Until the sin was uncovered and he was forced to see the bigger consequences of his action, the guilt had festered to the point of death when he could no longer hide.

The grandmother is also guilty of hidden guilt and an unrepentant heart. She could have told authorities what had transpired and intervened for mercy on the part of her son. She did not. As her granddaughter lived in a comatose state in a hospital, completely detached from her family, she could have confessed and ended the child's torment. But she didn't. She, too, is guilty of an unrepentant heart that destroyed the lives of the one she claimed to love.

The girl had witnessed the most natural process of womanhood—the birth of a child. It was a beautiful thing gone horribly wrong. The grandmother was apparently capable of helping her daughter-in-law through the birthing process. It was the hemorrhaging that followed that she had no control over. She probably took care of everything that needed to be done for the birth by herself, leaving the little girl to mind her brother. In her pride, she failed to explain what was happening to the girl. The screams of labor are terrifying enough for those who hear them; without medication or explanation, fear escalates. It is difficult to imagine what went through that child's mind as she watched her mother scream and squirm in her efforts to bring this child into the world. Then the birth itself was traumatizing as she saw this bloodied infant tear a hole in her mother as it forced its way into the world. And the blood. So much more than a skinned knee or that produced by a slaughtered chicken! Had mother and child lived, this eldest daughter would have learned that the pain of childbirth was erased by the bonding of mother and child. The instant forgiveness given when mother and child saw each other for the very first time, all this was torn from her. She was guilty of no sin yet paid the highest price.

Three generations felled by one single event. That is the curse of unrepentant sin in action.

Portrait of Paranoia

No matter where you go in the world, you will run into the concept of judgment, with variations in detail. The basic concept of judgment is simply that human beings are morally accountable.

—*AND HE DWELT AMONG US,* A. W. Tozer

Pamela walked down the long hallway in pursuit of a much-needed file. The person who had it was nowhere to be found. When she asked where Ms. Tellis could be found, she was told to check Ms. Soon's office. Ms. Soon's office was empty.

Pamela pondered the situation, then remembered that Ms. Tellis and Ms. Soon spent much of their free time gossiping in Ms. Flanders's office. Pamela walked the short distance to Ms. Flanders's office next door. There she found Ms. Tellis, gossiping with her cronies. Hesitantly, Pamela stepped into the room, drawing immediate attention to herself. The talking abruptly stopped, everyone turning to look at her.

Uncomfortable at having disrupted the discussion, she looked at Ms. Tellis and said, "I need to get that file to work on this afternoon."

Looking at her friends, Ms. Tellis grabbed her office key and mumbled something about being right back and to keep the place.

Ms. Soon joked back that she would forget where she was. Ms. Flanders just encouraged Ms. Soon to continue and that she would inform Ms. Tellis later of the rest of the details.

Pamela had been more or less snubbed by all three of these women before and didn't like having to deal with them. She always felt like they were watching her when she was in the same room with them. They always fell silent when she entered. Then they resumed their whispers as she was leaving. She didn't even feel comfortable around them in the copy room, waiting her turn politely.

Ms. Tellis unlocked the door to her office, opening it just enough for Pamela to enter. As Pamela searched the long table on the south wall for her file, Ms. Tellis stood just inside the door, with the door pulled closely to her, watching Pamela closely. Pamela tried to be polite.

"I can get the file early tomorrow morning, if that would be better for you," she said, smiling.

"No," replied Ms. Tellis shortly. Then as if she realized how sharp she had sounded, she said, "This afternoon would be best."

"I just hated to disturb your lunch," apologized Pamela.

"Oh, that's okay," stated Ms. Tellis flatly, retrieving the file herself and shoving it at Pamela and locking her door once more.

Pamela held the file tightly to her chest as she returned to her office to begin her work. She couldn't help thinking what would be said behind her back when Ms. Tellis returned to the hen coop. In her office once again, Pamela couldn't help but think how much nicer things would be if certain files didn't have to be kept in a central location under lock and key. Her mind began to wander back to the hen coop, and she could imagine the conversation going on with her as the central topic. Tears came to her eyes as the "talk" got more and more unrealistic and untrue.

She knew her imagination was going to get her into trouble by allowing these thoughts to continue, so she tried to put them out of her mind so she could continue to work on her file. She had a deadline to meet, and she couldn't let these feelings take over as they had many times in the past. Her work was shoddy, she knew that, but her paranoia just wouldn't let up. She would have to redo the entire thing, later, after she had calmed down. At last, she shoved the file aside and allowed the tears to run rampant.

When her tears had dried and she was able to resume her work, she realized it was late, and she had to return the file to Ms. Tellis's office to be locked away until tomorrow. Pulling her mirror from her purse, she quickly checked her face for redness or puffiness. After looking at herself for several minutes, she decided she had better stop at the lady's room before going to see Ms. Tellis.

Clutching the incomplete file to her chest, she walked, head down, to the lady's room, passing Ms. Tellis's office on the way. When she finally deemed herself presentable, she inhaled deeply and strode confidently to Ms. Tellis's locked and empty office. Pamela's heart fell at the sight. *Now where could she be?* thought Pamela, discouraged. Then she remembered Ms. Tellis's other favorite spot, the lounge, and started in that direction.

Relieved to find Ms. Tellis sitting there, smoking, Pamela, acting cheerful, handed her the file. Ms. Tellis, not reaching for it, gestured to the seat next to her and said, "Just put it there," and dismissed Pamela merely by turning her head away to take another draw of the cigarette.

Pamela quickly withdrew to her own office, gathered her purse and papers, and left, still feeling uncomfortable about what had occurred that afternoon. She just knew she was the topic of many hen sessions at that time in diverse parts of the building.

Waiting impatiently for the bus, she tried to dispel her fears by studying the buildings and cars. She never studied people. People could be dangerous. They could talk...talk about you. They would carry on conversations about you as if you weren't even there. They never mentioned you by name, though. They would always say "he" or "she" instead of your name. They were too smart to mention your name with you standing so close by. So she studied nonliving things instead.

The bus arrived on time, relieving her of the fear that the one man waiting with her was some nutcase who was watching her, thinking bad things about her. He looked like he was reading the newspaper, but she knew he wasn't. They both got on the bus. Pamela took the first vacant seat she came to. Holding her breath and trying not to be obvious, she watched the strange man, fervently praying that he wouldn't sit next to her in the half-empty bus. She relaxed a little when he passed her by and moved toward the back of the bus, was greeted, and then sat next to another man he apparently knew.

She tried to look busy throughout the long ride to her stop but was unsuccessful. With every stop, she found herself watching the comings and goings of every passenger, watching each in fear they would sit down next to her and start a conversation. Today she was lucky; no one sat with her. She was beginning to feel better about her day.

When the bus came to her stop, she quickly got off and began walking away from the bus stop. She was in the habit of walking with her head down, watching her feet, in order to avoid anyone taking notice of her. Walking thusly, she found herself colliding with another person, whom she hadn't seen. In fear, she dropped her papers.

As she bent to retrieve her lost work, she saw a very masculine arm also begin to reach for the papers. Trembling inside, she gathered the papers she could, then reached for the papers being held by an average-looking man who was looking at her apologetically. She recognized him as the man she had seen at her work bus stop.

Stunned, she took the papers from him, mumbled, "Thanks," then pushed her way past the man. She quickened her pace as her thoughts began to race. *Why is this man following me? What does he want? I've never seen him at my stop before. He could be dangerous!*

When she reached her apartment building, she quickly darted through the front door and hid behind the large plant next to the window. She stood there, peering out from between green leaves, waiting for the strange man to follow her into the building. When she didn't see him anywhere, she heaved a sigh of relief and started toward the elevator.

When the doors opened, she entered the elevator and punched her floor. Seeing the elevator was empty, she allowed herself to relax and crumple, still standing into one corner. When other people got on, she drew herself tighter into her corner and stood quietly as her floor was passed several times. When she was alone in the elevator once more, she again punched her floor. This time, she made it there in solitude.

She left the elevator behind her as she physically shook off her fear. She hated public areas, especially elevators, where people were forced to be so close. She would have taken the stairs, but they were so lonely, and anyone could be waiting there for someone like herself to come there alone so they could do terrible things that are done in a lonely stairwell.

Reaching her apartment door, she began fumbling in her purse for her keys. When she didn't find them immediately, she began to imagine pickpockets and purse snatchers going through her purse, finding only her keys of value. When her hand brushed against the cold metal of keys, she grasped them tightly, pulling them from her purse. Automatically, she began to check her wallet to be certain everything was there. It was.

Her hands trembled as she put the key in the lock and slowly turned it. She pushed the door open widely with a strong push of her hand. With the same hand, she began feeling along the wall for the light switch, even though there was enough daylight coming through the closed drapes to tell if anything was in the room.

As the light came on, Pamela thought she saw a shadow sneak deeper into the shadows of the hallway. Hesitantly, she stepped into the living room, staring fearfully into the dark shadows of the hallway. When nothing moved, Pamela closed the door behind her, checking to be sure no one was in the hallway observing her.

Fearful of intruders, Pamela locked the door, then fondled the chain lock. If she locked the chain, she would have difficulty getting out of the apartment quickly if there really was an intruder in the apartment already. On the other hand, one lock wasn't enough to keep other intruders from coming in. She slid the chain into place anyway.

"Hello! Anyone here?" she questioned the darkness of the hallway. *This is silly*, she thought to herself. *If anyone is in here, they certainly aren't going to talk to me.*

She walked a little more confidently toward the hallway, stopping only to turn on several more lights in the living room and kitchen. Fortunately, the hall light was in the living room just as you entered the hallway, and she was able to dispel the shadows before entering the hallway. That left only the bathroom and bedroom.

After Pamela had turned on every light in her apartment, she checked every closet, under her bed, and behind every item of furniture that could possibly conceal a person. She found nothing, just as she knew she would. She had never found anyone in her apartment in the two years she had lived there. She had never had a break-in either. Hers was a very secure building.

Laughing at herself, she returned to the living room and placed a chair under the doorknob of the door to the apartment. *Just as a precaution*, she reminded herself. She had bought that extra chair just for this purpose, and it had worked.

She fixed herself a small salad, being extra careful with the sharp knife so as to not cut herself. She was terrified of blood. That was just one of many reasons she did not own a television—too much violence.

After dinner, she gathered her papers and sat at the snack bar, facing the door. She had only one entrance to the apartment, and she had it covered. Relaxed somewhat, she threw herself into her work.

Around nine o'clock, she set aside the papers, stretched, and walked to the bathroom to take a hot bath. She never closed her bathroom door so she could hear if anyone came into the apartment without her consent.

Slipping into the warm bath water—never too hot or too cold—she allowed herself to relax further. She was working too hard. She shouldn't let the little things get to her. After all, she was a big girl now, and she had to learn to take care of herself.

Just as she was getting out of the tub and was drying off, she thought she heard a noise in the living room as though someone was trying the doorknob. Wrapping her robe tightly about herself, she tiptoed through the apartment, checking to be sure all the lights were still on. As she passed through the kitchen, she carefully picked up a butcher's knife she kept in a special drawer as a means of protection.

Standing nervously beside the door, against the wall, knife raised and ready to plunge, she slowly slipped the chair from beneath the doorknob. Watching closely, she touched the doorknob and unlocked it. Still staring fearfully, she slowly turned the doorknob and opened it just enough to peer around the chain and into the hall.

She saw no one. The hall was empty as it usually was at that time of night. Not even the shadows moved. The halls rang with the silence of the evening.

Cautiously, Pamela closed the door; she prided herself on her bravery. One step into the hallway, she could see the carpeted length of her floor, empty and silent.

As she turned to enter the apartment once more, she noticed an envelope lying on her threshold. She picked it up and opened it. Inside was a picture of herself, waiting for the bus outside the apartment building. There were no captions, no writing of any sort. Just the picture.

Frightened, she ran into her apartment and slammed the door shut behind her, forgetting to lock it. She continued running until she reached her closet. There she hid in the dark corners behind her clothing. The closet door was pulled shut, and she refused to turn on the light. If someone was watching her, she would be safe hiding in her closet, safe from the outside world.

When the neighbors finally found her three days later, hidden in the dark closet, she was found to be holding an envelope containing a sample photograph taken by a local photographer as an advertisement. Everyone in the building had received one, including Pamela. Each photo was a picture of the tenant that had received it. Pamela's picture had been sent without the enclosed advertisement by mistake.

Pamela was taken to the local hospital and admitted for psychiatric evaluation. She had a history of paranoid behavior and had been under a doctor's care for several years. It is rumored she sits in dark corners, repeating, "He's watching me! He knows all about me!" No one can get near her without her stabbing at them empty-handed as though she was wielding a knife. At those times, she screams hideously and states, "No! You can't have me. I belong only to me."

Poor Pamela. So afraid of herself she can't accept others, even when they just want to help her.

Proverbs 29:25, NKJV

> The fear of man brings a snare, but whoever trusts in the Lord shall be safe.

Notes of Lurlene Joy McCoy

After rereading *The Haunting of Hill House* by Shirley Jackson, I have drawn some new conclusions that can be directly related to this tale.

Dr. Montague, the instigator of the investigation of Hill House, describes his theory to his test subjects—Theodora and Eleanor, with house heir-to-be Luke—that ghosts can do no physical harm to the living and cannot do harm to the mind because the mind is invulnerable. As an anthropologist, he operates on very concrete and objective data to explain the supernatural as attacking the weak modern mind that has abandoned its protective armor of superstition and has no substitute defense. He goes on to explain fear as the "relinquishment of logic, the willing relinquishing of reasonable patterns. It's all or nothing. There is no meeting halfway."

Dr. Montague's wife, on the other hand, actively seeks out and encourages manifestations she can easily recognize as the cry for help from the souls suffering in the presence of her husband and his entourage. As such, she is pleased with her cold-planchette session in the library immediately following her arrival. She and her stoic friend, Arthur, are pleased with the "facts" of their efforts, particularly the alleged presence of a walled-up nun and a monk, which is not plausible according to the known history of the house. Neither of these individuals recognizes the true manifestations of Hill House's core spirit(s) when they do manifest.

A careful reader will not pursue paranormal inferences, however, as it is Eleanor Vance who is the true "haunt" of this house. Psychologically speaking, she is a victim of arrested development. It is hinted at in the absence of a father figure and the overpowering presence of her sister and mother that kept her from experiencing a fulfilling childhood and developing normal social interactions of adolescence since she and her family were ostracized by their neighbors. Just as she reached legal adulthood, she finds herself as sole caregiver to her demanding mother until her death. Though well into adulthood, Eleanor is still emotionally a child—living in fairy tales of her own making, desiring both freedom to go and a deep need to withdraw and be alone.

Notice the manifestations of Hill House the first night it reveals itself—the running of some energy through the hallways and pounding on the doors of all the rooms of that floor's wing. Later, Eleanor acts out that scene, like a naughty child given free run of a house in which she had previously been confined only to the nursery. She acts out childhood songs, endangering herself in the process.

She sees the otherwise normal adults around her and discovers she cannot relate to them on their own level, no matter how she tries. She is the odd stray kitten everyone feels sorry for but refuses to take responsibility for. The house uses this inconsistent maturity to draw her deeper within her psychosis.

The house itself was built to odd specifications in an otherwise ideal location. The unhappy history of girls growing up there reminds Eleanor of her own unhappy childhood. Those girls grew up motherless, with a father of perverse mind. Eleanor grew up fatherless with a mother of a perverse mind. The similarities gave her a false sense of fitting in. Theodora would never be her "cousin," Luke had no intention of becoming her lover, and Dr. Montague was uninterested in being her "father." Only the house, "the mother house" as Luke describes it, provides her with a sense of "home" she has never felt before.

Dr. Montague chose Eleanor for her experience with unexplained raining of rocks after her father's death. Perhaps he should have put her through a full psychological profiling before inviting her to his experiment. In hindsight, it would have been scientifically necessary to have such a profile before subjecting her to the history of Hill House.

Imagination is not limited to an individual. Documentation of mass hysteria in seeing visions or phenomena exists.

The book could have just as easily been titled *The Haunting of Eleanor Vance*, with no alteration of text with just as much effectiveness.

We all carry unconscious superstitions ingrained within us by our experiences and our upbringing. Even if we do not claim to believe in them, we do things obsessively to prevent bad things from happening to us. Though obsessively done, they so subtly blend in with our everyday behavior they become invisible or identifiable as "quirks" in our personalities.

Fears come when we are surprised by something unexpected in our environment—internal or external. We are taken by surprise, go into fight-or-flight mode, but having no experience, we try to use logic and reasoning to help us escape. Creativity forms "worst-case scenarios" in our minds, which heighten our emotions. Every part of our body accelerates its activity, bringing awareness to us in a new and unfamiliar way. Chaos ensues in our psyche.

Until we accept that unexpected events are something we simply cannot explain or control, or discover it is something we can do something about, fear stays with us, escalating into a temporary psychosis that alters our perceptions and responses. We call this the paranormal or supernatural because it is not our normal or what we consider natural.

Unexplained does not equal evil, bad, or unnatural. There are infinite mysteries in our world. Careful curiosity may yield answers, or it may lead to new questions. Recklessness only breeds chaos and misunderstanding, misinformation, and theory presented as fact simply because one person has declared it to be so.

Angels and demons exist. They can and do influence us mentally, morally, and spiritually. They can touch us and either protect or harm us. Whether through our psyche or through actual physical contact, we can feel their presence—for good or bad. As for ghosts, spirits, or souls of deceased humans existing on our plane, the jury is still out. The presence of cosmic fractals falls into this gray area regarding the origin of the unexplained.

Our protagonist, Pamela, also demonstrates a form of arrested development, combined with self-fulfilling prophecy fueled by fear. Somewhere along the line, she failed to develop a sense of security and self-confidence. Feeling insecure within herself, she turned to the world outside of her as her predatory power. She was safe nowhere, even in her otherwise secure apartment. Because of her insecurity, she was unable to develop relationships with others, which left her friendless and alone. She isolated herself from others at work, and they left her alone accordingly.

She projected her fears onto every scenario, fueling the lies she was already telling herself, causing them to grow. Though she was under a doctor's care, Pamela had not been able to move past the surface issues and discover the core problem that had built her into this enormous, dense lump of darkness she had hidden herself in.

Fear begins with a lie. If that lie is accepted, new lies join in their voices to the first, until the individual becomes slave to those lies.

Only truth could have set Pamela free.

Topic: What Is Paranoia?

Source: www.healthline.com

Summary

- A thought process that causes you to have an irrational suspicion or mistrust of others.
- May feel like they're being persecuted or that someone is out to get them.
- May feel the threat of physical harm even if they aren't in danger.
- People with dementia sometimes have paranoia, and it can also occur in people who use drugs.
- Can be a symptom of a mental illness or a personality disorder.

Symptoms of paranoia vary in severity and can interfere with all areas of life:

- Constant stress or anxiety related to beliefs they have about others
- Mistrust of others
- Feeling victimized or persecuted when there isn't a threat
- Isolation

Makes relationships and interactions with others difficult, causing problems with employment and personal relationships.

May feel others are plotting against them or trying to cause them physical or emotional harm.

May be unable to work with others and may be suspicious and guarded.

May also have delusions or believe that others are trying to hurt them.

A person with schizophrenia, a possible partner with paranoia, also experiences hallucinations.

Usually occurs due to personality disorders or other mental illnesses such as schizophrenia.

May be caused by a combination of factors, including the following:

- Genetics
- Stress
- Brain chemistry

Can be caused by drug use

- Methamphetamines
- PCP
- LSD

Can occur in people with bipolar disorder, anxiety, depression.

Treatment includes medication and psychotherapy to accept their vulnerability, increase self-esteem, develop trust in others, learn to express and handle emotions in a passive manner, develop coping skills, and improve socialization and communication skills.

Topic: Anxiety and Fear

Source: *Invincible*
Author: Dr. Robert Jeffries

Summary

- Anxiety is often described as worry.
    - In Greek, it means "to be [unduly] concerned"—an excessive concern about things, often about things that are out of our control.
    - German, *wurgen*, choking or strangling.

- Latin, *anixus*—implies a choking or strangling.
- Mark 4:7—Jesus used the word *sumpnigo* to describe the seed that fell among thorns; they were *choked out*

➢ There are at least three reasons for anxiety.

1. Misguided perspective—we put our focus on the wrong things.
    - Traced to fear, which is an emotional alarm to a real or perceived threat; may lead to overprotectiveness
2. Unconfessed sin—whenever we deliberately violate God's laws, we experience a general sense of uneasiness (Psalm 32:3–4). We fear our sin will be uncovered, and we'll be exposed. Or worse, we fear God is going to "get even" with us.
    - When we confess our sins, God will forgive us (1 John 1:9; Psalm 94:19)
3. Satanic attack—lust, doubt, materialism, etc. Anxiety diverts our attention away from the faithfulness of God and what He's doing in our lives in the present. The past is unchangeable, and the future is unknowable. Yet both can paralyze us with worry. Satan uses "If only" and "What if" to strangle the joy out of our lives.

- Anxiety produces distortions about the truth—Jesus called Satan "the father of lies" (John 8:44).

➢ Consequences of anxiety

- Burdens our minds to the point that fear replaces peace, leading to physical and psychological trauma.
- Strangles our ability to distinguish between what is incidental and what is essential, leading to distractions and distortions.
- Divides our hearts and displaces God as the center of our lives, leading to conflict with others—the old cliché of getting kicked at work, then coming home and kicking the dog.

- Such self-centeredness shouldn't be found among believers—Romans 12:3; Philippians 2:3

➢ Matthew 6:25–34—Do not worry

- Make plans, but do not worry about what comes to fruition.
- Do be concerned about what *might* happen, but don't make those things your focus.
- There's a difference between being carefree and careless.

1. Worrying is *unreasonable.* God created you. He knows what you need; He will provide.
2. Worrying is *unfounded.* God loves us; He will take care of us. We are valuable.
3. Worrying is *unproductive.* Unproductive people are usually anxious people. Productive people, on the other hand, are usually relaxed people—at peace with themselves and others. Valuing things like coins or inches of height is about perspective (a comparison with something or someone else), but things that are of value to the life of an individual are available only to that individual—beyond comparison.
4. Worrying is *unnecessary.* God will always provide (Hebrews 13:5)!
5. Worrying is *ungodly.* To worry is to forget God's past provision and to deny God's present power—to say that His grace is limited instead of limitless. According to Jesus, that's the mark of ungodliness.
6. To stop worrying, "seek first His kingdom and His righteousness, and all these things will be added to you. So do not worry about tomorrow; for tomorrow will care for itself. Each day has trouble of its own" (Matthew 6:33–34).

a) Dedicate your life to glorifying God (Matthew 6:9; 1 Corinthians 10:31).
b) Declare God's sovereignty over your life (Matthew 6:10).
c) Determine to do God's will (Matthew 6:10).

Facts about Fear

- According to medical experts, the physical effects of fear include a suppressed immune system, a disturbance in the sleep/wake cycle, eating disorders, headaches and migraines, muscle aches and fibromyalgia, body aches and chronic pain, difficulty breathing and asthma, and learning difficulties.
- Mood swings.
- Obsessive-compulsive thoughts.
- Chronic anxiety.
- The prevalent thought that you are a victim.
- Inability to develop feelings of love and compassion.
- Bitterness toward God and others.
- Loss of trust in God's goodness, mercy, and grace.
- Confusion as to what God is doing in our lives.

How other people perceive us is often dictated by how we perceive ourselves.

Fear distorts the size of our problems.

When we allow fear to fog our thinking, we're saying that God is either incapable or unwilling to take care of us.

- Eight times in the scripture we're assured that *nothing* is too hard for God:
  - Genesis 18:14
  - Job 42:2
  - Jeremiah 32:27
  - Zechariah 8:6
  - Matthew 18:26

- Mark 10:27
- Luke 1: 37; 18:27

To act on our fears is to deny our faith and commit the sin of disobedience.

Topic: Five Levels of Demonic Possession

Source: Citation unconfirmed

1. Manifestation—the beginning stage. In most cases, the demons have been "invited" in some way. (They are always present but are attached to individuals who have opened themselves up mentally and spiritually to their presence.) This can occur through participation in spiritualist games, using Ouija boards, taking part in séances, emulating activities seen on TV, or in books/media. Some experiences may be felt and/or seen, often as blurring lines between right and wrong, goodness and evil. Perception of things of the occult as "cool," no matter the consequences, influences individuals to experiment and dabble in things of the darkness they do not understand and cannot control. The main objective is to find its target—usually those who are emotionally, physically, and spiritually weak are the most obvious targets. Young children are also more vulnerable.
2. Infestation—things are starting to pick up fast. A demon may start recruiting help, and more will cross through this doorway that was opened. More physical experiences may start—cold spots, voices, lights, shadows. Quickly bends into infestation once the target(s) have been chosen.
3. Oppression—once infestation has started, it will immediately go into oppression. The reason it seems to start and build aggression is that the infestation is still going on. More demons are attracted and adding their energy/power to the assault. Usually there will be one main demon that is focused on the target while others are "outside" causing

havoc. The purpose of oppression is to isolate the target. To isolate the target, they simply play mind games. They may even cause depression because of some of the experiences and even by what the "voices" are telling them. It's all done to harm, and the faster it is done, the quicker advancement to the next stage. The target may become violent, so great care should be taken around the person oppressed. Their sense will be a great disdain to God and anything holy.

4. Possession—also known as full possession or integration. The demon at one level will actually possess and control the target. The person may or may not "come out of it" at different times. The demon will want as much as possible, but there are lapses. Don't be fooled, the demon is still in control! It will relinquish control at times, either to rest or in an effort to trick those around the target that nothing is wrong. The demon has an ultimate goal, which is the next and final stage, if not dealt with. Some things that would be seen of the target would be reaction to the Bible, liturgies, holy relics, even when hidden under clothes, and a definite disdain for God and all that follow Him. This stage is where the possessed is extremely dangerous to him/herself and those around, especially physically.
5. Death—all demons may have only one person in all stages of possessions. They seek to destroy and kill God's creation. The more pain they cause, the better for them. The more they can destroy relationships, marriages, etc., the happier still. But the ultimate goal is to definitely kill the possessed target, and if they can take another with the target, so much the better.

Topic: Signs of Demonic Possession

Source: Citation unconfirmed

1. Signs of ghost possession
    a) Mysterious shadows.
    b) Mysterious noises.

c) Hot or cold spots.
d) Lights going on and off.
e) Strange behavior in animals.
f) Disappearance and reappearance of items.
g) Feeling like someone is watching.
h) Feeling like someone is touching.
i) Drawers, doors, and cabinets closing and opening.
j) Objects moving on their own.
k) A place that feels creepy. You cannot tell why you do not want to be there alone.
l) Many deaths have occurred in a place, including suspicious deaths. The location of several traffic accidents could be a sign of sudden demon infestation.
m) Businesses start and go bankrupt repeatedly in a location.
n) Phenomena occurring in a place such as power going off, thumping noises, sounds of howling and whining, and flying remote controls.
o) Feeling a lot of negative emotions in a certain place. People suddenly feel depressed, heavy, and develop bad thoughts toward themselves. For example, you may feel fine and happy before getting into the place but feel negative immediately after entering the place. And then you feel fine shortly after leaving the place.

2. Signs of demon possession
   a) Having thoughts that are unlike you or which seem to come out of the blue or from somewhere else.
   b) Felling hopeless.
   c) Severe arguments with friends or your spouse.
   d) Suicidal thoughts.
   e) Sudden depression that can be very subtle or severe.
   f) Feeling controlled at times or all the time by something else or someone else.
   g) Feeling creepy.
   h) Inability to pray.
   i) Feeling like something has touched, scratched, or attacked you.

j) Feeling oppressed or negative in one area of your house or neighborhood.
k) Hearing one or multiple commanding, persuasive, and negative voices requiring you to do something. For instance, a voice may persuade you to avoid a friend or allow them into your life.
l) Inability to contact spiritual or religious items, for instance, or one may incur an aversion to touching a crucifix or going to the temple or church.
m) Phenomena such as things falling off shelves or walls, scratching sounds, or spiritual items moving by themselves.
n) Extreme personality changes. For instance, an outgoing person starts to stay at home all the time.
o) Feeling attacked is sometimes accompanied by inexplicable physical pain while others experience no attacks. The feeling is often accompanied by psychological pain such as anguish or terror.
p) Feeling like someone or something is pushing you to do something.

The Catholic doctrine has recorded the following signs of demonic possession:

1. Early warning signs, according to the Catholic church, include vocal outbursts, stomach cramps, palsy and tremors, vomiting, and violent headaches. It is possible for an individual to be physically ill and possessed at the same time. The church cites Matthew 8:16 from the New Vulgate Bible. The verse outlines the events on one evening when people brought possessed persons to Jesus. He cast out evil spirits from them with his word and healed the sick among them.
2. Possessed individuals sometimes get new physical abilities. A possessed individual may become violent if driven out of his or her hiding place. For instance, a child can throw

four men off or lift heavy items. A provoked demon can react aggressively by lifting people or objects and throwing them across the room. The provoked demon may also carve words into walls or human skin.

3. Another sign of demonic possession is sudden changes in personality. The changes may manifest as aversion to religious items, violent outbursts, and sudden knowledge of archaic languages. Peaceful individuals may act out by threatening others with fear and violence or make lewd or obscene comments about them. The Greek word for demon is_*daemon,* which is sometimes translated to mean a fallen angel or an unclean spirit. Hence, it is not unusual for individuals who were once virtuous or spiritual to incur sudden changes in their normal behavior.

Topic: Demonic Possession—How Demons Take Control (Part 2)

Source: Wake Up America Seminars
Author: Larry W. Wilson
Date: August 2017 (Updated August 31, 2018)

Summary

- God gives each person gifts and talents at birth.
  - The demons want to use and twist these assets for evil purposes.
  - God's gifts include a measure of faith; the ability to hear the Holy Spirit; intelligence; the ability to reason, reanalyze, and remember; the capacity to love and be loved; and *most of all,* free will (Romans 12:3; John 16:13; Joshua 24:14; Revelation 22:17).
  - When a person reaches maturity, God's gifts and talents enable that person to be a self-directed adult who becomes responsible to God and his neighbors for his actions.

- The curse of sin mars God's gifts and talents in various ways
    - Each person is born with a propensity for selfishness, rebellion, and wrongdoing.
        - If this propensity is allowed to dominate God's gifts and talents, the results will be harmful.
        - Demons prey on our natural propensity to do wrong.
        - The shameful and vulgar ways of talented and gifted people today, a bulging prison population, and thousands of years of sordid history reveal their many successes.
- Demons understand free will.
    - Each deliberately *chose* to rebel against God.
    - Their greatest delight occurs when they can lead people to make foolish choices which can produce misery for a lifetime.
    - They carefully study us from birth to determine how best to most effectively mislead us, no matter how long that process takes.
    - They watch to see which temptations are most effective, which natural traits of character are most dominant, which opportunities for entrapment are most likely, and even monitor which kind of person an individual develops relationships with as relationships with the wrong people will increase the likelihood of making bad decisions (1 Corinthians 15:33).
    - They are intelligent and can speak their minds (Matthew 8:29; Luke 4:33, 34; Acts 19:15).
    - They are permitted to speak to human beings just as the Holy Spirit speaks to us.
        - Identifying sources of communication may be difficult.
        - Human imagination can create evil thoughts because all sinners have a natural propensity for doing wrong; demons can insert their knowledge of evil through the power of suggestion, though humanity can create evil thoughts on their own.

        - The Holy Spirit also uses the power of suggestion to put thoughts into our minds and prompts us to obey God, do what is right, and to think and do things that are beyond man's natural ability to think of good things to do.
- "Mob mentality" occurs when demons use the same evil thought to influence individuals within a group at the same time.
    - The power of suggestion leads to action, making the mob appear to act as if of "one mind."
    - Anger, hatred, violence, and destruction, combined with adrenaline-induced anger beyond reason.
    - Matthew 8:32—the pigs displayed "mob mentality" when Jesus sent the demons into them.
- Demons know our fears, weaknesses, likes, and dislikes and are masters of tempting and tormenting people accordingly.
    - They cannot penetrate the "hedge of protection" placed around us by God unless we willfully and knowingly do wrong, which removes this hedge and allows demonic influence to begin.
        - Willful continuation of wrongdoing weakens the hedge, allowing more access to us by the demons.
        - Free will allows us to choose to do what is wrong, but it also allows us to choose to do what is right, which allows God to repair the hedge and renew our protection from demonic attack.
- Billions of demons are hovering over humanity, ready to destroy.
    - People are desensitized to the decadent state of humanity and live lives totally unaware of lurking demons.
        - What is presented in media or given attention to around us—drug use, robberies, corporate crimes, political hatred, infighting, etc.—are deemed to be normal, and "the world is a crazy place."
        - First Peter 5:8 states the devil is behind this desensitization process.

- Mental illness and demonic oppression are not synonymous, though they may co-occur.
  - Demon possession can mimic mental illness.
- There are different degrees of demonic oppression and many different routes to oppression or possession.
  - The doorway is always free will.
  - Possession is always involuntary—demonic possession is a condition in which the victim can no longer exercise free will because demons have complete control (Matthew 8:28; Mark 1:23–26).
- Demonic oppression and possession are different in that oppression does not necessarily end in possession.
  - Oppression occurs when demons torment willful and deliberate sinners.
    - They agitate, incite, and upset the victims in various ways.
      - Rob a person of sleep, which creates a train of physical problems.
      - Magnify innate tendencies, such as paranoia to extreme states; an angry person becomes explosive and violent.
      - Rash and unpredictable behavior in which personality states are turned on and off.
- Special spiritual discernment from God is necessary to detect these oppressive spirits.
  - First Timothy 4:1—The spirit clearly says that in later times, some will abandon the faith and follow deceiving spirits and things taught by demons.
  - First Corinthians 12:8–11—To one there is given through the spirit the message of wisdom, to another the message of knowledge by means of the same spirit, to another gifts of healing by that one spirit, to another miraculous powers, to another prophecy, to another distinguishing between the spirits, to another speaking in different kinds of tongues, and to still another the interpretation of tongues. All these are the work of one

and the same spirit, and He has given them to each one, just as He determines.

- Oppression begins with knowingly and willingly choosing to do wrong and violate our conscience.
  - Demons begin with a gentle insertion of thought that becomes more aggressive over time.
  - Oppression continues until the victim stands up to these thoughts and stops doing what is wrong. God then causes the demons to back down; they must respect our free will.
  - Continued oppression and persistent choice of wrong over right hardens the heart against God and makes the victim more vulnerable to the demons.
  - Oppression only ends when a victim repents of sin and determines to live by faith through forgiveness of sin and acceptance of the authority of Jesus Christ as Savior.
    - The individual is given additional strength to fight the good fight of faith.
- Demonic oppression can begin with an innocent violation of free will through addictive devices such as tobacco, drugs, alcohol, pornography, or violent movies and games; or it may start with exploring the occult, sexual lust that leads to sexual immorality or through abusive and unloving parents (care providers).
- Children are often targeted because they can grow up to hurt their own children.
  - Demon-possessed parents can make a child feel self-loathing and shameful, which results in the child having no self-esteem, self-worth, or self-value.
  - Evil parents can physically, sexually, and emotionally abuse a child, resulting in great psychological damage, causing a child to inordinately thirst for love and friendship, good or bad.
- Matthew 9:32 and 12:22 demonstrate that in ancient times, certain physical defects or illnesses were to be the

result of demonic possession. This is still true in certain parts of the world today.

- Matthew 17:13–20; Mark 9:17–29; Luke 9:38–42—Jesus heals a boy who suffered from a condition that caused him to foam at the mouth and fall involuntarily into water or fire; the father believed his son to be demon-possessed and took him to Jesus's disciples, who could not heal the child; Jesus rebuked the demon, and the boy was healed.
- Luke 9:1 commissioned the disciples to heal sickness and cast out demons, which had drawn the attention of this father, yet the disciples could not heal the boy.
- Jesus reminded the disciples that the power to cast out demons came from God and at God's discretion; God had chosen that this demon be cast out by Jesus, not the disciples.
- God uses men; men do not use God.

- Demonic prompting can lead a person to do a greater evil than would be within that person's normal range of behavior, prompting denial by the individual when confronted with proof of indiscretion.
    - Demons keep careful watch of when an individual is unaware of a lowered expectation and expression of a baser behavior and pushes just a little more the next time opportunity arises, causing the event to be minimized and forgotten, resulting in a downward spiral of character that leads to greater and greater transgressions.
    - Everyone who sins becomes a slave to sin (John 8:34).
- When an individual is freed of demonic oppression, the next step is to prevent it from reoccurring (Matthew 12:43–44).
    - The sin must be forever severed from the person, even if it means changing jobs, friends, and possibly separation from family for a time to allow God to work in and through the individual to strengthen them against renewed attacks.

The Skeptic

A man must not swallow more
beliefs than he can digest.

—Havelock Ellis, *The Dance of life*

The people of Satan's Den are true believers in the things of the supernatural, even those who move in from outside. Eventually, everyone is struck close to home by some tragedy or chance encounter with a devil or ghost. There are some families that have been here since its settlement well over two hundred years ago, nearly three now. People remain tight-lipped when it comes to these things. It's just not told to strangers. What happens in Satan's Den stays in Satan's Den.

Our next encounter took place not long after the turn of the twentieth century. Spiritualism was on the rise, and high society was jumping on the bandwagon—holding séances, attending meetings with like-minded folks. It was in vogue to pursue the deceased. The great Harry Houdini was one such seeker. His pursuit, however, was as a debunker. He would observe a séance by a medium, then reveal all the tricks that had been used to deceive the eager audience. Before he died of a ruptured appendix, Houdini vowed to communicate with his wife, Bess, when he reached the other side—if there was some way to truly contact the dead. He died on Halloween in 1926. Every year, on Halloween, Bess held a séance to try to hear from her beloved Harry. She died, having proven there was no communication with the dead, and anyone who believed otherwise was being deceived by money-grubbing hucksters. Even today, a group of Houdini fans holds a séance to try and communicate with the great magician or his beloved wife. There has never been a response.

Prominent universities took up the study of the supernatural as a science to prove beyond the shadow of a doubt that the supernatural was no more than science, utilized in such a manner as to be frightening and misunderstood. One of these scientists—a psychologist by the name of Dr. Emmanuel Babbitch of Boston—sought out the town of Satan's Den when its reputation was brought to his attention by a man of the town who had claimed he could prove to the good doctor that there was truth in the supernatural. Science could not explain the things experienced in his community. It was relentlessly haunted and uncommonly full of tragedy. The doctor was so moved by the man's petition he arranged to spend some time in Satan's Den, not out of professional curiosity but as a skeptic so sure of science that he could set the people straight. And so begins our story.

Dr. Emmanuel Babbitch stood in the center of the parlor, his back to a warming fire in the overly large fireplace. His hands were clasped behind his back; his legs at shoulder-width as if to balance the barrel-chested body. While the doctor appeared at ease, the two well-dressed couples that sat on durable and expensive divans on either side of him appeared less sure of themselves.

"There are no such things as ghosts," Dr. Babbitch began. "They are merely figments of a guilty conscience. We all have our secret sins, and they may manifest themselves as auditory and visual illusions that are harmful only if we allow our secret sins to consume us rather than freeing ourselves by confessing them."

"How can we be so certain, Dr. Babbitch? Aren't such things private?" The inquirer was John Adam Brown, homeowner and writer of the letter that had brought the doctor to Satan's Den.

"Simple, careful observation of the habits of those around you will give you the subtlest of clues that will ultimately reveal the hidden secret. For example, Mrs. Brown..." He addressed Amelia, his hostess.

She stiffened slightly as she was singled out. She held her breath in anticipation of the next words from the doctor. John Adam studied his wife curiously. He had never seen her this anxious before.

"Mrs. Brown," the doctor pressed. "What is in the drawer of the side table beside the divan Mr. and Mrs. Scott are occupying?"

"Why...," she stammered. "I assume, maybe needles and thread. I...usually keep some there for quick fixes that don't require me to get out my sewing basket."

"So if I were to open the drawer in question, I would find only needles and thread. Perhaps some sewing scissors?"

"I...suppose so."

The doctor moved to the tall side table with a single drawer in its upper section and open shelving beneath. He reached for the knob and began to pull the drawer open. Before he could open it far enough to glimpse the contents, Mrs. Brown let out a tiny moan. It was barely audible yet drew the attention of the other adults present.

She squeezed her eyes shut and whispered a simple "Please..."

"What is in this drawer that you don't wish anyone to see, Mrs. Brown?"

Tears formed in Amelia Brown's eyes, threatening to slip through her lashes and onto her cheek.

The drawer slid open a little further.

"Wait!" Amelia cried out. "I'll tell you. I feel so ashamed. I keep a journal there."

John Adam took his wife's hand.

"Darling," he said comfortingly. "There is no shame in keeping a journal. Many people do."

She met his eyes as the tears broke loose. "I know, but this one is so personal. I just don't think it would be of any interest to anyone other than myself."

"What could be so personal that you could not share it with your husband?"

Her pale face became flushed with embarrassment. She lowered her eyes to where her husband held her hand. "It's just...that I... sometimes...write...stories."

The truth came from her slowly and painfully.

"Stories? What kind of stories?" John Adam was more curious than concerned.

"Romance," she mumbled.

"Romance? Did you say romance?"

"Yes," she squeaked.

John Adam broke the intensity of the moment with a raucous laugh. "My wife writes romances," he stated proudly. Then to his wife, he said, "Why did you feel the need to hide them from me? You know I am always proud of you, proud to be your husband."

"I know, but…they are so silly. You are classically educated, the owner of a lucrative lumber mill, the master of your home. I am but your humble wife, educated only in the things necessary to run a household and raise children. Nothing I write could meet your expectations of propriety."

"Sweetheart, your thoughts and feelings produced the words upon each page, I will treasure them all the more for being yours. That's all that really matters."

Amelia contemplated her husband's words. Feeling calmer, she lifted her eyes to meet her accuser. "How did you know—?"

The doctor gave a harrumph.

"My dear, your eyes tended to this drawer many times during our conversation. You appeared distracted at times and scratched at your hands as if in anticipation of holding something. Though I did not know about your journal. So you see, the interpretation of your observations can be a form of self-fulfilling prophecy.

"Oh, poo," interjected Emily Scott from her place next to her husband, Errol. "It's all well and good to interpret what you see, but how does that apply to what you don't see? Like ghosts."

"Your brain senses your environment and tries to make sense of it. It names what it recognizes and files the unfamiliar as unknown. When fear or anxiety accompanies the unknown, a ghost is created."

Dr. Babbitch smirked as he hooked his thumbs in his vest pockets and proudly thrust out his chest.

"Hmmm." Errol Scott hummed thoughtfully. "Have you ever been in a position to experience the unknown? Perhaps sitting in the dark when an unexpected moan sounds behind you, yet you are home alone. Or perhaps, you awaken in the middle of the night to see a pale figure standing over you, a faceless phantom that slowly fades away as you watch."

The doctor grumpily cleared his throat before responding to the challenge presented.

"In the first case, only the wind blowing down the chimney could have produced a low moan under the right conditions. As to the second, it can easily be explained by an extra white nightshirt hanging on a peg beside the bed. The fullness of the moon piercing through the window illuminated it, making it appear as if alive. As a cloud passes over the moon, the figure appears to fade away as the amount of light is slowly snuffed. The figure appears to be faceless due to the shadowing of the neckhole drooping forward from the peg."

"While all that makes simple sense, how would you interpret a series of events that have no real or logical explanation?"

"My explanations are all based on observations and interpretations, so I suppose I would need to be present at the manifestations in order to debunk them for you."

Errol Scott leaned forward in his seat, making eye contact with his business partner and best friend, John Adam Brown. They nodded to each other conspiratorially.

"There is a place...," Errol drolly began. "Almost everyone says it is haunted. Those that don't say it out loud think it to themselves. The cabin has such a reputation that young people refrain from daring one another to enter it. Too many have taken the challenge and not lived to talk about it. At least, they were presumed dead. No one ever saw them leave the house, and no one ever saw them again."

The doctor contemplated his options.

"How close are we to this cabin you speak of? Would it be possible to go tonight? I wouldn't want to give anyone time to set up an elaborate hoax, after all."

The twinkle of delight in the doctor's eyes assured the local men that he had taken their bait.

"Very well then." John Adam smiled. "I will have the touring carriage hitched immediately, and we shall go. It is two hours before midnight, so we shall have no trouble with our timing."

When their host had left the room to make arrangements, the doctor rubbed his hands together in anticipation. Amelia and Emily sent for their warmest wraps as the nights could become quite cool.

"Are you ladies accompanying us then?" the doctor inquired.

"Of course," replied Amelia.

"I wouldn't miss it for anything." Emily giggled.

"Are you certain you should be going in your condition, Mrs. Scott. This little trip is not for the faint of heart or those of delicate constitution."

"I beg your pardon," Emily huffed. "I assure you I am no frail Southern Belle to faint at the hint of scandal."

"I assure you, madame," the doctor retracted, "you are as healthy as you appear. It is the wee babe you carry that I am concerned about."

Emily strangled on the words that tried to come from her mouth. It was Errol who came to her rescue.

"How dare you to be so familiar with my wife's health. If she were expecting, I do believe I would know of it!" Turning to his wife in disbelief he said, "Wouldn't I?"

Emily blushed and pressed her hands to her abdomen.

"I don't…I'm not…oh, maybe…," she said. "I'm not certain yet, but it does appear I may be with child."

A broad grin broke out on Errol's face as he took his wife in his arms and hugged her to himself.

"Darling! How wonderful! When…?" He broke off and turned back to the doctor. "You are not a physician, and you have not examined my wife. How could you tell? Do you also read minds?"

"Alas, no, sir. I simply observed her throughout dinner and our subsequent discussion. First, she ate very little of a scrumptious repast and was very pale when the more pungent items were served. She has frequently stroked her abdomen or held her hand over it gently, as would a woman in the family way. I assumed you already knew the news but were not ready to reveal it. I apologize for letting the cat out of the bag."

"You are quite forgiven, Doctor," Errol assured the older man. "These are all things I should have already been aware of as her husband. You have humbled me and reminded me of my place as her husband."

The doctor nodded in acquiescence.

"As to the event at hand, my wife is capable of judging her suitability for participation."

Emily smiled a quiet smile. "Wild dogs couldn't keep me away," she said.

John Adam returned at that moment and announced the preparedness of the carriage.

The night was clear, and a cool breeze brought the couples closer together. Having no partner, the doctor pulled his overcoat more tightly about himself. The matched pair of blacks blended with the shadows, giving them unnatural movement that fueled the expectancies of the ghost hunters and the one great skeptic. The driver turned down an overgrown rutted path. Branches reached out to the passengers, snatching at them as they passed. The women were all a-giggle, the men teasing them with "ghost" sightings along the way. Early autumn was a delightful time for a late-night excursion.

The cabin loomed up out of the darkness, a skeletal tower peering from empty, glassless eyes and a gaping mouth where the front door once stood. It had been two stories tall, but the roof had caved in on itself, giving the building a hunchbacked look. The clearing where the house sat had become tangled and overgrown through ages of neglect. The carriage driver was forced to stop just inside the crowded space. There was scarce allowance to turn the carriage as it was. The passengers were forced to disembark and wade through the tangle in order to achieve their goal of entering the desolate cabin.

"Tell me about this magnificent masterpiece." The doctor's voice was gleeful.

John Adam took up the narrative. "As far as anyone knows, this cabin has been here since before the town itself began. It hasn't been occupied in all that time. People have tried to settle the land here, but they have never succeeded. Every tree cut for building rotted overnight. Those who camped here to prepare for settlement had their livestock slaughtered in the night, despite a watch. Some people grew sick unto death after spending time here. After a time, people stopped trying to settle this spot and moved closer to town. All that's left are tales told by old-timers to scare youngsters on stormy nights."

There was neither porch nor stairs leading to the front door. The threshold was only inches off the ground, allowing a person to simply step into the house without breaking stride. John Adam did not step blindly into the house, however; he stopped on its verge and thrust the carriage lantern he was carrying into the ebony abyss. The darkness was so dense that the light appeared to have been cut from paper and pasted to a black background. The light was absorbed by the darkness.

Dr. Babbitch pushed his way past the others and stuck his head into the darkness. Laughing in anticipation, he stepped inside and was engulfed by the darkness. The ladies gasped at the illusion and held hands as they drew closer to one another. Their husbands followed the doctor's example. The light moved out of their line of sight. Eyes wide and shivering from head to toe, the ladies inhaled deeply and stepped into the black interior.

The floating lantern drew them to the back of the moderately sized room where the men had found a small square table with four chairs. All were rough-hewn and very old but still solid-looking. The husbands had thoughtfully pulled out chairs for their more delicate wives to sit in. The women perched on their chairs tentatively on either side of the table, their husbands within reach. The doctor stood behind the chair pulled up to the table between the two other men. He leaned expectantly on the chair.

No one dared move or make a noise. The empty darkness became pregnant with anticipation. The silence of death surrounded them, crowding them closer together.

At first, there was just a whisper of sound that slowly became the clawing of tiny feet within the log walls.

"Mice," whispered the doctor appreciatively.

"In the logs?" questioned Errol, trying to point out the flaw in the doctor's reasoning.

John Adam shrugged.

The tiny clawing became louder and more persistent. Something big was trying to dig its way out of the hardwood the cabin had been built from. The tearing and ripping of wood became nearly unbearably loud. All but the doctor covered their ears with their hands to try and block the sound from reaching their stressed and strained brains and spare themselves the increasing agony of the unseen creatures trying to join them in the darkness.

The women began to weep and moan in response to the excruciating pressure. Their moans were joined by the unseen entities around them until the moaning and crying overtook the clawing, and the clawing faded away. A cold breeze spun around the observers, causing their breath to come out in white-cold streams of steamy fog. The women shivered so strongly now their chairs rocked back and forth beneath them. Errol and John Adam feared for their wives at this point, particularly Emily, with a child on the way. Touching the ladies' shoulders with a hand and giving a gentle lift, the men guided them to the open door. They stumbled some in the darkness but eventually found the open portal to the real-world night they had so recently left. The women stepped quickly over the threshold. Clinging to one another, they pushed themselves forward to the comfort of the touring carriage and the safety of the carriage driver.

Back inside, the men were once again established at the table. Silence had returned. It was merely an intermission that allowed the women to make their exit. Act 2 began with Dr. Babbitch's criticism.

"Is that all you've got?" he cried out to the abyss. "Lousy noises that could just as easily be the wind flowing down the chimney and out the fireplace. The sheer size of the thing is enough to produce that level of sound."

The fireplace the doctor referred to was directly behind the table where the men stood. It was wide and tall enough for all three men to stand abreast. The blackened hearth held years of ashes concreted to its surface and a cast-iron cauldron with a fitted lid still hung from the hook it had become welded to from rust. The hinge that held it to the stone wall of the fireplace had also become corroded. Nothing would move that cauldron from its frozen position ever again. The fieldstone used to create the fireplace facade were blackened where flames had once burnished them. Other stones were blackened from age and neglect. Any wind issuing from that fireplace with strength to create the moans they had heard would have blown over anything in its path. The men had felt nothing.

"Show yourselves!" the doctor provoked. "Show us what you are made of!"

There was a loud thud from upstairs, followed by a softer thunk. Shuffling footsteps crossed the ceiling above the men's heads. They knew the upstairs was inaccessible due to the roof collapse. There was no way for anything living to be up there and make that much noise. When the footsteps reached the narrow staircase and started down to the main room, the darkness receded to allow the observers to see the steps clearly by their lantern light. The heavy steps, accompanied by a soft shuffle, continued their downward trek. No physical bodies accompanied the echoing footsteps. At the bottom of the steps, the unseen feet shuffled for position before falling silent.

Dr. Emanuel Babbitch's eyes glowed with excitement. Perspiration slid down his face in contrast with the frozen exhales of breath emitted by his mouth. Errol and John Adam did not share this state. They stood riveted to their places, growing paler and bluer with the fleeting autumn coolness to deep winter temperatures.

"Ah, there you are," said the pleased doctor. "So glad you could finally join us. You see, I came here specially to meet you. My young friends here have been unable to fill me in on your story. I would be much obliged if you were to share it with me."

There was no response.

"Come on, cat got your tongue? Or are ghosts not able to speak?"

Still no response.

"Can you at least show us what you look like? I've never seen an apparition before. I hear they are quite frightening. I am not afraid of you, and you have no reason to fear me. I only want to believe in you."

What sounded like a gravelly laugh filled the air. It was not of a friendly nature.

"Come, now," the doctor cajoled. "I have given you the privilege of seeing my personage. Now let me see yours."

An air of hesitancy was followed by the silvery shimmer of a thin shaft of mist. A second, smaller shimmer appeared beside the first. The larger shaft grew tall and broad as it took shape. The image of a man, maybe fifty years of age but looking much older from a hard life and harder work, seemed to solidify before the amazed doctor and his astonished friends.

The man had dirty, dark hair, unkempt and hanging to his shoulders. Heavy, dark brows overshadowed the depth of his sunken eyes. Dark-brown pinpoints of light glared from their darkness. A broad nose flared above a mouth with full lips, now dry and cracked with the drought brought by death. They were pale caterpillars crawling parallel to one another across his unshaven face. His beard was somewhere between "I forgot to shave this week" and an intentional growth of hair. Gray streaked the hair on his head as well as the beard and moustache on his gaunt but once blocky chin. The upper portion of faded and torn long johns hung loosely over atrophied musculature that had once been impressive. Large bony hands extended well past the hems of the sleeves. The fingernails still bore the dirt of farming and the calluses of labor. Homespun pants slouched around his narrowed hips and long legs. Streaks of dirt and mud overshadowed patching and darning. Quite large work boots had made the louder thuds on the stairs. They, too, were dried out and peeling from age and use.

The smaller shimmer came into focus as a woman, approximately half the age of the man she was standing beside. Her dirt-brown hair sprang wildly from the loose knot at the back of her head. Her eyes were a glowing emerald green. Thin eyebrows punctuated them with a look of perpetual surprise. The skin of her face was dried parchment stretched tautly over her more delicate skull. High cheekbones framed what was left of a delicate button nose, which was little more than nasal slits created by dried cartilage. Particularly thin lips had been pulled back by her shrinking skin to reveal the missing teeth in her mouth. She was not toothless but had lost enough molars to have made chewing dense food difficult for her. A long, thin neck attached her head to narrow shoulders and a sagging bosom. Scrawny arms beneath a dust-colored blouse ended in hands that were more skeleton than skin. The fingers had been long and elegant once upon a time. The nails were shorter than they should have been and were ragged as if she had been digging with her bare hands. A mud-brown skirt and dingy apron covered in unimaginable stains offset the delicate, slender hips. Her feet were bare and covered in nearly transparent skin. She may have been quite attractive before the hardships of life had taken its toll on her.

"I see you!" the awed doctor whispered in a stage voice.

The other two men were just as awed. They had never dreamed of seeing the sights they had seen on this night. Deep within, they each were grateful their wives had departed when they had. Else, their nightmares would haunt them for years to come. Neither relished dealing with a distraught woman night after night.

The doctor pushed his way past Errol Scott, who was closest to where the apparitions had manifested. He stopped just short of touching the two people before him. Both were taller than he was. Puzzled, he looked down and was surprised to discover that the spirits stood eighteen inches above the floor, with nothing to keep them there! He stretched out a hand to touch the male but pulled it back quickly when he encountered the frostbite-cold aura that oozed from the couple. He stepped backward to evade the frigid emission.

"Can you speak?" The doctor was flushed with delight.

The man nodded.

"Tell me—us—your story. We really want to know…so we can help you."

A rusty, gravelly voice creaked from the man's long-unused vocal cords. "It's been sooo long…" He sighed sadly.

"Sssoooo long…" the woman's husky voice echoed.

"We came to this place to be the first ones here. To be alone, just us two."

"Sssoo lonely." The woman's voice was hollow with sadness.

"Even the Injuns left us alone. Oh, they'd pass through, but they never stopped. We made a good go of it. Grew our own food, raised our own meat, and milked a cow. Didn't need no well 'cause water was plentiful in the crick behind us."

"Water…," the woman whispered longingly. "So thirsty…"

"It was all goin' good till it went bad. The crops failed. We et what we had put by. When that was gone, we started on the livestock. The horses was the last to go. We nearly died that winter. If it weren't for the trappers acomin' through, we'd a been gone fer certain."

"So hungry…," groaned the woman.

"Them trappers travel alone, you know. Most are old and grizzled, but they's enough young'uns to satisfy us. We'd take 'em in, an' they'd share the tack they had with us. They slept on a pallet in front of the fireplace in the luxury of a real home."

The pride in the man's voice made the doctor smile. City-born and raised, the doctor had no clue how hard life on the frontier could be, especially in those early days of exploration. John Adam and Errol knew about hard living. They had worked themselves up from the field to the co-ownership of a successful lumber mill. They were more empathetic with the plight of this deceased couple.

"They never stayed more'n a night. They was always gone afore the sun come up, but we made due for a time after that. My woman here is a real good cook. She could make a stew from a rock and a cauldron of water. Add a bit of meat and bone, and a man could et for days."

Errol and John Adam exchanged glances at this revelation. They turned to stare at the cauldron waiting patiently for its next stew, boiled over a roaring fire. They felt their stomachs churn.

Unaffected by the tale so far, the doctor urged the spirit to continue.

"Can't say how many trappers came and went, but spring found us near starvation. Didn't have no seed to plant, no horse to pull a plow. Not even manhood left in me to try. She was the first to take to bed. Couldn't do nothin' no more. She made me promise if she was the first to go that I would see that she was taken good care of. It didn't take long. When she had gone, I was able to go a few days more afore I took to my bed. There was no one to take care of me the way I had had took care of her and the way we had took care of them trappers. I passed on alone and empty inside. When the darkness was claimin' my soul, she was a'waitin' for me. We been here ever since. Doin' our penance."

The doctor was astonished at that. "Why are you doing penance? Didn't you find the peace you deserved? Wasn't there a heaven or a hell to go to? Where was God in all this?"

"'Twas God that declared our penance. We had sold our souls to the devil just to survive as long as we done. It come at a higher price that we imagined."

"Doooomed...," the woman wailed. "We are doooomed to never rest again."

"You mean you can't do your penance and then move on to something better? How horrible! What do you do for your penance? How can I—we—help you?" The doctor was truly concerned for these lost souls. His skepticism had been overruled by his human sympathy.

"We hunger," the woman responded.

"We wait here...waiting...waiting...always hungry. We must eat...or we suffer."

"What do you need? I can provide it for you. I have enough wealth to fill your bodies sufficiently for a long while."

"We only have one desire," the man declared.

"What's that?"

The woman's skin creaked as she leaned forward and stretched her hand out to the doctor. He took her bony hand in his.

"Your soul..." She grinned, revealing more of the missing teeth in her mouth.

Realizing what was happening, Errol and John Adam rushed forward and grabbed at the doctor's coat. They tried to pull him away from the wraiths that now floated before them. The sorrowful couple that had manifested had transformed into hideous blood-sucking, soul-eating creatures hell-bent on consuming the doctor as they had consumed the trappers long ago. The doctor was frozen in place, abject fear drawing his face into a caricature of himself.

Errol and John Adam tried to pull the doctor off his feet so they could carry him from the cabin. They failed. The woman had already wrapped her arms around the doctor and was greedily sucking the breath from his body. The man floated toward Errol and John Adam, arms outstretched, tongue licking at the dry dusty lips.

Errol was the first to release the doctor and began backing away. He grabbed John Adam's elbow as he went, alerting his friend to the danger. John Adam had no difficulty releasing the doctor and backing away himself. Leaving the burning lantern on the table, the two men stumbled their way to the door and fell out on the overgrown path they had previously trod. They ran to their wives in the touring carriage and ordered the driver to get them as far away as possible from this evil place. They climbed into the carriage as it began to move and threw themselves into the seats beside their wives.

The women were wide-eyed and were crying profusely on their husband's shoulders. The men clung to their wives, trying to shelter them from the blood-curdling scream that was the doctor's last breath on this earth.

Morning found the four adults sitting in the same divans they had sat on the night before. The fire was out, and the hearth was cold. The friends still wore their coats from the night before. No one had lit a candle or spoken a word. When the housekeeper discovered them, she assisted her mistress upstairs to bed and called for the cook's husband to assist with John Adam. The Scotts were taken home in their own carriage and cared for by their own servants.

Slowly, over time, they all recovered from the shock of their experience, although their lives were dramatically altered. They never spoke of that night, not even when an inquiry into the doctor's disappearance was made.

The story emerged many years later, only after a young boy, playing cowboys and Indians with his friends, scaled a large boulder and discovered a mysterious symbol covered by centuries of moss.

John 20:24–31, NKJV

> Now Thomas, called the twin, one of the twelve, was not with them when Jesus came. The other disciples therefore said to him, "We have seen the Lord.'
>
> So he said to them, "Unless I see in His hands the print of the nails, and put my finger into the print of the nails, and put my hand into His side, I will not believe."
>
> And after eight days His disciples were again inside, and Thomas with them. Jesus came, the doors being shut, and stood in the midst, and said, "Peace to you!" Then he said to Thomas,

> "Reach your finger here, and look at my hands, and reach your hand here into my side. Do not be unbelieving, but believing."
>
> And Thomas answered and said to him, "My Lord and my God!"
>
> Jesus said to him, "Thomas, because you have seen me, you have believed. Blessed are those who have not seen and yet have believed."

Notes of Lurlene Joy McCoy

Some people never learn. When all evidence is on the table and the jury allowed to review it in order to produce a verdict, human free will becomes crucial. A jurist seeking truth will find it and act upon it. One who is unsure and still in need of time to think and reason will delay with questions and the seeking of a verdict that will allow them to live with themselves in continued uncertainty but the self-content of having done their best, whatever that means. Then there is the jurist who refuses to see nothing but lies and will torment others with their belief that all evidence, no matter how convincing and reasonable, is wrong, simply because they choose to disagree with the presentation. This type of scenario ultimately ends in a hung jury. There is no agreement, no verdict, and no consequences or answers. For a criminal, a hung jury is a dream come true as they are able to walk away from accusations and the legal process that fails to condemn him. He is exonerated. He gets the idea that he is somehow above the law. This is our skeptic.

Dr. Emanuel Babbitch had studied medicine and then became an expert on the human mind and its intricate workings. He felt he was so secure in his belief in science and the answers found within its laboratories that there was nothing that could not be experimented upon and observed to discover rational, reasonable, and explainable cause and effect. He was so secure in his ability to see through all that is unknown to discover the known behind it that he was willing to seek out and experience the unknown for himself.

This is natural for humanity in its fallen state. The initial lie in Eden was to question God's faith in humanity by proving humanity could not trust God. The serpent asked Eve if it was true that God had forbidden the man and woman to eat from all the fruit of the garden. He then pointed out to her the consequence God had given for eating that fruit and implied that God had lied to them. Finally, he convinced Eve there was nothing wrong with the fruit of the Tree of the Knowledge of Good and Evil. Here was the first courtroom trial. The serpent prosecutor examined witness Eve with leading questions that were designed to fill her mind with doubt. Eve fell for this ploy as she had no experience with anything other than a benevolent God who had provided all she had needed. The questioning made her doubt what she believed to be truth, which led to her questioning of her own loyalty to God and the decision that there was no crime in wanting to be like her benevolent God by eating of a fruit that would make her so.

There was an incongruency in the facts as presented by her Creator and the slightly varied facts presented by her accuser. It was a tough call. Her jury of one chose to eat the fruit. She then gave it to her husband, who had watched the trial unfold, and he ate the fruit. They chose the lies over truth. Free will allowed them to weigh their options and choose for themselves. All this took place in front of the Judge Himself. The Judge then gave forth the verdict—guilty—and doled out the consequences for their poor choices.

Mankind has progressed far beyond that first courtroom. We have grown in knowledge and understanding of the world around us. There are many things we have not come to understand, however, and it bothers us. That fruit that was supposed to make us like gods has, instead, given us fragmented understanding of our world, albeit more greatly understood as technology opens up new pathways for gaining knowledge. Knowledge does not equate wisdom. Knowledge does not equate power. We have not become like gods, except in our own minds. We believe we can achieve the state of godhead if only we know "a little more" about something. We believe the next big breakthrough will reveal to us all the answers. We continue to fail in that pursuit. And we always will.

The tree bore fruit of the *Knowledge* of Good and Evil. We have discovered that knowledge is meaningless without the recognition of *good and evil.* We must recognize these opposing forces exist. We must recognize that the wrong choice will lead us down the spiral of evil that ultimately results in the loss of our humanity and the proper choice which draws us closer to our Creator, whose image we bear. The closer we follow His guidance and obey His precepts, the more we become like God.

Sadly, there are those who fail to understand how this continuum works. They believe only in their own efforts. They demand evidence, then deny evidential proof. Even when faced with ultimate irrefutable truth, they turn a blind eye and walk away unenlightened, more ignorant than before. Knowledge is their god; ignorance is their worship.

Topic: A Message from Hell to You from the Fire of Hell Past Redemption Point

Author: Dr. Bryam H. Glaze
Date: Unconfirmed

Dear Unregenerate Soul

My name is Dives, and I lived over two thousand years ago. But I know you will be interested in my life's story and my present condition.

I was born in Palestine of rich Jewish parents, five years before Christ was born. My father and mother had six sons born into their home. I was the oldest and was the first to die while in my middle thirties.

My father was very rich and devoted most of his time to his "god"—making money. He did not have time for any of us boys. Never do I remember his having taken time with us for play or for teaching us the right things in life. He did not find much time for religion and left the home and children with my mother. Mother, being wealthy, attractive, and educated, was invited to join all the clubs for women in the city. She spent most of the day away from home attending teas, luncheons, parties, and other social functions, leaving us boys with a maid who did not care about us so that we did as we pleased. Father told us boys not to associate with the poor trash in our community or with our poor kinfolk. He said we were better than most people. But he did not care about how wicked and mean our rich associates were. The older boys and girls taught me to drink, use dope, commit adultery, and curse, but Father did not worry or seem to know about these things. Mother and Father never had much time for each other. Mother seemed to live for the praise of women and every night wanted to tell us how the women complimented her during the day. My parents tried to go to the synagogue and to the temple once a year. My dad would give a donation each time when he went, and the rabbi seemed to think he was a very nice fellow. His donations were always small in comparison to what his tithes should have been.

Because my parents did not have much time at home and never taught us the better things of life, I soon fell into bad company and sin. Father always gave me anything I wanted just to get me to not disturb him while he thought of another scheme to make money. He disobeyed God and desecrated the Sabbath by keeping his business open seven days a week. Early in my life, he bought me the finest horse and chariot that Egypt produced. I was the envy of all the boys in our city and had more friends than any other boy. I wanted to take trips into foreign countries and all across our nation. Once, I went to Rome to see the capital of the world.

I was not more than fifteen years of age before I started drinking and living a very sinful and wicked life. I seemed to have more girlfriends than I knew what to do with. When I went into foreign countries, I always found the places where the wild parties were being held. Assured of plenty of wine and a beautiful girl, we had a good time sinning and fulfilling the lusts of the flesh. I thought I was young, handsome, smart, and tough, and that being rich, I could do anything and get away with it where others could not.

The only time I ever remember hearing my father say anything about religion was when someone invited him and his family over to the synagogue. He told the man he went once a year and gave for its support. Then he told the man he did not believe in forcing religion on his children. Therefore, he did not send them to religious services. He said, "When they grow up, if they want religion, they can choose the kind they want." He seemed to say this with a great deal of pride. His closing statement went something like this. "I hear the Pharisees and Sadducees as to which is right that I don't want much religion." As a result, I never gave religion a thought. I thought Father was a very smart fellow, successful in making money, and if he could live and die without it, that religion was surely not important or worthwhile for an intelligent young man who wanted to have a good time in life.

One day, everybody began to talk about a strange prophet who was baptizing in Jordan. The people thought he was the Messiah, but he denied being such and said, "The Messiah will be coming soon." Not many weeks later, the man appeared, and the prophet announced that this man was the Messiah. There was much discussion over Him. Those who loved Him would die for Him, while those who hated Him wanted to kill Him. The religious leaders of our nation, the Pharisees, were doing all they could to have Him put to death. Father said He was a troublemaker and would come to no good end, so I dismissed religion from my mind again.

By the time I was twenty, I was well on my way to being a first-class drunkard. My body was diseased, and I went to a doctor each week. But I continued my high living and good times, sowing my wild oats, staying out late into the night, not thinking of death or harvest time. I began to use dope with the gang. By the time I was thirty-five, I could hardly go, and I died in awful pain two days after my thirty-sixth birthday.

Death did not keep me from being conscious. I seemed to enter into another body that could not die and fire could not destroy. As I lay dying, suffering such awful pain in my body, the devil and his demons came for my soul to torment me. I heard the demons arguing with the devil as to which would take me into OUTER DARKNESS and the PIT OF HELL. Finally, the devil gave permission to carry my soul to the place which seemed to be a furnace of fire, and when he had finished speaking with the demon, I stopped breathing. The demon grabbed my soul, and in hellish glee and gladness, he traveled faster than light, rejoicing that he could carry my soul to the FLAMES.

In seconds or less time, he had cast me into a place so dark I could not see anything except in a distance.

I thought the demon had cast me into a LARGE DARK FURNACE OR BLACK FIRE AND SMOKE.

There seemed to be tens of millions of other people there screaming in the fire of the dark pit. When the demon threw me into the darkness, I thought surely I would soon hit the sides or bottom and dash my brains out. Then I fell feetfirst for a while, again backward, face downward. Then I seemed to spin round and round like a windmill. I have been falling through smoke ever since, bumping other millions as they fall.

Soon after my arrival in the fire, I passed the great gulf that separates me from the beautiful lighted place across the gulf which I saw when I was first cast into the darkness. I saw the father of our nation over on the other side with millions of other happy people. There was a man with Father Abraham whom I knew back on earth. He was a beggar and was placed on the street in front of our door. Every time I went by him, he would beg for food, but I did not have time to be bothered with him. When I saw him, I called to Father Abraham and asked for Lazarus to come over and put just one drop of water on my parched and burned tongue, but he wasn't allowed to do so.

For two thousand years—they seem like millions—I have been in this awful place without getting one drink of water, one wink of sleep, or one mouthful of food. Every minute of the time, you hear the shrieks and screams of the damned, sounding like raving maniacs being tortured. People pour into this place every second by the thousands from the earth like grain from a hopper. You should hear them scream when they first hit the fire and have a sensation of falling. As I fall through the fire, I come in contact with those just from the earth, and they tell me of all the changes on earth. The modern inventions amaze me. The people are still living for the devil, refusing to listen to the preachers or go to church—just like I did. My heart aches, and my mind is troubled to know that people will not listen. Father Abraham told me that preaching was the only method God had for me to know the plan of salvation. Millions of young people from all nations are coming here in their early teens and twenties—just boys and girls. All of them had no time for God on the earth. They lived as though they would never die, and now it is too late. They come from ungodly homes where parents are godless.

I have come to believe we are locked in the heart of the center of the earth, and as the earth spins through space, we are continually falling through the fire. It is like rolling a barrel about three-fourths full of apples. They roll over one another; so do we here. We call this place the BOTTOMLESS PIT!

I had not been in hell many years until the man who was called the Messiah back on earth, when I was living there, came to be with Abraham for a very brief period of time. Then all at once, he took all the people who were so happy and disappeared with them. From that time, we have not seen one ray of light. I have had that nerve-racking sensation of falling all this time. Never have I been able to put my feet on anything solid, nor have I been able to rest my head or body on anything solid. Every time I open my mouth, I swallow fire into my stomach. My lungs are filled with fire every time I breathe. I am covered in fire like someone covered underwater. My body has been tormented until my nerves seem to be leaping like wild steeds at night whipped by crazy men. My head is so hot until my mind and thoughts seem to run on hot wires. The entire body feels as if it had been baked, for a million years. My eyes feel like hot balls of fire ready to burst as the smoke and fire torture them. As I fell through fire, smoke, and space, I fell onto something like a horse with iron scales and woman's hair and a tail with great stings to torment us even more than the fire. One day, these horrible creatures will come to earth to torment people there for five months. One time, I fell onto an angel tied on the hands and feet with chains. I held to his chains for a while as we fell through space and fire bumping into millions of other lost people. Between the horrible sensation of falling and grabbing for something solid and screaming with anguished pain, I talked to the angel. He told me that he had been a holy angel in God's presence doing His will at one time. At that time, the devil was the most beautiful and powerful creature God had made. He said, "The devil told me if I would help him, he would give me a place of honor. So I and millions of others joined the devil in a war against God. We were conquered, chained, and cast here. It was at that time God made hell and put every angel that helped the devil into this place of torment. God told the devil that He would cast him here for a thousand years, in the future. We were such fools for listening to the devil. The people back on earth who now live for the devil are even greater fools, for they could repent, accept Christ, and escape this place of doom."

Once, my father fell on me as we came tumbling through space, and I recognized him as he spoke to me. I asked him why he did not live for God and teach me how to be saved while a child and not permit me to come to this place. He replied, "I'm sorry." Then I hit him with my fist and kicked him with my foot and cried, "I HATE YOU! I HATE YOU!"

There is not a person here who loves his parents or those who influenced them for evil while on earth. When they come in contact with one another, they fight and curse one another for influencing them against God. You hear the blows being passed and the awful cursing by these benighted souls, every second. Everyone here seems to hate, curse, and fight one another. Hell is a good name for this place.

I feel so lost, alone, hopeless, and helpless without a single friend. All those you knew on earth hate and curse you because they blame you for their lost condition. I cry, "How long must I be tortured and tormented?" From a distance, I hear someone like the crying and hissing of a wild demon saying, "Forever! Forever!" I cry and ask, "When can I have a glass of cool water?" Another voice sounding like a mad demon cries to me, "Never! Never!" Every flame, cinder, spark, and the very smoke of hell all seem to cry "Doomed forever and ever!" The cries of the lost and damned souls here sound so fatal and hopeless. What the Bible says about us having no rest day or night, forever and ever, is so true. When I think of eternity and my future, I seem to go stark mad and raving, yet there is nothing I can do but endure the pain, curse, and fall through the dense fire and smoke.

Amid the screams of the millions, I hear the drunkard crying for his bottle. He wants to get drunk and forget it all, but there are no liquor stores in hell. Their operators and owners, the manufacturers of whisky, and all drunkards are here. I hear the blasphemers cursing God. I hear one screaming, "My punishment is greater than I can bear." I knew that was Cain. Another was crying, "I have betrayed innocent blood." That is Judas. The educated, the uneducated, men, women, young people, boys, and girls are here. I have come in contact with popes, kings, dictators, presidents, infidels, college and seminary professors, and earth's rulers of every position, crooked politicians, who forgot God and did not believe in the Bible. They all turned a deaf ear to the preacher and thought God did not mean what He said. But there is no doubter in this place. Even infidels believe what God said. There are multiplied millions of devout religious people here. They realized when it was too late, that church membership, being confirmed, taking mass, baptism, keeping the Sabbath, or rituals would save. It takes more than religion and sincerity to keep people out of hell. Unfaithful church members by the millions are her lamenting their sins and suffering the judgment of God. The only person who escapes this place is the one who has accepted by faith the atoning blood of Christ. All the other horrible creatures of humanity are crying and cursing because of God's fierce wrath upon their sins. But all the time they are FALLING! FALLING! BURNING! BURNING! FOREVER AND EVER! I have been here over two thousand years and will have to stay here at least another thousand years suffering untold agony. Plus the fire, hunger, thirst, and the need for sleep, there seems to be millions of worms to cover the entire body. Everybody suffers alike here, for there are no degrees of punishment in hell. This is God's jailhouse where we wait for His great Judgment Day. One day, I must go before the Messiah who lived on earth the same time that I did, the one my father said was a rabble rouser, and I rejected Him. But He is God's Son who died for my sins, and I refused His love and mercy, with no time or thought to God. There I will be compelled to bow my knees before Him and use my tongue to confess Him as God's Son, but it will be too late. He will judge me for my sins and set my degrees of punishment, then cast me into the lake of fire for all eternity. There I will be swimming in liquid fire, brimstone, melted sulfur, forever fighting to keep my head above the surface, yet the flames above the surface will torture it. The lake of fire is called the second death. It is here where all unsaved people, of all ages, fallen angels, all demons, and the devil spend eternity suffering the pains of death every second but never dying. The lake of fire is called the cup of God's anger, where His indignation and wrath are poured undiluted with the torture of fire and brimstone. Here the smoke of our torment ascends forever and ever, and we have no respite—no pause, no intermission, no rest, no peace, day or night. In this black night of eternity, people grit and grind their teeth and chew their tongue because of the unbearable pains. Here the fierce and strong winds of God's wrath and judgment dash great waves of liquid fire over every creature. As the waves of brimstone roll over us, the deafening thunder peals and rumblings of the great deep add to our terror and agony. The lake of fire is the ultimate, the climax, the everlasting exhibition of the fierceness of the wrath, indignation, and anger of God Almighty against the devil and those who love and serve Him. You have heard it said, "If you went to hell, you would have plenty of company." This is a very true saying, but they are no comfort or help to you. They are Christ rejectors, God haters, liars, morally upright people who thought they were good and the very trash and scum of the human race who lived for and honored the devil.

I have cursed the day I was born and my father and mother for bringing me into the world. They are the ones who caused me to forget God and live in sin. Furthermore, I blame them for my being here because if they had taught me about God and carried me to the synagogue services, I would have known and loved God as my savior. As I said, my father and mother are here in this place and also are my five brothers. They blame my parents and me for being here. How I hate the thoughts of my parents because of the lack of interest they showed in their children's spiritual welfare and the bad example they set before us. I am so glad that I never did marry and have a family. The way I lived would have kept my wife and children from knowing Christ as savior and probably my grandchildren down through the centuries. They all would have been here in hell with me, and I would be responsible. Many of the young people I led astray are here in the flames with me. They hate me almost as much as they hate the devil.

Young people, let me urge you to forsake sin and the devil. Repent of your sins and live for God and do not come to this place. I am here because I did not repent. I was too busy having a good time to think about God and eternity. Never did I think about dying and going to hell and burning forever. Every creature in hell would cry aloud, if they could, and warn you of the awful agony that is suffered here. They would cry aloud, "The devil is a liar, a thief! Don't believe him. Forsake him and live for God." They would say, "Flee the wrath to come." If you die without being saved, you will believe all I am telling in less than sixty seconds after you die, for doomed you will be forever.

Fathers and mothers don't be like my parents were, with no thought of God and eternity. You owe your children a Christian home, Christian parents, and a church-centered life. You should lead them to trust Jesus as soon as they are old enough to understand and teach them to live for God. This will make them happy and God-honoring citizens of earth and heaven. If you do not, they will be wicked, mean, possessed of the devil, evil citizens of earth and hell. No one escapes death, and no unsaved person will escape this place of torture. No saved person is here. Please make your peace with God now by accepting Christ as your Savior.

Your sinful, lost, and tortured friend,
Dives

After reading this message and realizing that hell and the lake of fire is far worse than human tongue can describe, will you now repent and accept Jesus?

Here is the way to be forgiven, cleansed of sin, and become a child of God.

1. Realize you are a lost sinner.
    a. "There is none that understandeth, there is none that seeketh after God. They are all gone out of the way, they are together become unprofitable; there is none that doeth good, no not one… For all have sinned and come short of the glory of God" (Romans 3:22, 12:23).

2. Believe Jesus died for your sins.
    a. "For I delivered unto you first of all that which I also received, how that CHRIST DIED FOR OUR SINS ACCORDING TO THE SCRIPTURES" (1 Corinthians 15:3).
    b. "Who his own self bares our sins in His own body on the tree, that we being dead to sins, should live unto righteousness" (1 Peter 2:24).
3. Confess our sins.
    a. "And the publican, standing a far off, would not lift up so much as his eyes unto heaven, but smote upon his breast, saying, 'God be merciful to me a sinner.' I tell you this man went down to his house justified" (Luke 18:14b).
    b. "If we confess our sins, He is faithful and just to forgive us our sins, and to cleanse us from all unrighteousness" (John 1:9).
4. Accept and believe in Jesus as your savior.
    a. "But as many as received him, to them gave He power to become the sons of God, even to them that believe on His name" (John 1:12).
    b. "Believe on the Lord Jesus Christ, and thou shalt be saved, and thy house" (Acts 16:31).
5. Confess him publicly.
    a. "Whosoever shall confess me before men, him shall the Son of Man also confess me before men, him shall the Son of man also confess with thy mouth the Lord Jesus, and shalt believe in thine heart that God hath raised him from the dead, THOU SHALT BE SAVED" (Romans 10:9).
6. How to have assurance.
    a. "He that hath the Son hath life; and he that hath not the Son of God hath not life. These things have I written UNTO YOU THAT BELIEVE ON THE NAME OF THE SON OF GOD, that ye may KNOW THAT YE HAVE ETERNAL LIFE" (1 John 5: 12, 13).

This message was written by Dr. Bryam H. Glaze, for twenty-five years pastor of Calvary Baptist Church, Columbus, Georgia. One night after an unsuccessful attempt to interest his deacons in a soul-winning effort, he went home heavyhearted and grieved for a sleepless night. About 2:00 a.m., he began to pray and asked God to send the rich man from hell with the smell of fire and sulfur to hold a revival in his church to let the people know what hell is, Luke 16:19–31. As he prayed, the Lord spoke to him in a voice which sounded almost audible, "You know that I am not going to send the rich man back to earth. You know the Bible and what I have to say about Hell. Get up and write it and send it to the people." He got up and obeyed, writing as God gave the message. At 5:00 a.m., when he finished, he felt so relieved that he slept for two hours before getting up for the day. After a short time, the tract was printed for distribution.

I can't recall how or when I received this tract. It was already careworn at the time I picked it up. The last page was missing, and I have been unable to determine publication date or if the tract is still in print. Dr. Glaze has now passed on, and there is no other information on this tract or how copies can be obtained. It would be interesting to discover what this account of a biblical skeptic who came face-to-face with what he once denied had in impact upon that specific congregation and those who have received the tract as published.

Pondering Eternity

It should be said that the Holy Spirit
always creates in accord with His character
as truly God. He stamps whatever He
does with the mark of eternity; it has
upon it the quality of everlastingness, the
dignity and holiness of Deity set apart.

—*The Alliance Weekly/Witness*,
A. W. Tozer (1960)

Some people are lucky enough to escape Satan's Den, but they carry a small part of it away with them, wherever they go, even into outer space.

Simon Anderson had been a letterman athlete in nearly every sport offered by his schools in his hometown, known colloquially as Satan's Den. Only the sports reserved for girls only had evaded his efforts. He also graduated at the top of his class, a feat so unknown to those who followed the dumb jocks through their miserable academic years and into a miserable life as a virtual nobody, married to his high school sweetheart, a cheerleader, who had become pregnant her senior year, graduating with a distended belly for everyone to see her shame and hadn't stopped reproducing since.

Not so with Simon Anderson.

No, Mr. Bigshot Simon "Brains" Anderson was a top-notch athlete recruited by many scouts but never accepted any, on principle. College is strictly for academics, not sports. On graduation night, he was awarded numerous medals, trophies, and certificates of merit. His teachers and coaches had only good things to say about him and wished him well in his collegiate pursuits. He was also presented with a full scholarship to study mechanical engineering at the most prestigious university.

As expected, he mastered all his courses and went on to achieve a doctorate in mechanical engineering. His designs were written up in the trade journals; he was admired by the other great minds in his field. His only dream, however, was to work for NASA, to design better equipment and safer spaceships for earth's astronauts. In particular, he wanted to design the ultimate space station, where families could dwell together, generation after generation, never setting foot on their native land. He wasn't a sci-fi junkie, but futuristic ideas spurned him to analysis and restructuring of past and present air and spacecraft, reporting his findings to his peers and to the officials he slaved for, with minimal pay.

The day NASA called and asked him to interview for an open position, he politely accepted, then broke into a geeky dance that belied his athleticism after hanging up.

In addition to his earthbound work, Simon trained as an astronaut. Once completed, he would be propelled into space with other team members to the International Space Station. There, he would get a close-up of the inner workings he had only studied in schemata and models before. He was anxious to put to trial the restructuring ideas he had formulated in his studies. Calculated into the total weight capacity of the redesigned and recommissioned space shuttle program were countless tools and space-friendly parts specifically created for the ISS. He would personally lead a team of engineers on a space walk that would make history.

His team was young, made up of individuals with master's degrees and a hunger for experience that could propel them through their own doctorates. Both genders were represented, and a cross section of humanity was represented. There was no discrimination here. Space knew no distinction of life-forms, only feeding its own vast vacuum, spewing out what it found inedible into the atmosphere of earth where it burned up as it passed through the atmosphere, leaving little to return from whence it came.

Once launched into "the wild blue yonder," excitement faded into restlessness. Discontent rose among some of the junior team members as they compared universities and courses they had taken, argued theory, and proposed truths yet to be discovered. Simon quietly but firmly redirected them to what their individual and collective roles would be once they reached the space station. He kept them focused by having them recite their specific duties and warned them about crossing lines as that could cause their mission to go off course, wasting their time and taxpayer's money. A faulty mission could result in the dismissal of the entire program and its participants. He challenged them to not only do what they were assigned to do but also be prepared to share notes with the team and suggest possible solutions and/or improvements, each of which Simon would evaluate. One lucky member of his team could walk away with a full scholarship to pursue his or her doctorate with the promise of a position at NASA upon completion of their program.

The stakes were high, the competition tight, but there is no "I" in teamwork. Only by working together would they accomplish their goal. Though each had only a single piece of the puzzle to work with, they would need to work with those around them to draw the correct conclusions and connect the parts to form the bigger picture. An international team such as this one could help unite the planet earth into a peaceful entity, moving toward the future confident in their ability to communicate and problem-solve without conflict. For them, the scientific method was the healer of all wounds.

Upon arrival, they were debriefed by the astronauts who were taking their leave of duty from the space station and returning home to the chaos of life that keeps the earth in rotation. They reviewed the work done by these astral pioneers, commenting when appropriate. They were given instructions on how to maintain ongoing experiments while completing their own tasks. All too soon, the debriefing was over. They bid bon voyage to those who had served their term and settled into their new roles within the claustrophobic world of the space station.

Within twelve hours of their arrival, the individuals were in their proper stations, busily at work after a brief period of rest in their quarters. None seemed the worse for wear. NASA had chosen these young spacewalkers well—mind over matter, a healthy body to resiliently deflect the torments of space travel while remaining sane. It is a rare person, indeed, who can become trained as an astronaut.

Astringently, they were sifted as candidates began to fail the physical and mental tasks of their training, leaving only this elite group chosen for this daunting task. Many apply, but few can cut the muster. Discipline is the key without which they would have failed as well. Brainy yet brawny, they told themselves, the perfect balance. Even the most well-balanced can fall apart in the cosmos.

The day of their first space walk began well. Nutritionally balanced food products had been provided and consumed. Bodily functions had begun adjusting to the new normal they would experience for the next year. Simon chose one member of his team to accompany him on his walk as they inspected the outer casings of ISS for flaws in need of repair or improvement before beginning their mission. Inside, other team members were monitoring the conversation and making notes. Everything went smoothly. The following day, a different team member accompanied Simon and began the initial phase of work they had decided upon after the initial inspection. Each team member would be given a chance to spacewalk and get hands-on experience to apply their individual expertise that would develop their weaknesses into satisfactory strengths.

Thus, each "day," marked only by NASA observers, passed. Progress on the ISS became routine. Earlier squabbles were squelched as new insights triggered the genius within each team member, and they began new sketches of designs that could build on current technology. Any and all romantic inclinations became stifled by the busy work schedule. Even during their downtime, their minds continued to produce ideas which were analyzed, criticized, and revised. NASA would richly benefit from these innovative schemata and applications of new technological proposals by these "mighty brains," as they had dubbed themselves. Already, the ground crew was abuzz with the creativity of the new designs, and bets were being taken as to which of the brains would walk away with the scholarship. Other space programs were actively petitioning NASA for dibs on individual minds that were currently in orbit and unaware of the proselytizing going on beneath them. Had they known, they would have specialized their designs for one program or another. As it was, they remained uninformed and focused on the task they had been chosen for.

Dr. Simon Anderson was secretly proud of his young protégés. Outwardly, he maintained the cool temperament of the tough but fair commander. His team matured into one unit, versus the individuals who had begun this journey. The new maturity built an unbreakable cohesion that would have been fractured had they known of the recruiters awaiting them upon landing.

Eight months into their space walks, repairs, improvements, and new designs were well into their implementation. Simon Anderson took two of his more mechanically adept colleagues on a space walk to install an advanced oxygen-producing mechanism. The individual parts had been specially manufactured on earth, transported with them in their shuttle, and partially assembled within the zero-gravity confines of their workspace in the ISS. A Russian team had replaced a Chinese team two weeks earlier, and establishing communication was still ongoing due to culturally bound language barriers. The Russians were deeply involved in astro-agriculture and studying the effects of growing root crops in a gravitationally challenged environment. They didn't understand the schemata of mechanical design any more than the brains had understood the chemical formulas and data produced by the agri-botanists.

The limited space provided for the two teams led to proposals for better usage of space and the potential expansions feasible with current technology to allow teams freedom to move about and still maintain separation of workspaces. Occasionally, the work tools of one team would be found mingled with the tools of the other team. Arguments about how the tools had been mingled occurred. Simon and the team leader of the "space farmers" mediated these conflicts.

Dr. Anderson, Michelle Chan, and Phillipe N'gamo donned spacesuits, complete with their tool kits designed to tether their tools to their suits at the ankle of one leg and fitting into a pocket on their thigh, and float within reach of the engineer when in use. The tools were, in turn, tethered to the tool kit with retractable cords that allowed the engineer to pull them from the kit and handle them without floating away before being reeled back into their locations in the tool kit. Drifting tools would not become a nuisance or cause issues that could result in an accident.

On this day, Chan would be carrying the box of parts they would need, and N'gamo would be working under Dr. Anderson's supervision to install an improved oxygen exchange system, designed for the very specific needs of the ISS. N'gamo began his task as the others looked on, passing him tools or parts as requested. No surgeon could have been more concise than this French African brainiac whose skill with using the finest tools with an uncanny adeptness, despite the thick, heavy gloves they wore. Chan, on the other hand, was so petite the gloves made her clumsy, meaning she was more suitable for the role of assisting on these space walks. She knew the schemata of the planned project in depth and was able to direct her partner well if he tended to err in his judgment. N'gamo was irritated by the usurping of the traditional male role over that of the female and tended to only barely comply with her redirection or expounding of information related to the theory behind the design of the OES. Dr Anderson spoke only when necessary. These two were emotionally volatile and worked well together only when necessary. They were prone to arguing semantics or interpretation. As a trained observer, Simon would note their behavior and make recommendations for the fair and unbiased choice of candidate for the promised scholarship.

N'gamo was struggling to perform a task prescribed by Chan. His frustration was growing, and he was beginning to tremble as he clutched tools in a too-tight grasp that made it difficult for him to manipulate the tool properly, which led to more criticism by Chan.

Simon spoke to the young man softly and with encouraging words in an attempt to calm him down. Instead, the words only fueled N'gamo's anxiety. He growled a low rumble, prompting his commander to stop talking and simply observe.

Observe Simon did; he saw N'gamo's hands stiffen as he tried to continue with his task. Silently, Commander Anderson told N'gamo what to do, and when N'gamo seemed to hear his silent words and comply, he silently praised the young man. He would give voice to these praises, along with some critical analysis regarding the young man's need for anxiety reduction during their debriefing. He also made a note to discuss Chan's communication techniques to try and improve team integrity.

N'gamo reached for a tool on his utility belt. The release cord seemed to jam, and he had to yank at it several times before it released its self-retracting cord and allowed him to return to his task. In the process of recovering the tool, N'gamo lost his balance and started to slip from his precarious perch. Anderson reached out to stabilize him, trying to avoid a time delay that would be required to reel the young engineer back into the space station, effectively throwing the renovations off schedule.

Anderson stabilized N'gamo but slipped himself. As he felt himself beginning to drift at the end of his tether, his sleeve caught on the tool clutched in N'gamo's hand. The mirror affixed to his sleeve to help him see what was occurring in the tight space in which they were working came loose and began floating away from him. As it slowly turned in the vacuum of space, Simon caught a glimpse of the terror on his face in the reflective object.

He saw himself—a look of terror on his face. He was drifting away from the space station while N'gamo struggled to catch the tether of his commander's suit. He heard N'gamo's panicked voice on his communicator. He saw his own body relax into a comma of unconsciousness. How could he see all this if he was trapped at the end of a tether. He should have felt his body collapse. How could he see and be aware of what was happening if he was unconscious?

The darkness of absolute absence of light overcame him momentarily. Then the lights of a billion stars filled the space around him—colorful nebulae, the creamy consistency of the Milky Way. He saw a glimpse of the earth as it rotated slowly beneath him. The sun, nearly too bright now, caused him to squint. He saw a side of the universe he had never thought possible with current technology. It was all so clear, so bright, yet so dark. Absolute silence sliced though him, deafening him, not that it mattered as long as he could see this wondrous vastness.

His hearing slowly came back. He heard rhythmic hums, thrums, and echoes—the voices of the universe, all alive and singing to him. Not only was his eyesight attuned to a far greater acuity than that acquirable on earth, his hearing had been deafened to all but the music of the universe itself.

He didn't want this dream to end, this once-in-a-million-lifetimes opportunity to study the cosmos in its purest state! If only he had some way to record all this new information and study it for the benefit of mankind. He reached for paper and pen to record his findings, but his body would not comply. Frowning deeply, he thought back to the incident he had moments ago witnessed. He had slipped and was floating at the end of his tether, unconscious. Impossible! He couldn't have seen it if he had experienced it.

Then he remembered the mirror as it was launched from his wrist by the impact of N'gamo's tool. He remembered seeing the look of terror on his own face as it was reflected in the surface of the mirror. No, as it couldn't have been a reflection he saw; he had seen himself! That meant…he…was…the…reflection—not himself but a mere reflection of himself.

He remembered some of his early undergraduate work that included the exploration of supernatural phenomena and superstition among various groups of undereducated peoples. One that stood out most to him then, and now, was the belief that creating an image of a person, whether through photography or other artwork media, equated trapping the soul of the subject. There were cameras to record the work both inside and outside of the ISS. Images were sent via satellite to the earth where those with access to the video could join in the activity, albeit vicariously. No artist could produce any replication of actual activity as it occurred before them as the work being done did not allow for such personal activity. To capture a soul in such a manner would require the physical presence of the individual, wouldn't it?

The only remaining factor was the physical presence of the mirror. A mirror captured the reflected image of the one looking into it. Through the reflection and refraction of light, an individual can clearly see a clear, albeit reversed, image of themselves. The image held no life force of its own. It merely mimicked the movement of the original.

Crawling through the subtext of his thinking were memories of mirrors. His grandmother had once told him that mirrors had to be covered with a black cloth when a person died so that the freed soul would not become trapped in the mirror and become forever earthbound. Windows and doors were opened to give the spirit egress into the spirit world, where it would be judged and sent to its proper eternity. He had thought that all silliness as he grew up with his mind on logical rather than magical thinking. He had erased all things of the spirit and, with it, religion from his mind. Science became his god.

Though it seemed so impossible to his science-honed mind, he had somehow transferred his consciousness, his very soul, into the mirror, leaving behind the shell of his mortality. Trapped in the spinning vacuum of space, he was truly alone—no one to share his new-found knowledge with, no one to share himself with, no one.

In space, no one can hear you scream.

John 5:37–40, NKJV

> And the Father Himself, who sent Me, has testified of Me. You have neither heard His voice at any time, nor seen His form. But you do not have His Word abiding in you, because whom He sent, Him you do not believe. You search the scriptures, for in them you think you have eternal life; and these are they which testify of Me. But you are not willing to come to Me that you may have life.

Genesis 1:27, NKJV

> So God created man in His own image; in the image of God He created them: male and female He created them.

Deuteronomy 4:15–24, NKJV

Take careful heed to yourselves, for you saw no form when the Lord spoke to you at Horeb out of the midst of the fire, lest you act corruptly and make for yourselves a carved image in the form of any figure: the likeness of male or female, the likeness of any animal that is on the earth or the likeness of anything that creeps on the ground or the likeness of any fish that is in the water beneath the earth. And *take heed*, lest you lift your eyes to heaven, and *when* you see the sun, the moon, and the stars, all the host of heaven, you feel driven to worship them and serve them, which the Lord your God has given to all the peoples under the whole heaven as a heritage. But the Lord has taken you AND BROUGHT YOU OUT OF THE IRON FURNACE, OUT OF EGYPT, TO BE HIS PEOPLE, AN INHERITANCE, AS YOU ARE THIS DAY. FURTHERMORE, the Lord was angry with me for your sakes, and swore that I would not enter the good land which the Lord your God is giving you as an inheritance. But I must die in this land, I must not cross over the Jordan; but you shall cross over and possess that good land. Take heed to yourselves, lest you forget the covenant the Lord your God which he made with you, And you make for yourselves a carved image in the form of anything which the Lord God has forbidden you. For the Lord your God is a consuming fire, a jealous God.

Notes of Lurlene Joy McCoy

As an anthropologist, it is my duty to observe and record information about the culture of a group of peoples. There is to be no judgment, simply objective recordings of observed interactions of the peoples with one another, outsiders, and the natural world around them. However, being human, subjectivity arises. Having been raised within very specific Western philosophy and cultural experiences, it is only natural for me, or any other observer, to bring judgment or impinge beliefs and interpretations upon what is observed. No matter how objectively presented, the material presented by these outside observers will be interpreted in the predominant cultural beliefs of those reading or interpreting those presentations. Personal philosophical and religious beliefs will influence interpretation. A fully immersed practitioner of anthropological research will still remain biased. Only a person born and raised in a culture can explain their culture's beliefs and customs. In many cases, they do not understand these things themselves. It is simply the way it has been done throughout the existence of their cultural group.

In the United States, as with all advanced countries, there is a mishmash of smaller cultural groups that form the overall national population with culturally related beliefs that compel them to settle in culture-friendly clusters alongside the broader culturally diverse peoples around them. Chinatown, Little Italy, Little India, and other such neighborhoods are found in larger cities. The Southwest is culturally known as a combination of Spanish and American tradition. The Southeastern coast surrounding the Gulf of Mexico has a rich French influence that often follows the Mississippi River northward to Canada. Along the Canadian line, there are communities with strong Scandinavian and Norwegian ancestry. The Appalachian Mountain region is rife with old-world influences of Swiss, Irish, German, and British ancestry. All these groups have formed our modern American traditions as they blended with Native American traditions and those traditions that became integrated through those of African descent who have richly influenced our country, regardless of which side of the war you may stand on. Yes, there is still a war going on in our world. It is said to be based on the issue of racial superiority but is really a war on human pride as each determines to reign over the other. Slavery began when one man determined he was more powerful over another and forced the weaker into submission. Thus, the first slave was born. It is arguable as to whether the first murder (Cain having slain his own brother) could have been an attempt at Cain attempting to subdue his brother's will to his own as a result of having his own sacrifice to God rejected and his brother's accepted.

Regardless of the circumstances that led to the first slave, and all other inhumane events that followed the first murder, a Great Exchange took place. Adam and Eve instructed their sons in the manner of worship expected by God. God savored the burned offering of a slain lamb given by Abel. It is a reflection of the later sacrifice God Himself would make in sending His only begotten Son, a part of Himself, to live among humanity, to live a sinless life in a sinful world, to then be killed in the most cruel manner available at that time, buried in a tomb, and raised again to life so that any human being who accepted the truth of their sinful nature and a desire to be reconciled to God could find forgiveness and restoration through that very act of sacrifice. These boys knew God is *real.* They knew evil was *real.* They had been taught the consequences for rebellion against God—separation from God in their earthly existence that would lead to eternal separation from God in eternity unless there were some atonement made on their behalf to return to a trust relationship with God. Abel died for his faith and trust in God. Cain was exiled. He later is associated with the cultures that descended from him as the antagonists of those who descended from the younger children of Adam and Eve, primarily through their son, Seth. Paganistic religions and rites can be traced to these descendants of Cain. The one whose sacrifice was rejected because he failed to heed God's requirements, murdered his brother in jealousy, and then refused repentance when confronted by God became the father of those who oppose God.

Through the line of Seth, Noah was found righteous. He and his family were saved from destruction when the earth was destroyed through a vast flood. Within two generations, the Great Exchange had revived and continued to grow in prominence. God called a man named Abram to step out in faith, leave all he knew behind, and pursue a single God who claimed to be above all others. Through the line of Abram, later renamed Abraham, a nation dedicated to the worship of this one God came into existence. They weathered four hundred years enslaved by a paganistic culture yet remained unscathed in their faith in the one God who rescued them. Though they fought all along the way, they eventually returned to the Promised Land once owned by their ancestors, overcame those who refused their God, and established the nation of Israel and the Jewish faith. Through that cultural group, Jesus Christ came to earth as both man and God. A new faith was born. For those who choose to follow this Savior, Jew or non-Jew, all humanity can be reconciled to God.

The Great Exchange continues today, not so much in traditional beliefs in the supernatural and paranormal but in the pursuit of science. Superstitions revolve around the unknown alone. They are established through observations of recurring patterns and oral traditions that are a mixture of scriptural truth and traditional pagan worship as they have become blended within the fabric of history. Science, as demonstrated by the Middle Ages thought, was deemed dangerous as it often challenged established cultural beliefs. During the Renaissance which followed, science began to replace religion as the prevailing thought of truth. Many of the mythologies and legends arising from the Middle Ages gave rise to fantastical mythology as philosophical thinkers tried to explain religion through science exclusively. Our modern world continues to reflect this blended philosophy. "Show me the science" seems to be the prevailing thought, rising above the "Show me the scriptures" and "Show me the proof" of the religious and spiritual cultures.

Though there is a definite separation of natural and supernatural in modern thinking of so-called advanced cultures, there are subcultures in which superstition will likely prevail regardless of science. For example, the Amish and Mennonite population eschew modern technology, refusing to allow electricity into their home, and refusing to own or operate transportation vehicles. They do allow others to take them places in those vehicles. They employ the use of batteries for flashlights and provision of light in their homes. It appears to be selective to outsiders but fits with their Ordnung, laws. Onc thing they refuse any compromise of belief is in the area of image creation. They refuse to allow their pictures to be taken unless their faces are unseen, such as with their backs to the camera. Any artwork in which someone of their order is depicted, the individuals must be represented without facial features. If they allow dolls for their daughters, they must be of this faceless nature, or they will be denied or destroyed. There are stories of demonic possession that occurred as the result of a doll with a human face, purchased or created by someone outside their order being presented to a child or brought into a home. These nonviolent people also refuse to have whatnots, figurines, or other decor in their homes as that violates God's Word. Mirrors are forbidden. They take their beliefs seriously and will not tolerate violation of this rule.

In his Evans Grove series, Jim Shaver uses an *Alice in Wonderland* theme to explore a modern conflict in a fictional California town. It begins with a girl who is accused of murdering her parents after acquiring a mirror very reminiscent of the one the girl had seen in an illustration of Lewis Carroll's *Alice's Adventures in Wonderland*, her favorite childhood story. As the story unfolds, it is discovered that the mirror in question is, in fact, one of five specially created to be used by a Satanist who wished to raise the demon Baphomet. The books are not for the faint of heart and are of a spiritual warfare nature as the young women at the heart of the story are torn between their faith in a loving and benevolent Father God and the very real threat of a woman who has sold her soul to Lucifer himself and has plans to destroy as many people as she can in her effort to rise to power on earth.

The use of mirrors is not uncommon in occult practices as demonstrated in the variations on the Bloody Mary legend. Superstitions around mirrors, such as those shared with Simon Anderson by his grandmother, abound. Greek mythology speaks of Narcissus, a man so vain he fell in love with his own reflection in a river. Breaking a mirror is said to bring on bad luck lasting for seven years. Even the modern man and woman seem to have a great need to affirm that they exist by the number of mirrors in public places and the use of mirrors in trick photography and visual effects for visual art displays. Mirrors are prominent in the use of optics equipment. Our society could likely collapse without mirrors.

In his book *Fantasy, Horror, and the Truth: A Christian Insider's Story*, Benjamin Szumsky chronicles his journey from hard-core consumer of "dangerous" fantasy and horror literature as a teen and adult years to writing as a lay critic of those who write such literature and his subsequent salvation experience that led him to writing this book in which he exposes these genres for the unholy material he believes them to be. While not a fan of science fiction in general, fantasy and horror do bleed into this genre with regularity. Some of Mr. Szumsky's cautions are easily arguable as his mere opinion, while others have real scientific support to uphold his viewpoint. Among his observations is the accepted definition of science-fiction as employed in the literary world. This outline is quite complete and reflects the thoughts I have here inscribed.

As outlined by Szumsky, science fiction has two unscriptural messages that become abundantly clear in all such works. I feel both can be found in the story of Simon Anderson. May God deal with his soul faithfully, and may others be warned by his experience.

1. The primary message of sci-fi is the propagation of macro-evolution of belief as demonstrated by modern science as process theory with the inevitable outcome that over time, nature and science will converge to the point where religion will no longer be needed by humanity. Instead, God and His scriptures will be replaced with the fallible theories of mankind based on the ironic blind faith that transmutation of species in which all kinds of life are related and produce man's character accordingly. As a result, the future belongs to the life-forms that outlast all others—the survival of the fittest. God is not a part of this process as man has determined himself to be god.
2. The secondary message is that there are other life-forms, not of this earth. Mr. Szumsky denies the existence of life

> anywhere else in this universe as we have on earth. In these literary works, alien life-forms of an extraterrestrial origin are defined as the progenitors of life on Earth—the theory that life on this planet was "seeded" by aliens in an effort to create a place for them to dominate in some way, to control or become the gods of, for some ulterior purpose. If they are not progenitors of life, they come as our destroyers. We are seen as being in their way and in need of removal, annihilation, in order to achieve their agenda. He rightly describes this thinking as being Satanic in nature as demonstrated by a careful study of the scripture.

I question some of Mr. Szumsky's conclusions as merely opinion formed from his own experiences but very valid for his life. In general, however, I agree that the fine line between what is of God and what is of Satan has become undeniably blurred as our humanity has progressed from the Paradise of Eden to the fallen and very broken world in which we now live. The choice of subject for our entertainment can and will influence our thinking as I have tried to outline in my notations for those within the AD family. We are more privileged than most in our access to things of the truth and the nature of our fallen world, but we are still, first and foremost, human. We are chosen, gifted, and trained for our missions here on earth, with the purpose of preparing humanity for God's coming kingdom. We fight battles no others know and are tasked with righting wrongs done by the enemy through our various pursuits. We are human and fallible, just as those we are sworn to serve and protect. I am tasked with the gathering of folklore, tales of the supernatural, and compiling the unexplained. I distribute my collection to the world, but it is ultimately what they take away from it that determines their interpretation. I observe and report. I must remain neutral unless called upon for instruction and interpretation. Even then, I am limited by my audience as to what I am allowed to impart to them. Where the truth is accepted, it will be heard. Where lies prevail, I cannot change their minds. May God bless my efforts for His kingdom. May those who read my words read truth in their hearts. Pray for my work and those others who are doing the same, my brothers and sisters.

It is equally dangerous to read truth and call it lies as it is to read lies and declare them to be truth.

Topic: Spacewalking Astronaut Loses Mirror, Newest Space Junk

Source: *Associated Press*
Date: June 26, 2020

Cape Canaveral, Florida

Commander Chris Cassidy lost a small mirror attached to his sleeve as soon as he emerged from the International Space Station for battery work. The item posed no risk to either the space walk or the space station as it quickly floated away.

More than 20,000 of the millions of pieces of space debris are considered big enough to track via satellite for the purpose of safety of those who work in and travel through space. The mirror is of no concern.

At 5-by-3 inches, and including the band that attaches it to the astronaut's sleeve, it has a mass of barely one-tenth of a pound.

Commander Cassidy had no idea how the mirror became dislodged.

The loss of the mirror did not affect the six-hour space walk to replace the last of the old batteries used by the space station.

Both men involved in the space walk were on their seventh space walk.

When the Giggle Hounds Come

The lone hope for a sinning man is that for a while God will not accept his sinful conduct as decisive. He will hold judgment in suspension, giving the sinner opportunity either to reverse himself by repentance or to to commit the final act that will close the books against him forever.

—*A Word in Season*, A. W. Tozer

Ben Jonson leaned back in his bright-green camp chair, allowing his head to fall back so he could see the last quarter moon of the month above him. The clear skies allowed him to see the vast expanse of the Milky Way in vivid detail. Mentally, he located and named the constellations that danced in the sky in that part of the summer season in Kentucky. His fire crackled in counterpoint to the harmonious cacophony of the tree frogs and insects around him. A slight breeze added an underlying susurrus of leaves brushing against one another. On nights like this, he didn't mind watcher's duty.

The tiny one-room cabin was well prepared to the individual tastes of the watchers assigned for each season. The only exception was alcohol and any form of narcotic or illicit drug. Alcohol and drugs dulled the senses and invited exaggeration and hallucinations à la Pooh Bear's heffalumps and woozles. It was particularly atop the crown of Blind Man's Peak, the highest point in the area, where even a blind man could see for miles on a clear day. It wasn't the most haunted place in Satan's Den, but it had a track record spanning centuries of being the focal point of manifestations of the supernatural world. Though it could not be proven, it was believed to be the location of one or more portals.

As far back as oral tradition can recall, a watcher has always been on this mountaintop, watching, listening, feeling with their very souls, any disturbances in the veil between what is known and what is unknown. Young men who were ready to be real men would be sent to this sacred place for seven nights and days, learning from what they experienced. At the end of their stay, they were declared men and allowed to join the other men on hunting parties. If a young man returned less than he was—his mind altered irretrievably—he was placed in the care of the tribe's shaman, who touted that the boy had become an oracle, an omen-sayer, a sacred position many desired but few were willing to make the sacrifice to achieve. Sometimes, the boys did not come back, swallowed by the portal itself and enslaved in the secret lands of the gods. If ever they were seen again, they were considered the embodiment of the trickster god and full of vile mischief.

These superstitious beliefs were passed to fur traders, explorers, and early settlers, each learning the lessons of the watchers. Those who did not believe experienced great tragedy. Unbelief was not an option, regardless of the state of faith within the individual. It was essential to believe if one were to survive in this wilderness, one became a watcher, or one would die at the cost of ignorance. Many unmarked graves laid beneath the dense forest floor, their secrets lost forever.

When settlement led to civilization and the rise of towns with self-sustaining industry, people set aside the old ways for the new capitalism of progress. Money and power became the gods of these people. All else was superstitious prattle. The world of spirits faded into the shadows of reason.

Nonetheless, there were those who clung to the old beliefs, knowing from personal experience that there was more to this world than the material objects so coveted by society. Those people had gifts or had been trained from birth to believe in haints and things that go bump in the night. Some were scholars in the occult or practitioners of the traditional mountain witchcraft, including a form of faith healing, incantations, and dreadful charms. Of course, there were those who had been converted to their beliefs after encountering something they could not explain away with modern science and religious reasoning. These people tended to keep themselves off the radar of mainstream America and quietly lived their lives of spiritual desperation. They met in secret in times of need or prophecy to plan their defense against the known darkness, carefully chronicled by many hands across time, and against the darkness yet to come, unknown and terrifying in their own ways. Thus, the watchers of Blind Man's Peak were born.

No more coming-of-age rituals, gone were the random experiences of unfortunate travelers and settlers. The watchers were organized. They were armed with knowledge. They were willing to sacrifice themselves for the greater good of mankind.

Now it was Ben Jonson's turn on the mountaintop. He was a third-generation watcher. His sons would take his place one day. That was his hope as he counted the stars on that summer night. His hand found the water bottle secured in the cupholder built into the arm of the chair without looking. He used his other hand to twist and remove the cap from the bottle. Instinctively, he raised the bottle and took a big swallow, never taking his eyes from the stars.

The sudden cessation of all sound caused him to choke on the second large gulp of the cold water. A gurgling sound erupted from his mouth as he struggled to breathe. With a watery gasp, he spewed the offensive liquid from his mouth, spraying the grass at his feet. Broken coughs followed, interspersed with gagging and dry retching.

The spell passed. Ben could breathe somewhat better. Reluctantly, he took another drink from the plastic bottle he had nearly crushed in his fit. It went down smoothly, moistening his parched mouth and throat. A second, larger gulp allowed him to collect his senses.

The vacuous absence of all sound was unnerving, causing all the exposed hairs on his body to stiffen and stand straight up. The swiftly thickening five o'clock shadow on his face exposed the skin he had forgotten to shave that morning. He shivered with the exposure and the imagined fears. Static electricity in the air stung his face; it could not be heard as it scraped at the exposed skin.

Frozen in place, he attuned his ears to locate the hint of any sound. There was nothing. The sound of his own heart throbbed in his ears and echoed throughout his head. It wasn't really sound but the memory of a heartbeat, culled by his brain to explain the absence of true sound. The pressure from the vacuum of the atmosphere around him punched at his ears, escalating the intensity of the imagined throbbing. He clasped his hands over his ears, dropping the water bottle to the ground without a crinkle or plop. The more he pushed against his ears, the worse the invisible pain became. He grimaced as he tried to bear the pain like the man he was. The pressure continued to increase. A silent scream of agony disturbed the bubble of consuming silence with an audible *pop*! The last of his screams echoed from the mountaintops around him.

Realizing his torment had ended, Ben lowered his hands to his lap. The silence remained, but the vacuum had gone. Where his hands had landed, he discovered a cold, wet sensation. He glanced down, expecting the worst, but found only large spots of water where the bottle had dropped and spilled before rolling to the ground. He wanted to curse but remembered the deafening silence of his agonized scream. He was also afraid to move.

"Hee."

The voice came from behind him.

"Hee."

This time to his right.

"Hee."

"Hee."

To his front and his left.

"Hee."

"Hee."

"Hee."

"Hee."

They were all around him, laughing and mocking him. "At least seven. Maybe ten," he muttered.

The giggling abruptly stopped. An eerie silence wrapped itself around him like a blanket.

A single, large shadow pulled away from the shadows of the dense tree line. Red eyes glared at Ben. No other features were discernable. An inaudible signal must have been given as the unseen creatures began to scream in unison.

"EeeEeeeeEeEE!"

Silence fell as yet another unheard signal was given.

"Ben Jonson…," growled a voice inside the man's head. His eyes widened in surprise.

"Ben Jonson…" The voice echoed inside his skull.

"Yes," acknowledged Ben, barely above a whisper.

"You have sinned." The voice was ominous.

Ben began to sweat as cold chills wracked his body.

"You have sinned!" The voice was more forceful.

"Who hasn't?" countered Ben.

"YOU have sinned, Ben Jonson."

Sweat dripped into Ben's face. He couldn't move to wipe it away.

"D-doesn't everyone?" Ben's chattering teeth made it difficult for him to speak.

"YOU…HAVE…SINNED!"

Ben couldn't think of an appropriate response that would satisfy the voice.

"BEN JONSON, YOU HAVE SINNED!"

The voice shouted in his head, causing him to cringe inwardly. His body would not move. He was frozen in fear or by some other, more sinister force.

"BEN JONSON, YOU HAVE SINNED!"

"Have pity on me," he pleaded. "I don't know what you mean. What sin have I committed?"

"You know, Ben Jonson."

"No, I don't. Honestly."

"You DO know."

"No, I don't!" His emphatic scream flew defensively from him in stark contrast to his previous whispers.

Silence.

Was it gone?

No. Unblinking red eyes continued to float against the darkness near the tree line.

He chuckled nervously.

"Ben Jonson..."

"That's my name. Don't wear it out," he replied in a more normal tone.

His flippancy didn't affect the red-eyed creature.

"Ben Jonson..."

"WHAT!" His agitation began to show.

"YOU have SINNED!"

"You keep saying that, but I don't know what you mean?"

"You know your sin. REPENT!"

That was new. What did Ben Jonson have to repent about? He couldn't think of anything at all.

His heart was racing; he could feel it pounding in his chest and coursing around his brain. His breath was labored. The air filled with puffs of condensation, quickly absorbed back into the heavy atmosphere of the night.

A sudden grip around his heart, as claws into prey, began to squeeze, escalating the pressure and speed of the blood coursing through his body. He cut off a scream of agony before it could escape, resulting in a pained growl.

"Repent!" the voice demanded.

"I don't know what you want me to repent of!" Ben's voice hissed through clenched teeth.

"Review your memories." The voice was not sinister, just deadly insistent.

Shutters of light flickered in his mind's eye like strobe lights on a disco floor. Snippets of his life could be seen as they fluttered past at great speed. Minor transgressions of childhood were resurrected and interwoven with faulted behaviors of adolescence, poor decisions of early adulthood, and the intentional trespasses of middle age. Memory upon memory swept emotional pain and disdain out from beneath the rugs that had hidden them from time. Ancient anger, resentment, embarrassment, defiance, greed, and lust swirled about him, irritating his senses, tantalizing him anew. The guilt weighed heavily on him. Regret brought him to the brink of depression. He had not always been a nice guy. He admitted it. He apologized when he had to. Wasn't that enough?

Suddenly, the same scenes began to repeat, as if in a loop. Only this time, he was witnessing the same scene from the viewpoint of those he had wronged. He felt their shock, disappointment, resentment, feelings of vengeance, and despair. He experienced their anger, their rejection, and felt their anguish. While he laughed at the funny-looking kid in third grade, that kid was inside of him, crying, not understanding the rejection of the boys he just wanted to be his friends. He didn't understand the words these boys were using. He had trouble understanding what people said to him. He struggled to learn in school. All he wanted was someone to play with. Why did they treat him so mean?

He became his junior high girlfriend on the day he broke up with her. She wouldn't give him a kiss behind the bleachers of the football field. He had called her a tease and a few choice names that besmirched her character. She was devastated. She didn't know what those names meant, but she knew they were said about bad girls, and she didn't want to be a bad girl. Her mother had taught her that girls her age could hold hands with their boyfriends, but only bad girls kissed. She felt ugly and rejected. He remembered that girl refused to go out with anyone for the remainder of her years in public schools. The other boys had called her a prude and stuck-up. They made up stories about what she really did with men who came to her house and even said she only liked girls. That girl had never married.

His mother came into his mind—it was the day he had told her he hated her because she wouldn't let him have the car to go to his girlfriend's house for a party. She had offered to drive him there and pick him up. She needed the car to go to church that night. She was picking up some neighborhood children for a special program he had promised to attend with her. When he had stolen her keys and took the car anyway, she had broken down and cried as she called everyone she could to try and find another way to get those children to church. She refused to tell them why she didn't have her car. His father had tried to convince her to call the police and report the car stolen, but she had come to the defense of her beloved son, declaring he had made a mistake and that she would take care of it later. That night, he drank too much with his buddies at the party at his girlfriend's house. Her parents hadn't been home, and they would not have allowed that party if they had been there. On the way home, he had been speeding and missed a particularly sharp curve. When he awakened in the hospital, his mother was by his bedside, telling him he was going to be okay. Only later did he discover the car had been totaled in the accident and that his mother had lost her job because she had no way to get there without a car. Their insurance was raised because of the accident, and his mother was unable to buy another car right away. She had stayed by his bedside until he was able to get out of bed and become mobile once more. He never asked about the car or the insurance or herself. She had never outwardly blamed him for anything, yet her pain remained.

He remembered when his girlfriend told him she was pregnant. They were still in high school. He had called her a stream of bad names, accusing her of infidelity and declaring the baby wasn't his. He declared he would never marry her and told her to get rid of the baby. He would not be responsible for another guy's kid. He could see the hurt in her eyes then. Now he felt the terror in her as she had broken the news to him. She was scared he would leave her. She was scared to have the baby. She was scared to tell her parents. She had been faithful. He had been her first and only lover. She had been reluctant, but he had pressured her until she gave in. She had lived with that guilt but felt if she didn't give in to him, she would be abandoned. She also feared that he would dump her for another girl of easier reputation. And he would have. He recognized that now. He had compromised her, and he had forced her into something she was not ready for, just as he had tried to do with that girl in junior high. He considered dumping her anyway. Somebody else could have her. She was spoiled goods. He had reluctantly married her. He loved her, but he still resented being trapped by her. His boys were the best thing about their marriage.

Then he recalled the night not so long ago that he was in a bar with his friends after work. A woman had begun flirting with him from across the room. He had tried to ignore her, but she refused to be ignored. She had leaned forward provocatively to reveal deep cleavage barely covered by what she wasn't wearing beneath her blouse. She had crossed and recrossed her legs enough to reveal she was similarly unclad beneath her very short and tight skirt. He tried to remember he was a married man, but scenes of that woman and himself began to play out in his mind. Before long, he had excused himself from his buddies and approached the woman. He got her phone number and promised to call her later that night. When his buddies questioned him, he told them she was an old friend and he just wanted to say hello. He knew they didn't believe him. Late that night, he hid in a hallway closet and called the woman. They exchanged pleasant conversation that was sexually charged with innuendo, and both were panting hard by the time they hung up. He had felt guilty for making the call but did not believe he had done anything wrong. They had just talked. He wouldn't really meet with her, not in person. As long as they just talked, it wasn't an affair, was it? The phone calls continued for days. He agreed to meet her at another bar for drinks. He would break it off. It wasn't fair to his wife. They had ended up at her apartment. He crawled home late that night, her smell heavy on his clothes. He showered before getting in bed beside his sleeping wife. She rolled over and snuggled up to him and asked him if he had finished the work he had stayed late to do. He mumbled something that seemed to satisfy her. She went back to sleep. He remained sleepless. He had seen this other woman twice since then. His wife didn't seem to notice his late nights were becoming more frequent or that he had started doing his own laundry. As this crossed his mind, Ben saw his wife's face swim before him. She was crying. She lay in the bed next to her husband's empty space, holding his pillow as if she were holding him. He heard her talking into the pillow as the tears made it wetter and wetter. She was asking herself what was wrong with her. She wanted to know if she had grown fat and ugly. Was she no longer good enough for her husband. Had she done something to push him away? She *knew* he had been unfaithful. She loved him anyway. She thought she had done something to push him away.

Oh god, what had he done to her? He had been angry when she got pregnant. He loved her and wanted to marry her; the baby just took them both by surprise. He had tried to do right by her, given her a home and children. He had been a decent husband and father. He gave her what she needed as best he could. Maybe he worked too much. Maybe he spent too much time with the guys. Maybe he didn't listen like he should when she wanted to talk. Had he ever asked her what she would have done with her life if she hadn't gotten pregnant in high school? Had she ever talked about her plans for her life? Her hopes? Her dreams? Was she happy being a wife and mother? She wasn't a perfect wife, but he had nothing to complain about. So why was he messing around with this other woman. She only wanted one thing, and he could give her that. But so could any other man—a man who wasn't married, a man who didn't have responsibilities for others besides himself, a man who cares for her the way a man should, as a husband should.

"Ben Jonson…," growled the voice in his head.

"Yes." He sighed. "I am he."

"Ben Jonson…you have sinned."

It was a simple statement, no condemnation or judgment. He knew the truth. He *had* sinned. He had been selfish and rebellious. He had hurt others without contemplating the consequences of his actions regarding himself or those of the ones he had sinned against. *Sin*—one word he had heard in the little church his mother had dragged him to every Sunday until he refused to go. There were too many rules, and they wouldn't allow anyone to have any fun. Sin was the only thing fun in life, and he wanted to experience it all. He had not only told his mother he hated her for not giving him the car but that he hated her God who couldn't love us, or He wouldn't have given us the Ten Commandments and then send us to hell when we couldn't live up to them. God wasn't love. He was a dictator. That night, he had nearly died. If he had, he would have stood before the very God he had denied that night. He would have been condemned to hell, but not because God didn't love Him. It would have been because he didn't love God. God was not evil. God did not give rules, then punish us because we couldn't follow them. No, God loves us. He gave us rules to help us love Him in return. We are His children when we obey Him. When we rebel and choose to go against His rules, He disciplines us. He shows us that we are going the wrong way. It's called a conscience. It's called guilt. It's called sin. He proved His love in sending Jesus to die for the sin of humanity. *My sin*, Ben admitted. *He died for me!* Ben wouldn't die for anybody—not even his family. Yet Jesus had died for *him*. Jesus became sin so Ben Jonson could be forgiven of his. Why? Why would God do that?

"You are loved, Ben Jonson." That voice was so gentle. It couldn't be the same beast that had spoken before. That voice was condemning. This voice was…forgiving?

"God?" The question hung in the air.

There was only silence in return.

"Jesus?" A warm breeze began to warm him.

"God? Jesus? I'm sorry. I didn't know. I had no idea how bad I was. I was a terrible person. I hurt so badly inside. I thought I was above Your law. I didn't need you. I thought because my dad was never at home that being a father meant you didn't have to love your family as long as they were taken care of. Mom did all she could. She had to be both Mom and Dad when Dad wasn't there. Dad loved us…in his own way. He didn't know what it was like to not have a dad come to your ball games or be there when your friends rejected you because you liked a girl and wanted to spend time with her and not them. He wasn't there when I got beat up on the playground because I stuttered. He pushed me to get a job when I turned sixteen so I could help pay my way in life. He was angry when I told him he was going to be a grandpa. He refused to help us when the baby came, and I was looking for a job and some way to care for my family. He never told me he loved me or that he was proud of me for doing the right thing by my girlfriend. He complained a lot. He made my mom get a job to help pay the bills. He didn't want her doing things for me because she would make me a sissy. She stood by me after the accident that nearly took my life. She nursed me until I was able to go back to school. She stood by my side at the courthouse when I married Becky. She was there the day little Cody was born and baby-sat for us whenever we needed her to. She was the one who loved me the way You wanted to love me. And I rejected her—You! I am so ashamed of what I have been and of what I have become. I deserve whatever punishment you have reserved for me. Surely this is my day of reckoning. I sit before You now a broken man. Send me to the hell you have created for those who have rejected You. I deserve it.

"Ben Jonson…repent and be forgiven."

"I am not worthy of forgiveness. I am too far gone. I give myself to You right here and right now to do with as You will."

"Ben Jonson…you are forgiven."

"I am not worthy."

"Ben Jonson…you are my child. Repent!"

"What is this repent business? You keep telling me to repent, but I don't know what that means."

"Ben Jonson…you are forgiven. Go and sin no more."

"Sin. I am a sinner. How can I sin no more?"

"You are forgiven… You are My Child… You can be born again and sin no more."

"I've heard about that before…being born again. I don't understand it though."

"Cease your sin…be forgiven…ask forgiveness…seek forgiveness…begin anew."

"Can I stop sin? Isn't that a part of being human—original sin and all that?"

"Created in love…to be loved…to return love…to be forgiven and restored in love."

"You love me? I've messed up too bad. I don't even like myself. No one can love me."

"I love you."

Ben felt his body relax and allowed himself to crumble into his chair. He bent forward with his head between his knees as he tried to keep from hyperventilating. His tears fell in a river down his face and into his hands as he covered his face. Was it possible? God loved him? God forgives him for all he had done? He had cheated on his wife. He was in danger of losing his family because of that one mistake—no, because of the many mistakes he had made throughout his life. How had he been so stupid? Not his fault! The devil made him do it, didn't he? No, he had made those choices all on his own. It was solely his fault his life was falling apart. And God was willing to forgive him? Too much. Too much.

He pulled himself from the chair and fell to his knees where he was in front of the chair that had been his watchtower. He tilted his head back to look at the stars in the sky he had been admiring such a short time before. God had made those.

"And I made you…"

God had made him, Ben Jonson, out of love. He had sent Jesus to die for Ben Jonson, out of love. He wanted to forgive—no, *had* forgiven Ben Jonson, out of love. Could Ben Jonson love God in return? Yes, he could! He would!

"Forgive me, Jesus."

"You are forgiven. Repent."

"I don't want to sin anymore. I want to straighten up and fly right from now on, but I don't know how."

"Let Me help you."

"Help me, Jesus!"

In that moment, the night noises returned. It was if there had been no giggle hounds, no judgment, no encounter with God.

But Ben knew it had happened. He felt the pain he had carried for so long melt away. He felt the stirring of the Holy Spirit within him as he began to contemplate how to share his experience with the other watchers, with his buddies, and most of all, with Becky and his boys.

As the sun rose, Ben Jonson cleaned up the refuse of his watch and threw the small bag into the back of his pickup truck. For the first time, he was thankful his watch was only twelve hours every three months and not the weeks his father had endured or the months his grandfather had endured. They had done their duty but had not learned their lesson. He, Ben Jonson, had faced God and lived to tell about it. He had been broken in the midnight and risen healed in the sunrise. This was a legacy to pass to his boys as they, too, take up their place as watchers in Satan's Den.

Romans 10:13, NKJV

> For whoever calls upon the name of the Lord shall be saved.

Notes of Lurlene Joy McCoy

It's as easy as ABC.
Admit you are a sinner.

> But now the righteousness of God apart from the law is revealed, being witnessed by the law and the Prophets, even the righteousness of God, through faith in Jesus Christ, to all and on all who believe. For there is no difference; for all have sinned and fall short of the glory of God. (Romans 3:21–23, NKJV)

Believe Jesus is God's Son, who shed his cleansing blood upon the cross, was buried, and rose again on the third day.

> But what does it say? "The word is near you, in your mouth and in your heart" (that is the word of faith which we preach); "that if you confess with your mouth the Lord Jesus and believe in your heart that God has raised Him from the dead, you will be saved. For with the heart, one believes unto righteousness; and with the mouth confession is made onto salvation. For the Scripture will not be put to shame." For there is no distinction between Jew and Greek, for the same Lord over all is rich to all who call upon Him. For whoever calls upon the Lord shall be saved. (Romans 10:8 -13, NKJV)

Confess Jesus Christ *as Lord over your life.*

For it is written: "As I live, says the Lord, Every knee shall bow and every tongue shall confess to God." So then each of us shall give account of himself to God. (Romans 14:11–12, NKJV)

Brothers and sisters, we are truly privileged to be born into the families we have been given. More privileged are those who are chosen to be adopted into our number. As children of God, separated from the world at large for the sole purpose of serving our Creator King, we have been brought up in the ways of the kingdom. We are gifted and trained to fulfill the roles destined for us from the foundations of this world. We are watchers over humanity as we go about our kingdom work both overtly in our lives and covertly in our chosen professions. As such, we are held to a greater level of accountability. Those of us who know God are challenged to live fully for Him so that those who do not know Him may come to seek Him and, by seeking, to find Him. How will we be found when the giggle hounds come for us?

The Forbidden Five

Remember that it is not the truth that hurts
you; rather it is the evil. The 95 percent
truth is trumped by the 5 percent evil. This
our archenemy knows only too well.

—A. W. Tozer, *The Crucified Life*

Children all over the world delight in telling ghost stories around the campfire and playing tag after dark. There's something thrilling about facing your friends in a creative game of cat and mouse, playing ghost in the graveyard or flashlight tag. Ordinary objects take on surreal and supernatural forms in the transforming moonlight. Add tingling nerves and spine-chilling tales, and you have the perfect scene for the undead to walk up to you and begin a conversation, dance with the devil, exchange recipes with a witch, lose your soul to the unknown.

The group of adolescents stood with their eyes closed. A chill breeze stirred their hair to stand on end. One young lady slipped gently among her comrades, speaking in low tones. She took care not to touch anyone as she passed among the group. When she did choose to touch someone, it produced an eerie chill that ran from the person's toes to the tips of their fingers, up their spines and to the ends of their hair. Ripples of shock and gasps of fear escaped their lips.

"And so they became known as the *Forbidden Five*," intoned the girl. She fell silent. No one moved. It seemed as if no one breathed. The air was filled with fear.

One by one, the listeners began opening their eyes, realizing the story had ended. When everyone's eyes were opened and they had resumed breathing, the girl stepped up on a log to regain the center of attention.

"You think this story has ended, but it hasn't." She had their full attention once more. "The story will never end. You see, those five unfortunate men, doomed to walk the earth forever, are here among us tonight."

Kids shuffled and looked around them.

"They have walked among us tonight, choosing five of you to join them in their hideous quest. You have been touched by their chill fingers and must now walk among your friends, choosing one to take your place among the *Forbidden Five*. None of us know who the chosen are. Not you, not I. There are only a few rules. The chosen ones cannot touch anyone who is on the hay wagon, hereby known as the *Holy Ground.* Anyone not on Holy Ground is fair game. The Forbidden Five are not permitted to touch Holy Ground. Holy Ground can only be sought if you know who *all* the Forbidden Five are. The game will last until no one is left or until the Forbidden Five are driven from the land and everyone else is on Holy Ground. To capture someone and make them Forbidden, a Forbidden One must touch his or her opponent. That person then becomes Forbidden as well. Any questions?"

A young man in the back spoke up. "You mean we can't touch anyone until the game is over, unless we are Forbidden?"

"That's right," said the girl.

"Man, this is going to be hard," muttered another boy.

Slowly, the group spread out further, each person eyeing the others around them. They tried to recapture the fun they had been having before the game began. The food was still out and available to be eaten. Some of the teens bravely filled a plate with roasted hot dogs, chips, and cookies. Soft drink cans popped open. Small talk began with safe distances between participants.

As the mood began to relax, participants began moving closer to one another once more; talk came more freely. The party returned to a more normal level. People began to forget about the *Forbidden Five.* Couples drew closer to each other as they had grown accustomed to each other's touch. Tactile friends returned to their normal modes of communication through touches, brushing near, but not quite making contact. Friction static built up between their flesh and that of the ones being air-touched.

The cool evening darkened into an even cooler night. Jackets, sweaters, and sweatshirts were taken from the haphazard piles the warmer afternoon had produced. Couples began separating themselves into the ever-decreasing circle of light provided by the bonfire. Those without dates and those who preferred the light of the fire drew closer to preserve the warmth.

A piercing scream shattered the casual interactions. A silence fell over the field. Even the flames of the bonfire flickered in silent consumption. If the wood cracked or split under the heat, it was done without an accompanying *pop*. Even the creatures of the night lost their voices.

Young bodies stilled, as if by death. Wild eyes danced in their whites, trying to see the source of the scream without actually moving the head their eyes peered out from. A wave of shudders made its way among the fireside observers, each passing along the fear to the person beside them. Couples and small groups of adolescents emerged from the shadows, first as amorphous beings with glowing eyes, then solidifying into familiar faces. For the alert participant, a head count would reveal a full complement of teens. No one was missing. Nor did anyone appear to be in the type of distress that would have warranted such a scream.

Whispers began to hiss as each partygoer began his or her own take of the event. The scream belonged to a female. No, a male. It was more like a panther, thought one young man who considered himself a seasoned hunter and "in the know" about such things. Those who refused to attribute the sound to anything living listed spooks, wraiths, werewolves, and hungry zombies as the source. The scream that had split the night was thought to have come from a specific locale, but even that differed from witness to witness. All agreed it had come from nowhere and that it weirded them out so badly they wished to leave.

The hostess of the party, who had told the tale of the Forbidden Five, warned her friends that leaving before the Forbidden Five had sated their bloodthirst or were driven away could be dangerous. It had been told over the generations that anyone who heard the Five or were touched by their icy fingers and left the area were haunted by the dead men's spirits until they were driven into madness and killed themselves or died of sheer fright. Rattling car keys were quickly muffled by hands shoving them back into jeans pockets.

Chilled bodies crowded around the bonfire, many sitting; the brave or too scared to move, standing. As close as they all were, none touched. Real fear threaded the air, weaving a blanket of darkness so thick the kids should have been warmed by its presence. Instead, they were shrouded in cold death. Even the suffocating depth of the grave appeared to be warmer.

A thin, reedy voice, surprisingly belonging to a hulking football player known for his fearlessness on the field, split the preternatural silence.

"Who got touched?" His usually deep voice crackled.

Accusing eyes flitted among the group, seeking the guilty parties. There was no response.

"Come on," squeaked the brunette cheerleader with the football player. "Someone had to get touched. Otherwise, we wouldn't all still be hanging around here like pigs for the slaughter."

Her unfortunate choice of words resulted in someone crying out in tear-soaked exasperation. Other sobbing voices joined the first. Amid the gasps and snuffles mingled the deeper sounds of males clearing their throats.

A tiny female voice spoke up.

"I didn't get touched," she said. "But I think someone near me was."

"How can you tell?" said another female voice, shaking with terror.

"It got really cold. It was all around me. Then there was…a… movement…in the air. Like the air was being pushed. Like something invisible was trying to touch one of us."

"How do you know it didn't touch *you*?" accused a tall, thin youth wearing a red hooded sweatshirt with their school's name and mascot, BAND GEEK proudly stretched across his chest.

"I…" the girl began. "I didn't… I mean…someone…" Her voice trailed off into the darkness, helpless to absolve herself of the accusation.

"I think she's one of them," a boy's voice whispered loudly to a blond girl near him.

"Yeah. Why don'tcha just admit it so we can all get out of here," demanded a girl nearly hidden by the oversized jacket bearing the name of her boyfriend.

"Really…I…" the girl blubbered as she broke into gut-wrenching sobs and buried her face in her trembling hands.

The boy to her right raised his arm as if to comfort her. He stopped just short of contact and yanked his arm back as if he were a kindergartner afraid of catching girl cooties.

A tall solidly built girl wearing a letterman's jacket proudly indicating her position as captain of the girls' basketball team frowned deeply and raised an accusing finger. "She's guilty! Can't you see it on her face?"

Murmured agreements and accusative comments blended together, adding to the already volatile atmosphere.

As if in response to the accusation, the smoke rising from the fire shifted from its upward pull to drift intently toward the pale young lady, seemingly wrapping itself around her slim form to imprison her.

"See, I told you so!" her accuser exclaimed with another condemning finger wag.

The girl's sobs intensified into wails of fear. Fearing the darkness more than the accusations, she slipped to the ground, rolling into a fetal position. The accusing smoke stroked her one last time before returning to its upward spiral.

The party hostess, a redhead of medium build, spoke up. "It's just a story, guys." She didn't sound convinced herself as her voice trembled with each word. "I mean, I *did* touch some of you during the story, but that was only for effect. I don't even remember who I touched."

"You mean it was all a joke?" an angry voice filtered through the grumbling, complaining partygoers.

"It wasn't a joke," defended the hostess. "It was just a ghost story made up to be told around the campfire. It's not even a true story."

"Then why did my blood turn to ice when you touched me?"

Everyone turned toward the speaker, a tall lithe brunette with short hair and overly large brown eyes. Her naturally wan face glowed palely in the darkness; the rings of black around her eyes only emphasized the exposed whites. Dressed all in black, she was a ghostly presence among the living.

"I didn't touch you," replied the hostess. "With your goth look, you would have been too obvious."

"If you didn't touch me"—the girl gasped—"then who did?"

As one, the teens nearest her moved out and away from her until she stood in an ebony fog only she could see. She wrapped her long, slender arms around herself in an attempt to find warmth that would no longer be her companion. A bluish tint appeared around her blackened lips. Her white face developed veins of blue, giving her the appearance of a comic book zombie.

"That's one," a young man stammered.

"Four more to go," a girl whispered.

"It was just a story," squeaked the hostess to herself. She was becoming less convinced as her friends were falling apart before her eyes.

"It figures it would be her," muttered a girl just behind the hostess. "She's already a ghoul. It was just a matter of time before the dead claimed their own."

"I'm *not* a ghoul!" retorted the goth girl. "Just because I wear black and enjoy dark culture doesn't make me evil! I'm just expressing myself!" Tears dragged mascara down her cheeks, fueling the cruel taunt. "I thought you were my friend!"

"Friends with a ghoul?" The accuser stepped forward. She was a bottle blonde with dark roots dividing her scalp. "I wouldn't be caught dead hanging around with you!"

"Be careful what you say," began the husky young man with a mop of curly hair to his shoulders, who had come with the accuser and the accused. His large black-framed glasses magnified his green eyes into owllike orbs.

Realizing what she had just said to her own best friend, the brunette-blonde pulled back into the shadows, turning her back to the others. Her own sobs nicked at the frayed nerves of those who could hear her.

"Okay. Let's look at this through rational eyes," said a serious-looking boy wearing a North Face fleece jacket.

No one spoke.

"First," said the young man, "how many here really truly believe in ghosts?"

Two hands were raised tentatively.

"Then what is a ghost?" he addressed those two specifically.

"A dead person," offered a girl all in pink.

"That's a zombie, stupid," reprimanded a geeky-looking boy, rolling his eyes in disgust.

"A restless spirit of someone who has died," declared the second believer.

"So it isn't alive. Right?" the moderator summarized.

Nods and words of agreement from a handful of adolescents encouraged his line of deduction.

"A person who is dead cannot be alive. Therefore, something that is not alive cannot hurt you. Your fear is just in your head. It's psychosomatic."

"You mean you aren't scared?"

"Of course not. A work of fiction has only a brush with reality. It is designed to make us *think* it is real by imitating a known reality. Take from it what you will. It's still make-believe."

"Hah! You got touched didn't you, you little rat?" The booming voice came from a popular basketball player known for picking on the little guy.

"Believe the lie if you must," returned the man of reason indignantly.

"He did! I saw it! He got touched!" shrieked a girl.

"See here…" the boy tried to defend himself.

"Cootie boy!" shouted the basketball player, chuckling with half-hearted gulps.

A third person became isolated by his peers moving hastily away from him, while trying to stay out of reaching distance of their peers.

For a while, no one spoke. The accused settled into disquiet as their emotions drained them of energy.

"We have to know all five who were touched, right?" a chocolate-skinned girl asked.

"That's what she said," snorted a pimple-faced boy.

"In the story," added the hostess, "that's true. Then *I* said that the hay wagon was Holy Ground and that you had to know who the five were before you could go there. Until then, you are in danger of being touched and dragged into the world of death by the Forbidden Five. It's just a story, though, something my grandpa used to tell us to make sure we didn't stay outside after dark."

"Where did your *grandfather* get the story? Did he make it up?"

"I don't know." The redhead frowned. "I always just assumed he made it up to scare us."

"*He made it up*," mocked the basketball player with an immature sense of humor.

"What's wrong with you?" accused the band geek. "Did you get touched, or are you just *touched* in the head?"

"Me? Get touched?" The self-proclaimed big man on campus laughed out loud. "Those things wouldn't *dare* touch me. I'm too important to the team. They'd lose without *me* on the court."

"The guilty dog barks," snarled the band geek in sarcasm.

"Bark? I'll *bite* you in a minute!" he flared as he started toward the band geek. The group parted to let him pass unmolested.

A bookish girl moved away from the circle of safety around the fire and ran toward the wagon for hay designated as Holy Ground. She scrambled her way to the top of the hay and stood firmly in the center of the wagon like the Queen of the Hill, secure in her position of power.

"What are you doing?" questioned a young man with sparse facial hair he was attempting to grow out. All eyes turned to the new prey.

"I know who the Forbidden Five are," she chattered. "You've all given yourselves away. I won't let myself be dragged into your destiny by ignorance. Begone, foul fiends!"

"Who are the Five?" cried out several voices. "Who are they?"

"Tell us!"

"It's for me to know and you to find out," she said with a firm pout.

The group turned back to their hostess.

"Tell us the truth!"

The redhead dropped her eyes to the ground and let her shoulders droop.

"I don't know." Her voice was barely audible.

"What do you mean you don't know? It's *your* game."

"It *is* my game, but I don't know who you think the Forbidden Five are. I touched about half of you while I told the story. It was just to make the story scarier. I only meant it as a party game. Everyone loves a party game. Everyone loves ghost stories around the campfire.

"Not everyone, it seems," grumped the rational man.

"So we accused our friends for nothing?" The bottle blonde glanced hopefully at her best friend. The goth girl glared back at her from ruined raccoon eyes.

Tempers were rising as fear washed away. The guilt-ridden hostess sobbed as she tried futilely to apologize to her peers, who had been her closest friends at the beginning of the party but were now alienated from her, possibly forever. Her life was ruined, as well as altering the course of the lives of others. Life after high school laid in the darkness of destiny's fickle fingers.

"So it's over?" the boy with curly hair and owlish glasses asked.

In reply, the partygoers began to move toward their cars. Their silence spoke volumes.

The girl on the hay wagon watched the others go, her mouth agape.

"You're really going to walk away now? They are still out there. You need to find them!"

A few teens stopped. Others slowed down dramatically. The rest defiantly continued toward their cars.

The dying bonfire suddenly and unexpectedly flared up, its flames roaring, wood cracking and popping deafeningly. Sparks lit up the sky with their brief but poignant flares. Newly released smoke billowed upward and outward in a black mushroom, blocking the natural light of the sky. A hiss of burning sap in greenwood rose from the accumulated ashes. The hiss became a wail; the wail, an eerie laugh.

"We are here!" the blended voices of many people bled through the crackling laughter. "Find us!" they commanded.

The girl on the hay wagon dropped to her knees. "I told you!" she cried out.

The group quickly gathered around the once-again-dying bonfire. There was no longer heat coming from the remaining flames. Light came only from the autumn moon and stars above their heads. Shadows prevailed, making it more difficult to see one another.

"We're back to square one."

This deflated remark came from the rational-minded young man who had previously concluded that the spirits of the dead could not hurt them. He now shuddered within his dark-green fleece. It wasn't because he was cold.

The autumn night turned to a chilly autumn morning as the youth remained where they stood, unmoving, unspeaking. Mute as clay pigeons, they watched the moon set in the west and the sun began to paint the east. An early-rising rooster crowed from the direction of the chicken coop. A dog barked its displeasure, and the rooster grew silent.

The last star, likely some planet, lingered well into the sunrise, fading slowly into the sky as the sun's fiery corona pushed its way upward. A slight breeze stirred the cold ashes of the bygone bonfire.

Wan, ashen faces, each limned with fear, raised to the cleansing power of the new day.

"It's over," the hollow-eyed hostess rasped.

"Are you sure?" someone asked.

"I think so," the girl replied. "We made it through the night. *They* cannot come out during the day."

"How do you know?"

"I just suppose so. They're ghosts, right? Ghosts only come out at night. I just assumed that at sunrise."

"That's the problem," guffawed the wise-cracking basketball player. "You *ass*umed. You made an *ass* out of *you* and *me.*"

"Not funny," corrected his girlfriend, a natural blonde with puppy ears and small wire-rimmed glasses.

"Time to go," a boy stated almost questioningly.

This time, as the teens started toward their cars, no one tried to stop them. The girl on the hay wagon slid to the ground, embarrassed by her behavior during the night. She shuffled toward her best friend's car. The two girls who had been put at odds by accusation stopped to embrace, each apologizing to the other. Their tears of reconciliation mingled with the cold sweat stains left from the nocturnal drama. The boy they were with rolled his eyes but smiled at their renewed relationship. One, after all, was his sister; the other, the girl he could only dream of someday dating.

The basketball player lifted his girlfriend and threw her over his shoulder in a fireman's carry, saying, "Me, Tarzan. You, Cheetah." The girl giggled and made monkey noises while she playfully pounded him on the back with her fists.

Mr. Rational stood beside his car, keys in hand. He contemplated the events of the previous night. His back window was partially plastered with vinyl clings proclaiming him a Darwinist, president of the debate team, Beta Club vice president, and a member of Future Scientists of Tomorrow. Maybe he should add a decal of a ghost, declaring himself to be a "beLIEver." He shook his head and silently unlocked his door.

"Great party!" a young man called out to the redhead still seated by the firepit.

"Yeah," she replied uncertainly, then mumbled to herself, "We'll have to do it again some time. *NOT!*"

Shaking off fear for the fearlessness of adolescence, the young people returned to their lives as they had left them. No one had felt the icy cold finger of death turn their blood ice-cold as they walked away.

Proverbs 24:8–9, NKJV

He who plots to do evil will be called a schemer.
The devising of foolishness is sin,
And the scoffer is an abomination to men.

Notes of Lurlene Joy McCoy

This sounds like the plot to nearly every adolescent scream film made in recent decades—a bunch of kids in the woods on a really dark night. Something happens to give them a scare, and they start turning on one another. The only thing missing is the psychopathic killer and the gratuitous blood and guts. Otherwise, cue the spooky music and shocking sounds that grate the nerves and throw the brain into survival mode.

Psychologists will tell you that the greater a fear is, the more irrational the individual becomes. Movie producers combine a creepy storyline with music of such a pitch and tempo that your heart rate accelerates, and sudden extra-loud sounds designed to startle the body into flight or fight, and visually assaulting special effects to produce pulse-pounding adrenaline rushes that leave us breathless and wanting more. A good storyteller can set the scene psychologically and guide their audience to explore their own phobias and respond with an associated fear. Our young party hostess is such a storyteller. Her friends responded to the natural temperature changes of the autumn evening and their own fears of social isolation as implied by the game.

I deliberately omitted the story the girl told as there are already far too many urban and rural myths abounding in our world. It is not my intention to add to these, hence the inclusion of these notes for my AD associates. We are all trained in our fields of expertise, our areas of giftedness, but often encounter situations in which we find ourselves facing a dilemma because we are unsure of an overlapping concern. I have mentioned this regarding areas of physics and the cosmos in general that fail me miserably. Insight from my brothers and sisters is necessary for us to all share in greater understanding of God's universe and our part in it, while combating our common enemy and his forces.

There is so much to discuss presented by this event. The true nature of this storyline is that of humanity since the fall of Adam and Eve. When we fail to recognize truth and to remain in a trust relationship with our Creator, we can fall for every lie of the master of lies. It begins with a single thought, something that leads us to doubt if we truly know truth or if we truly understand the nature of truth. When we begin to doubt, we are open to new ideas that may or may not align with what we already understand to be truth. The more we entertain these ideas and try to align them with our foundations, the more frustrated we become when they don't "fit" or remain unsatisfied with the evidence we have, and we begin grasping at straws, using logic and reasoning to talk ourselves into a comfort zone explanation, no matter how irrational or unreasonable it is.

These kids knew their hostess was telling them a story as part of a party game. If they had remained focused on that fact alone and played along accordingly, relationships would not have been damaged, no one would have gone home in fear, and they would have all lived happily ever after. Instead, these kids had been exposed to horror films and literary endeavors about supernatural creatures of evil intent. They had preconceived notions that evil exists and is out to get them. That's what the movies say. They let their experiences with fiction determine their real-life experience responses. No matter how much bravado you may have while watching a scary movie and yelling at the screen, when you are in the situation live, there is no room for audience participation, not that any audience has ever changed the recorded actions of actors in a film, no matter how many times you see the film. "If it was me, I'd…" doesn't work when it *is* you. It becomes a self-fulfilling prophecy. Ignorance of options should never be an excuse.

First Thessalonians 5:21 advises us to "test all things; hold fast what is good." If it doesn't feel right, it probably isn't good. If you don't have the answers, seek them. Don't seek a single source as our Darwinist skeptic or ignore all possibilities as did our big-mouthed athlete. On the other hand, too much information can be chaotic as well. Explore options and alternative explanations. Take everything you discover with a grain of salt. Do your homework and make an informed decision accordingly. While we know the Source of all Good and shun the source of all evil, we can be deceived when one takes on the form of the other. Do not entertain the things of the devil as we have seen in each of these stories. Pursue the Creator and all He freely gives.

Thrills and chills are cheap. Your eternal soul is priceless.

I have struggled with what the message of this story is. There is so much I could expound upon. I have decided to save my historic and theological explanations for an appendix to this volume for those who have the time and interest in chasing the myriad rabbits of this twisted warren. The primary issue at the heart of this story is fully stated in and expounded upon by the plot itself.

Here, a young woman repeats a story told to her by her grandfather, and she turns it into a party game. We do not know the origin of the story or its integrity. Was her grandfather telling of an actual event, tagging on a warning message, or was the entire piece a fabrication of a skilled storyteller? In our modern world, we have eschewed mythology and superstition for cold hard facts, or so we say. Yet a study of our modern literature and media consumption reveals that we are as superstitious now as our ancestors were, if not more so. We now call these things fiction—movies, books, magazines—that are just-so-happens about the supernatural and are billed as simply entertainment. Then there are the "reality shows" that center around individuals and groups that hunt and try to film paranormal events and mythical creatures. In the latter case, the same concepts are treated as nonfiction. Billions of dollars are spent annually on such "entertainment" and the merchandise it spawns. We are very much believers. Our consumer patterns clearly demonstrate what sells.

Sadly, with the rise in the supernatural and paranormal market, the church and all it stands for have failed to countermand with teachings that this stuff is very real, albeit not in the sensationalized form presented by the media, and that we are all victims of it in some form. The church not only tends to downplay such topics or expound only upon their detrimental effects on our kids, but it also flat-out denies that such exists and declares that the "born again" cannot be bothered by these things. A mixed message at best, it is fully dangerous. Just as happened at this party, a story is presented, complete with warnings and rules for play, but there is no clear definition of the true dangers involved. "The Bible says so" is far from an adequate explanation.

Hosea 4:6 declares, "My people are destroyed for lack of knowledge, Because you have rejected knowledge, I will also reject you from being priest for Me; Because you have forgotten the law of your God, I will also forget your children."

I believe Paul had this in mind when he penned Colossians 2:8, "Beware lest anyone cheat you through philosophy and empty deceit, according to the tradition of men, according to the basic principles of the world, and not according to Christ." He further expounds on this in his second letter to Timothy, chapter 3, verses 1–9, "But know this, that in the last days perilous times will come: For men will be lovers of themselves, lovers of money, boasters, proud, blasphemers, disobedient to parents, unthankful, unholy, unloving, unforgiving, slanderers, without self-control, brutal, despisers of good, traitors, headstrong, haughty, lovers of pleasure rather than lovers of God, having a form of godliness but denying its power. And from such people turn away! For of this sort are those who creep into households and make captives of gullible women loaded down with sins, led away by various lusts, always learning and never able to come to the knowledge of truth. Now as Jannes and Jambres resisted Moses, so do these also resist the truth: men of corrupt minds, disapproved concerning the faith; but they will progress no further, for their folly will be manifest to all, as theirs also was."

Here are the true FORBIDDEN FIVE:

1. Rejecting God and His Word as Truth.
2. Removing God from truth as explained by human context, even where there is evidence that points to God's Word.
3. Proclaiming human interpretation as sole source of truth, denying God or declaring God's Word as fallible or inaccurate and in need of revision to reflect modern understanding of truth.
4. Teaching human interpretation as sole source of truth and that it is hatred to not accept that one person's or group's truth must be accepted as equal with other truths; truth is not absolute but relative and is therefore valid, except

when it contradicts one's own truth. This leads to mixed messages and chaos that creates hostility.

5. Claiming to be a follower of God but denying Him power over your life, twisting His Words and commands to benefit self or harm others through judgmentalism, condemnation, and hatred; using God as means of declaring status or establishing superiority over another person or group. This is *self-righteousness*, not *God-ordained righteousness.*

These young people had little to no knowledge or understanding of good and evil, no concept of heaven or hell, and did not recognize either God or Satan. In our stimulus-response world, they heard the story, related it to what they had been exposed to in their limited cultural experiences, and responded in the only way they understood how. Without being able to see both sides of this spiritual coin, their world made no sense. From the atheistic philosopher to the scoffing athlete, each adolescent made his or her own decision about the truth and relevance of the story. They missed the point that it was just a game. Satan plays this game well. He is the master and creator of this game. He takes perverse pleasure when we fail to see the truth that ends the game and sets our feet on stable ground. The greater we fear our world, the less likely we will see truth and peace that only comes through Christ.

It is our responsibility, brothers and sisters, to ensure the truth is presented so that no one can claim ignorance. We are accountable for our actions; let us not fail in our efforts.

The Night the Wind Came In

We have within us temptations, which
if yielded to would destroy our soul.

—*Fellowship of the Burning Heart,* A. W. Tozer

There was once an old woman who lived way up in the mountains in a little house all by herself. Every night when she went to bed, she would blow out the candle and pull the covers up under her chin. Just as she was about to go to sleep, the wind came blowing with a mighty whoooooooooooooosh! It rattled her windowpanes.

Every night, the old woman would cry. "Wind, wind, why do you rattle my windows so?"

The wind replied, "I've come to visit, Old Woman. I've come to visit. Let me come in."

Every night, the old woman told the wind, "No! Go away and let me be!"

This went on for many years.

One night, the old woman decided to let the wind come in.

That night, the old woman blew the candle out and pulled the bedcovers up to her chin. She waited for the wind to come calling.

Whoooooooooooosh! The wind charged around the house, rattling the wooden windowpanes.

The old woman sat up in bed and said, "Wind, wind, why do you rattle my windows so?"

The wind answered her, "I've come to visit Old Woman. I've come to visit. Let me come in."

Expecting to be told to go away, the wind was surprised when the old woman opened the window a very tiny bit.

"Come in, Mr. Wind, come in," the old woman said.

With a gentle puff, the wind came in. A tiny whirlwind danced around the tabletop and whispered stories of faraway lands. It told the old woman of different-colored peoples who wore brightly colored clothes. It whispered of strange trees it had rattled and waters it had rippled. The old woman laughed with glee.

When the sun came up, the wind had to go. The old woman let it out and watched it blow merrily on its way.

That night, she decided to open the window just a tiny bit more.

As she blew out her candle and pulled the covers up to her chin, she heard the wind coming racing around her house. Whoooooooooooooosh! She waited until the windows began to rattle before she called out, "Wind, wind, why do you rattle before my windows so?"

The wind replied, "I've come to visit, Old Woman. I've come to visit. Let me come in."

The old woman opened the window just a tiny bit, and then just a tiny bit more. The wind came rushing in. It was too big to dance on the tabletop, so it danced on the floor. It told the old woman more tales of faraway places.

When the sun came up and the wind had to go, the old woman sadly watched it go.

That night, she jumped into bed, blew out the candle, and pulled the covers up to her chin. Quietly, she waited for the wind to come.

Soon, a loud whoooooooooooosh! announced the wind. The windows began to rattle.

"Wind, wind. Why do you rattle my windows so?" The old woman giggled.

"I've come to visit, Old Woman. I've come to visit. Let me come in."

The old woman opened the window just a tiny bit, then just a tiny bit more, then gave a hard shove until it was halfway open!

With a long howl, the wind came dancing in. It was too big for the tabletop. And too large for the floor. So it danced from wall to wall, picking up everything it saw. It danced with logs from the fireplace. It danced all night from wall to wall as the old woman laughed at the stories it told.

When the sun rose, the wind had to go. The old woman waved goodbye and wiped a tear from her eye.

That night, she could hardly wait to jump into her bed and listen for the wind. She blew out the candle and pulled the covers up to her chin.

The wind climbed over the mountain and raced to her house with a loud wail! The windows began to rattle.

"Wind, wind, why do you rattle my windows so?" The old woman laughed out loud.

"I've come to visit, Old Woman. I've come to visit. Let me come in."

The old woman ran to the window and opened it just a little bit. Then she opened it just a little bit more. Then she gave a great shove and opened the window all the way up!

The wind pushed her aside as it came SCREAMING in. It was way too big to dance on the tabletop. It was way too big to dance on the floor. It was so big it couldn't bounce from wall to wall! The wind was so big it didn't seem there was any room in the little house for the old woman.

The wind looked for places to go. It danced with the fire in the fireplace. It pushed on the walls. It rattled the windows. The old woman danced with the wind as it whistled about and told wonderful stories of faraway places.

Creeeeeeeeeeeeeeak! came a noise. The old woman stopped dancing.

"What was that?" she asked.

"It was nothing," said the wind.

They began to dance once more.

Creeeeeeeak! came the sound again.

The old woman stopped dancing once more.

"It is nothing," said the wind. "Come dance with me!"

They danced, and they danced, not caring what came.

Creeeeeak! came the noise. The old woman stopped.

"I know I heard something," she said. "What can it be?"

The wind tried to scoop her up into a dance once more, but she stood solid as a tree.

Creeeeeeeeeeeeeeeak! came the sound once again. The old woman stood firm, planted in fear. She watched as one wall fell away. The wind began to chuckle. Another wall fell. The wind began to laugh. A third wall fell down. The wind began to bellow with glee. The fourth wall fell. The wind twirled wildly about as it snatched the roof and carried it away over the mountain.

The old woman stood on the floor of her house, watching the fire burn in the lonely chimney.

Quietly, she climbed back into her bed and slept beneath the starry sky.

The next day, her son came to visit. He saw the house scattered around the yard.

"What happened here?" he cried.

"I've been dancing with the wind," replied the old woman.

"Mother, you must come to live with me," said the son.

So they packed up her bed and all her things, and the old woman went to live in her son's house in the valley.

She was very happy there, except at night, when she could hear the wind up on the mountain, calling, "Where are you, Old Woman? I've come to visit you."

The old woman would whisper from her bed, "I'm here, oh, Wind, far from home."

One day, she told her son. "Son, I miss the mountain. Please build my house back where I belong."

A new house was built for her. She moved in as soon as it was done.

That night, she blew out the candle and pulled up the covers to her chin. She could hear the wind whisper, "Where are you, Old Woman? I have come to visit you."

The old woman whispered back, "I am here, oh, Wind. Back where I belong."

The wind spoke louder, "Where are you, Old Woman? I've come to visit you."

She spoke louder. "I am here, oh, Wind. Back where I belong."

The wind began to shout, "Where are you, Old Woman? I've come to visit you!"

The old woman shouted back, "I am here, oh, Wind! Back where I belong!"

The windows began to rattle, and the wind screeched outside.

The old woman shouted, "Wind, wind, why do you rattle my windows so?"

The wind gently replied, "I've come to visit, Old Woman. I've come to visit. Let me come in."

The old woman opened the window just a tiny bit. A puff of air blew past. A tiny whirlwind danced across her tabletop. The old woman sat to hear the stories of the wind.

Proverbs 25:28, NKJV

> Whoever has no rule over his own spirit is
> like a city broken down, without walls.

Notes of Lurlene Joy McCoy:

In literary terms, this is called a circular story, in that the plot circles back around to the beginning, indicating the story will simply repeat itself with no end. This can also be classified as a cautionary tale as it appears to warn against behavior that can lead to destruction for those who fail to learn and apply the intended lesson.

Self-control is listed as one of the fruits of the spirit (Galatians 5:22–23). This old woman seems to have struggled with this concept. In her initial interactions with the wind, she seemed to fear what the wind could do to her. Perhaps she had seen the effects of the wind, from gentle ripples of water to the devastation of a tornado, and she realized it was an unpredictable force. She had every reason to fear the wind as it rattled her windows as she tried to sleep. It produced insecurity in her.

The wind enticed her with gentle whispers that it had secrets to tell if the old woman would only let it. A gentle breeze feels nice on a calm day, with just enough sun to produce a heat that needs to be cooled. The wind whispers that it can cool you down and teases us with its caress. That same wind can just as quickly rip the hat from your head and toss it about just out of reach, making you chase it, or bend a tree over until it breaks and blocks your escape to safety. Just as the story of the competition between the sun and the wind to determine who was stronger, the wind can be gentle and cool you on a warm day, or it can be so forceful and cold it makes you put on a coat to protect and warm yourself. However, the sun provides warmth that makes you take your coat off (and sometimes more) in order to find warmth and to relax in comfort. Yes, the sun can be brutal, too, especially if you are prone to sunburn. The point is, there is always a balance somewhere in between. It takes time and experience to find that balance.

Temptation does not have to be a bad thing. It does not have to lead to destructive decisions or self-destructive behavior. It can be a learning tool to determine where your personal line lies in that area. You must learn how far is too far. Is it okay for me to do this, or is it bad for me? Addictions are temptations that have become destructive. Sometimes, abstaining from all exposure to those temptations is required to overcome the temptation permanently. It is a lifelong abstinence. Other times, it is necessary to abstain for a period to learn how to deal with the temptation appropriately when it comes again. Once we understand why something is a temptation for us and what our alternatives are, we can face the temptation without falling prey to it.

This is exactly how Satan works in our lives. He begins with whispers that something isn't really bad. You should try it; you'll like it. When we give in and find pleasure or success resulting from giving in to the temptation, Satan ups the ante just a little bit. He lowers the bar so that other temptations don't look quite as bad as they once did. With each lowering of the bar, we compromise our self-control and begin to lose control. A fortune cookie I once received had this to say—"Don't give the devil a ride. He'll just want to drive." Once you give in to temptation, that temptation only gets stronger. Soon, an addiction arises. Addictions are difficult to break as I have already discussed.

This old woman was taken away from the mountaintop to her son's house in the valley. She claimed happiness there, except for the memory of the wind. She seems to have forgotten the loss of her home to that very wind. She insisted her home be rebuilt, then looked forward to the return of the wind. The story ends where it began, opening the window to let the wind come in. Because she failed to develop self-control and master her fear of the wind in an appropriate manner, she is seemingly doomed to repeat that mistake.

There is always hope that she did indeed learn her lesson and will refuse to open her window no more than a tiny bit for a refreshing breeze to cool her on a hot night. But the temptation for more will always be with her. Self-control is a lifelong development. May she live to tame the wind.

Labyrinth

The sin nature is so repelled by the purity of
God's nature and seeks other consolations.
These two natures are incompatible, which is
the practical outcome of alienation from God.

—*Experiencing the Presence of God,* A. W. Tozer

When you are mad, life becomes one big maze, with no apparent way in or out. No matter which way you choose to turn, you find yourself in a dead end. Marking your path for an easy retreat only results in a mess of bread crumbs, quickly snatched by scavenger birds seeking a free meal. You are left with a trail of feathers and bird droppings.

After a while in this maze, you begin to doubt not only your sanity but your very being. You don't remember who you are, where you originally intended to go, or how you came to be in this dark labyrinth. You begin to imagine evil minotaurs in every shadow, even you're on your own. You feel its venomous breath scorching your neck. You know your moments are numbered.

When you least suspect it, the minotaur is going to bound from the shadows, rip your head from your shoulders, and devour it whole while your heart continues to beat its lifeblood from your tattered neck. Time in this dark abyss makes you long for that finality.

You find yourself no longer seeking a way out but a way in… to the deeper reaches of this everlasting madness. You no longer care about escape. Darkness is your only companion. Its cool fingers embrace your cooling body. You feel warmed as you slip into the numb darkness of death.

Job 10:20–22, NKJV

Are not my days few?
Cease! Leave me alone, that I
may take a little comfort,
Before I go to the place from
which I shall not return,
to the land of darkness and the shadow of death,
A land as dark as darkness itself,
As the shadow of death, without any order,
Where even the light is like darkness.

Notes of Lurlene Joy McCoy

Here is a description of what it must be like to die without Christ. There are stories of people who died screaming, complaining of hellfire and demons coming for them. It is a horrific thing to come to the end of your life and enter into eternity knowing there is no more chance at redemption. Many people have written their accounts of having experienced hell, whether in a dream, an out-of-body experience, or as part of a near-death encounter. Remarkably, these experiences have some things in common. There is always a sense of hopelessness and despair. Sometimes there are physical flames eating at their eternal corpses. Some describe tormenting demons that seem to take great pleasure in tormenting fallen humanity. At times, they are in pits with others or in an isolated cell or cage. None of it is pleasant. There are no parties or orgies there. There is no compassion. There is only emptiness and cries of despair.

Mary K. Baxter wrote about her nocturnal visits to hell in her book *A Divine Revelation of Hell.* She spoke of the inhuman torment of those condemned there. As she walked through hell with Jesus by her side, the souls would cry out for release and repentance. Jesus then revealed the person's earthly lives and the decisions they had made that had resulted in them rejecting Jesus and leaving them to this eternity. Mary learned that the decision to follow Christ *must* be made before entering into eternity. Once the soul was released from the flesh, that decision was final. Each of the condemned souls then began to curse Jesus and remained unrepentant, even amid eternal torment. Christ knows our hearts. He loves us anyway. He tries to reach out to each of us personally, offering forgiveness and salvation; it is ultimately our own decision to accept or reject that offer. It saddens Him when we turn away. He does not want any of us to perish, but He will not force us to follow Him. It is our choice. It is called free will.

In *23 Minutes in Hell,* Bill Wiese chronicles his own trip to hell in the company of Jesus. He, too, describes many of the torments he saw. The most impacting event for him was being suspended in absolute darkness in a small cage, with absolute silence surrounding him. He recalls crying out to Jesus and receiving no response. The sheer terror of being separated from his Lord and savior nearly broke him mentally in that moment. Before that could occur, Jesus snatched him from that pit and took him to a point in space where he could see the entirety of the earth, as if from space. Jesus revealed the love He has for His creation and the desire to protect it from the evil that is necessary for humanity to understand His love and goodness.

Other writers have created fictionalized accounts of hell, such as Dante's *Inferno*, the first of the three parts that form *The Divine Comedy.* Hell has become a part of modern culture and has been incorporated into the modern mythology of the graphic novel and comic book superhero genre—with characters such as Hell Boy and demonic characters that are being rewritten as heroes. Hell is money to those who seek to exploit it. Modern horror films tout characters that come from hell to drag you to hell before they are sent to hell for eternal torment. People pay to see hell portrayed on the big screen. They court the terror of confronting hellish creatures and living to tell the story.

Many who pick this book up and peruse its pages are such thrill seekers. In its secular form, this is simply another book to read with the lights on at midnight. Some will take the stories to be urban or rural myth and will perpetuate them around the campfire without caution of their potential harm. Remember what happened with the

Forbidden Five. Spread the gospel to offset the reality of hell. Don't go uninformed about the flipside of fear. There is peace in knowing a loving savior who gave His own life so that we will never have to see hell for ourselves. Choose life. Choose Christ.

Like Father, Like Son

If man were not made in the image of God,
redemption would not be possible. Those who
have tried to think of man as coming into this
world without a Creator are, in fact, denying
man's redemption. Only what was created in
the image of God can be restored by God.

—*Living as a Christian,* A. W. Tozer

A small boy holds the key to his daddy's soul.
Daddy is his to bend and shape as he wills.
Playtime comes at childish demand.
Daddy howls, the small boy laughs.
Together, the two sing in harmony.
The small boy toddles into his father's arms.
They wrestle and play until bedtime calls.
Monsters bring delight to the child's play,
Until he begins to fear hidden things.
Daddy's howls take on new meaning.
Daddy becomes a monster each time he sings.
Only his son can save him now.
A kiss, a hug, the reassurance of love
Can tame the wild beast that howls at night.
Who will kiss away the monsters
when the boy is grown and gone?
As the boy grows, he overcomes the fears.
Together, they howl once more.
Secret nights, they play.

Away from friends and those
who wouldn't understand.
The bond between father and son.
The day the boy leaves home,
the father howls alone.
His lonely nights are unfulfilled.
The moon rises many nights; unsung, it sets.
The man waits; the son doesn't come.
Time passes, the boy becomes a man.
The father howls, calling his son.
No answer comes; the echoes die.
A tired old man lies down,
Tears in his eyes as he sleeps.
Monsters come to claim their king.
Howling fills the night as warriors seek
The one who can free a father's soul.
The son comes; is it too late?
Can his kiss still tame the beast?
His manly arms embrace his dad.
The snarl becomes a smile.
Father and son rejoice, sharing a soul once more.

Proverbs 22:6, NKJV

Train up a child in the way he should go,
And when he is old, he will not depart from it.

Notes of Lurlene Joy McCoy

This poem demonstrates the parent-child relationship as it is in a fallen world. When our children are small and naive of free will, they follow our example blindly and with delight in knowing we are finding pleasure in them. As they grow and mature, they begin to see there is more to their world than Mom and Dad. They see things that seem to be contrary to what they knew and wish to understand these new things. The authority of parents becomes questionable, and they rebel as they investigate these new ideas. Sometimes, this results in them viewing their parents as unrelenting monsters, trying to control them. If the world has its way, they cut off the relationship with their parents as one would cut off an offending appendage. The parents continue to cry out to their children that they are there for them; their love has not disappeared. Parents set rules and boundaries to protect their children, but when children move outside of those boundaries, the parents cannot follow. The "monsters" remain penned up far away from influencing the children they spawned. The children hear them snarling and growling, threatening them if they don't return. Eventually, they escape even the sound of their parents' voices. They claim to be free. When life gets tough, they seek out others with like minds for advice but rarely find solutions. It is only when a child reluctantly or willingly reconnects with the wisdom of their parents and admits the parent was right about the rules and boundaries keeping them safe that the child sees that the parent was never a monster. They acted in love. They fiercely defended their child from all harm as long as they could, then cheered their children as they set out to discover life for themselves. Those cheers were intended as reminders that they were loved and could always come home. Sometimes those cheers were intended to guide the children away from trouble. Sometimes there were tears of sorrow when the parents saw the child chasing disaster and they called out to their children to try and bring them back to where they belonged. Far too often, the needed reconciliation only occurs when either parent or child is near death. Far more than known are the parents and children parted by death without reconciliation. For those children who reconcile with their parents, a new relationship begins in which the authority the parent once had over the child is now shared authority between parent and child, with each being accountable to the other.

This is how it is with God, our precious Father. He designed us in love, through love, for love. He provided everything we could ever need or desire. There was just one rule. We were to not partake of the Tree of the Knowledge of Good and Evil. As long as we trusted the goodness of Papa, we were safe. Only when we were persuaded that we could be like God were we introduced to the dangers of disobedience. It was when we chose disobedience to the One Who Provides that we become slaves to our own passions. We blamed God for our failings. We blamed Papa for taking away our toys. In our eyes, our Creator became a destroyer of all pleasure. It is the true destroyer, Lucifer, who has drawn us away from true love. It is Satan's lies that made us into the rebellious monsters we have become. Jesus cries out to us in love. He came to us and walked among us to show how much He loves us. He died in our place so we could be redeemed. He rose again from the grave so we could be reconciled to Papa. He cheers us along and cries out to direct us back to Him. We hear only dictatorial and judgmental roaring that seeks to enslave us against our will. We have lost the first love of our Father and traded it for the song of a liar. Only when we see the strength and love of Papa once more and crave that relationship once more are we able to return to the family we were born into and take our place as children of the Most High, safe from the fallen deceiver for all eternity.

May we never leave the bounds of His great love. May we never walk away to never return. May we always hear the voice of the One Who Loves Us Best.

Dead Man's Inn

God has buried something deep within the soul of every man and woman. It is simply and profoundly a longing for immortality.

—*And He Dwelt Among Us*, A. W. Tozer

The house was quite large—too large, really, for a family of four, but they loved it. The family stayed mainly on the first floor, shutting off the second floor completely to save energy. The rare excursion to the second floor was for the moving in and out of stored items such as Christmas ornaments and seasonal clothing. Even on those rare occasions, the family never explored beyond the main room designated as storage. It wasn't until one child braved the second floor to seek out a bedroom all her own away from the rest of her family that the secret life of the second floor was discovered.

She was twelve, that age when privacy became important to a young girl. The single bathroom on the main floor was always occupied by some member of the family, meaning she was always waiting in line to bathe, brush her teeth, do her hair, or take care of basic needs. It was a constant race to get the best of the hot water. The bathroom on the second floor was closed off, unused. She could have it all to herself if she had her own room.

The room she had downstairs was always noisy, thanks to her brother's loud music, her mother's frequent laundry runs, and her father's constant lecturing just outside her door. Though private, her room was too accessible to the public parts of the house. Her mother was constantly saying they needed a home office / guest room. If she moved to the second floor, her mother could get her wish. In her small downstairs room, she had trouble concentrating on her homework; frequent headaches and eyestrain in the brightly lit room sent her seeking shadowy spaces where darkness eased the pain and she could find peace. The second floor had one room that seemed to fit this need. These issues disrupted her school days and led to the slipping of her grades. Her parents spent more time invading her space in their concern, leading to more headaches. These issues and impending puberty drove her to seek refuge on the second floor.

She found a quiet room as far from the stairs as she could get. It was fully furnished in feminine florals and brought her peace. Whoever had lived in that room before her was a kindred spirit. She brought her most important belongings to this refuge, her private paradise. She could sit for hours in the dark, relaxing and contemplating peace, before returning to the chaos of her family downstairs.

During one of her frequent visits to this private Eden, she felt the presence of others in the room. Feminine odors or soft touches alerted her to the presence of others within the upstairs space. Sometimes she imagined the tinkling laughter of a child or heard the rustling of skirts. Rather than being fearful, she instead embraced the events as a natural part of her private world.

Eventually, the silent visitations became more audible. Their voices could be in the hallway or from behind the closed doors of the other rooms. The female presences were joined by those of males. A mustiness sometimes invaded, as if an elderly individual had been there only moments before. Toys mysteriously were moved or appeared where they hadn't been before.

The girl, Julia, adjusted to these events as if they were a normal part of life. In fact, as she lay there in the dark, fending off a headache, she would listen for the voices and try to interpret their sibilant sounds. She made out occasional words and phrases but could not make out the conversations. The voices became a comfort to her, a soothing source of peace in her increasingly more difficult world.

Julia began retreating to her private space more and more frequently, and she stayed there for longer and longer periods. It seemed days would go by before she returned to the world of her family downstairs. No one mentioned her absences. Life continued as usual, though her mother appeared tired, and her father more reserved. Even her brother walked lightly around her.

The day arrived as she lay in the dark that silent figures entered her room and watched her sleep. When she awoke, she was not afraid. She had been expecting these guests. She smiled dreamily.

An older woman in an out-of-fashion print dress stepped forward and brushed the hair from Julia's forehead. She, too, smiled.

"We were wondering when you would wake," said the woman, brushing back a bit of her own flyaway hair that had come loose from the bun at the nape of her neck.

"My headache is gone," stated Julia. She sat up on the edge of the bed, facing her visitors. She reached for the bedside lamp to turn it on but realized it was already on. Her brow furrowed as she distinctly recalled turning it off earlier.

A young woman sat down beside Julia and placed her arm around Julia's shoulder. Julia looked at the young woman curiously. The young woman used her free hand to wipe a tear from her cheek.

"Why do you cry?" asked Julia.

"She is relieved to see that you are okay," replied the older woman.

"Who are you? What are you doing in my home?"

Julia looked at each of the five women of varying ages and ethnic backgrounds that were in the room with her. She sensed others standing unseen in the hallway, beyond the closed bedroom door.

"Who we are is no longer important," replied a woman with olive skin who stood partially in the shadows near the door.

"We are who we will be but not who we were," implied a gray-haired matron in the chair by the window.

"As for why we are here," began an elegant black woman of indeterminant age, "we are here until we move on to where we will be."

"I don't understand," said Julia, confusion and fear causing her voice to quiver. The young woman beside her began rubbing her shoulders gently but did not speak.

The older woman who had spoken first knelt on the floor and took Julia's hands into her own.

"We are friends, Julia," she said. Julia was startled that this woman knew her name. "We hear your parents and brother speaking to you, and we have tried for so long to speak to you too. As soon as we knew you sensed our presence, we tried to talk to you. At last, you have broken through."

Julia stood. This was too much. She still didn't know who these people were. She crossed her arms to ward off the chill of the room.

"What do you want from me?" she stammered.

"Someone to talk to, mostly," returned the olive-skinned woman, stepping into the light. Her green eyes sparkled. Her long, black hair hung to her waist. She was beautiful by any standard, and young.

Julia thought for a moment. She eyed each woman in turn. Finding only acceptance in their eyes, Julia sat on the bed once more.

"Why me?" she asked.

"Only you would understand," stated the grandmotherly woman.

"We are 'Between,' as are you," explained the olive-skinned woman.

"Your riddles confuse me," said Julia. "Please tell me what is going on."

The elegant black woman was the one who finally spoke. We are Between. That means that we are no longer a part of your world. Neither are we a part of the next world. This house, among others, is a waiting place. A Dead Man's Inn if you will. When our lives cease to be lived in the way you know it, we come to a place like this to await our time to move into the next life, the everlasting life. Sometimes our stay is brief, sometimes long. We know not when our time comes to pass on. It just happens. Then someone else comes to take our place."

Julia stood, stunned into silence, contemplating what she had just heard. Her house was a waiting place for dead people! Chill bumps crawled up her arms. The hairs on the back of her neck stood on end.

"I think I understand your Between. You said I am Between too. Do you mean I'm dead? Or dying?" The fear was clear in her young eyes.

The elderly grandmother leaned forward, chuckling.

"Law, child, you do go on. Your Between is the most natural thing that could happen to a girl your age."

Julia's brow continued to wrinkle in confusion. The young woman sitting on the bed started nodding her head in quick, fluid motions. Her mouth also moved, but no sound came out.

"She says you are no longer a child but becoming a woman. You are between youth and womanhood," interpreted the grandmother.

Understanding peeled away from Julia's eyes and face. She had been told by her doctor that her headaches and moodiness were related to emerging hormones and bodily changes as puberty approached. He had assured her the symptoms would lessen or disappear over time. He had not, however, mentioned that she would also be able to see ghosts.

Julia began spending her "quiet time" on the second floor, getting to know the residents of the second floor "hotel." She learned that though the population frequently changed, there usually tended to be an equal number of males to females, ranging from newborns to the very elderly. Each occupant spent anywhere from a few hours to many years occupying the second floor.

Julia's favorite was an elderly occupant who had been a resident longer than anyone else. Even he knew not how long he had waited. Mr. Ezekiel Greene had no memories of his previous life and was bedridden even in death. He spoke to Julia of the life he was waiting to go to. He spoke of green mountains, sparkling streams, and animals so tame they would eat out of your hand. She would sit for hours listening to Mr. Greene's dreams of heaven.

Julia blossomed into full womanhood one July afternoon as she approached her thirteenth birthday. She had the worst headache she had ever experienced accompanied by the expected cramping. As soon as she could, she retreated to her special place on the second floor. She fell onto the bed in her darkened sanctuary, praying the pain medication she had taken would take effect before she exploded. Being a woman could be a terrible thing, if you asked Julia.

Her friends came to comfort her, but even their experienced wisdom could not alleviate her pained tears. Jodi, a six-year-old who had come to stay just three weeks before, came skipping into the room, asking Julia to play. Kitari, the olive-skinned woman, pulled Jodi back into the hallway, offering to play with her instead. Jodi wasn't particularly upset; one playmate was as good as another. They were met in the hallway by a teary-eyed young man named David Miller. David had been a college student before coming to this house. He was usually jovial and upbeat but was disturbingly down at that moment. He stopped to whisper something to Kitari. Kitari strangled her response and ran down the hall, Jodi in tow.

David stepped sorrowfully into the room, eyeing each of the others who were present. He lowered his eyes before he spoke. "Mr. Greene has passed on," he said.

"Oh, no!" wept Diana, the grandmotherly woman seated in the chair by the window, her personal favorite.

"When?" asked Jamika, the elegant black woman.

"Only moments ago," replied David. "I checked on him not more than ten minutes ago, and he was fine. When I felt a sudden warm breeze, I was drawn back to his room. I found the bed empty."

The hidden household mourned the passing of their mentor and friend. Yet, they rejoiced that he had finally found the heaven he had spoken of for so long.

2 Corinthians 5:1–15, NKJV

> For we know that if our earthly house, this tent, is destroyed, we have a building from God, a house not made with hands, eternal in the heavens. For in this we groan, earnestly desiring to be clothed with our habitation which is from heaven, if indeed having been clothed, we shall not be found naked. For we who are in this tent groan, being burdened, not because we want to be unclothed, that mortality may be swallowed up by life. Now He who has prepared us for this very thing is God, who has also given us the Spirit as a guarantee.

So we are always confident, knowing that while we are home in the body we are absent from the Lord. For we walk by faith not by sight. We are confident, yes, well pleased, rather to be absent from the body and to be present with the lord.

Therefore we make it our aim, whether present or absent, to be well pleasing to Him. For we must all appear before the judgment seat of Christ, that each one may receive the things done in the body, according to what he has done, whether good or bad. Knowing therefore, the terror of the Lord, we persuade men; but we are well known to God, and I also trust are well known in your consciences.

For we do not commend ourselves again to you, but give you opportunity to boast on our behalf, that you may have an answer for those who boast in appearance and not in heart. For we are of sound mind, it is for you. For the love, it is for you. For the love of Christ compels us because we judge thus: that if One died for all, then all that those who live should live no longer for themselves, but for him who died for them and rose again.

1 Corinthians 15:42–45, NKJV

So also is the resurrection of the dead. The body is sown in corruption, it is sown in dishonor, it is raised in glory. It is sown in weakness, it is raised in power, it is sown a natural body, and there is a spiritual body. And so it is written, "the first man Adam became a living being." The last Adam became a life-giving spirit.

Notes of Lurlene Joy McCoy

I have had more backflash from this piece than any others I have published. It is a coming-of-age story, and some people are offended at the personal language of such an event in a girl's life. It is traumatic at its very core, no matter how prepared the young woman is. It has nothing to do with seeing ghosts, however. For those who have deemed this story to be inappropriate for public eyes, I apologize. In our modern society, such private matters are becoming more public in advertising and media presentations, such as movies and books for the preteen. It is a fact of life.

That is merely a surface complaint, however.

Truth of the matter is that this story is more allegorical in nature than folklore. For many, the allegory is simply fantasy and has no bearing on real life. For the informed, allegory is real life explained in a fantasy format. Much like the parables Jesus told, only those who understand the story behind the story will get the point. It requires reading between the lines and ferreting out the symbolism and the patterns to make sense of the secret code. That is one reason for this selective edition of this book that contains my notes and research. By having this information, each of you will be able to break the code behind my other works and those who have been charged with this same chronicling of truth in the form of fiction.

This is the story behind the story.

We are born into a fallen world, in a fleshly tent we call our body. The eternal soul and spirit are trapped within this mortal flesh. Because of free will, we experience both pain and joy as we navigate through life. We are born innocents into a broken world. As we begin to grow and experience the harsh realities of this broken world of mixed messages, we face decisions that will impact our present and determine our future. We undergo a form of spiritual puberty as we learn right from wrong and determine the path we believe will achieve whatever goals we have decided upon. We are in the Between of accountability. Some will choose the path of disobedience and grow increasingly disruptive in their lifestyles, crowding out and pushing aside any who dare confront them or try to redirect them.

Most will veer side to side, unsure as to what is truly right or wrong as they lack guidance and knowledge to show them the proper way. A third group will take the path of righteousness and seek the peace that path provides. Whichever path one takes, they are between mortality and immortality that begins with the release of the spirit and soul from this flesh.

In the case of our story, Julia expressed distress in the way her family went about their daily lives—a brother who made his presence known through loud music, a mother who spent her day in busy activity that never seemed to end, and a father who seems to be dissatisfied in the unruliness around him but hopeless to do anything about it. Julia became confused as to where she fit into this familial chaos. She tried to keep to herself in her room, but life interfered. She began to experience a very real illness as she became pressured to find her niche in the world around her. She withdrew as a means of escape. Her schoolwork suffered. Her parents began questioning her and monitoring her more closely. She began seeing a doctor who tried to assure her she would grow out of her condition. Her brother became estranged from her. She began to hear the voices of people who cared and were willing to help her as she bridged the gap from childhood to adulthood. When she came to terms with the fact that these people genuinely loved her and accepted her as she was, she developed a relationship with them. They helped her find her niche in life. They aided her in developing a maturity and security she did not have before. She found true friendship and a family that would not give up on her, though the members of that family came and went. She found the peace she needed. When she lost the man who had become her mentor, she mourned, yet she rejoiced. She knew he was no longer between what he had been and was now fully what he was to become. Mortality had given way to immortality in the desired paradise he had thought to be long in his past.

This is a picture of the church as she should be, the Bride of Christ. Our world is a confusing place. We, as believers, are called to be there for those who are struggling to find their way in this world. There are those who cannot or will not respond to the ministrations of compassion. We are still to be there for them, even though they refuse to acknowledge our presence. We are to continue our love and support, never giving up. Some will eventually begin to see that we are agents of good and mean them no harm. They will coexist with us, recognizing that we are there, but choosing not to respond to us. Those who decide to give heed to our voices will see us and talk to us, listen as we show them the Creator who loves us and died for us. We are at the age of accountability and must make a decision of how we wish to enter adulthood. Everyone makes this decision at some point in their life. Unless there is some extreme circumstance that robs us of our mental faculties and ability to respond to stimuli in the world around us, we are accountable for our actions. Small children are capable of recognizing right and wrong. There is no excuse for adults. Even the six-year-old Jodi in the story had made that decision and joined the family of believers in the second story of Julia's home. That second story is the family of God. Everyone is welcome, no matter their age or circumstances. When we make that decision or are brought into the church as babies, we begin the learning process of what it means to be a child of God. We all begin as spiritual infants and grow in faith as we age in body. We don't know how long we will remain here in our earthen vessels before being called home to be with Christ. Mr. Greene had served the Lord for so long it was all he knew. He no longer desired to walk in the ways of the world and had dedicated himself to service in Christ alone. His loss was felt greatly by his friends, but they rejoiced in knowing that they would one day be reunited with their friend and mentor.

As we begin to grow and develop in our faith, we do fail in the things the world has to teach. We no longer need the things of the flesh to satisfy us—materialism, consumerism, self-righteousness—as we are fully sustained by our Creator. We grow into a new creation. We do leave this earthly vessel behind. All humanity does. But our eternity is entered into immediately upon that transition. Our soul is present with God as His children. Those who do not have that assurance are ushered into the presence of God to receive their eternal punishment—separation from the One Who loves them best but whom they failed to love in return. Immortality exists. But the state of immortality is only determined while mortal. Someday, all will be judged. The unrighteous will be separated from the righteous. Our spirits which sleep will reunite with our souls, and we will receive a new body that is incorruptible. In heaven, we will feast with our Bridegroom, Christ Himself. For those who have failed to reunite with the One Who made them, there will be eternal separation, no chance of redemption. The wedding invitation has been sent. Will you walk down the aisle as bride or eternally be the onlooker who longs for a different partner that will never come?

Our time on earth is an opportunity to create for ourselves a preparedness for what we will become. We can never go back to what we were. The present is the only "Between" we have. How will your time in this Dead Man's Inn be spent?

The Night Train Element

"There are many opinions that our life is exactly like a train. You start the ride and through the ride you meet some passengers. Some stay longer, some get off out of your train sooner, but when you reach your final destination, you reach it all on your own."

—www.dreamingandsleeping.com

Lonely calls the night train as it passes through
The dark moonless night.
Sleeping passengers dream fearless fantasies
As the tracks lead ever deeper…
Into the mountainside.
Black gates open and close
As each passenger finds his or her private Eden,
Disembarking, seeking pleasure as the night train pulls out.
Private dreamers, private pains
All are one and the same.
Haunting echoes of the night train's whistle abound
As sleeping minds awaken to the reality of their dreams
And find they are trapped in their own private hells.
Screams blend with whistle calls in the lonely distance
As trapped souls beat against their steel cages.
The night train knows no man from another.
No respecter of persons; one soul is as good as another.
All who come to these mountains are prey.
Sleep well in the darkness of night.

Hide not your sins from yourself or others,
Else the night train will seek you out
And carry you away to a place of private regret
From which there is no escape.
Hear the whistle in the night; the conductor is calling you.
"Step aboard, dreams can come true.
Face your fears, come away free," he cries.
Hidden darkness, hidden pain, found in every man's heart,
Leads to this moment of trial in Satan's own den.
Bring the darkness or bring the light.
The power lies solely within you.
Choose wisely, my child...
The ticket is one-way.

I have a problem with a recurring nightmare, or at least one element of a nightmare. I don't know how to get rid of that darn antiquated train. The only way I know to exorcise a dream is to talk about it or write about it. Well, I'm killing one train with two stones so to speak. I am writing it all down for you to read. The story is being told.

I can remember the first time I dreamed about the train. I was in my late teens. I don't remember if I was married or not, but I do remember that most of these dreams have occurred during my adulthood.

Why the dreams always use a train as an antagonist I have never known. I have loved and respected trains my whole life. In fact, one of my grandfathers was a railroad man. I have ridden on a train. I have even explored the inner workings of a steam engine courtesy of a museum from the time I was at least five years old. My husband owns a toy train which never fails to keep my attention for hours. I always ache to build it a little town, complete with people, tunnels, trees, everything.

Perhaps therein lies my problem. I have an insatiable need to create. I am a poet and a writer. I sew. I do needlepoint. I am a romantic, a daydreamer, a seeker of knowledge. Even my dreams take on this desire for creativity when I literally stop the action and step in as director, turning a nightmare into a comedy.

While there is one basic recurring element, the train, there are other elements of the first dream that occasionally recur. That is why I will begin with the original dream. It was innocent until things began to go terribly wrong.

My father owns the family farm he grew up on. The house sits in a wonderful valley between magnificent green hills. One hill has been consistently used as pasture; the other was briefly lumbered but has been sitting undisturbed as long as I can remember. It is the latter hill which concerns me.

A creek separates this hill from the rest of the farm. There is a small stretch of flatland acting as a front porch between the creek and the hill itself. Our property only runs to the top of the ridge, and there really isn't that much land, but the dream always seems to magnify it and turn it into more than it is. But isn't that the way nightmares operate?

The dream opens with a dream. My own dream is to set up and operate my own attraction. It would begin with a train ride through various villages and towns, allowing people to experience different times and activities by interacting with real actors and actresses. At the end of the ride, participants would slide down a huge slide from the top of the hill to the bottom, experiencing the thrill I had rolling down these hills as a child.

The ride begins in the valley, winds slowly uphill for what seems to be a half mile before coming to a huge gate that conceals the first stage. As the train approaches, the gates open to reveal a Western town, circa 1880 or so. Cowboys wander through the town, eyeing the strangers disembarking at the train depot. As the visitors begin mingling with the actors, other characters begin to appear. Shopkeepers, ladies, and saloon girls make their appearances, playing their parts as if the modern intruders didn't even exist. Somehow, one feels one has been transported back over a hundred years to a bygone era.

Tumbleweeds roll through the streets as desperadoes ride into town. The hired townspeople seek their assigned places, waiting for the gunfight to begin. It is at this point the hint of something going wrong begins to show.

During the gunfight, a bystander is shot—only a flesh wound, but frighteningly unplanned. The poor man is rushed off to the first aid center to be tended to.

Contrary to my initial reaction, the shooter was an employee. The young man seems to show an uncharacteristic apathy for his victim. The guns were to have been loaded with blanks.

"Well, obviously they weren't," snarls the shootist.

The visitors are hustled to the train to cross into the next pavilion. Nervously, they anticipate the next encounter—a Viking world.

The gates open on an Icelandic village. Great Viking dragon ships sit at harbor, glaring gruesomely upon the village. Costumed actors stomp heavily through the disembarking crowd, growling and fondling the strange clothing of the guests.

Slowly the crowd spreads out to enjoy the shops, food stands, and exhibits, some visibly shaken by the proximity of the Viking men.

A fight breaks out in an open area. Two Vikings have discovered a pretty, young tourist and are fighting over her. The girl in question nervously watches the two men, unsure whether to applaud their acting or be frightened at the reality of the scuffle.

A final blow with a war axe leaves one man wounded. The victor gives a war cry and snatches his prize, disappearing into the crowd with the girl screaming for help.

Some of the spectators, mostly male, cheer the victor. Others, mostly female, stare aghast at the bloody battle sight. Many others, men and women, are unsure how to respond. Children stare blankly, waiting for their parents to respond.

Several other tourists report assaults and robberies; three others are missing by the time the conductor calls for passengers to board.

Each new pavilion brings some new horror to these unsuspecting passengers. Eventually, some refuse to get off the train. Other, braver, more skeptical parties disembark, seeking excitement and adventure, refusing these actions to be real.

This type of interaction was not a planned part of the program. No one was supposed to get hurt. What was going so suddenly wrong? After a hundred or so safe runs, the nightmare began. How can it be stopped?

It is a much smaller group that steps from the train in our small alpine village. Pale and sick, they file to the long slide that will take them to the safety of the real world of their cars. Some have to be persuaded to pass through the artificial snow blizzard on the slope. Others push their way forward to get to the front, shoving one another down the hill in the process.

Everyone is finally gone. I am alone with my nightmare. It and I stare at each other. Steam begins to puff from a cold furnace, empty of fuel. The wheels begin to turn. The nightmare continues. This time I am alone.

Jude 12–19, NKJV

> These are spots in your love feasts, while they feast with you without fear, serving only themselves, they are clouds without water, carried about by the winds; late autumn trees without fruit, twice dead, pulled up by the roots, raging waves of the sea, foaming up their own shame; wandering stars for whom is reserved the blackness of darkness forever.

> Now Enoch, the seventh from Adam, prophesied about these men also, saying, "Behold, the Lord comes with ten thousands of His saints, to execute judgment on all, to convict all who are ungodly and the deeds which they have committed in an ungodly way, and of all the harsh things which ungodly sinners have spoken against him".

Notes of Lurlene Joy McCoy

The premise of an interactive entertainment attraction is not new. Amusement parks used to feature train rides through the Western frontier with staged scenes and costumed mannequins that were paired with live storytellers and actors that staged train robberies. Western towns with gunfights in the street rose up in the wake of the popularity of movie and television Westerns. Historical reenactments are performed across the country annually. Entertainment venues offer "A Taste of…" whatever culture they offer for consumers to experience. With the rise of Disneyland, people were able to experience new cultures in animatronics, billed as "It's a Small World" and offering a boat ride through the cultures of the world and how we all share commonalities as well as differences. These were all designed to bring out the best in humanity. They have also brought out prejudices and reinvented stereotypes. Not all these events were thought out to benefit humanity but were designed to give the consumer what they paid for. Consumerism reigns, with materialism and self-righteousness as consorts. Today, people get angry when they are presented with true history or ugly reality about what they had preconceived notions of. Culture and history are specific to those who experience it firsthand. They are the experts. Listen to their explanations but keep your own in reservation. Evaluate their truth and adjust your understanding of it. You cannot determine the truth of what you do not understand or even know. Therein lies the core of chaos.

Though likely influenced by the movie *Westworld*, starring Yul Brenner, the teller of this nightmare experienced other truths as well.

There are unhealthy factors in our world. What is meant for good is infiltrated by those who would cause harm, until what was erected in joy is torn down in disgrace. The first-century church faced this daily. They were still in their infancy as a culture. They had no models upon which to base their organization. Paganism was rampant around them. They had difficulty separating what they once did with what they were now being asked to do. Old habits die hard. Those who simply joined the early church without understanding the need to change everything they knew because it went against what this new faith stood for made it difficult to worship in the new way. Some of these people were intentional troublemakers, trying to discredit this new God. Others were stubborn and could not give up their old habits easily. It interfered with the growth of the new faith based on belief in a savior, the Son of God, who had died for them and risen from the dead again.

We continue to face this situation in our modern world as the church redefines itself in an attempt to prove our God is "inclusive." Consumerism and materialism are replacing benevolence and personal worship in a corporate setting with God alone as focus. "Warm bodies with cold cash" have replaced an open door for all comers. From the beginning of time, this has been a problem. It will only continue to grow worse if we do not learn the lessons needed to overcome the problem of growing apathy among humanity. Hatred, the partner of apathy, cannot be allowed to prevail. The fight begins within each of us and radiates out to those around us, everywhere we go.

Topic: Trains and Fictional Symbolism

Source: THE BURNING, Signet, 2006
Author: Bentley Little

Summary

This fictional account chronicles one of America's unrepented holocaust stories. Little relates the tale of vengeful spirits of murdered Chinese immigrants who were murdered in mass after building the transcontinental railroad, in a form of attempted genocide. These spirits come together to take revenge on the descendants of the ones who murdered them. These individuals are drawn to a central location, surrounded by spectral trains which come from the four cardinal directions bearing the spirits of the murdered men, women, and children to enact a mass slaughter of their murderers. An elemental earth spirit calls together native Americans and non-white people to do physical combat with the living. This book is not for the faint of heart and is graphic in nature, as well as language.

Topic: Spiritual Meaning of Trains

Source: www.dreamsandsleeping.com

Summary

- Dreaming of trains is not uncommon.
- Not a reason for worry, in general.
- Symbol of our life, representing the course of our lives.
- Remembering the tiny details important for finding the true meaning behind the dream.
- *Being on a train*: thinking about your life and choices made along the way; may mean a bright future and many positive moments along the way; sign of possible positive surprising news likely to be heard soon; may be a sign you are ready for a certain opportunity along the way.
- *Seeing a train*: could be a sign you are on the right track in your life; means you are a type of person that loves peace; you are never making any action that goes against the rules or against someone's will.
- *Passenger train*: a sign you are working on your mental health; everything comes from our mind; the way we think is the way we live.
- *Someone being hit by a train*: Is the person familiar or a stranger? Friend or family means someone needs your help to live a healthier lifestyle; they are making destructive

choices and have destructive behavior patterns. A stranger represents yourself; you are making poor decisions and living life in the wrong way; change your life for the better.

- *Out-of-control train*: A sign you are actually steady; you have control and power over your life, ready to face everything on your own and do not have the time to spend it on nonsense.
- *Driving a train*: A sign you are not controlling your emotions the right way; feelings get in the way of something in your life, and that is not good at all: discipline your mind and learn how to be the master of your own emotions, or you will be emotionally manipulated by everyone in your life.
- *Seeing passengers on a train*: A sign you will experience a lucky period; high chance to get richer than you are now.
- *Hearing a train*: Missing out on some great chances in your life; could be a bad mindset or because of your social circle; you may have a fear of new situations, and that is why you are missing out on some great chances in your life. You may end up with great regrets without change.
- *Model train*: Someone is making huge decisions in your life for you. Take control!
- *Train crash*: A sign you are not surrounded by good people.

Topic: Biblical Meaning of Train in Dreams and Interpretation

Source: www.alodreams.com

Summary

For purposes of making a biblical connection, trains are equated with the chariot common to biblical themes.

Trains are symbolic of help arriving for you soon, symbols of looking into your spiritual life more, or symbolic of long-term plans.

Common Situations Where You Dream about Trains

- Seeing a derailed train in your dreams: This may signify you are being a good Samaritan to others, without expecting anything in return; may also be an unfortunate connotation of other people not appreciating your efforts or the help that you afford them; may also mean they are taking advantage of you while you let them abuse you; though your intentions are noble, you may be better off to just leave toxic and abusive people whom you give your whole heart to but end up harming you more than appreciating what you give them.
- Dreaming of alighting from a train: You have finally arrived at your destination in your waking life. This may symbolize that you have finally achieved what you have always set out to do; you may be working hard at a certain project at work or consciously trying to fix a relationship that you have with a partner, family member, or friend, or there may be an advocacy that you have devoted too much time and heart to. Getting off the train means you have finally reached your goals, and you are to reap the rewards of your hard work soon.
- Dream of being hit by a train: This may signify a decision or journey you are about to take in your waking life that you should probably avoid; may be some sort of warning sign that you should probably delay or not push through with that matter that you plan to do.
- Dream of riding a train: A positive sign of the journey you are on in life right now.
- Seeing train tracks in your dream: This could symbolize a path that you have been avoiding for the longest time in your working life; may be something you are not confronting; may mean that you can take a different journey, and you know this could be more beneficial for you and your growth, but are refusing to see how much wiser it is to take the leap. It could be a prompt to reflect on the path that

you are on and reevaluate if this is really helpful to you and your whole psyche and health; it may not be good to take on a different path instead.

- Dreaming of missing a train: This is a sign there are things in your life that are not meant to be; you could possibly be either just allowing it even if you know deep down that there is something not right about it, or you could also be forcing something that is not healthy anymore. Be brutally honest with yourself and see if what you are doing is selfish or if it is really benefiting the community you belong to as a whole; cut off these habits or actions from life.
- Dream of seeing a train pass you by: Symbolic of something that is not for you or you should not be a part of.

Biblical interpretations are meant to help you deepen your understanding of yourself and be more reflective and authentic, in order to have a more meaningful spiritual life as well.

Topic: Train

Source: *Understanding the Dreams You Dream*, Destiny Image Printers Inc., 1997
Author: Ira Milligan

To dream of a train represents continuous, unceasing work; the church; connected; fast.

Acts 2:42

> And they continued steadfastly in the apostle's doctrine and fellowship, and in breaking of bread, and in prayers.

Topic: Long Black Train

Songwriter: Fred Turner
Recording Artist: Josh Turner

Lyrics

There's a long black train comin' down the line
Feedin' off the souls that are lost and cryin'
Rails of sin only evil remains
Watch out brother for that long black train

Look to the heavens, you can look to the sky
You can find redemption starin' back into your eyes
There is protection and there's peace the same
Burnin' your ticket to that long black train

'Cause there's vict'ry in the Lord I say
Vict'ry in the Lord
Cling to the Father and His Holy Name
And don't go ridin' on that long black train

There's an engineer on that long black train
Makin' you wonder if the ride is worth the pain
He's just a waitin' on your heart to say
Let me ride on that long black train

But there's vict'ry in the Lord I say
Vict'ry in the Lord
Cling to the Father and His Holy Name
And don't go ridin' that long black train

Well, I can hear the whistle from a mile away
It sounds so good but I must stay away
That train is a beauty, makin' everybody stare
But its only destination is the middle of nowhere

But there's vict'ry in the Lord I say
Vict'ry in the Lord
Cling to the Father and His Holy Name
And don't go ridin' on that long black train
I said cling to the Father and His Holy Name
And don't go ridin' on that long black train
Yeah, watch out for that long black train
The devil's a drivin' that long black train

A Taste of Licorice
Return to the Rock

Prologue

Mark Collins and Andrea Fuller sat beside a crackling campfire. Each was leaning as close to the other as possible, his arm around her shoulder, her head on his chest.

"It's a beautiful night for our last campout of the season," Andrea said contentedly.

Mark hugged Andrea more closely.

"Made all the sweeter with you by my side." He grinned.

She raised her face to his. He leaned in to kiss her. His playful peck led to a longer, more intimate kiss. The night sounds of the woods around them serenaded them.

September leaves rustled as night creatures went about their business of foraging or hunting.

As the couple's passion rose, so did the night sounds around them. A full moon spotlighted the small clearing.

Without warning, all sound ceased, even the crackle of the fire, which seemed to become cool coals in that brief second. A cloud passed over the moon, and the couple were thrown into near darkness.

Andrea was the first to notice and pulled away from Mark. She looked around her, unsure of how to respond. She saw the cold fire-pit and thumped Mark in his chest. He opened his eyes, and his contented smile slowly slid from his lips.

"What's going on?" he asked.

"I don't know," Andrea replied. "I've never seen this before."

"You know," he said teasingly, "they say that the forest goes silent when a large predator is present. Maybe we are being stalked by Bigfoot!"

He broke into a laugh when Andrea's eyes had widened in fear, and she gasped as she looked around in fear. When she realized Mark was only teasing, she relaxed and laughed with him.

"Oh, you!" she exclaimed.

Mark leaned in to kiss her once more. As his lips touched Andea's, however, she jerked her head back and sniffed at the air, her nose wrinkling in disgust.

"Do you smell that?" she asked.

"Smell what?" Mark replied, trying to divert her attention back to kissing.

"It smells like…"—she continued to inhale deeply in order to identify the odor—"licorice? Yes, definitely licorice."

Mark shifted gears and also sniffed at the air.

"You're right. I smell licorice. Disgusting stuff!"

Andrea scooted away from Mark but remained within arm's reach.

Mark stood and drew his jacket closed, fastening it as he began looking around the edge of the clearing for anything that could be giving off that scent. At first, he couldn't see much beyond the hand he held out at arm's length as if ready to defend himself if necessary.

A darker shape moved out of the darkness behind the bright-orange dome tent.

"Stop right there!" shouted Mark.

Andrea stood and moved to stand behind Mark.

"What is it?" she whispered.

"I don't know yet," he whispered back without taking his eyes from the now-still shape.

"Who are you? What do you want?" he shouted again, moving his arm back and forth in front of himself to establish his territory.

"Please," a pleading voice came from the dark shape, "I need your help."

The dark shape moved closer and began to take on very human features. The young girl, about ten or so years old, had large black eyes that glittered with unshed tears and long, thick braids that trailed down her back. Her smooth clay-brown skin and high cheekbones gave away her Native heritage. She wore a T-shirt, jeans, and tennis shoes caked with dried mud. She looked at Mark pleadingly and very vulnerable.

"Please, you must help me. My little brother is lost, and I can't find him."

Mark lowered his arm and turned to look at Andrea. She looked more concerned than frightened now. She gave Mark a slight nod. Mark turned back to the girl.

"Where did you last see your brother?" he asked in a gentler voice.

"By the rocks. We were playing hide-and-seek. I was it. He hid, and now I can't find him."

"I'll get the flashlights," said Andrea, already in motion. She retrieved them from inside the tent and gave one to Mark. They both clicked on their flashlights and pointed them at the ground so as to not blind anyone.

Mark nodded at the girl.

"Can you take us there?" he asked.

She nodded silently and turned to reenter the darkness. The young couple followed. The girl moved quickly through the darkness, avoiding all obstacles in her path. Mark and Andrea were not so capable. They consistently tripped over tree roots, bumped into low-hanging tree limbs, and slid on damp leaves trying to keep up with this child who apparently knew the woods so well. The scent of licorice led their way through the darkness.

The invisible trail followed the natural contours of the mountain they were slowly climbing. Neither Mark nor Andrea knew the way back to their campsite. They would have to rely on their mystery girl and her missing brother for help. In the meantime, they would search for the boy in question.

The girl came to an abrupt stop, causing Mark and Andrea to fall over each other to keep from knocking the child over. The girl raised an arm and pointed to the darkness in front of her.

"There," she said. "We were playing there."

Mark trailed his flashlight across the path in front of the girl. At first, he saw nothing. As he moved the flashlight beam to hip level, the grays and whites of a large limestone boulder rose up from the ground. Ground cover, moss, and climbing plants had nearly engulfed the stone in places. Using his flashlight, Mark estimated the rock to be roughly twelve feet across and eight feet in height. It was roughly rectangular in shape from this angle. The growth around the stone, including tall, sturdy trees that abutted the stone itself, was older than expected and appeared to have been undisturbed for ages.

"You were playing here?" Mark asked in disbelief. "How did you even find this place? It looks like no one has been here in years."

The girl made no response. She stood stiffly, arms at her side, staring at Mark.

Andrea pushed past the inert girl and joined Mark beside the rock. She ran her hand along the limestone where it hadn't been overgrown.

"It's so cold," she observed.

"Well, it *is* rock, Andrea," taunted Mark.

"No," she replied seriously. "It's *really* cold. Like ice. It's definitely limestone, but it feels like an Ice Age glacier."

Mark placed his hand tentatively on the rock. He then pressed more forcefully. He yanked his hand back with a scream.

Andrea rushed to his side. He was holding the hand he had touched the rock with in his opposite hand. The hand that had touched the rock was reddened, like a burn, with dead, white edges, and blue tips on his fingers.

"It looks like some sort of frostbite." Andrea breathed in amazement. She looked at her own cold hands. They were red, as if she had been handling ice, but had not advanced toward frostbite in the same way as Mark's had.

"What the—" Andrea began.

A giggle behind her cut her off.

Andrea and Mark turned to see the girl laughing, still standing stiffly in the same place. Only the girl saw what happened next.

Two very large and hairy arms materialized from the side of the boulder and reached for the two campers. They screamed as basketball-sized hands took hold of their jacket collars and dragged them backward, roughly, toward the stone. Two flashlights fell to the forest floor where they laid, shining into the night.

Part 1

The candy-apple-red Mustang with bright-white racing stripes cruised its way into town, people on the streets stopping to admire its original paint and glossy wax job. If not for the other vehicles of much newer make and model, the 1964 Mustang would have fit right into the overall atmosphere of the small town. The well-kept buildings looked to have been built pre-Depression of the early twentieth century but had been given little modernization on the exterior. Cars were parked on either side of the street; people strolled casually along the sidewalks. The two men in the car scanned the storefronts as though looking for a particular business.

"There." The younger passenger pointed to his left.

The driver located a parking space for his much-loved vehicle and deftly parallel-parked between an aging Ford pickup and a newer Toyota Corolla. There was no traffic to impede their jaywalk to the store they were looking for.

The window had old-fashioned lettering that hadn't been updated in at least thirty years. INCENSE AND OLD LACE it read. A variety of items sat on the floor of the display shelf, declaring the store to be A PLACE OF WONDER AND CURIOSITY. A slightly worn antique doll dressed as a bride stood next to a small table set for a tea party with a child's tiny china tea set. A teddy bear stared out from where it sat in a chair at the table. A tray of costume jewelry laid to the left of the tea table. To the right, a handgun and a wicked-looking knife were on display. Mixed among the antiques were scented candles, bottles of goat's milk lotions, and soap bars scented in the same fragrances as the candles. Jars of dried herbs and spices clustered there. A variety of herbal teas were arranged in front of the tea table to encourage the potential buyer to associate childhood play with the relaxing teas for the overly stressed adult. The careful observer would see that the teddy bear had been placed on a stack of books in its chair, spines facing the window shopper. All were on Eastern Kentucky folklore.

The taller of the two men pointed to the window display and quipped with a slight smile, "Well, I'm curious. How about you?"

Before his companion could respond, the tall one opened the door and entered the shop. The tinkling of bells alerted the proprietor that a customer was present. A slightly musty smell caused the stockier man to stifle a sneeze. He continued into the main display room as the taller man closed the door behind him. Mountain music with a strong banjo riff filled the store.

"Paddle faster! I hear banjo music," the tall one quoted.

"Don't you ever tire of that old quote from *Deliverance?*" asked the stockier man.

"Not really. It's too good to not use," the other replied. "Hello? Anybody here?"

"Can I help you?" came from somewhere in the back of the store. A dark blond woman stepped from behind a tall bookshelf, dust rag in her hand. She didn't reach five feet five inches and was mildly overweight. Stormy blue eyes twinkled from behind her glasses. A friendly smile welcomed them.

The older, taller man spoke first. "We're looking for the writer of the *Walking through Satan's Den* website," he said expectantly.

"You found her," she said, approaching the two men. Her short hair framed her squarish and mostly unlined face. She was in her mid-fifties but wore no makeup to hide her age lines. A silver-gold streak blended into the hair at her right temple. She stuck out her hand before her.

"Lurlene Joy McCoy, at your service," she announced as she shook their hands.

"*You're the writer*?" the younger, stockier of the two questioned in surprise.

"Sure." She laughed. "What were you expecting? Some nerdy adolescent with a passion for folklore and ghosts?"

"Yeah," said the tall one.

At the same time, the stockier man shook his head and said, "No." The two men looked at each other in exasperation and exchanged messages with their eyes.

Lurlene continued to laugh. "I take it only one of you is a fan of my writing. My guess is…you." She pointed at the taller man.

The stockier man looked up at the taller man and chuckled.

"I'm Deven…Thompson," he stated. "This is my cousin, Marcus Quinn."

"Thompson…and Quinn…," said Lurlene thoughtfully. "I've heard of you two. You're pretty famous in our circle too. Proud to meet you!"

"Your…circle?" Marcus hinted.

Lurlene didn't clarify. Instead, she reached behind Deven, locked the shop door, and flipped the sign to CLOSED.

"Follow me," she said more seriously.

The cousins felt they had no other choice. The two wove their way through the curiosity shop—mostly antiques and folk crafts, with some artifacts native to this region of Kentucky: a polished antique wooden jewelry box with an exquisite inlay design had been placed next to a creepy-looking taxidermic raccoon and a rag doll made from muslin and wearing a blue gingham dress sat staring at them with green button eyes, one large and dark, the other small and bright, and a roughly stitched mouth that gave it a wicked leer. The hair consisted of six hanks of brown yarn, knotted and sewn onto the head, which was proportionately smaller than the doll's body suggested. The frizzled yarn stuck out at odd angles, as if the doll was terrified by something it saw. Along the back wall, beneath a small window with red checkered curtains, was a bookshelf filled with books of folklore, folk crafting, local history, fiction, and poetry displayed casually.

Lurlene stopped at the bookshelf and drew out a key ring from her pocket. The cousins waited patiently while she found the key she required. Deven examined the titles and authors of the books as he followed Lurlene through a door clearly marked as an exit. Lurlene McCoy's name was on many of them. Lurlene locked the door behind them and started walking toward a large, white Victorian house on the lot behind the store.

Being sat back farther from the street, they arrived at the front of the house, which would not have been easily seen from the storefront. Lurlene stopped abruptly, hand on the doorknob of the large front door painted in a very loud aqua. She turned to the cousins, wearing a very serious look on her face. Only the twinkle in her eyes gave her away.

"I need to warn you boys about my sister before we go in. We're twins, near identical but fraternal nonetheless, but as different as night is from day. Where I'm casual and laid-back, she's...well... intense. It's hard to explain. You'll see for yourselves soon enough. Just...don't...stare. It sets her off."

Thinking the worst, the cousins followed Lurlene into the foyer.

"Glory!" Lurlene shouted. "We've got company."

"Coming," a gruff voice replied.

Lurlene led Deven and Marcus into a comfortable parlor and gestured for them to sit down. They chose either end of a pink floral couch with an antique traveler's trunk as a coffee table.

"Deven, Marcus, this is my sister, Glory." Lurlene gestured to the woman next to her. The resemblance was easy to see, but the fact that these two women were twins was belied by the other woman's appearance.

Glory had the same height and basic shape as Lurlene. There the resemblance ended. Glory's long hair had been brushed back and wrapped in a messy bun. Her hair was the same dark honey blond as her sister's but seemed to fade to cornsilk blonde somewhere in the center, creating a halo around the near brown-blond of the bun itself. Her eyebrows were darker and thicker than Lurlene's and formed a slight unibrow above hooded eyes. The blue of her stormy blue eyes was hard and cold. The hint of a light-brown mustache sat above her thin upper lip made even thinner by the overly exaggerated frown on the woman's face. A hairy-looking black mole accented the frown near her chin on the right side of her lips. As if in opposition to her sister's simple T-shirt and jeans, she wore a loose blouse that overlapped a nearly ankle-length skirt of matching fabric. Beneath the skirt, she wore brown orthopedic shoes that had a Velcro strap across the top.

The cousins had seen some pretty frightening supernatural creatures, but this little woman had to be the most frightening human being they had ever seen. Surely, she scared small children and made adults cry. If anyone was the model for the wicked witch of fairy tales, here she stood.

"Glory, this is Deven Thompson and his cousin Marcus Quinn."

Beady blue eyes looked the men up and down. The frown seemed to deepen in response.

"Pleased to meet you," grumbled Glory in her coarse voice.

Lurlene watched the men's response to her sister. She chuckled to herself.

"Glory, why don't you get these gentlemen some fresh lemonade and a piece of apple pie?" She turned to her guests. "You do like pie, don't you? Would you prefer iced tea or soda?"

Deven grinned broadly. "Yes, ma'am. And tea for me, please."

Marcus just nodded his head.

Glory disappeared back into the depths of the house.

Lurlene moved to sit in an overstuffed easy chair with tiny pink rosebuds on an off-white background. She leaned back and made herself comfortable.

"Don't say I didn't warn you." She grinned mischievously as the two young men breathed a sigh of relief.

"Yes," said Deven. "You did warn us."

"She isn't much to look at, but she's a very compassionate person deep inside."

"Real deep," muttered Marcus.

Lurlene pretended not to hear the comment.

"So what brings you to this little no-name town? Besides my website."

Marcus brightened and began to explain that he had been following the website for some time. An anonymous email had recommended it as being "of interest" to him and his cousin. He found the stories compelling and wondered how much truth there was in the accounts she had posted. As an amateur anthropologist, he had a deep interest in literature and religion of ancient cultures and their impact on the modern world. The more pagan the better.

Lurlene looked down at her hands where they were neatly crossed in her lap. When she looked up once more, the twinkle in her eyes was gone, and she had taken on a dark pallor.

"I know your history, so I know you will understand what I am about to tell you."

She looked each of them in the eye.

Glory chose that moment to return with a tea cart bearing four glasses of ice, a big pitcher of lemonade and one of iced tea, and four saucers with generous slices of apple pie, still steaming from the oven. A quart of vanilla ice cream and a bowl with cheddar cheese completed the hospitable spread.

Deven watched closely as Glory distributed the refreshments, checking each of the young men's preferences before handing them theirs. When he received his slice of pie, he inhaled the scent of cinnamon deeply, with his eyes closed and a big grin.

"It sure smells good," he said happily, picking up his fork.

"Thank you," grumbled Glory. "Cheddar? Ice cream?"

"Both, if you don't mind."

The edges of Glory's frown almost turned up, as if a smile was trying to fight its way out. She served generous portions of cheese and ice cream to Deven. Marcus declined both. Lurlene accepted the cheese, while Glory topped her own with a carefully measured scoop of ice cream.

Glory sat down in the twin of Lurlene's chair.

"You were saying…," reminded Marcus as he gathered a bite of pie on his fork.

Lurlene glanced at Glory, who simply nodded, message received.

"We, our family, has been around for over two thousand years, traceable through written records going back that far. We evolved from an older group. Alpha Domini, or simply AD, is comprised of individuals descended through the bloodlines of the original twelve apostles, daughters, sons, nieces, and nephews. We even have members who are direct descendants of the half-brothers and half-sisters of Jesus Christ Himself."

She paused to let that sink in. Marcus looked astonished. Deven gave a low whistle.

"We have been given the mission to oversee the spiritual health of the people of earth."

"Like the pope?" Deven inquired.

"*Not* like the pope," Lurlene replied as Glory let out a sound of disgust. "We are what the pope aspires to be. The pope is the head of the Catholic Church. Protestants don't recognize his authority. AD operates between heaven and hell, preventing an imbalance between the light and the dark. We recognize only true believers. Denominations are meaningless drivel that serve only to divide. We unify. We can be found in most churches that follow Christ and his teachings. Each of us is born with a particular gift which determines our role in AD operations. I was given the gift of knowledge and history. I keep the lore of the watchers in this region. I have been trained and entrusted with the chronicles of AD activities. I have a doctoral degree in cultural anthropology with an emphasis on the folklore of the Appalachian, Blue Ridge, and Smoky Mountains. A very small part of my historical knowledge is available in the form of both fiction and nonfiction, including books, articles, and my website. Generally, the facts are rearranged or fictionalized in order to be pleasing to the average human palate. The full truth would destroy society as we know it."

Marcus paused with the last bite of apple pie halfway to his wide-open mouth. Slowly, he closed his mouth and set his plate on the trunk table in front of him.

"So you're going to try to stop the Apocalypse," he stated flatly.

"Again, no," replied Lurlene. "We chronicle history from the spiritual realm. What happens in the veil affects earth, but certain prophecies cannot be stopped. Delayed, perhaps, but not stopped. It has been decreed, so it will be."

"Said Pharoah to Moses," muttered Deven.

"*The Ten Commandments*," provided Marcus.

Deven nodded in agreement.

Marcus swallowed a deep gulp of lemonade. "Every prophecy has a loophole. We've—"

"We know what you two have done," snapped Glory. "Your reputation precedes you!"

"No offense, ladies," Marcus continued. "We just want to know the facts behind your website."

Lurlene inhaled deeply, then let it out slowly. She leaned forward in her chair.

"All of it," she confirmed. "Everything you read there is absolutely true. Watered down and candy-coated but true. It's one way I share my research and observations with other chronicle keepers around the world. My so-called folklore is very real."

"How many of these chroniclers exist anyway? Why not just use a phone?" Deven tried to cover up his unease flippantly.

Glory laughed loudly, almost a cackle.

Lurlene fought back her own laugh. "Industrial spies," she said in a stage whisper. She let her own laugh join that of her sister.

"Ha. Ha. Very funny," said Deven drolly.

"You sort of asked for it," teased Lurlene.

"Yeah, yeah, we did," agreed Marcus with sarcasm.

"Okay, all kidding aside. We do have enemies who want to get their claws on the information we have. Our identities as AD are held a closely guarded secret for our protection. We don't advertise our services, but we're always there when we are needed. We can be called into active service anywhere at any time."

"Kind of like the National Guard," Deven scoffed with a grin.

"Yes." Lurlene was serious.

Marcus decided to break the building tension in the room.

"I've been following your website since the anonymous message. That's what I do. I research things. Anyway, I started to notice parallels between your accounts and accounts being reported in the media in other parts of the United States."

"Surely you don't believe everything you read, young man." Glory all but snarled.

Marcus glanced at his cousin, who gave him a cheesy grin and a shoulder shrug. Deven had seen Marcus perusing all sorts of magazines and books for far too many years to comment.

"No. Of course not!" said Marcus, almost apologetically.

No one spoke for a few moments.

"As I was saying," Marcus began again, "I've seen some parallels between the media and your articles and stories."

Lurlene nodded knowingly.

"The most recent event was that couple that disappeared from their campsite last month." Marcus continued. "There have been other disappearances in that same area, haven't there?"

Lurlene nodded, still silent.

"Just how many have there been?"

Lurlene leaned back in her chair once more. "Nine," she said. "In the last year."

"Nine," Deven implied. "That's an awfully high number of people to disappear in one year. What? Do you have hillbilly cannibals living up in them thar mountains?"

Glory glared at Deven until he leaned back onto the sofa and slid down like a disciplined child trying to disappear. "I was just joking," he mumbled, rolling his eyes.

"We've managed to keep most of the disappearances out of the media," Lurlene returned to the topic. "Those that did make it into the media were carefully edited to reduce suspicion."

"You lied!" Deven shouted triumphantly.

"We did," admitted Lurlene. "It was necessary to protect the truth."

"And the truth is...," inquired Marcus.

Lurlene sighed. "It would be easier to show you."

Glory spoke up. "You're the expert. I'll go mind the store while you three explore the truth." With that, she left the room. In seconds, they heard the front door open, then close.

Lurlene broke into a big smile. "I told you she was intense."

"Yep," agreed Deven. "Are you sure you two are related?"

"Quite sure. At least that is what our daddy always said. Mama wouldn't say either way." The twinkle was back in her blue eyes.

Catching on, Deven let out a short laugh. Marcus shook his head at the attempt at humor.

Lurlene rose from her chair. "Follow me, and I will reveal all," she said in the exaggerated voice of a mysterious storytelling sorceress.

Part 2

The stone walls of the basement were cold but dry. The mortar that held the stones together was old, very old. Where it had dried and cracked or fallen out, there was evidence of more modern repairs. The wooden steps that led down to the basement, however, had not had the benefit of modernization and were becoming hazardous. The three made their way carefully down to the hardened dirt floor. Shelves of home-canned food lined two walls. A third wall held a workbench and shelves of tools so ancient they could have been used by the earliest settlers of this area nearly three hundred years before. Projects in various forms of disrepair gathered the dust of old age. Along the fourth wall, the modern furnace stood out in its newness. Odd boxes and old furniture were also stacked along this wall.

Deven wrinkled his nose, then rubbed at it to prevent a sneeze as dust assaulted him. Marcus pushed away cobwebs and spider-webs where they dangled from the low ceiling and tried to entrap his forehead and hair. Lurlene didn't seem to be affected by any of these things. She led them to the area beneath the steps they had just descended. She brushed at the accumulated dirt at her chest level. Finding what she was looking for, she pressed a specific stone with the palm of her hand. A section of wall three feet wide and five feet high slid backward and to the side to reveal a dark chamber. Lurlene stepped easily into the chamber with the slightest stoop and reached to her right. She turned and handed heavy-duty flashlights to the men. She reached for a flashlight for herself and turned it on. When all three were safely inside, Lurlene pressed another stone, and the door slid closed, locking them in.

"That's just dandy," quipped Deven, beginning to feel slight anxiety.

"Believe it or not, that door and this tunnel are centuries older than the house above," Lurlene explained.

"I believe it," replied Deven.

"Where does this tunnel go?" asked Marcus curiously.

"You'll see," answered Lurlene.

The walls of the hand-dug tunnel were lined with the same stone and mortar as that used by the builders of the basement. Wooden beams reinforced the ceiling. The tunnel took a downward slope that might have challenged them to fight against the pull of gravity if not for the wide plateaued steps that allowed for a gentler pace. The tunnel ended abruptly at a solid-looking wooden door.

Lurlene pulled an ancient iron key from her jeans pocket and inserted it into the keyhole. She turned to look at the cousins, a deeply solemn look on her face.

"Gentlemen," she began, "you are about to see what very few outside of Alpha Domini have ever seen. I must swear you to secrecy, upon your very lives. Our mission must not be compromised."

The men agreed and swore to secrecy. Deven even offered his blood to seal the Blood Brothers pact. Lurlene pushed the heavy door open and entered a vast underground chamber. It wasn't until Lurlene began lightning kerosene lanterns spaced about the room that its size was detectable.

Shelves and tables filled the room. Every surface held a book or artifact of some kind. One table held arrows, spears, and other ancient weaponry related to the Native American heritage of the mountains. On the next table were guns of many ages and varieties. Swords, some with scabbards, littered another table. Marcus picked up a scabbarded sword bearing a Nazi swastika. He pulled it out to examine its condition.

"My grandfather took that off an SS officer during World War Two," informed Lurlene. "He was one nasty son of a gun, that officer."

Marcus raised his eyebrows in both curiosity and awe.

Deven had discovered a table containing gas masks, helmets, and odds-and-ends paraphernalia of past wars. He was examining a leather pouch dried and cracked with age. Inside, he found hardened leathery objects, all similar in size and shape but bent at different angles. He picked them out one by one, sniffing them, then replacing them by dropping them back into the pouch.

"My great-grandfather got that from the corpse of a Cherokee warrior that became demon-possessed. Those are the fingers of people he killed. That's his trophy bag, made from the skin of his first victim."

Deven made a sound of disgust and quickly dropped the bag back onto the table.

"Is there anything in this room that wasn't taken from a dead person?" he asked with a frown.

"Plenty," replied Lurlene. "We keep the most dangerous artifacts down here for their own protection. If they fell into the wrong hands..." She left the thought unfinished.

"Over here is what I want to show you," she said as she moved to a solid-looking seventeenth-century desk in a far corner.

When Marcus and Deven had made their way to the desk, she pulled a stack of cloth-bound books from a bookshelf next to the desk and placed them on the desk for all to see. Marcus picked up the one on top and examined it.

"Manly Wade Wellman?" he inquired.

"Yes," Lurlene whispered. "My father's colleague and mentor."

When she didn't say more, Marcus examined the other books in the stack. They were all by Manly Wade Wellman, and first editions, signed to "Joseph, my boy. Rise tall and conquer giants."

"These are all fiction," said Marcus. "How are these going to help us understand what is happening here?"

Lurlene refocused her attention from her memories to the present.

"Remember how I told you I hid truth in fiction on my website and in my books?"

Marcus nodded.

"He did the same."

She paged through the book in her hand.

"He kept the chronicles down in the Carolinas. These are his public records. The full, true records are kept in a secret archive by his descendants.

"He communicated with other AD members through the names of Silver John and John Silver. The two characters were one and the same. Two sides of the same coin. Silver John carried a guitar with silver strings, and John Silver carried a walking stick with a silver sword hidden inside."

"Silver," stated Deven. "Did he see many werewolves by chance?"

"A few," returned Lurlene. "Among witches and not a few elder gods. Molech, in particular."

"Molech. The baby-eating god?" Marcus asked.

"The one and same," said Lurlene. "Molech is first mentioned in the Judeo-Christian Old Testament, though he appears in older texts of the civilizations around the area now known as Israel," Lurlene began. "He was one of the many false gods the Israelites were warned against. Many times, the places of worship used by pagan worshippers of these gods were torn down. They always arose somewhere else just as or more powerful than before. It really hasn't been too many centuries that these pagan cults have been driven underground, at least in modern civilized countries. In third world and primitive areas…" She shrugged her shoulders.

"We've seen our share of big-shot demons, haven't we, Marcus?" bragged Deven.

"Yeah, but I'm not sure that's what she's talking about here."

"What's worse than a demon? Satan himself? Been there. Done that. No contest."

Lurlene eyed Deven up and down carefully.

"Marcus is right," she said. "We aren't talking about demons here. Even Satan fears these creatures."

Deven released a loud expletive.

"You called them old gods," Marcus said. "What are they?"

Lurlene gathered her thoughts carefully before responding. "In my many years of seeking and archiving the folklore of these mountains, I've heard and read many versions of the Creation, each varying in detail. Usually, they have a central theme. None of them are as complete as the ancient secret texts of Creation and history of earth. I have a very old copy of this text, translated into English, for those of us who do not speak the language of angels."

She turned to a table beside the desk. It held seemingly random items and books in disarray. Lurlene stooped and reached into the darkness beneath the table. With both hands, she withdrew a large wooden box with a hinged lid. She set the box on the desktop beside the Wellman books. Lifting the lid, she used both hands to remove an oilcloth-wrapped object. From a desk drawer, she withdrew white gloves and distributed them to her guests, keeping a pair for herself.

"To protect it from the oils on your hands," she explained.

Marcus and Deven hastily put the gloves on.

Lurlene carefully unwrapped the oilcloth to reveal a leather-bound book that had seen better days, before Lincoln ran for president. The gold embossed lettering and decoration had nearly worn away, giving it the feel of dating to the Middle Ages. The fragile spine showed hand-threaded pages in places where the leather had worn away. Marcus looked on in awe, while Deven appeared bored and ready for some action.

Lurlene grasped the cover gently with blunt-ended tweezers and opened the book. The title page was brown with age but clearly portrayed the same lettering and designs as the cover. It was in a language Marcus had never seen before.

"I thought you said it was in English," Marcus accused Lurlene.

"Oh, it is," she assured. "At least that part of it that can be translated. Some parts of the language of the cosmos cannot be translated easily. Where that occurs, we are left in the dark. Even the angels themselves cannot read it."

"Are you saying this is so old it predates Creation?" Deven was skeptical.

"Yes," Lurlene said in a small voice.

"Oh my god!" exclaimed Marcus in fascination.

"Yes, indeed," Lurlene confirmed.

"Indeed what?" Deven said, now more interested.

"God. The Creator of the universe. The author of all things. These are His very words. A diary of sorts."

Marcus stroked the page with his gloved hand.

"This is the Word of God? I thought the Bible was supposed to be—"

"This is the Word of God for the universe. The Bible is only God's Word for humanity."

"Hey, we know someone who met God!" interjected Deven. "And he didn't seem to care enough to have written this kind of…

diary, journal, or whatever. He seemed more interested in everything but us."

"The man described as being God was *not* the Jehovah of the universe. He was an impostor. We, Alpha Domini, have watched him for millennia. He is quite delusional and quite resentful. He can cause chaos when he wants to."

"If he wasn't God, then who was he?" demanded Marcus. A purple vein in his forehead had risen and become visible, pulsating in rhythm with his rapidly beating heart.

"He is…what we call…a fractal."

"What the—" Deven began.

Anticipating his comment, Lurlene cut him off.

"A fractal is a piece of the shattered universe. God has always been. When He decided to create our universe, He released the darkness He had kept in check for the eternity that came before. Goodness is inherently good, light, and love. There is no evil in Him. In order for there to be a balance of all that is natural or, in this case, supernatural, there must also exist an inherent darkness or evil. God's shadow, if you will. It's infinitely more complex than that, but it's the easiest way to explain it. Anyway, the energy used to create our universe required God to pinch off a bit of that darkness and put it into the mix to allow free will in the sentient beings he would put in charge of maintaining His creation. On earth, it is humanity. On other planets? Only God knows.

"Anyway, that pinch of darkness left a dusty remnant unused in other portions of space and time.

"Those particles of dust took on a life of their own and scattered throughout the universe in search of places to hide and grow strong. As life grew and intelligent beings became the caretakers, the fractals set themselves up as gods and demanded sacrifice to gain their favor."

"So Lucifer-Satan is a fractal," Deven surmised.

"No," Lurlene returned. "Lucifer is exactly what the traditional Bible says he is—a fallen angel. Created by God. Fractals were not created in this way. Their essence has always been, just as God has always been. Without beginning and without end. God created from Himself."

"What you described on your website," began Marcus, "that's a fractal?"

Lurlene nodded.

"What's it doing here?" asked Deven.

Lurlene sighed. "It's hard to say. It has always been here, according to the oral history of the Natives of this land. Even the little we know from the prehistoric Adena people demonstrates they were aware of this fractal. Its presence may have been why the mound builders disappeared from this area without a trace. We have some cave paintings from that time, but interpretation is open to conjecture."

She began leafing carefully through the book, page by page, using the tweezers. The pages had faded, fine print, diagrams, and drawings on nearly page. Marcus longed to sit down with the book and examine it cover to cover. Deven only rubbed at his nose to prevent sneezing as the moldy, musty books around him added their dust to the air.

Finding what she was looking for, Lurlene stabbed a finger at a full-page illustration in wood-block print.

"This, for all practical intents and purposes, is a fractal," she said, turning the book so Deven and Marcus could see.

A very large ape-man-like creature had been carved in terrifying detail. Large fangs protruded from the upper lips and large tusks from the lower. The eyes were small and cruel, and the nose broad and flat. If ears were present, they were hidden by the creature's hair. A broad powerful neck sat squat between the squared chin and the wider-than-expected shoulders. Its massive biceps looked like the trunks of California Redwoods. Its forearms weren't much smaller and ended in hands that could dwarf a basketball. Clawlike nails extended from the long, thick fingers. The chest was full and well-developed, leading to a lean abdomen and broad hips. Thighs thicker than its biceps looked as if they could crush cattle just by squeezing. Knees, like the elbows, were nearly nonexistent, as if the thing could bend its arms and legs in any direction, like tentacles. Bulging calves and thick shins led to strong ankles and very large feet.

Deven let out another expletive. "A fractal is a sasquatch?" He laughed at the idea.

Marcus looked up at his cousin in embarrassment. "It's more than that, Deven. It's a sasquatch on cosmic steroids, from what I understand."

Deven sobered but didn't quite buy what Marcus was saying. He bent over the book to read what it said for himself. He cursed once more when he could make no sense of it.

"You have one of these around here?" Deven asked in astonishment.

"Yes and no," Lurlene replied mysteriously.

"What do you mean, yes and no? You either have a fractal problem, or you don't." Deven was becoming agitated.

Lurlene closed the book, carefully rewrapped it in the oilcloth, and returned it to the wooden box. Before she closed the lid, she gently caressed the oilcloth-bound bundle. The box was returned to its hidden location beneath the desk. Lurlene removed her gloves and gestured for the men to remove theirs as well.

"The rest of the story, as Paul Harvey used to say, is in the shop." With that, Lurlene went around extinguishing each lantern until the only light came from their powerful flashlights.

Part 3

Glory was standing behind the cash register when they came into the showroom from the rear. Glory didn't seem any better. If anything, her frown had deepened. She looked like a large-mouth bass when she spoke.

"It's about time," she said to her sister.

Lurlene smiled at her twin. "You know how I am when I'm down in the archives. It's just who I am," she stated unapologetically.

Glory made a curt nod.

Lurlene led Marcus and Deven back through the store. She stopped at the side door they had just come in but chose to examine the bookshelf instead. She took one book from the shelf and led the young men to the other side of the rear of the store. A door marked PRIVATE—EMPLOYEES ONLY led to a small office. Beyond the office, another door led to an area where overstock was kept. A comfortable arrangement of old but still nice living room furniture had been set up as if expecting guests. Lurlene took a seat in a recliner that rocked. Marcus sat in the matching armchair, and Deven took up a position on the couch.

"Go ahead. Put your feet up if you like," Lurlene invited.

Deven stretched his lanky arms to meet at the back of his head, leaned back, placed his long legs on the coffee table in front of him, and crossed his legs at the ankles. The old coffee table wasn't quite wide enough, and his feet dangled over the far side. He closed his eyes and smiled in comfort.

Marcus remained on the edge of his seat.

Lurlene opened the book in her hands and thumbed through the pages. Finding what she was looking for, she handed the open book to Marcus.

"Here. Read," she commanded.

While Marcus read through the pages he had been assigned, Lurlene released the footrest of her chair and leaned back into a relaxed position.

Marcus read through the pages quickly, then went back and read it again. Several times.

"How much of this is true?" he asked Lurlene.

"As I told you before, all of it," she replied.

"Can you take us there?" Marcus asked excitedly. His creamy well-tanned skin became flushed with emotion.

"Whoa! Whoa there!" interjected Deven, his fairer skin reddening with anticipation. "Go where?"

Marcus silently handed the book to his cousin. Deven sat up and put his feet back on the floor. He glanced at the page, then looked up at Marcus and Lurlene. He began to read.

"I'm game," Deven said after reading for himself, several times. "But first. I want to know what the story has to do with the disappearances."

Lurlene pulled her chair to an upright position. "The fractal is about to be freed. The sigil is nearly broken. The missing people have all been sacrificed to feed the fractal and strengthen it before it is released."

"Now you're talking!" rejoiced Deven. "Dispensing bad guys, demons, and monsters is my specialty. I use our real-life exploits in the design of my video games. Of course, they are all rated 'M for Mature,' but it hasn't stopped people from buying them." He rubbed his hands together in anticipation.

"I'll take you there," Lurlene promised. "After dinner. You boys will eat with us, won't you?"

"Well. We don't know where we're going to stay tonight, so maybe we should find a motel," said Marcus, disappointment in his voice.

"Hah!" Lurlene laughed. "A motel in this town? Ain't gonna happen. If you boys need some place to stay, Glory and I have plenty of room. I hear the food is good too."

Deven's eyes lit up. "Much obliged. Will there be more pie?"

Part 4

Deven was finishing his third helping of apple pie with cheddar cheese and ice cream after eating a dinner of pot roast with potatoes, carrots, and onions, homemade corn bread, and a choice of jellies, jams, or fresh honey from a local hive. Marcus sipped at his lemonade. Glory and Lurlene were busy cleaning up the kitchen and doing dishes.

"You're being awfully quiet, Marc-Marc," said Deven, licking his fork.

"Just thinking," replied Marcus.

"About…," hinted Deven.

"Fractals."

"Ah, the beastie of the week," Deven teased.

Marcus leaned closer to his cousin and, in a stage whisper, said, "Deven, we've never seen anything like this before. All we know about it comes from an ancient manuscript and a book of folktales. What if we can't kill it or whatever?"

"We've been in situations like this before," Deven stated. "We've always managed to come out alive."

"Yeah, barely."

"Hey, I haven't gotten you killed yet, have I?" Deven smiled but without conviction.

Marcus stared at his cousin, broodingly.

"Oh, yeah," admitted Deven. "I have let you down. Look at the bright side. You made a comeback, didn't you?"

"Death or near-death stinks, you know," Marcus pointed out.

Deven cleared his throat and put his fork on the plate in front of him.

"Yeah," he said. "We've both gone that route before. I still haven't recovered from that six-week coma I was in. The nightmare never ended."

"And I don't want to do it again," said Marcus firmly.

"You're the one who said we should come here, bookworm," Deven accused.

Before Marcus could reply, Lurlene announced it was time to go.

From the front passenger seat, Deven was thankful Lurlene had insisted that they should take her rugged Jeep to the site. The roads were barely wide enough for one vehicle, and passing a car going the opposite direction was a hair-raising experience as both vehicles seemingly dove off the road into whatever ditch, field, or hillside was at hand. Lurlene drove like a pro. When she turned up a hidden and overgrown path that threatened to swallow the Jeep whole, passengers and all, Deven found himself clinging to the door handle to keep from being jounced right out the door, despite his seat belt. He hit his head on the roof more than once.

Marcus, though he was shorter and stockier, was also being thrown around quite a bit in the back seat. His seat belt made less difference to him than it did for his taller cousin. He, too, clung to the door handle. In this case, it was to keep from being thrown into Glory's lap. Marcus didn't even want to imagine that happening.

The road dead-ended. Lurlene put the Jeep in park and unbuckled her seat belt.

"This is as far as we can go in this thing. From here on out, its mare's shanks all the way."

"Mare's shanks?" Deven looked around to see what Lurlene was talking about. There was nothing there but trees.

Lurlene stepped to the edge of the woods in front of the vehicle.

"It's not far from here. Hardly anyone goes there anymore. Not willingly anyway."

She entered the shadows of the trees.

Marcus, Deven, and Glory followed.

Deven leaned toward Marcus. "I thought we were going by mare's shanks. I don't see anything else out here. Do you?"

Marcus shrugged and started to answer, but a cackle cut him off.

"Mare's shanks." Glory laughed. "She meant, city boys, that we're having to hike the rest of the way. Hoofin' it, if you will." She continued to cackle lightly as Marcus and Deven looked at each other and shrugged.

Lurlene didn't follow a visible path but seemed to know exactly where she was heading. Glory was humming off-key to herself. "The Battle Hymn of the Republic" never sounded so bad.

The shadows beneath the trees darkened the deeper they went. Animal and insect sounds decreased, then stopped all together. With unexpected suddenness, the dark shadows brightened as the trees became farther apart and early evening sunlight broke through the canopy.

"Well, I'll be—" Deven started to say. Glory had elbowed him on the ribs in anticipation of his choice of words. She glared at him when he realized she was standing next to him.

Before the hikers, enormous boulders sat among the trees like stone temples, with guardian trees protecting them. The green of the glen was brighter than the forest around them, where autumn had already started turning the leaves orange, gold, and red.

"It's like summer in here!" Marcus exclaimed in wonder.

"It only looks that way," explained Lurlene. "It's actually colder here than in the woods we just traipsed through. The only time it changes is in winter, when there's a beautiful snowfall."

"Incredible!" said Marcus. He stepped into the glade and began to examine the mossy stone before him.

The angles were nearly even and the sides rough but not enough to hurt Marcus's hands. Fine cracks had appeared over the years, telling the story of the stone since its exposure.

"Which one of those monoliths holds the fractal?" Deven asked, getting right down to business.

"Over here," said Lurlene.

The nearly rectangular rock rose majestically above them. They had to crook their necks to see all the way to the upper edge, even the statuesque scarecrow Deven.

"That kid you wrote about," Deven started, "you're telling me he climbed that thing by himself. He was what, eight?"

"Ten," corrected Lurlene. "And yes, he did climb it."

"How?" asked Marcus.

Lurlene shrugged. "I assume the fractal made a way for the boy to get up there. Or perhaps it was the spirits of the Natives that fought, captured, and entombed it. I have no further evidence to explain it. And it's not for lack of trying."

"Okay," said Marcus. "According to your book, this ten-year-old kid is dared to climb this rock just to see if it could be done. He somehow succeeds and finds the sigil beneath the moss. When Ancients did long ago trap this fractal in this rock. He never tells anyone about it. How did you find out?"

"First, our people were already here long before the boy discovered the sigil. We have chronicled activities and lore for many generations, including that of the Natives that frequented this area. We were not unaware that there were unusual activities and rituals concerning this rock. Though our chronicles only identify what was experienced here, there is little else known. Much of what is known has been shared through my writing as needed.

"Second," she continued, "Luther came to me quite some time ago, after I had published my first book. He said he didn't know why, but he felt compelled to share his story with me. Of course, I chronicled the interview and gained his permission to print it as fiction, with proper alterations. He reluctantly agreed.

"When the first disappearance occurred ten months ago, I went on alert. I filed away my findings, thinking that was that. Two months later, there were two more episodes of people disappearing. No bodies were found, and no new clues discovered. I added these to my file. When two more disappearances occurred within weeks of each other, I began searching the archives for anything that could explain these events. That's when I discovered that disturbing picture in the *Cosmic Compendium*. I paralleled what I learned about fractals, what little is known, with Luther's story and chronicle entries. I drew my conclusions from that evidence. There are still a lot of unknowns, but I am beginning to make some sense of it."

"Can we meet this Luther?" asked Marcus. "That is, if he wants to talk to us. And is still, you know, alive."

Glory let out another cackle. Lurlene smiled broadly.

"Already done," reported Lurlene. "We meet with him after breakfast tomorrow morning."

As Lurlene led her party back out of the woods to the Jeep, a pair of black eyes watched from the branch of the tree she had chosen to hide herself in. A sly smile touched her lips. Her thick, black braids briefly became hissing snakes that writhed against her shoulders and chest.

Part 5

Marcus sat at the side of the twin bed he had chosen the night before. He watched Deven pace the room.

"Okay, bookworm," Deven proposed. "What do you know about these fractals that I don't already know?"

"Not much. There's nothing on the web about them. My contacts have never heard of them or Alpha Domini. I really thought we were dealing with a run-of-the-mill demon or some other monster we have dealt with before."

"So do you believe what these women are telling us?"

"I don't know. I guess we'll find out."

Deven stopped pacing and looked around the bedroom. Twin beds sat side by side along one wall, a nightstand between them. Opposite the beds was a solid-looking antique desk and a dresser that matched the beds. Posters of classic rock guitarists lined the walls. A guitar-shaped lamp sat on the desk. Other guitar-themed decor filled the tops of the dresser and bedside table.

Deven nodded in approval. "I think I'd like the guy who lived in this room. He's got good taste."

"Lurlene said it was her son's room. He's somewhere east of Knoxville, Tennessee, right now. She said he's an incredible musician in his own right. He plays several instruments I hear. I'm a drums man myself."

"Still, this is one cool dude. I'd jam with him some time. You'd sing for us, wouldn't you, Marcus?"

"Not in my job description, cuz, and you know it. I'd play drums, though." Marcus played air drums, shaking and nodding his head in beat to the imaginary rhythm.

Deven accompanied Marcus on his air guitar.

There was a gentle but firm knock on the bedroom door.

"Yeah," grunted Deven.

An unfamiliar, and very feminine, voice answered, "Breakfast is ready. Mom sent me up to get you."

Marcus and Deven looked at each other in surprise. Deven stepped to the door and quickly opened it. A tall redhead stood in the hallway, her green eyes twinkling with mischief. Marcus stood respectfully, trying to see past Deven. The heart-shaped face looked impish as she grinned, checking out both men.

"Mom told me you two were here. She just didn't tell he how handsome you both were."

Deven mentally preened. Marcus gulped down embarrassment at her unexpected boldness.

"I'm Mercy, by the way," she said, extending her hand.

Deven took it and shook it, introducing himself. Marcus made his way to the door, shook her hand, and introduced himself as well.

"Come on. Mom doesn't like to be held up if you hadn't noticed yet."

Her red curls bounced as she bounced down the stairs.

Marcus and Deven followed quickly.

In the kitchen, they found another surprise. A petite young woman with strawberry-blond hair was placing a bowl of hot fried potatoes on the table. She straightened up when the guys came into the room.

"Good morning," she greeted with even, white teeth and deep dimples that made her Cupid's bow lips fuller and rosier. "I'm Grace, Mercy's not-identical twin."

Another set of twins! These were much easier on the eyes than Glory for certain and outshone Lurlene.

Mercy hugged Glory where she stood at the stove taking up sausage and bacon. "Good morning, Mom. Let me get that plate for you." She took the plate from Glory and took it to the table, where she arranged it carefully to make room for the remaining dishes.

Marcus and Deven stared in astonishment, first at Glory, then her twin daughters. How could such beautiful girls come from the same stock that produced Glory? Maybe there *is* a God, and he dwelled in this house!

"Well, come on," grumped Glory in her usual gruff manner. "Don't let it get cold."

Deven and Marcus quickly took their places, as did the girls, their mother, and their aunt. Lurlene said grace while Marcus and Deven waited impatiently.

While they ate, Marcus and Deven answered questions posed by Mercy and Grace. They also asked questions of the girls. They discovered that Mercy was working on her doctoral thesis for an advanced degree in archaeology. Her research was on the Adena Indians that had populated Eastern Kentucky and the Ohio River Valley during prehistoric times. She was currently working with professionals at Serpent Mound in Adams County, Ohio. Grace was completing doctoral work in forensic science. Both had taken a break to come help return the fractal to its stony grave.

When breakfast was complete and the kitchen cleaned, Lurlene led her troop of warriors into the formal dining room which doubled as a conference room when needed. The Cosmic Compendium was laid out and waiting.

Before they could all get settled, the doorbell rang. Grace excused herself to go see who it was. When she returned, a frail-looking elderly man followed her into the room. He had been tall in his youth but was now beginning to bend and create a hunched back. He had been portly at some time as well. The skin of his neck wobbled from side to side as he shuffled through the door and took the seat closest to him.

"Good morning, Pastor Rowe," said Glory in an almost cheerful voice. Her deep frown didn't change, however.

"Good morning to you, too, Sister Glor-ee Hal-lee-loo-yah!" He shouted her name with his drawn-out Kentucky twang.

Deven looked astonished at the strength in the man's voice, while simultaneously using his fingers to assure his eardrums hadn't busted with the man's trumpeted greeting. Marcus glanced backward and forward between the man and Glory. The state of his hearing was not indicated.

"Glory Hallelujah Mason is her full name," explained Lurlene. "She likes it when it is said like a Pentecostal praise. Many people around town oblige her. It makes her happy."

"If she's happy, I'll kiss a snake," Deven whispered to Marcus.

"Oh, Luther isn't a snake handler," clarified Mercy as she had overheard the comment. "He's a Baptist." The innocent look on her face nearly fooled Marcus, but he caught the tiny upturn of her lips as she tried not to smile.

"Tell them you're just kidding," Marcus whispered to his cousin. "If you don't, they just might pull out a snake and make you kiss it."

Deven looked at Marcus as if his cousin had grown a second head.

"Uh...yeah," Deven said to everyone. "Let's get this meeting started, shall we?" He rubbed his hands in anticipation.

Lurlene introduced Luther Rowe to the cousins, explaining that he was the retired pastor at Community Baptist Church. He was also the boy that had witnessed the binding ceremony of the fractal long, long ago.

Marcus was the first to speak once the introductions had been made.

"Sir. Mr. Rowe, could you tell us your story, from your point of view?"

"You've read the book, ain'tcha?" He was more inquisitive than angry.

"Yes," replied Marcus. "But you may remember it better now than you did then."

The old man laughed, his dentures jiggling loosely. "Son. I am well past eighty years old. I am lucky if I remember to breathe. If the nurses at the home didn't remind me, I'd forget to eat."

When he stopped laughing, he began coughing. Grace got up and got him a bottle of water. After a long, refreshing drink, the former pastor was able to speak again.

"You already know the gist of it, so I'll just hit the highlights."

"That would be good," said Deven, trying to be patient.

"I was just a kid, somewhere between believin' in the Easter Bunny and discoverin' girls. My brother, Paul, and my cousin Will knew I wasn't afraid of nothin', or so I said, so they dared me to climb that big ol' rock out in Rock City. That's what we kids called it. Only superstitious folk called 'em the Haunted Rocks. I did. Don't know how I did it though. I've never been able to do it again since. I never quite believed what I thought I saw. I wanted to prove it to myself. I'd always go there alone to the rock as I was the only one who knowed what happened up there. I finally give it up when I got too old to try and climb that rock. Wouldn't do to fall and break my hip."

He took another long drink of water.

"I put it out'n my mind and concentrated on pastorin' my little church. Life was good. When I started thinkin' 'bout retirin' from preachin', I started havin' nightmares. Ever-thing that happened on that ol' rock come back to me in the worst way. I got so's I couldn't sleep. I didn't even take my usual afternoon naps.

"When it got so bad, I come to Sister Lurlene Joy. I knowed she would help me. She done wrote all them books and all. Well, she believed me. I took her out to the rocks. It weren't all new to her. She believed me."

"Tell me about the Native Americans you saw!" interjected Mercy.

"They was just Injuns to me. I don't know one bunch from another."

"Too bad," she said thoughtfully. "If they were Adena, it could help me with my thesis." Mercy sensed the others staring at her. "Sorry," she said apologetically. "I just dig history."

No one laughed.

"Just a little archaeology joke," she muttered under her breath.

"I do know two things I didn't tell Sister Lurlene Joy."

"Luther, you old rascal. You withheld information from me. Shame on you." Lurlene wasn't upset. She was just teasing her guest.

"I knowed it, and I'm sorry. To be honest with ya, it didn't even occur to me. Until last night. It all come back to me in a dream. It's like I was there again. Ever' bit of it."

"Well, Luther. Are you going to tell us, or do we have to beat it out of you?"

Luther laughed. "Now, Sister Glor-ree Hal-lee-loo-yah, don't get your nylons in a bunch. I'm a-gonna tell ya."

He took another long, slow drink of water, draining the bottle to the last drop.

"Its name is Achimoth, or somethin' like that. Least that's what them Injuns called him. Hit's the onliest thing I understood. It come from a great light that come out'n the sky. That great light grabbed ahold of that monster and verily shoved it into the ground. When that earthquake come, I figure it musta disturbed that ground, causin' it to rise up out of the ground and that one big ol' rock broke into all them that are called Rock City. Course that also 'splains why they call 'em the Haunted Rocks."

"Brother of death," replied Mercy. "Its name Achimoth is Hebrew for 'brother of death.'"

"What's the second thing you learned?" Grace spoke for the first time.

"Hit smelt like licorice," Luther said seriously.

Marcus and Deven exchanged looks of surprise.

"This thing smells like that black, chewy stuff that turns your teeth and lips black?" Deven let out a string of profanity. A kick to his leg put an end to it.

"Ow!" he yelped and looked around the table. Only Glory didn't seem surprised by his declaration of pain. She glared at him from across the table.

Lurlene quickly opened the book in front of her to the picture of the fractal. She turned it around so the others could see it, especially her nieces, who were seeing the creature, and the book, for the first time. Her gloved hands were a curiosity.

Grace touched the picture with her finger. "It looks familiar."

Mercy leaned in to examine the picture more closely. "I'm sure I've seen this guy before. Only he didn't look this friendly."

They continued their discussion well into the early afternoon. They made strategic plans and drew up diagrams until everyone understood and agreed with the plan.

Part 6

It was an hour before sunset, and a crowd had gathered at the end of the road that led to Rock City. A large group had arrived on a school bus. Led by Luther Rowe, the party of believers represented all the churches in the area. The youngest was a young man of fifteen or sixteen, adolescent acne marking his face. The eldest was a woman with a walker, who claimed she was ninety-one but still spry. There were forty people in all. Pastor Rowe informed Lurlene that at least fifty others had gathered at the Methodist church to pray for their success. These were the saints too young, infirm, or unable to participate due to familial obligations.

The other vehicles were beat-up pickup trucks, older cars, newer SUVs, and two minivans. The people exiting these vehicles were far from the believers as possible in appearance. Native Americans in full ceremonial dress mingled with the believers, and a group of odd characters stood off to themselves. Lurlene made her way from group to group, welcoming the people and explaining the arrangements.

A scraggly haired woman who closely resembled the hags of fairy tales stood next to a well-dressed younger woman. They were talking and gesturing like two homemakers exchanging recipes. The older woman's clothes were faded and patched. Her skirt hung down to the tops of the ancient work boots she wore. Bags of leather and burlap were strung from the belt at her waist. The younger woman looked like she had just stepped out of an L. L. Bean catalog. Her jeans were a comfortable fit beneath the oversize flannel shirt she wore beneath a khaki vest. She unconsciously ran her hand through her short black hair when she was speaking. At her feet was a backpack bulging with its contents.

Nearby, staring intently at Marcus and Deven, stood a quite large middle-aged man. He wore an actual buckskin tunic and pants with soft deerskin boots to his knees. His brown hair and long beard were beginning to gray. He had an ancient saddlebag thrown over one shoulder. His piercing green eyes were unnerving when paired with his scowl. He was so large Deven, at six feet four inches tall, looked nearly dwarfed.

"Does Glory have a brother we don't know about?" quipped Deven in jest.

Marcus just shrugged.

A second man, also middle-aged, squatted next to a doctor's satchel, going through its contents. He looked like a fatherly or grandfatherly type in sneakers, jeans, and a denim jacket over a black-and-white checkered shirt.

A woman of indeterminate age brushed still golden but laced with silver braids off her shoulders. Several reusable shopping bags sat at her feet. She was busily reviewing the contents of an old book she held in her hands.

Lurlene called for attention. The large crowd quieted in a wave as each group took its cue from the group closest to them.

"Thank you all for coming," Lurlene nearly shouted to be heard by all. "Each of you has been called here tonight to put a stop to a creature as old as the cosmos. Each of you have specialties that will allow us, collectively, to achieve this goal."

She looked around the crowd.

"I have invited shaman from both the Cherokee and Shawnee Nations. These, our brothers and sisters, once shared this land, for hunting and trading. Those who came long before them somehow captured the creature we will battle tonight and entombed it in the rock beneath their feet. Earthquakes, great and small, have brought forth its tomb. As the elements chipped away at the rock, the sigil began to decay. Pastor Luther Rowe was fortunate enough to find this and was transported through the mists of time to witness the interment of the beast.

"When the white men came and settled the land, there was peace. They heard tales of monsters from the Natives who knew of them from their ancestors. Generations have gone by. Life has gone on. New traditions were brought here as more people came. The folklore of Satan's Den is filled with the exploits of the mountain witches—some who healed, others who destroyed. Their magic lingered and mingled with the spirits of the Natives and their gods. Together, the Shawnee, the Cherokee, and our local witches will draw down their magics to take down this nightmare.

"With settlers came their religious beliefs that were contrary to the Natives and the witches. Their belief in One All-Powerful God challenged the spirits bound to this plane. They will now combine their beliefs with the others. Each will call upon the light that can defeat this darkness. It cannot die, but it can be weakened and imprisoned. Together, we can renew the seal upon the rock and prevent the destruction that would occur if this thing is freed.

"This creature is known by many names. In my research, I have discovered that it is most frequently referred to as Achimoth, 'brother of death.' Feel free to use its name against it.

"This creature can spawn minions by implanting a part of itself into a sacrificial body. We know of nine such recent sacrifices. The more sacrifices made, the stronger the creature becomes. Don't let it or its minions close to you. My sister, my two nieces, these two brave cousins, and I will be your front line of defense. If we fall, retreat at any cost. The battle will be lost.

"We call now upon our guardian spirits to fight by our side. To protect us as we pray, chant, or recite a spell. With diligence and great faith, we will be victorious!"

The crowd whistled and cheered.

"Get your stuff together and move out!"

Lurlene's order brought more shouts and much shuffling as people gathered boxes, bags, and drums. Lurlene motioned Marcus, Deven, Mercy, and Grace to the back of her Gladiator where Glory had pulled a large wooden box to the tailgate. When they had all gathered around, Glory opened the box to reveal swords of different sizes and styles.

"These weapons," Glory began in her stern voice, "have been made from the same substance as the cosmos of the Master Creator Himself. They are indestructible but must be wielded with great care. If you miss your mark and leave yourself open, you can and will be killed. Do you understand?"

Everyone nodded.

First, Glory removed two huge and heavy two-handed swords, both edges sharpened to a deadly blade. She handed Marcus and Deven the swords, one at a time.

"You do know how to use these, don't you?" Glory asked them with a glare.

"I guess we'll find out," said Marcus with uncertainty.

"It's just like an angel blade, only much bigger," encouraged Deven. Two lighter, but just as deadly looking, swords were presented to Mercy and Grace, who seemed thrilled with their weapons.

"I haven't held one of these in years." Grace reminisced with a grin.

Mercy examined her blade intently. "Just like the ones we trained with at the academy, only sharp," she replied.

"That must have been some academy!" Marcus exclaimed, envy in his eyes.

"Yes," said Grace. "You could say it was an out-of-this-world experience." She giggled conspiratorially, as did Mercy. Glory reached back into the nearly empty box. When she withdrew her hand, she held a two-foot-long metallic rod, which she handed to her sister. Lurlene grinned broadly.

"Oh, my favorite," she said cheerfully. Pressing an unseen switch, both ends of the rod expanded another twelve inches at each end to form a formidable staff. To the surprise of Deven and Marcus, eight-inch spear heads emerged from each end.

"Whoa!" cried Deven in admiration.

"I'm impressed!" concurred Marcus, looking at the spear-staff and comparing it to his heavy sword.

Glory drew out the final item from the box for herself. It was a simple wooden walking cane with a dull silver cap at one end and a simple silver handle at the other.

"How do you expect to fight this fractal with that little cane?" Deven asked in disbelief.

"Don't worry," she grumped. "It's made of solid oak."

"Druids," said Marcus.

"What?" asked Deven in sarcasm.

"Druids," repeated Marcus. "Druids worshipped oak as being sacred. The cane is made of oak, so it must represent some kind of Druidic power or spirit."

"Oh," said Deven, not particularly interested.

They followed Mercy and Grace into the crowd and stepped into the darkness of the woods.

Part 7

The sun had set, and the moon was rising. It was full and a bright orange. It was a perfect harvest moon, just as long as the harvest didn't include human sacrifices. Wood, smoke, and odd herbal scents mixed with less pleasurable odors of sulfur and unrecognizable foul mixtures.

Deven giggled and, in a slurred voice, said, "Dude, I hope the smoke doesn't make us stoned."

Marcus scowled and rolled his eyes.

Deven inhaled deeply, held his breath, then released it slowly, a goofy grin on his face. "The colors, man!" he mocked.

Marcus walked away from his cousin, hiding a slight smile. He knew his cousin's sense of humor was always at its worst when the level of danger was at its deadliest. It was probably Deven's least annoying bad habit. Marcus loved it anyway; he just pretended to be annoyed so Deven would keep trying to make him laugh in the face of danger.

Lurlene, Grace, and Mercy disappeared behind the monolithic stone, already assuming combat positions. Glory directed Marcus to the westernmost point of the stone, placed Deven in a central position, then moved to the eastern edge. For the first time since the boys had met her, Glory was wearing loose-fitting camouflage pants, an olive-colored short-sleeved Army-style shirt, and actual combat boots. Where she had found boots small enough to fit her tiny feet was a mystery. Somewhere along the line, she had strapped an Army-style helmet over her tricolor hair, the insignia designating her as a five-star general. The way it wiggled about her head when she moved gave away the fact it was most likely a hand-me-down from another generation, someone with a much larger head. She stood at attention, straight-backed, shoulders tensed, cane held straight by her side. She stared straight ahead at the rock as if waiting for an order to be given. Her usual intense and frightening appearance became a stony Medusa, waiting for the opportunity to ambush any invaders with her petrifying stare, just before bonking them on the head with her ridiculous-looking cane.

The Christians of Satan's Den had formed a circle, linking arms into a tightly woven ring. The elderly woman with the walker had been carried piggyback style by a large, and apparently quite strong, man in his thirties. A woman who appeared to be the large man's wife had carried the walker. The man and woman almost seemed to hold up their elder between them, the walker supporting her on three sides as well. Luther Rowe was praying loudly. The others in the circle were also praying, some in barely audible whispers, others shouting and repeating the word *Father* like a mantra every few phrases. Most used conversational tones. Oddly, what should have been a cacophony instead blended into a harmonic symphony.

Rhythmic drumbeats and serene flutes accompanied haunting chants of the Native American dancers. Erratic rattles from the shouting shaman pierced the darkness. Fires sparkled and popped as secret ingredients were tossed into the fires at intervals, creating varying-colored smoke that rose like sacrifices to the lunar god above.

Pagan ceremonies combined with Christian and everything in between in an effort to contain and defeat the fractal null. All believed in some power greater than themselves. Distinctively absent, however, were those who declared Satan as their god of choice. This seemed odd to Deven and Marcus, who had encountered people of that religion before. They seem to want to promote their beliefs in their Under Lord and should have come, if only to protest. Also missing were Jewish participants, as far as they could tell. It made no real sense, other than the population represented may have been reflective of the regional religious practices of historical significance to the people and the land. Marcus made a note to ask about that if he lived to survive this unknown. How much of what he saw was legitimate "religion" and how much was so much delusional drivel was left to personal opinion, he supposed, as he had no real beliefs himself, despite experience with the things of the supernatural and paranormal.

Fallen humanity, sin, and satanic influences, he gathered, had created perverse diversity of the truth taught by Christians. The fear of nature, leading to the worship of natural elements themselves, was found across cultures, from the most primitive to the more advanced and long-lasting cultures of countries in Asia. He understood that as cultures began to develop, gods and goddesses were associated with natural occurrences, making nature easier to explain—and to blame—as the gods and goddesses also demonstrated humanlike characteristics. Demigods were produced by the mating of these gods with humanity. Early Hebrew sources refer to these demigods as Nephilim, half-man, half-angel, believed to be of the fallen sort, and giants by comparison to humanity. Giant gods and goddesses also appeared in the pantheon of ancient Egypt but were said to come from the stars. Greek and Roman mythology had their giant—the Cyclops; sons of Poseidon, god of the sea; Orion, the hunter in the stars. Norse mythology speaks of frost giants. Where fact meets fiction remains in debate. When the concept of One Living God as Creator of all was introduced through the Hebrew writings of Moses in the book of Genesis, it was laughable and quickly rejected by all the nations. Abraham was the first to deal with the worship of this single triune God. Having come from a pagan culture himself, he must have been quite astounded to discover his error in worshipping a god that existed only in the mind of those who believed in them.

Didn't that make the God of the Jews and Christians a newcomer? That is the way it has been perceived and taught in schools and academies of higher education for generations. It is what the historical record shows, isn't it? Marcus was beginning to question his educational experience as being less comparative and more subjective. What he knew and understood from these things he had learned in school. Being raised in Hawaii by a Hawaiian mother who taught her children of the Hawaiian culture and old ways, it rose in conflict with a father who was apathetic to all belief as he was accustomed "to each his own." With their family history of fighting the things that go bump in the night, their only real belief came in that there were bad things in this world, and the forces of good seemed to be absent. Having met Lurlene Joy McCoy was beginning to make him reconsider his background knowledge. There must be a core of truth that gave birth to all these variations that seem so much alike yet were so different.

Where had God been hiding between the generations of Adam and Eve and Abraham? Marcus wondered. Why did He become so powerful and vengeful at that time? It seemed to him that God didn't seem to align with the God the Christians he knew, albeit very few and questionable churchgoers at that, talked about so much. Marcus had never read the Bible, though he had looked information up in it. It sometimes seemed to say one thing, then contradict itself. Yes, he had read those passages he had researched out of context, much as any researcher would do when seeking specific information, but didn't want to read an entire book to find one short passage. Maybe that was a flaw of researching. It is usually topical and specific, often to the exclusion of all other information connected with a topic that could be revealing of a better point or contradict the point the researcher was trying to make. Maybe the Bible wasn't intended to be read the same way as a reference book. Perhaps there was a bigger picture that could only be seen when taken in its entirety. Marcus vowed to make a study of Christian scripture if he lived—just out of curiosity, as a good researcher.

A veil of silence suddenly fell around the warriors. Activity continued as If nothing had changed. People could be seen doing what they had been doing previously, but there was no sound, as if someone had hit a mute button. The four women and two men watched as a dense fog rose up from the earth and engulfed the stony prison of the fractal. The full moon continued to shine down on the eclectic gathering, but its light could not reach the warriors caught in the invisible dome that seemed to surround only them and cut them off from their reinforcements.

A small figure began to form within the fog. As it solidified, it took on the features of a girl. Her black braids initially appeared to be suspenders, then were redefined as the girl's shirt took on a lighter shade that differentiated from her worn jeans as she became less shadow and more humanlike. When completely formed, her Native American features glowed softly in the darkness. It wasn't a natural light, as the reflection of the light of the moon, but more an inner glow as a jack-o'-lantern with a dark flame. Her eyes were large in her young face. They were also pits of pure darkness, as if their sockets were reflecting the eye of a black hole. She scowled menacingly.

"I thought this thing was big like sasquatch, not a demonic kid," stated Deven, relaxing his stance.

"It can take on the forms of its former victims as minions," reminded Glory, still standing at perfect attention.

"That's right, cuz," reinforced Marcus.

"So what are we supposed to do now? Spank her for being naughty and send her back to her parents?" Deven was still unconvinced.

Before anyone could answer, the girl raised her arms, palm up to the sky, until they were shoulder height. A wavering mini hurricane began at her feet and worked its way up to her head. Her braids began to unwind on impact and separate into individual strands. Each strand expanded in girth and developed diamond-shaped heads at their tips. Red-slit eyes glowed from each head, and extraordinarily long-forked tongues slid in and out of their snake-scale mouths.

"She's a Medusa!" shouted Marcus.

"A what?" asked Deven, raising his sword into battle stance once more.

"A Medusa," explained Marcus hurriedly. "She can turn you to one if you look her in the eyes."

"How am I supposed to fight her if I can't look at her?"

"Close your eyes and swing."

"What if I miss?"

"I'll try to cover you. You keep her distracted, and I'll try to get her from behind."

"It's your game." Deven closed his eyes and tried to listen for the girl monster to move. He was no Jedi and had terrible hand-eye coordination when blindfolded. In other words, they were doomed.

Subtle hissing seemed to come from everywhere at the same time. If she were moving, he couldn't tell. A subtle rustling of autumn leaves finally allowed him to focus on the thing's probable location. It wasn't moving toward him as they had planned. It was moving toward Marcus instead. Marcus was humming the funeral march, badly. Deven took it as his cue to act.

"Hey, snake-girl! Over here! I'll give you a haircut like you've never had before!"

Deven's taunts caused the creature to stop in her tracks. Shuffling leaves made him hope she was turning to come at him so Marcus could get in the first and preferably last blow. The shuffling *was* moving toward him. He braced himself for Marcus's signal.

Marcus was now humming the "Battle Hymn of the Republic," his signal that the ploy had worked.

Deven tensed. He knew the creature was near him but not how nearby, until a steely forked tongue tasted his neck. He had feared it had changed directions again.

"Do I taste good?" he asked, not expecting an answer.

Two more steely tongues caressed his neck.

"That's right, baby. Grade-A prime rib. Come on and get it!"

Icy-cold hands took him by the waist, the highest a ten-year-old would be able to reach on such a tall man. She leaned herself intimately into his body. Now multitudes of steely forked tongues tasted the parts of him they could reach. Deterred only by the fabric of his coat and shirt, the hair-snakes discovered his unshaven chin and ears, the lower part of his mouth, probing to try and make their way inside.

Deven shivered in repulsion. If his eyes hadn't already been closed, he would have screwed them shut as he puked, trying to expel the rancid taste left by the fractal-minion's kisses. He wanted to swing his sword at the head of his molester, but she was too close to his body, and he couldn't judge where her neck would be. Decapitation would be the only way to stop this thing. He hoped.

Marcus let out a war cry as he charged the child-demon embracing his cousin. With such a large sword, he would have to make perfect contact, or he could kill Deven instead of the Medusa girl. Having never really used a two-handed sword, he channeled his inner Highlander and slashed downward, shouting, "There can be only one!"

The impact of his downward blow threw him off balance. As if in slow motion, he watched the sword pass neatly between Deven and the little monster that clung to him. A number of hair-snakes were severed and dropped to the ground. The blade continued its downward course, neatly severing the creature's arms just below the elbow. The taloned claws that had not been noticeable before released their grasp and dropped to the ground, shattering in the impact, as they had turned to stone when separated from her body. The still living child of pure darkness let out an ear-splitting scream, revealing unnaturally sharp teeth that appeared to be made of obsidian. A shiny black tongue, forked like a snake, thrust out into the night air, writhing as if looking for something to grasp on to. The child's body stepped backward toward the rock from whence she came. Before she could pass into the thick ebony fog, Marcus repositioned himself and swung the heavy blade once more. This time, he was prepared for impact. His blade sliced cleanly through the creature's neck, her head toppling backward to land at her heels. As he watched, the black eyes dulled back to a more human size, the features softened, and the snakes on her head returned to their natural black strands, now chopped messily and unevenly. Just before the light left her eyes, a tiny smile of relief curved her lips. In death, her flesh became sunken as if she had begun to shrink from the inside out. The mutilated body fell forward unceremoniously as bone deteriorated rapidly and flesh began to rot. Within moments, only a putrid soup-like substance remained, seeping through the clothing left behind.

"You can open your eyes now," directed Marcus breathlessly.

Deven opened one eye, letting it roll about as if it could see everything of importance. The other eye opened and, together, took in the scene in front of him. He let his sword drop to the ground, grabbed his stomach, bent over, and emptied his stomach until only bile was left.

"How about you be the bait next time?" Deven admonished Marcus.

"Whatever, cuz. You know I will always have your back."

"Or front," pointed out Deven.

Marcus looked down at the remains of the Medusa. "Yeah," he replied solemnly.

On the other side of the fog-shrouded monolith, they could hear Lurlene and her nieces in apparent combat. Whatever they were fighting sounded large and smelled like sewage. Without thinking, they started toward the melee on the other side.

"Don't!" demanded Glory.

The men stopped and turned to stare in surprise at the older woman.

"They need our help," stated Deven sternly.

"They are well trained," replied Glory. "Light is on our side. What will be will be. Now pick up your sword and prepare for the next wave." She nodded at Deven.

"Next wave?" questioned Deven as he picked up the weighty sword he had dropped. "How many of these things are there?"

"There is only one fractal," explained Glory patiently, "but it has many minions. Remember, it cannot be killed. It is immortal. It can only be contained. That is why we are here."

Reluctantly, the two men took up their positions, fighting stances held confidently.

The black fog began to swirl as a new form began to solidify. It was large and broad across the shoulders. The massive legs appeared last. The man could have been a lumberjack cousin of Paul Bunyan or a world champion wrestler—not the entertainment-quality wrestling icon but the more refined sport of sumo wrestling for physically fit giants. Hercules? Maybe. Titan? Definitely!

"Uh, oh!" exclaimed Marcus. "I wrestled in high school, cuz, but I never went up against anyone *that* big, and I was the heaviest of the heavyweights."

"Remember, it's *your* turn to be the bait," taunted Deven.

Marcus inhaled deeply. He exhaled slowly, blowing the carbon dioxide through pursed lips and puffed-out cheeks. He looked at his sword. It was made of the same stuff as the universe. His sword could defeat the big, black-skinned ox, but he would never be able to get close enough to use it. It was mano a mano or nothing. With force he didn't know he had, he thrusted the tip of the sword into the forest floor beside him. He rubbed his hands together, sucking in air and blowing it out to relax himself for the attack. Bellowing like an enraged bull, he charged the enormous ebony-skinned man.

Aiming for the creature's chest in an attempt to tackle the beast by throwing him out of balance, he hit a brick wall instead. Staggering back, he fought to catch his breath.

"What are you doing?" shouted Deven. "Trying to get yourself killed?"

"I'm being the bait, cuz. You can jump in any time now and rescue me."

"As if…" Deven gasped.

"Don't go coward on me now. I nearly gave my life saving you from that Medusa. You owe me."

"She wasn't a bad kid."

"That was trying to eat your face off."

Marcus gave another bull roar and dove for the rock giant's knees. Again, he fell to the ground, the thing still standing undisturbed.

"Geez, what's this thing made of?" Marcus asked hypothetically.

"It is much older than the minion you fought earlier," interjected Glory. "He has had more time to become infused with the essence of the fractal. He won't go down easily. Judging by his clothing, he must have been a slave during the precolonial period. Probably brought here as a beast of burden because of his size. He could have carried as much gold as a mule if needed, and more manageable in the wilderness. Look carefully, and you can see the iron shackles left around his ankles and wrists. A heavy iron collar encircles his neck. If I could see him more clearly, I'd say there are scars from a cat-o'-nine-tails crisscrossing his back."

For the first time, Marcus realized this stony specter was shirtless and shoeless. His homespun pants were torn and ragged at the hems.

Marcus felt compassion rise within his heart at the plight this man must have endured. Being part Hawaiian, he knew what it meant to be a proud warrior and defender of his people. This man had fought to remain free but had been subdued into little more than an animal as he sought to simply survive. Had he been made the bait to allow his captors to run away? Being the prisoner of this fractal had to be worse than the fate of hell itself.

Knowing he couldn't begin to take on this giant, Marcus decided on a more humane approach. He climbed to his feet and stood just out of the man's lengthy grasp, he hoped.

"My name is Marcus," he said, tapping himself on the chest. "I want to help you be free."

The hardened black marble eyes narrowed, his nostrils flared, as if checking the air around him.

"Can you understand me?"

Slowly, the giant gave a single nod.

"I'm sorry I tried to hurt you. I thought you were going to try and hurt me."

A snarl appeared, revealing rotted yellow teeth. The hands formed fists, and the creature placed one in the palm of his other hand in preparation for a punch.

"I can see now that you do not want to hurt us. It is that thing that controls you that wants to hurt us."

He gave another single nod.

"We can free you of your captivity if you will let us."

The giant hummed to himself. A garbled noise followed.

"You can't talk, can you?"

The giant shook his head. He mimed pulling out his tongue and cutting it off.

Marcus's stomach churned at the horrific gesture.

"Who cut out your tongue?"

Another garbled response.

"It doesn't matter. We can still be friends, can't we?"

The giant tilted his head to one side as he tried to comprehend Marcus's offer.

"We are here to put this thing back into its prison so others can't be enslaved by it. We don't want to hurt anyone, but we will if we are attacked."

Understanding washed over the former slave's face as his snarl melted into relief. He let his heavy hands fall to his sides in a more relaxed stance.

To Marcus's surprise, the giant dropped to his knees, a pleading look in his eyes. Whatever he had been like in life, he was intelligent and knew the only way he could be truly free was to submit himself to the stocky little man who showed such sympathy for him. When Marcus didn't respond right away, the self-condemned man pointed at the standing sword beside Marcus. Realizing the meaning, Marcus reluctantly pulled the sword from the earth.

The condemned spirit lowered his head to bare his neck. His eyes were closed, and tears of relief fell to the dying leaves of the forest floor. A gurgle that resembled a form of laughter broke Marcus's heart.

His heart filling with regret and compassion, Marcus shifted his position to allow him access to the kneeling figure and raised the two-handed sword above his head. Blinded by his own tears, he brought the sword down in one swift motion. His sobs drowned out the crushing of the spinal column at the nape of the man's neck and the thud of the head dropping to the leaves on the ground below. He imagined he heard a great sigh emerge from the severed head as the fractal's hold on the once-man was broken.

A strange lull in activity fell as the others dispatched whatever they had been facing. The silence was deafening inside the sphere. Marcus and Deven exchanged curious glances. Deven's clothing was tattered in places, and some sort of black ichor splattered his face and clumped in his hair. Marcus wondered if he looked as bad as his cousin. He had no time to contemplate his appearance, however, as a thick black mist oozed from the limestone monolith and began to solidify. The smell of licorice became overwhelming. Marcus began to retch. Behind him, he heard Deven coughing and gagging as well.

"Remember, whatever it does, try to herd it my way."

The voice surprisingly came from Glory. Marcus and Deven looked at each other in surprise, while the voices of the ladies on the other side of the rock shouted their agreement. Deven shrugged.

"Gotcha," he replied.

"As you wish," quipped Marcus with a grin.

Deven nodded at his cousin's movie reference in approval, a wry smile on his face.

A tendril of ebony material broke away from the mass and wound its way across the forest floor like a perverse snake. A second tendril joined the first. Then there seemed to be countless tendrils, snaking over leaves and soil, leaving steaming, acidic-looking slime everywhere they went.

Marcus and Deven were too focused on the tendrils moving toward their feet that they were completely startled by the "Heads up!" that came from nowhere and everywhere at once.

Instinctively, they looked up.

Tentacles were coming from every part of the mass like a nightmare clump of giant squids, each seeking the tidbits of flesh flaunting themselves so temptingly.

Each man took up a firm stance, swords at ready. This was all new to them. This was strange beyond strange.

A tendril tickled Deven's left ankle as it began to wrap itself around the top of his boot. He pulled his foot loose but found himself off balance as a second tendril tightened around his other ankle and began pulling it forward. Deven fell backward, landing in a seated position, his sword lying beside him where he had dropped it in order to catch himself.

The anchored tendril continued to pull Deven toward the rock as the second tendril repositioned itself to wrap around Deven's wrist. He felt himself slowly being dragged across foliage, roots, and buried stones. He tried to grab his sword as he slid forward in an odd, almost sideways manner. It was just out of his reach. He had faced death before but never eternity as a slave to an indestructible cosmic force. That rock was already too crowded. He would not become the next unwilling tenant. He released a primal scream, digging his free foot into the ground to slow the tentacles. With one hand, he punched at the tentacles. When his punches had no effect, he began clawing at it. The squirming darkness was harder than any known mineral on earth yet was as pliant as putty as it sent out smaller tendrils from itself to entrap his fingers in their viselike grips. Deven screamed in agony as his fingers were crushed by the force of the deceptively strong tendrils that resembled black threads that wrapped themselves around and around, weaving a black mitten around his hand. Where his thumb was spread away from his other fingers, a single thread sought out the flesh of its tip. Deven stared in horror as the end of the thread thickened into a bulbous head that split open to reveal minute fangs, rows upon rows of minute fangs. He screamed again as the tiny mouth latched itself around his thumb and began to suckle like a frightened child.

Deven squeezed his eyes shut, tears flowing down his face and mingling with his sweat. He struggled to remain conscious as something seemed to course through his veins, lulling him into sleep. Whatever it was coursing through his veins was icy but light, nearly weightless. He felt himself becoming lighter, starting to float. Was this death?

A whoosh, combined with a primal scream, followed by a metal-on-metal clashing noise caused Deven to open his eyes. He saw the blade of a very large sword speeding down toward him. He tried to scream and reflexively turn away from the blade's intended arc but found himself frozen in place.

There was another metallic clang.

"You can thank me later, broh," a familiar voice said.

Finding he could move again, Deven turned toward the voice and found Marcus grinning down at him.

"Thanks, cuz," Deven mumbled helplessly as he took Marcus's offered hand.

Marcus pulled Deven to his feet.

"Seriously, thanks, cuz," Deven repeated with a much stronger voice. "Thought I was dead for a minute there."

"Me too," returned Marcus.

They both examined the ground where Deven had been attacked. The drag marks were clear, but there was no sign of the dreaded tentacles. The mass still surrounded the rock but seemed placid, as if waiting for its next imminent victory. Sounds of combat from the other side of the rock filled the background. The women were in active battle, yelling directives back and forth as they combated whatever was emerging from the mass in their section.

Deven stooped to pick up his sword. As he rose, something behind his cousin caused him to quickly place himself into a defensive position, both hands gripping the sword at the ready.

"Look out!" he screamed.

Marcus whirled around to discover a tidal wave wall of tentacles rising over his head and preparing to slam down on him.

It was Marcus's turn to be frozen in fear. He watched helplessly as the tentacles wove themselves into an enormous obsidian hand, fingers flexing in preparation for the swat.

"Oh no, you don't!"

Marcus heard Deven behind him, then he saw his cousin standing in front of him, sword thrust up and away from his body, tip buried in the center of the giant palm.

The hand stiffened, and the fingers spread in surprise. It seemed to be inert, for the moment.

Marcus raised his own sword.

"Send it to Glory!" he shouted.

Deven nodded and withdrew his sword.

The hand contracted and drew itself into a fist as if squeezing the pain. Marcus moved behind the hand from the outside so as to not trip over the thick corded "arm" attaching the hand to the mass. Deven moved to the side of the hand from the outside and took up a fighting stance.

As one, the men attacked the hand with the broadside of their swords, as if spanking the monstrosity.

Like any creature taken by surprise, it lurched forward, nearly falling to the ground. In instinct, it uncurled its fingers and positioned them to break its fall.

Deven and Marcus began a relentless attack on the creature, spanking it repeatedly in strategic places to keep it off balance and moving toward Glory's position.

It crawl-walked obediently.

The others were also making their move as someone was screaming, "Get along, little doggie."

Someone was talking to whatever they were encountering, disciplining it when it was errant and praising it when it was compliant, albeit reluctantly. A third voice gave directions to the other two, giving warning when necessary.

All six people converged at Glory's corner. They automatically took up a defensive perimeter as the black mass seemed to slide toward the very place they needed it to be, revealing exhausted limestone and decaying vegetation as its essence drained away.

At last, the mass huddled in a position free of the rock that had confined it. It shifted size and shape as if considering its options. Finally, it began to transform, taking on shape, shrinking to produce mass for its final form.

Marcus and Deven watched the transformation in awe. When the mist had concluded its transformation and solidified itself for the final battle, they saw only a massive humanoid creature, seemingly covered in the blackest of black hair. It slowly unfolded itself and stood erect. There before them stood the creature from Lurlene's book, only a thousand times larger.

"That ain't no sasquatch," stated Marcus.

"No, it sure ain't," commented Deven.

All twelve feet of the creature seemed to be composed of obsidian needles in lieu of hair. Its facial features were reflective of the primate-humanoid Bigfoot, but it made Bigfoot look like a child's soft teddy bear. There were no eyes, as such, but black-hole portals spiraled dizzyingly where they should have been. It was very disorienting when it turned its head to examine each of its opponents in turn. It showed no fear—or any other emotion. An icy-cold vacuum surrounded it, threatening to suck them in with every move it made.

"Are you ready for this?" Glory asked calmly as if they were preparing to partake of a country buffet.

The other combatants looked around at one another. All were battle-worn. Each nodded in turn.

"Let me deal with it," Glory reminded them sternly. "All you need to do is watch my back. Is that clear?"

Voices of agreement floated out of the darkness.

"Let's do this," Glory commanded. She broke her attention and assumed a fighting stance. She had stood by until this moment. Now she took over. She held the cane in her left hand, her right hand on the upper half. The light of the dome around them was not provided by any natural source, and shadows made Glory look like your worst nightmare as she stared sternly at the fractal.

In what seemed to be slow-motion, Glory separated the top portion of the cane from the lower portion. As the two parts moved in opposite directions, the glint of viciously sharp cosmic blades sparked around her. When fully separated, Glory held two short and narrow but very dangerous swords, one in each hand.

She feinted at the fractal. It responded by swatting at her with one massive hand. Glory danced backward, just out of its reach.

Glory jabbed at the air between herself and the creature. She repeated the air jab like a kid taunting a sibling. The fractal tilted its head to one side, a rumble of sorts coming from it. There was no visible mouth around the fangs and tusks, just needlelike hairs clacking together expressively.

Next, Glory stood at attention, arms above her head, swords crossed in an *X*. She still hadn't blinked, or at least it seemed that way. Her scowl was deeper than Deven or Marcus had yet seen. Her eyebrows were knit together into a formidable unibrow, giving her a fierce, primitive look. It was truly terrifying.

The thing made up of cosmic dust and earthen materials tilted its head in the other direction. It raised one hand and poked at Glory. The woman didn't move. She didn't wobble. She had become stone herself.

Finding nothing to fear, it turned toward Grace and Mercy. To their credit, the girls stood their ground as this thing approached them. One hand reached out toward Mercy, as if to pick her up, but it stumbled off balance when struck heavily from behind.

What the creature had not seen was Glory dropping her petrified stance and charging the creature. Gracefully, she had leapt into the air, extending her right leg, and made contact with the creature with the sole of her miniature combat boots, before dropping back to the ground in a fighting stance, swords at the ready.

Clumsily, the fractal staggered to regain its balance and turn to see what had attacked it. The needles of its body stood up and shook, creating an enraged rattle.

Taking advantage of the creature's rage, Glory performed a perfect roundhouse kick, landing a blow in the area of the beast's nearly nonexistent kneecap. The thing shook in rage, causing needles to fly from its body in all directions. Glory seemed unaffected by the needles that flew past her, one grazing her cheek.

For her next attack, Glory began swinging the swords around and around at her sides, then brought them in front of her, continuing to swing them in a furious fan. She maneuvered them over her head in the same furious fashion. The movement seemed to mesmerize the creature. It moved its head in rhythm with the swirling blades, trying to follow the pattern.

Without warning, Glory charged the wall of obsidian, making contact with each blow. It started to stagger backward under her assault. Glory moved forward as it fell back. It flung its arms around in an attempt to stop the blades from making contact. Its size and density in respect to Glory made it clumsy and reflective. It was soon backed against the rock that had been its prison for millennia.

Glory ceased her frenzied swinging, one sword in the air over her head and the other with the tip in the abdomen of the fractal.

"Thou foul creature," Glory snarled. "Conglomeration of Creation leftovers. Thou art an abomination. As such, thou art to be returned to this rock where thou canst do no more harm. To await the day when thou art undone and returned to the void from whence thou came."

She thrust the sword already at the creature's abdomen into its body. It shook with rage again, releasing more of the needle-hairs into the air. It flailed its arms and tried to stomp its feet. This time, it created a pained howl.

Removing her sword from the creature, Glory took up a different stance, both swords down to her sides at an angle, forming a sort of triangle with her body.

"God the Creator Father spoke all that is into being. And it was good.

"God the Son came to earth to right the wrong introduced by your kind, corrupting a perfect angel of light and twisting him into an instrument of evil."

She paused again. The creature seemed to be groaning. Whether in pain or at her words, it was difficult to say.

"God the Holy Spirit is here with us. Within us, around us. Strengthening us. The power of the Spirit will return thou to thine prison of stone until such time that all that is evil shall be placed in the lake of fire, never to be free again for eternity."

Glory's voice had risen with each sentence until she shouted the final declaration.

Without hesitation, she raised both swords and thrust them simultaneously into the creature's abdomen.

To the observers, light seemed to emit from the areas of the punctures, grow steadily brighter as the limestone monolith appeared to inhale the unholy prisoner back into itself. It was difficult to say as the light had blinded all observers. When the light had faded, the creature was gone, and Glory was standing erect, swords to her side. She seemed suddenly small and frail as she relaxed her frown and unfurled her eyebrows. Nonchalantly, she returned the blades to their places within the wooden cane once more.

"Fetch the ladder," Lurlene directed her nieces as she placed her arms around her twin, led her to a level spot, and sat down with her.

Deven and Marcus helped Grace and Mercy place the ladder against the boulder that now held the fractal once more. Lurlene climbed to the top of the stone monolith, walked around, and then sat down. She pulled a metallic stylus from a pocket and began marking the stone.

"She's resetting the sigil," explained Grace. "She's using her heavenly pencil to make sure it lasts."

"Heavenly pencil?" asked Marcus.

The girls giggled.

"It's made of the same thing as the cosmic blades we used in the battle," explained Mercy. "We always called it the heavenly pencil when we were kids."

"I get it." Deven laughed. "It's made from dust from heaven."
"More or less," replied Mercy cryptically.

Part 8

The sun was beginning to peek up in the eastern sky by the time the dome dispelled and allowed the warriors to rejoin the eclectic group outside. Individuals and groups were mingling, helping one another clean up the areas where they had each done their things. Everyone looked tired but at peace with one another.

Glory was replacing their weapons in the back of the Jeep. Grace and Mercy were helping her.

Deven and Marcus stood with Lurlene, watching as Christians helped pagans and witches pack up their gear.

"Were all these…religions…really necessary to put that thing back in its box?" asked Deven.

Lurlene shrugged. "We all have allowed evil into our lives. We are all responsible for ridding our world of evil. Each of these groups believes they have made their penance by performing their rituals here. It is not ours to judge. Though we believe in only One Way to overcome evil, it is not ours to force that knowledge onto others. It's a personal relationship, not a corporate endeavor. We just set the example and pray they will follow. By being open about who and what we stand for, without judgmental behavior that condemns them, we can share our faith with them in a way that satisfies their curiosity and allows them to ask questions or compare our ways with theirs. We can be friends who disagree about these things. We share our commonalities. We stand together for what we agree on. Those ties are more likely to win friends and influence people than verbal condemnation and prejudicial behavior. Diplomacy and prayer. Community and relationship. Not us versus them. Even Jesus surrounded himself with those who would otherwise have been condemned and thrown aside as unworthy of being in His presence. His greatest objectors were the Pharisees and Sadducees, *religious* people who thought they had a corner on the God market. In the New Testament, particularly in the book of Acts, the apostles spoke to pagan believers and practitioners of dark arts. Many repented of their spiritual error and were baptized into the new faith of Christ. It's a relationship with another human being that opens the doors of communication about a relationship with Christ. All Christians are called to this mission, but so many fail to understand how it works or to fulfill it."

"So Glory's church people are no better than the Native Americans or witches?"

"We are all sinners and fall short of the glory of God," replied Lurlene. "As sinners, we are blind to the light and chase whatever we believe will bring us peace. Right or wrong. Only God can open our eyes to the true light."

"What about those who don't believe in God?"

"Everyone believes in God, Marcus. Even the demons in hell acknowledge Him. It is denial of self that makes us believe we are alone on earth or above any intelligent Creator. Nature itself shouts the glory of God, but people choose to believe it is not so. God is everywhere. All you need to do is look for Him. It is dangerous for a man, or woman, to say there is no God. It is condemning eternally to say God exists, but I want no part of Him. That is the unpardonable sin—to deny God even in death."

"Marcus and I have seen our share of evil," said Deven, "and we've done our part to rid the world of it. Where is God in that?"

"That depends, Deven. Do you fight fire with fire, or do you fight fire with water?"

"I don't get it."

"Deven, what you and your cousin do is a calling. Not just anyone can do what you do without losing their minds. You do what you know to stop whatever you face. Sometimes you use witchcraft to summon or trap demons, take down vampires and werewolves. Witchcraft may be what is needed in those situations as witchcraft helped create them. But witchcraft is still a tool of the devil. You are using the devil's tools to fix what the devil broke."

"Ah." Deven sighed.

"I see what you mean," said Marcus. "But what are we supposed to do? Become priests so we can do exorcism's God's way?"

Lurlene chuckled to herself. "That's one way to do it, but I don't recommend it. Celibacy can be a real problem."

Deven cleared his throat and looked away. Marcus lowered his eyes and tried not to blush.

"Don't worry, boys, I'm just teasing you. The best way to put out the devil's fires is with the Water of Life. Jesus spoke to His apostles about exorcism. He told them it is not enough to merely clear the house of evil. If the house remains empty, evil will return and bring its whole family, making the situation even worse. You have to fill that house with something better, something stronger, that won't be attractive to the darkness anymore. The best thing to keep darkness out of your life is to fill it with light."

"Does that really work?" Deven was suspicious.

"You saw what happened in there. You tell me."

Neither man spoke. They withdrew into their own thoughts.

Part 9

"Is everything loaded, cuz?"

Deven nodded.

"Just waiting on you."

The two young men who had driven into this quaint old-fashioned town just days before were preparing to leave much wiser and sober regarding things of the supernatural world. They realized that good and evil will always have their gray areas, but ultimate good and ultimate evil would always be beyond human comprehension. They were rethinking everything they thought they knew about the beginnings of the universe, the origin of mankind, and the old question of whether humanity was born basically good or basically evil or a blank slate that is filled with the entire nature-versus-nurture argument. No amount of education could enlighten them the way this experience had.

Four women—two generations of fraternal twins—stood outside the *Incense and Old Lace* curiosity shop, laden with packages. Deven and Marcus fidgeted and looked at everything but the women. For some reason, this goodbye was so much more personal.

Grace stepped forward with her package. It was a small box with a lid that could be lifted off. She handed it to Marcus. The stocky man raised his brows as he accepted it. He lifted the lid and found a phial attached to a heavy chain. Inside the phial was a droplet of the black goo they had all been covered with after returning Achimoth to its prison.

"Gee, just what I always wanted," teased Marcus. "Cosmic goo in a bottle."

Grace was smiling broadly. The sun brought out the red in her hair, giving her a Strawberry Shortcake porcelain doll look. Her freckles were more evident in that light, he noticed.

"Yep. That's why I saved it for you."

She turned to Deven.

"I've sent your blood samples to the Alpha Domini lab. Their equipment is more sensitive and accurate than anywhere else on earth. They'll be in contact with you about the results. We've never had a sample before. Anyone who would have been able to give such a sample is never seen again. Let us know if you demonstrate any changes in behavior, develop odd illnesses, or have any odd changes in your physical appearance. Also, if your eating habits change dramatically..."

She left that sentence unfinished.

"I get it," Deven reassured her. "Anything that changes gets reported."

She nodded, choking back a sob. She put her hands in her pockets as she turned back to Marcus.

"That piece of goo is the one I took off your cheek. It's been inspected rudimentarily and declared as safe as long as it is inside that teeny tiny hermetically sealed bottle that has been specially treated by angels. And it's been blessed. If anything changes after analysis, and it isn't safe, I'll let you know how to dispose of it."

Marcus looked at Grace intently. She was quite sincere. Her blue-green eyes were watery, and her nose beginning to turn pink.

"Thanks," he said seriously.

Grace pulled a card from her pocket and handed it to Marcus.

"Here's my card. Keep in touch, you hear."

"Of course," he said, barely above a whisper. They both knew that was unlikely, but they could both hope.

Grace stepped back to allow Mercy to come forward. She ran her arm under her nose in a graceful yet gross manner. Marcus found it endearing.

Mercy's parcel was also small. She presented it to Deven with a great deal of ceremony.

"For you, sir," she said with a mischievous smile and a twinkle in her eye.

Deven unfolded the top of the small brown bag and peered inside.

"Cool," he said as he withdrew a beaded bracelet. "I always wanted one of these, but my sister refused to make one for me with her little weaving loom."

"I had it especially made for you." Mercy indicated a tiny figure on the band. "That is Jesus, the Great Spirit. The other designs represent prayers for the Great Spirit to be with you. With the possibility of fractal DNA being in your blood, you may need it. Never take it off. It's waterproof."

"Double cool and wow!" exclaimed Deven, sounding like Opie Taylor in an old *Andy Griffith Show* rerun.

"It was made by a Shawnee shaman friend of mine. She made it and overnighted it to me. She sends her blessings as well."

"Thanks." Devin grinned widely. "I really appreciate it. It really means a lot to me."

"Keep in touch," Mercy finalized. "Here's my card."

Deven took the card and slid it into his coat pocket before placing the bracelet on his left wrist.

"Perfect fit," he said.

Mercy kissed her fingertips, then touched them to Deven's chest before backing away.

Lurlene Joy carried a large shopping bag with the *Incense and Old Lace* logo.

"These are for both of you, but I believe Marcus will probably use them the most."

Marcus took the bag and looked at Lurlene Joy with a small smile of curiosity.

"To give you a new toolbox," Lurlene stated bluntly. "I've included my own notes to help you."

Devin leaned over to look into the bag. He saw a copy of *Sleeping in Satan's Den* on top and presumed the bag was filled with a copy of all Lurlene's books. He raised his eyebrows at his cousin.

"Right up my alley," said Marcus happily. To his cousin, he said, "Don't worry, cuz. I'll read them to you and explain all the pictures."

"Ha ha," replied Deven with a wry smile.

"These will also help you decode my blogs. Feel free to contact me—us—if you need us. Prayers go with you and angels on your shoulders."

"What's that about angels and shoulders?" asked Deven.

"It's something I used to say to my son when he was small and scared. It reminded him that God was always with him."

"Uh, huh," Deven scoffed.

Lurlene looked Deven over from top to bottom and back up. "My husband always told him, 'Know who you are and to whom you belong.' So far, he's lived by those words. Take them with you, even if you don't believe them. They can be powerful."

"Gotcha," responded Deven.

"Uh, Lurlene," Marcus interrupted softly. "I've got a question to ask, but I don't want to seem too...nosey."

"Shoot," encouraged Lurlene."

"How did she," he nodded to Glory, "do all that...you know...?"

Lurlene let out a belly laugh that took both men by surprise.

"I told you we were trained by angels in things of the Spirit. Well, that included weaponology and hand-to-hand combat. Turns out that what my sister lacks in personality was more than made up for in her ability to fight. She's a weapons master of the highest level achievable by a mortal. It comes in handy now and then."

The cousins exchanged shocked looks.

"Weapons...master?" repeated Deven. "You don't say." The look of awe on his face spoke of new respect for the middle-aged grump.

"Wow! Who'd have thought?" added Marcus with respect.

"That explains that," said Deven, "but what about us? We've never handled swords like those before. How did we know how to use them? And so effectively?"

"God provides what you need when you need it," Lurlene added with a shrug.

She hugged each of them and stepped back just enough to allow Glory to come forward with her plain brown bag that, while not big, seemed heavy.

Seeing that Marcus had his hands full with Lurlene's gift, she thrust her bag at Deven.

"Here," she grumped. "For tonight, after you are off the road."

The bag was heavier than Deven thought, and he nearly dropped it. Curious, he slid his hand into the bag, and he nearly dropped it. He drew out a quart jar of a clear liquid. His eyes lit up.

"Is this what I think it is?" he asked.

"Sure is. Kentucky White Lightning. You boys earned it."

"Glory?" Lurlene was both questioning her sister's choice of gift and her surprise.

"I've got my sources," Glory threw back.

Lurlene chuckled.

Deven returned the jar to the bag.

"Take it slow and easy. Sip it. Don't down it. That stuff will kill you even if you are used to it. Save it for when you are going to be off the road for a few days, just in case…"

"Just in case," repeated Deven happily.

Glory eyed the boys wearily, then grabbed each in a brisk hug before stepping back beside her sister.

Deven cleared his throat and shifted his feet uncomfortably.

Marcus was the one to speak up, give their thanks, and express goodbyes.

They loaded the books and moonshine into the back of the Mustang. Before closing the trunk, Marcus drew out the top book. Deven only nodded.

The engine roared as it came to life. Unseen by them, townspeople had gathered to say their own goodbyes. A new peace had come over Ṣatan's Den, and the people looked forward to the respite brought by the reentombment of the fractal that has plagued the land from the beginning of time and will remain until the earth is no more.

Ephesians 6:10–13, NKJV

> Finally, brethren, be strong in the Lord and in the power of His might. Put on the whole armor of God, that you may be able to stand against the wiles of the devil. For we do not wrestle against flesh and blood, but against principalities, AGAINST POWERS, AGAINST THE RULERS OF THE DARKNESS OF THIS AGE, AGAINST SPIRITUAL HOSTS OF WICKEDNESS IN THE HEAVENLY PLACES. THEREFORE TAKE UP THE WHOLE ARMOR OF GOD, THAT YOU MAY BE ABLE TO WITHSTAND IN THE EVIL DAY, AND HAVING DONE ALL, TO STAND.

Notes of Lurlene Joy McCoy

Brothers and sisters of Alpha Domini, I have no doubt that you have recognized and received the message clearly sent by my store window. People ask about it, and I must give them the vague responses they seem to seek and be satisfied with. We are an open book regarding our business for those who know our language. But for those who may not be familiar with our particular establishment, I will give you the information you will require to understand future communications from us.

Let us begin with our name. INCENSE AND OLD LACE alludes to the old story of ARSENIC AND OLD LACE, the story of two elderly women who poisoned some of their houseguests with arsenic-laced elderberry wine. No one suspects these gentle old women of being murderers until a body is accidentally discovered before it can be buried. It is a dark comedy. However, Glory and I are not murderers in any way. We are, however, warriors in God's heavenly kingdom. Incense was burned upon the altar of the tabernacle in the wilderness as a means of worship and communication with God. We carry that over by offering a line of scented candles which are handcrafted locally. The old lace of our name simply identifies us as lady antique dealers who happen to be edging on being antiques ourselves. We thought it was clever at the time we opened the store.

We chose a tea party theme to reflect the Arsenic and Old Lace story as well. The women poisoned their prey while serving them a meal or afternoon tea. In that period, the art of serving tea was considered to be hospitable. It was a way of welcoming guests into your home as friends. Our shop and our lives are open to each of you. We are here when you need us. No arsenic will be served, we promise.

The teddy bear at the table represents childlike faith and trust we must have in one another and in our Savior. We are called to communion and fellowship with one another and with Him.

The bride doll should be the biggest giveaway. Not only do we deal in antique toys, but we are a part of the Bride of Christ. The presence of the doll reflects our true purpose by placing it in the display with the tea set and teddy bear to complete our statement of faith. The candles, soaps, and jars of herbs represent our worship of Almighty God. The odd items are the handgun and knife, both of great antiquity. They are heirlooms of our family, going back many generations. We have artifacts going back even further than our presence in this country that have been passed down to us as well. My sister, Glory, is a celestial weapons master, and this is her signal to others who deal in combat with such weapons that she is available for your support as needed. We are all trained in spiritual warfare, and our weapons are not of this world. Here, you can find what you may need in completing a kingdom quest. My books identify our location as a safe place for our communications.

In this combination, our current mission is laid out for all to see but few to understand. Each generation has its own missions to fulfill, and our message may change as the next generation comes to the forefront and we retire, but we can always be found if you know the secret language of our group. We know many others out there communicate in much the same way. My greetings to you all, and may God's glory be with you.

In discussing fractals, it is interesting to search prehistoric cave art on the internet. It would surprise many to discover that the oldest-known cave art in North America has been found in the Smoky Mountain region of Tennessee. These prehistoric pictographs depict what we can only assume to be events of importance to those people. Some of the creatures depicted appear to be transformational in nature, such as doglike creatures with bird claws. Perhaps these people were giving us a warning that there are supernatural beasts that do walk, fly, swim, or crawl among us. Native American mythology is full of anthropomorphized animals that help explain their understanding of the universe. Some of the spirit beings and humanoid peoples in their stories should not be easily dismissed as imaginary. Our Native brothers and sisters, though speaking from a more primitive or pagan viewpoint, could hold the key to opening up our understanding of the unseen world around us. We should not be quick to discard these people or their culture as savage and anti-Christian. Instead, we should develop a parallel comparison of known literary references of the cultures that arose earliest, with those who have arisen in more recent history, and compile it with that of Jewish tradition that has most greatly influenced Christianity.

We are not truly in opposition to one another as humans but are influenced by the opposing forces of good and evil. This is played out in the mythologies of every known culture. Even the early chapters of Genesis give us clues as to how rapidly paganism became the norm for Cain and his descendants. Cain was raised to believe in God the Creator. It is only following the murder of his brother Abel that he is exiled by God. Cain is described as becoming a vagabond, a wanderer. He is later said to have founded a city, where he began his family. A city implies a great number of people. Cain was exiled alone and marked as a murderer so that he would not be killed by others. Who were these others? Watchers? Fallen angels? Fractals? There are numerous theories, but none have been proven with any more proof than human conjecture and cultural mythologies. I use the term *mythologies* in this context not as made-up stories to explain the supernatural but as human interpretations of events that led to the growth of a belief in their authenticity. There is a kernel of truth at their center. It is through comparative study that we can begin to discern these core truths.

It is my opinion, and that of others within the AD spectrum of knowledge, that these core truths can be traced back to those events leading up to the fall of humanity and the beginning of the dispersion of humanity into the world at large that came with Cain's exile. Jewish tradition teaches that the Sons of God that intermarried with the daughters of mankind introduced much of what we call civilization to the world, including metallurgy, music, the use of cosmetics by women to increase their seductive power over men, and the use of herbs and spells to manipulate and summon creatures of a supernatural nature. Hence, biblical witchcraft can be defined as the ultimate form of rebellion. It is not the spell casting as we believe it to be today but the refusal of humanity to allow God to be their source of provision and sustenance. It is the proclivity toward self-promotion and self-reliance that bypasses God and all that is required by God for a relationship with Him. Satanism as a religion is the newcomer. Worship of nature and the manipulation of creation for the purpose of self-promotion, however, began almost in the beginning. Satan is its source of perversion and author of the chaos but was not recognized as being "in place of God" in worship until much later.

Fractals are neither good nor evil. They are the void itself. They have no shape but what they choose for themselves. They seek only to devour the creation that was ripped from its bowels, leaving them desolate and unformed for eternity. It makes sense that they would desire to return to that unformed state in which they were born. If the theory that angels were created at the moment God said, "Let there be light," is to be taken literally, it is clear that the void came first. When God divided the light from the darkness, He tore the fabric of the void and created the balance that keeps our world and our universe in stasis. As these two forces pull against each other, the universe is pulled asunder. Fractals desire to reinstate the fabric of the void in order to undo Creation.

In the beginning, God created the heavens and the earth. The earth was unformed and void, darkness was on the face of the deep, and the Spirit of God hovered over the surface of the water. Then God said, "Let there be light," and there was light. God saw that the light was good, and God divided the light from the darkness. God called the light day, and the darkness he called night. So there was evening, and there was morning, one day (Genesis 1:1–5, *Complete Jewish Bible*).

Lucifer desires to take the place of God. The fractals desire to remain formless. There is a vast difference between the two concepts. Separately, they are formidable. Together, they will be the downfall of humanity and all creation.

It becomes imperative here to define the word *fractal*. In common usage, it applies to a complex mathematical term few have heard of. Not being a mathematician, I will give you the *Wikipedia* shortcut version. Generally defined, a fractal is "a geometric shape containing detailed structure at arbitrarily small scales, usually having a Fractal dimension strictly exceeding the topological dimension." The word *fractal* was coined in 1975 by Benoit Mandelbrot. A fractal is symmetrical and can be split into parts, each of which is (at least approximately) a reduced-size copy of the whole. A fractal can be simulated in sound, digital images, electrochemical patterns, circadian rhythms, etc. They can be created in models using a computer algorithm. They occur naturally and can be seen in some algae, animal coloration patterns, blood vessels and pulmonary vessels, crystals, heart rate patterns, lightning bolts, mountain goat horns, pineapple, snowflakes, geometrical optics, and trees. They can be found in cell biology. Computers using these algorithms have been able to replicate paintings of the artist Jackson Pollock with a 93 percent rate of similarity. The structure of mountains can be described using fractal algorithms.

Because there is so much evidence for the presence of this precision in Creation, the presence of a Creator becomes self-evident. Going back to Genesis 1:1–5 from the Jewish Bible, initially, the earth (and the universe) was without form and was void. Being the Great Mathematician God is, no doubt each particle of that formless void was precisely symmetrical but not arrayed into the form it would become. God then spoke into existence the vision of the universe as He had planned it, thus splitting the void into its smaller parts. We could call this the Big Bang as it was a shattering of a whole into parts. When anything shatters, there is always irretrievable dust that is left to fill the space around the shards.

A fractal is then a fragmentation of a larger mass. In the case of our antagonist, a fracture of the cosmos itself has taken on this form in an attempt to reunite with the shard of the cosmos that became earth. It consumes all matter it comes in contact with that can help it achieve this end. Our fractal consumes human flesh. By consuming the human life force, it is attempting to recreate the organic patterns of its own fractal biology. It is a living creature, though we do not understand in what way life applies to it. It is sentient. It plans and strategizes to obtain nutrients. It appears to understand its limiting constraints and fights against them to regain freedom. While the Cosmic Compendium has yet to reveal the secrets of this creature, something like it has been seen and documented for millennia, sometimes as monster, sometimes as demanding god. If we could succeed in gaining blood samples (if it has blood) and skin or hair samples (if that terminology applies), we could understand it better. However, our training in this area is limited. God only intends for us to know only what we need to know to fulfill our current missions. He reveals what is needed as needed.

For those of you who are grumbling and complaining that I would invite pagans to participate in so serious a ceremony, I say to you that it was necessary. Humanity was deceived by Satan. Some questionable source continued that deception through the establishment of heavenly knowledge in a perverse form as humanity began to spread across the earth. We are all deceived creatures. Each culture received this perverse knowledge and worshipped the beings that came to them as gods. We lost our ability to be one with our Creator and walked away from the opportunity for reconciliation. Within each culture, however, the concept of light and dark continued to thrive. There is a constant battle between these forces that is still taking place today. The wise men and women of each culture learned how to fight that spiritual battle. Their methods and techniques may be questionable to those of us who have returned to the Creator but should not be discounted all together. As Elijah fought the priests of Baal upon the mountain, so do we battle the forces of spirit around us. We recognize that evil cannot cast out evil. Only good has that power. Only God can defeat all that opposes Him. These people gathered in faith to overcome the fractal. Their faith in their practices gave them strength to face the unknown. The fractal is neither light nor darkness. It is void. It seeks only to reunite all Creation into the formless mass that spawned it. If the forces of good and the forces of evil were to combat it individually, each would fall. Together, they represent the balance of power that holds sway over humanity. It proves that we can and are willing to set aside our differences in a time of need to preserve our species. It isn't about who is right or wrong. God will always prevail. It is about coming together, sharing our individual beliefs to find common ground, to see we are not really in opposition to one another but have chosen opposing forces as our guides. Here is our opportunity to share our Creator and His unerring truth.

Forgive me for seeming flippant regarding our great mission, but some of us must act as referees between opposing armies. We must acknowledge each side and understand the basic tenets of each. We bear the cross of mediation. We have our loyalties firmly in our Lord and Savior Jesus Christ yet must enter the viper's nest to retrieve those who will be saved once they have seen and heard truth. It is said that we go where angels fear to tread, and that may be so. It is our calling. We are trained for this battle. Though you may not understand or agree, pray for us.

For those who wish to "fact check" my interpretations or to explore some of the ideas I have presented to you, I will give you references to other fiction writers who could just as easily present to you some of these ideas in a perhaps more palatable form. I have already presented James L. Rubart in other notations. I now submit to you two specific works he has produced. The first deals with the concept of the chronicling of humanity. In *Book of Days*, a man and his deceased wife's best friend go in search of the Book of Days which is reported to contain the past, present, and future of every human to have walked earth, are currently walking earth, and will walk the earth in the future. Would you like to know your future? Think carefully before responding. The other book is Rubart's *The Five Times I Met Myself,* in which a middle-aged man uses a technique known as lucid dreaming to revisit his younger self and make changes that affect his current reality. Dreams or time travel? You decide. The other series of novels I would like to recommend is the Cades Cove Series by Aiden James. In this series, a man accidentally releases a vengeful spirit in a rock in Cades Cove of the Smoky Mountains. The spirit follows him home to Colorado. He has no choice but to return to Cades Cove and team up with a Cherokee shaman and his granddaughter to return the spirit to the rock. A great awakening of vengeful Cherokee spirits sets off a series of battles that could mean life or death for the participants. Perhaps this series will appease some of your curiosity or assist in a clearer understanding as to why seemingly conflicting faiths were allowed to come together to put Achimoth back into its tomb. We are all guilty of setting these things free. We are all accountable for letting them remain free. Shouldn't we all come together to drive them back to where they came from?

Topic: Licorice

Source: Wikipedia

Summary

Licorice is a flowering plant of the bean family *Fabaceae.*

The aromatic flavor is extracted from the root and is fifty times sweeter than sugar.

The plant is native to Western Asia, North Africa, and Southern Europe.

It is used as flavoring in candies and tobacco, particularly in some European countries.

Excessive consumption of licorice may result in adverse effects, including unexplained hypokalemia (low potassium) and muscle weakness.

Licorice is used for indigestion and stomach inflammation, as a cough suppressant, ulcer treatment, and laxative.

Ninety percent of licorice is used by the tobacco industry as flavoring, with the remaining 10 percent divided about equally between the food and pharmaceutical industries.

Toxicity symptoms include sodium retention, potassium loss, electrolyte imbalance, edema, increased blood pressure, weight gain, heart problems, and paralysis.

A single death from licorice toxicity was reported in 2020—a man died of cardiac arrest after consuming a bag of black licorice daily for three weeks prior to the event.

Topic: Licorice in Witchcraft

Source: www.thegypsythread.org
Author: thegypsy
Article: Magickal Properties of Herbs, Nuts, and Branches Used in Spellwork, WITCHCRAFT, December 6, 2019

This is a list of ingredients used in spell casting by those who practice such craft. It simply identifies the plant and the type of spells it is used in. Licorice is listed as being used in spells for love, lust, and fidelity.

Other articles on the history and use of licorice indicate that this root is a good binder when used with other herbs and natural ingredients. It acts as an agent to deter some of the side effects that may occur with these other ingredients. It has been used in wine as discovered by the amount of licorice-based wine discovered in King Tut's tomb. Licorice root sticks have been chewed as candy, without the issue of tooth decay. It has been associated with sexual virility. It is listed as an integral part of Chinese apothecary. While it can be domesticated and grown in parts of the United States, it is not native.

Topic: Real-Life Disappearances in the Smoky Mountains

Source: Unsolved Disappearances in the Great Smoky Mountains
Authors: Juanitta Baldwin and Ester Grubb

Summary

The authors have researched and presented true stories of people who have disappeared in the Great Smoky Mountains since their inception as a national park. In the first five (of seven) cases presented, three are individuals that have disappeared without a trace. In the other two cases, years of research and new information has been discovered that have helped to determine the puzzling events that led to the deaths of those two individuals. There have been no new leads to assist in the closure of the first three cases. In all three cases, the individuals were with a group. The others in the group saw the person just moments before they disappeared, and extensive searches found no evidence of foul play or indications of accident. No bodies have been recovered.

Thelma Pauline "Polly" Melton was hiking with longtime friends when she began walking at a brisk and determined pace that left her friends behind. Her friends watched her atop a hill and presumed she would tire quickly and be waiting for them at a bench just over the hill. Polly was not there when they arrived not long afterward. There were other hikers in that area that day, and none saw Polly. She was afraid of snakes and would not have left the path voluntarily. Polly and her friends had been camping at the park for a considerable number of years, and she was familiar with the trail.

In the case of Trenny Lynn Gibson, the teen was on a school field trip when she went missing. She and her friends had hiked to the top of a mountain to observe the botanical variety for her horticultural classwork. She was with a close friend at the time, and other students were nearby. She, too, began walking at an accelerated pace, passing some of her classmates on the trail. At a slight bend in the trail back to the parking lot where their bus awaited, Trenny appeared to step to the right of the trail and disappeared from sight. The trail curved to the left at that spot. To the right of the trail, where

Trenny was last seen, is rough ground that is overgrown with thick underbrush and briars. A stream running next to the path makes the bank slick. There were no indications of Trenny or anyone else having exited the path there.

The third incident involves a young child, Dennis Lloyd Martin. He was playing with several other children when the children decided to "sneak up on and scare" the adults who were watching them nearby. The adults saw the children and played along with them. Dennis, who was wearing a red shirt, would have difficulty sneaking up on the adults from the front, so he had run to the rear to make his "attack." He disappeared as soon as he broke from the pack and ran to the rear of the shelter. Less than five minutes passed between the inception of the attack and the discovery of Dennis missing.

Topic: Spiritual Warfare: Ephesians 6:12–18

Source: The Jeremiah Study Bible
Author: Dr. David Jeremiah

Summary

People often think of war as glamorous—until they or someone they know becomes a casualty. The same is true in the spiritual arena. Spiritual warfare seems to be a popular subject for movies, lectures, books, and preaching, but many believers are casualties of Satan's schemes.

Make no mistake: whether they are aware of it or not, all Christians are engaged in a very real spiritual battle between two opposing kingdoms. And those least in the know are often the first casualties. Thankfully, Paul provides believers with a self-defense course in Ephesians 6, and Jesus equips us with all six dimensions of our spiritual armor. He is our truth, our righteousness, our peace, the object of our faith, the source of our salvation, and the living Word of God. When we "put on" Jesus Christ (Romans 13:14; Galatians 3:27), we are protected by the only person Satan has never defeated.

Using the armor of a Roman soldier as a model, the apostle Paul describes how the Christian can stand strong in the midst of this ever-present, but unseen, spiritual battle:

1. The belt of truth (6:14). The soldier's belt served as the foundation of his armor, holding his sword and breastplate. Because Satan is the father of lies (John 8:44), he cannot stand against the truth. Jesus said, "I am…the truth" (John 14:6). Victory in spiritual warfare starts with truth.
2. The breastplate of righteousness (6:14). The breastplate guarded the heart—the source of the soldier's life. In a similar way, righteousness protects the spiritual life of the Christian. Our righteousness comes not from ourselves but from Christ (Philippians 3:9).
3. Feet protected by the gospel of peace (6:15). The soldier's heavy, armored sandals gave him traction and security in the heat of the battle. So our peace with God through Jesus Christ gives us security in the face of Satan's accusations (Philippians 4:7).
4. The shield of faith (6:16). The soldier's leather-covered shield could be soaked in water to extinguish the flaming arrows of the enemy. Faith in God's promises deflects and extinguishes the lies of Satan (Proverbs 30:5; 1 John 5:4).
5. The helmet of salvation (6:17). The armored helmet protected the soldier's brain. Since the primary battlefield in spiritual warfare is in the Christian's mind, assurance of salvation defeats the doubts Satan uses to attack us (John 10:28).
6. The sword of the spirit, the Word of God (6:17). Paul noted only one offensive weapon, the soldier's sword. For the Christian, the sword is the Word of God.

Thankfully, our spiritual armor is to be used in a war that has already been won. It is said of Napoleon Bonaparte that as he attempted to conquer all the kingdoms of the known world, he spread out a map on a table, pointed to a specific place, and said to his lieutenants, "Sirs, if it weren't for that red spot, I could conquer the world." The red spot to which he pointed was the British Isles, the very nation that met Napoleon at Waterloo in Belgium and defeated him in league with a group of nations.

There is no doubt that when Satan talks with his minions about conquering the world, he says the same thing about the red hilltop of Calvary where Christ's blood was spilled: "If it were not for that red spot, I could rule the world!"

But that red spot is what makes all the difference in our spiritual battle. We do not have to live in fear of the devil. We need only enter the spiritual battle to which we have been called, aware of its reality and its subtlety, and armed with the truth that the ultimate victory against Satan has already been achieved. Therefore, right now at this moment, we are "more than conquerors through Him who loved us."

For Further Reading

Isaiah 59:17
Luke 4:1–13
Romans 12:21
2 Corinthians 10:3–6; 11:13–15
Colossians 1:13, 14
1 Thessalonians 5:5–8
James 4:7
1 Peter 5:8–9
1 John 5:19

Topic: Popular Children's Rhyme

If I had a little red box to put my Jesus in,
I'd take Him out and share him with a friend.
If I had a little black box to put the devil in,
I'd take him out and STOMP HIS
HEAD, then put him back again.

Topic: Get Back, Satan! Five Tips for Using Scripture as Defense

Source: https://www.crosswalk.com
Author: Alicia Purdy
Date: August 8, 2019

Summary

Jesus warned us, in John 15:18–19, "But because you are not of the world, since I chose you out of the world, the world therefore hates you." In John 16: 33, Jesus said, "In this world you will have tribulation."

Combine human troubles with those created through spiritual turmoil. The two are interconnected.

We wrestle not against flesh and blood (even if we want to).

Ephesians 6:12 states, "For our fright is not against flesh and blood, but against principalities, against powers, against the rulers of the darkness of this world, and against spiritual forces of evil in the heavenly places."

It is not necessarily the *people or their behavior* we must battle; it is the powers that are working *through* them that we must battle.

Second Corinthians 10:3–4 states, "For though we walk in the flesh, we do not war according to the flesh. For the weapons of our warfare are not carnal, but mighty through God to the pulling down of strongholds."

The enemy is fighting to the death; so must we.

The Word of God goes forth and doesn't return empty.

The battle is *always* spiritual for the Christian. Satan roams the earth looking for people to use to turn and devour you (1 Peter 5:8).

Stay in the light of Jesus; Satan cannot get to you there.

Isaiah 55:11 states, "So shall My word be that goes forth from My mouth; it shall not return to Me void, but it shall accomplish that which I please, and it shall prosper in the thing for which I sent it."

Jeremiah 1: 12 says, "The Lord says He watches over His Word to see it performed: 'Speak the Word over your situation! There is true power there!' When we agree with God's Word and refuse to speak against it or disagree with it, we speak faith into existence."

Five Tips for Using the Word of God to Push Back and Win the War against Satan in Your Situation

1. Use fighting words.
    a. Speak faith. Read Psalm 18, a psalm of battle worship.
    b. Personalize your declaration: "The Lord lives! And blessed be my Rock! May the God of my salvation be exalted. It is God who avenges me and subdues the people under me; He delivers me from my enemies. You lift up above those who rise up against me; You have delivered me from the violent man. Therefore I will give thanks to You, O Lord, among the nations, and sing praises to Your name" (Psalm 18:46–49).
2. Own your truth.
    a. Know your identity in Christ.
    b. Read Romans 8:3 –39. God is who He says He is, and you are who He says you are; you were made to walk with Him, to overcome Satan, and to live a life of victory. Know who you are fighting, why you are fighting, and how to fight with the weapons you have been given.
    c. Personalize your declaration: "In all these things [I am more than a conqueror] through Him who loved us. For I am convinced that neither death nor life, neither angels nor demons, neither the present nor the future, nor any powers, neither height nor depth, nor anything else in all creation, will be able to separate me from the hand of God that is in Christ Jesus our Lord."
3. Speak supernatural power statements.
    a. Use God's Word. The enemy isn't afraid of your words, but he fears God's Word; because God resides in you and protects you, you can call upon the name of the Lord (Romans 10:13).

   b. God sends His angels to camp around you (Psalm 34:17).
   c. You cannot control what comes, but you can control your response to it.
   d. You are not a victim, unless you choose to be: the battle isn't over until God says its over (James 4:7).
   e. Read Psalm 118:5–18; it's victorious, powerful, declarative, and filled with images of the victory of the Lord.
   f. Personalize your declaration: "The voice of rejoicing and salvation is in the tents of the righteous: 'The right hand of the Lord is valiant. The right hand of the Lord is exalted; the right hand of the Lord is valiant.' I shall not die, but I shall live and declare the works of the Lord" (Psalm 118:15–18).
4. Know your enemy.
   a. Satan is a liar; don't believe any message he is sending. Every thought or word you speak that goes against *even one word* of God's Word is a lie. God's Word is the only source of truth; don't doubt it!
   b. We have been given the power, authority, and obligation to cast down imaginations and "every high thing that exalts itself against the knowledge of God, bringing every thought into captivity to the obedience of Christ."
      i. Requires knowing what constitutes the "knowledge of God" and what things are exalting themselves above that knowledge: imagination, fear, anger, doubt, trauma, bad memories, guilt, shame, unforgiveness, bitterness, worry, and more.
   c. If God didn't give it for His glory, Satan can use it. Cast it down!
   d. Read Revelation 12:1–2. Remind Satan of his ultimate fate. He has already been defeated.
   e. Personalize your declaration: Matthew 18:18 states, "Truly I say to you, whatever you bind on earth will be bound in heaven, and whatever you loose on earth will be loosed in heaven."

i. Luke 10:19 says, "Look, I give you authority to trample on serpents and scorpions, and over all the power of the enemy. And nothing shall by any means hurt you."

5. Fight to the death.
   a. First Corinthians 14:8 states, "If the trumpet makes an uncertain sound, who will prepare himself for the battle?"
      i. It's time to attack! God will fight for, in, and through you in the battle for his victory.
   b. Read 1 Timothy 6:11–12; make this your challenge.
   c. Personalize your declaration: Ephesians 6:10–13 states, "I am strong in the Lord and in the power of His might. I will put on the whole armor of God that I may be able to stand against the schemes of the devil. For our fight is not against flesh and blood, but against principalities, against powers, against the rulers of the darkness of this world, and against spiritual forces of evil in the heavenly places. Therefore, I take up the whole armor of God that I may be able to resist in the evil day, and having done all, to stand."
   d. John 10:10—this is a fight that can be won!

Topic: Six Things Satan Wants More Than Anything Else

Source: https://crosswalk.com
Author: Victoria Riolanno
Date: May 13, 2022

Summary

There is a real enemy—Satan, Lucifer, Beelzebub, the devil.

In Genesis 3, he has nothing but malicious intent for God's creation.

In John 8:44, he was a murderer from the beginning and has nothing to do with the truth because there is no truth in him when he lies. He speaks out of his own character, for he is a liar and the father of lies.

There is no truth, no good, no love, and no hope that can come from the devil. When we allow the words of the enemy to have power in our lives, we come into agreement with things that directly oppose God's Word. His desire is to kill, steal, and destroy "anything that brings God glory, including bringing destruction to mankind themselves."

1. To make you doubt God's Word (Genesis 3:1ff)
    - Convinced people to doubt the inerrancy of the Bible and even the promises listed in His Word.
    - Many have become skeptics.
    - Spend more time trying to prove God wrong than accepting God's love for them.
    - By doubting one word of what God has spoken, we start to second-guess all other things that have been said and that will be said.
    - One seed of doubt can spread like an infection across entire families, causing many to stumble, just like we see in the Garden of Eden.
    - God does not lie.

    Numbers 23:19 states, "God is not human, that he should lie, not a human being, that he should change his mind. Does He speak and then not act? Does He promise and not fulfill?"
2. To paralyze with fear
    - If our lives have become riddled with fear, we will find that we are consumed with the "what ifs." Life becomes focused on what we can and cannot control versus putting complete *faith in God.* Fear will keep us from taking a step of *faith* into a new career, praying for a friend who may reject us, and even being able to rest. God does not give us fear. Instead, His Word brings peace, wisdom, love, and a sound mind.

First John 14:18 states, "There is no fear in love, but perfect love casts out fear, for fear has to do with punishment, and whoever fears has been perfected in love."

3. To silence you from sharing the gospel
   - "A Christian who hoards the gospel to themselves is an ineffective Christian one of our primary roles as a follower of Christ is to make more followers of Christ."
   - Matthew 28:19
   - Modern social media—Christians feel nervous to share God's Word for fear of being virtually attacked or not wanting to bc associatcd with thc "church."
   - "Followers of Christ should take every moment they aren't being a *Christian* influencer for Christ, the enemy will certainly find opportunities to influence those around us. Let us not be ashamed to share the gospel by any means necessary."

   Romans 1:16 states, "For I am not ashamed of this Good News about Christ. It is the power of God at work, saving everyone who believes—the Jew first and also the Gentile."

4. Cause you to live in shame
   - Reminding you of your past indiscretions or current insecurities is another scheme of the enemy—to convince you that your past can disqualify you from receiving God's love or grace, you will never come to accept the Word of God fully, you will remain defeated and frustrated, only accepting some of God's Word. Shame keeps our eyes focused on ourselves, reminding us over and over of what we did wrong or how we don't measure up.
   - Shame will keep you from praying to God and even sharing the gospel with others. If the enemy can keep you in self-pity, you will never walk in God's peace. We are not a sum of our past behaviors; when we turn away from sinful desires and walk toward God's love,

He will show us how to live a life that is rewarding and where we can be free from condemnation.

First John 1:9 states, "If we confess our sins, he is faithful and just to forgive us our sins and to cleanse us from all unrighteousness."

Romans 8:1 states, "There is therefore now no condemnation to them which are in Christ Jesus who walk not after the flesh, but after the Spirit."

5. For you to worship an idol
   - An idol can be anything we place before the Lord.
   - Old Testament people worshipped literal objects.
   - Favorite celebrity, social media, life focused on self.
   - We can spend years worshipping things that seem good on the outside but suddenly become an obsession to where "it" becomes our primary focus on life. What began as a positive thing can become our primary source of hope and happiness.
   - We look to those things more than God.

   Exodus 20:3–6 states, "You shall have no other gods before me. You shall not make for yourself a carved image, or any likeness of anything that is in the heaven above, or that is in the earth beneath or that is in the water under the earth. You shall not bow down to them, for I the Lord your God am a jealous God, visiting the iniquity of the fathers on the children to the third and fourth generation of those who hate me, but showing steadfast love to thousands of those who love me and keep my commandments."
6. For you to be deceived
   - Satan will do anything to cause confusion, including using Christians, with so many different beliefs that it appears to be dozens of different religions mixed into one.
   - We must know that anything we believe that contradicts the Word of God is simply another ploy of the enemy. Let us not give the enemy any more power over our minds and action and walk fully in God's Word.

> Second Timothy 4:3–4 states, "For the time is coming when people will not endure sound teaching, but having itching ears they will accumulate for themselves teachers to suit their own passions and turn away from listening to the truth and wander off into myths."

Topic: Witchcraft in the Bible
Source: www.Biblestudytools.com

Summary

The word *witch* appears in Exodus 22:18 and Deuteronomy 18:10. The Hebrew word is *kisheph*, meaning "to practice the magical article."

First Samuel 28 (KJV) refers to "a woman who has a familiar spirit," literal meaning, "a woman who is a mistress of an 'obh, or ghost.'"

While Saul visited a medium in Endor, the term *witch of Endor* is a literary phrase not found in the Bible.

The word *witchcraft* is described as a form of rebellion in 1 Samuel 15:23.

The writer argues that the words *witch* and *witchcraft* should be removed from the English Bible as the modern concepts presented by these words were not known in Bible times. And they suggest a revision to *divination* as recognized by the revisers of 1884.

The word *witch* means "one who knows"; historically, a witch is both masculine and feminine.

Anglo-Saxon derives *wicca* as masculine alone.

The word *wizard* has no known connection with *witch*.

In Shakespeare's *Cymbeline*, the witch referred to is male.

In the Wycliffe translation, Acts 8:9 refers to Simon Magus as a witch (wicche).

During the thirteenth century, the word *witch* has come to refer to a woman who has formed a compact with the devil or with evil spirits, by whose aid she is able to cause all sorts of injury to living beings and to things; in modern English, *witchcraft* has come to refer to the "arts and practices" of such women.

In 2 Chronicles 33:6, the king of Judah, Manasseh, is said to have practiced paganism by sacrificing his children to an idol, practiced divination and witchcraft, sought omens, and consulted mediums and spiritists.

In Galatians 5:20, the Greek word *pharmakeia* is translated as "witchcraft" or "sorcery." The Greek literally refers to the act of administering drugs and of giving magical potions; it then comes to stand for the magician's art, as in the Wisdom of Solomon 12:4; 13:13 and the Septuagint of Isaiah 47:9, where the Hebrew word is *keshaphim*, translated "sorceries."

The plural *witchcrafts* (found in the King James Version and Revised Version—British and American) is seen in 2 Kings 9:22, Micah 5:12. and Nahum 3:4, in which the proper rendering would be "sorceries" or "magical arts." The word *witchcrafts* is inaccurate and misleading.

The verb *bewitch* is used in Acts 8:9, 11 (Greek, *existemi*—"amazed") and Galatians 3:1 (Greek, *baskaubaino*—a blinding effect of the evil eye and perhaps has an occult reference but has nothing to do whatever with *witch* or *witchcraft*).

Common elements are found in witchcraft and ancient Oriental magic.

The fundamental thought involved the activities of the English "witch" concept.

It is familiar enough to ancient Hebrews—other nations of antiquity (Babylonians, Egyptians, etc.)—that there exists a class of persons called by us magicians, sorcerers, etc. who have superhuman power over living creatures including man and also over nature and natural objects. This power is of two kinds—cosmic and personal.

In Assyrian and Babylonian literature is found the most complete account of magical doctrine and practice. Male practitioners are called *ashipu*, while female practitioners are called *ashiptu*.

This corresponds to the Hebrew *mekhasheph* (male) and *makesheshphah* (female) in Deruteronomy 18:10 and Exodus 22:18.

These cognate to *ashphaph* in Daniel 1:21 and 2:2, 10, where they translate as "magician" and "enchanter."

Babylonian refers to *kashapu* (male) and *kashaptu* (female) practitioners.

There are no words for "one who traffics with malicious spirits for malicious ends."

The magician (male and female) was considered a source of good, as conceived by the Babylonians, especially the ashipu and ashiptu, to the state of individuals, as well as of evil, and was often therefore in the service of the state as the guide of its policy.

The Hebrew concept is similar, though the true teachers and leaders of Israel condemned magic and divination of every sort as being radically opposed to the religion of Yahweh (Deuteronomy 18:10).

Topic: Magic in the Bible

Source: Cultural Background Study Bible, Zondervan

Summary

Ancient magic varies greatly from the modern concept of illusion or some intrinsic power that a person has.

Ancient magic involved tapping into external sources of power or knowledge, including hexes, spells, incantations, and exorcisms, used to wield power. Necromancy was used to gain information from the dead; divination was practiced in many forms to gain knowledge from the gods or about the gods. Therefore, these practices became an integrated part of the practiced religion, not an opposing force. Magic had its distinctive uses but was not classified as "black," "white," or "gray" as it is today. Destructive or constructive use was determined by the individual practitioner's agenda rather than the nature of the powers that were tapped. Power came from either the gods or spirits and was prominent in the practice of medicine, working alongside herbal specialists, as each was seen to have skills to combat illness.

The Israelites were forbidden to practice any of these forms of power-wielding magic. Only God could and would work these wonders through specific individuals (Moses and Elisha, for example). Divination in general was forbidden, with the exception of binary forms such as casting of lots, which required no interpretation, or God-inspired forms where God provides an interpreter, such as dreams and prophecy.

Topic: "What's a Biblical Description of Witchcraft?"

Source: www.probe.org
Author: Sue Bohlin, Probe Ministries
Date: May 27, 2005

The author references Deuteronomy 18:9–14 and Leviticus 19:26–28, 31 in response. She then offers the glossary of terms presented by Kay Arthur in her book *Lord, Is It Warfare?*

1. Casts spell: the act of charming; "tying up" a person through magic; used in the sense of binding with a charm consisting of words of occult power.
2. Divination: the act of divining sorcery; soothsaying or prophesying; man's attempt to know and control the world and future apart from the true God using means other than human; foretelling or foreseeing the future or discovering hidden knowledge through reading omens, dreams, using lots, astrology, or necromancy.
3. Interpret omens: a type of divination; seeking insight or knowledge through signs or events.
4. Medium: necromancer who foretells events by conversing with spirits of the dead; conjurer.
5. Necromancer: one who calls up the dead; medium.
6. Spirits: familiar spirit, one who has esoteric knowledge through nonhuman means; diviner.
7. Soothsaying: witchcraft, observing clouds for augury; foretelling future events with supernatural power but not divine power; interpreting dreams; revealing secrets.

8. Sorcerer: magician, conjurer, enchanter; one who practices magic arts, sorcery, charms, with an intent to do harm or to delude or pervert the mind; one who claims to have supernatural power or knowledge through (evil) spirits.
9. Witchcraft: soothsaying; practice of witches; the use of formulas and incantations to practice sorcery; act of producing extraordinary effects by the invocation or aid of demons; the use of magic arts, spells, or charms.

Topic: What Does the Bible Say about Witchcraft/Witches?

Source: www.gotquestions.org

Summary

Deuteronomy 18:19–20 addresses the practices of nations surrounding the Promised Land that are in opposition to the worship of Yahweh.

The penalty for practicing witchcraft under Mosaic Law was death (Exodus 22:18; Leviticus 20:27).

In 1 Chronicles 10:13, King Saul died for his disobedience in consulting a medium.

In the New Testament, the word *sorcery* is translated from the Greek *pharmakeia*, which gives us our modern word *pharmacy*. It is found in Galatians 5:20 and Revelation 18:23.

Witchcraft and spiritism often involve the ritualistic use of magic potions and mind-controlling drugs. Therefore, using illicit drugs can open ourselves up to demonic spirits, so engaging in a practice or taking a substance to achieve an altered state of consciousness is a form of witchcraft.

There are only two sources of spiritual power: God and Satan. Satan only has the power that God allows him to have, but it is considerable as demonstrated in Job 1:12, 2 Corinthians 4:4, and Revelation 20:2.

To seek spirituality, knowledge, or power apart from God is idolatry, which is closely related to witchcraft, as stated in 1 Samuel 15:23.

Witchcraft is Satan's realm, and he excels in counterfeiting what God does (Exodus 8:7).

At the heart of witchcraft is the desire to know the future and control events that are not ours to control—those abilities belong to the Lord. This desire has its own roots in Satan's first temptation of Eve in Genesis 3:5.

Since Eden, Satan's major focus has been to divert human hearts away from submission to the Lord God; witchcraft is merely another branch of that enticement. To become involved in witchcraft in any way is to enter Satan's realm, including seemingly harmless modern entanglements such as horoscopes, Ouija boards, Eastern meditation rituals, some video and role-playing games. Any other practice that dabbles in a power source other than the Lord Jesus Christ is witchcraft. Revelation 22:15 includes witches in a list of those who will not inherit eternal life.

We should not fear Satan's power but respect it and stay away from it (1 John 4:4; 1 Thessalonians 2:18; Job 1:12–18; 1 Corinthians 5:5).

If we belong to the Lord Jesus Christ, there is no power that can ultimately defeat us (Isaiah 54:17).

We are overcomers (1 John 5:4), and we "put on the whole armor of God so that you can stand against the devil's schemes" (Ephesians 6:11).

When we give our lives to Christ, we must repent, including renouncing any involvement with witchcraft, following the example of the early believers in Acts 9:19.

See Also

Isaiah 8:19
Micah 5:12
Galatians 5:19–21
Only Jesus has the words of life (John 6:68).

Topic: Why Are So Many Christians Practicing Witchcraft?

Source: www.charismanews.com
Author: Jennifer LeClaire
Date: April 27, 2013

Summary

Rebellion is equated with witchcraft.

In 1 Samuel 15:1–9, King Saul is ordered to utterly destroy the opposing Amalekites and everything they had—man, woman, infant and suckling, ox and sheep, camel, and ass. Saul found victory in the battle through the grace of God, but he spared the Amalekite king, Aga, and kept the finest of the livestock. When confronted, Saul told God that the cattle had been saved to be used as sacrifices to God. He refused to admit his disobedience and justified his actions.

First Samuel 15:22 declares that obedience is better than sacrifice. As such, one way Christians are practicing a sin that is within the realm of witchcraft is when they are disobedient to God because their fear of man is greater than their fear of God (vv. 23–24).

Saul continued to be disobedient and eventually lost his kingdom, and his life, because of his rebellion against God. Rebellion grows from many roots but all end in the same result.

Jezebel (2 Kings 9:22)

The spirit of Jezebel is essentially a spirit of seduction that works to escort believers into immorality and idolatry (Revelation 2:20), uses witchcraft against its enemies.

Jezebel's witchcraft was rooted in rebellion, but she also used incantations, spells, and curses against her enemies,

In modern times, we practice this form of witchcraft when we "curse" others by speaking negativity over someone's life—judging appropriateness of dress, length of a marriage, or other judgmental opinion statements. By using such negative speech, we're in agreement with the enemy's plan and giving power to it with our anointed mouths.

Works of the Flesh

Anything that goes against the spirit of God is witchcraft, and the spirit of God opposes it. This includes everything from divination to magic to rebellion to word curses—to works of the flesh.

Galatians 5:19–21 identifies the works of the flesh as sexual immorality, impurity and debauchery, idolatry and witchcraft, hatred, discord, jealousy, fits of rage, selfish ambition, dissentions, factions and envy, drunkenness, orgies, and the like.

Witchcraft is listed alongside adultery and fornication—a serious offense in any manifestation. It violates the first commandment (Exodus 20:1–6). The flesh opposes the move of the spirit and resists all things spiritual. Galatians 5:21 makes it clear that a person practicing witchcraft will not inherit the kingdom of God.

Galatians 5:16 advises that "if you walk in the spirit, you will not fulfill the lusts of the flesh."

Galatians 5:22–23 identifies the fruit of the spirit as love, joy, peace, forbearance, kindness, goodness, faithfulness, gentleness, and self-control.

Repent, stop what you are doing, and crucify your flesh with its passions and desires.

Afterword

"Gentlemen and lady, this is just a sampling of the history of our little slice of mountains."

The older woman who had been giving the Kentucky Educational Television team the tour of Satan's Den abruptly stopped speaking and waited for the responses of her captive audience. A gentle breeze played with the sprigs of her hair where they had escaped from her loose bun. Her careworn face was free of makeup, but there were no issues with her camera image. In fact, the camera loved her. The cameraman had commented that he had never captured such a clear and flattering image in his entire career.

"You've been an excellent guide and storyteller, Matilda," complimented the thirtysomething woman in tight-fitting jeans and light sweater which clung to her curves. "I'm sure that when my producer sees the promo video, he will jump on the chance to create a 'Tales from Satan's Den' series. He'll want to premiere it in the fall season lineup in order to capitalize on the Halloween trends."

"What about Christmas?" the old woman asked.

"What about Christmas?" the younger woman repeated. "Christmas has nothing to do with scary stories. It's best to premiere around Halloween."

Matilda let out a cackle of amusement.

"Young lady," she said, "it has everything to do with Christmas. Why, in England it's the custom to tell ghost stories at Christmas. That's why Charles Dickens had three ghosts to scare ol' Scrooge into bein' a better man at Christmas. Did you know that story about that Frankenstein monster was writ by Mary Shelley in a storytelling contest on Christmas—to see who could write the scariest story, her, her husband, or their friend? I guess you see who won that one."

She cackled again.

The woman made notes in the notebook she carried. There was no cell phone service on this side of the mountain, so she had to old-school it.

"I'll check into that," she said, more to herself than anyone else. "It could make an interesting angle."

"We need to get her to do our storytelling. She looks great on camera, and that costume is so authentic its perfect."

The young woman thanked the cameraman for his suggestion and made more notes in her notebook.

"Vintage clothing...old boots...long skirt...looks heavy... long-sleeve, button-up blouse...nice for cold weather but probably hot in summer...maybe add a bonnet or hat of some sort for outdoor shots."

The boyish intern also took notes. He was shadowing the cameraman and the associate producer in this interview for the experience.

"I hope I'm still around when they start filming this thing. It'll be so awesome. Which format will you use—single storyteller only, storyteller voice over with reenactments?"

The associate producer glanced quickly at the intern with raised eyebrows before returning to her notes.

"I'd like to see Matilda do the introduction and closing of the show with live actors performing the stories. That way, the audience feels like they are a part of the show. Expensive, but may pay off. Risky. Ed'll probably nix it for a cheaper format. It *is* public television, you know, and fundraising can be tricky. Budgeting issues... quality programming..."

Her voice dropped off as she wrote. The intern nodded sadly. He was learning there were so many tiny details that could make or break a program.

"Could we use performers from the theater program at the university? Give them class credit and their names listed in program credits or something?"

"Good idea, but very complicated logistically," she replied absently.

"I think we're done here," said the cameraman. "We already have so much material to go through it's going to be tough to cut it down to a promo video. Could be an entire show on its own. You up for some heavy editing, kid?"

"Yes, sir!" The intern smiled broadly, his earlier concern forgotten.

"Before you go, I'd like to show you a special place no one around here knows about. Just me, And now you all."

"Exclusive!" sang the woman as she closed up her notebook and slid her pen behind her ear.

The cameraman prepared for this final shoot. The intern looked on in interest.

"You won't be needin' that thing," Matilda said, nodding at the camera. "This here isn't for recordin'. It's for learnin'."

The KET trio looked at one another curiously. None could guess what they were about to learn.

"Follow me."

The three followed the spry elderly woman as she began winding her way up the mountain through the dense forest. She was the only one who saw any pathway as she ducked under branches, skirted around fallen trees, stumps, and large rocks. She pushed between overgrowth bushes like butter, while her followers fought brambles and briars, their clothing snagged and torn in places. They tried not to complain, but the young woman gulped back tears as she commented on the cost of her sweater being unraveled by Mother Nature. The intern talked under his breath, questioning his choice of career. The cameraman cursed when his equipment caught on something, and he had to stop and untangle it.

At last, they reached their destination—a level and treeless meadow. They were all three amazed at the contrast of the murderous trail they had to take to get there and marveling at the simplicity of this natural clearing. The autumn grass was greener than would be expected, especially when framed by the colorful leaves of the forest around it. The meadow appeared to be endless where it met the western horizon. The sky was clear and filling with the sunset palette as night drew near.

"Wow, this is beautiful!" exclaimed the associate producer.

"Never seen a sunset this amazing before," stated the cameraman.

"Now this was worth it." The intern gasped through asthmatic breaths.

"It gets better," warned Matilda. "Watch the horizon."

Silence reigned for several moments—no wind, no animal or insect sounds, just peaceful silence.

"Here they come," Matilda said.

Shadows removed themselves from the horizon and began moving toward the humans. As they came closer, they began to take on recognizable forms.

"Horses?" The associate producer was surprised, but distant, as if she were unsure about the creatures.

As the shapes came closer, it was clear that they were indeed horses. Tiny miniatures strode alongside massive draft horses. Ponies trotted alongside sleek show breeds. Each animal was of a different breed or coloring. No two were similar.

The KET team was engrossed by the fluid movement of the graceful beasts.

"Pooks," said Matilda.

"What?" asked the intern. "Did you say 'poops'?"

"No, spooks," corrected the associate producer.

"They're incredible," admitted the cameraman.

"Pooks," repeated Matilda. "You've heard of nightmares, right?"

The three agreed without taking their eyes off the equines.

"Well, nightmares are harmless compared to pooks."

"These are horses, not bad dreams," philosophized the intern critically.

"If you say so," conceded Matilda.

"When our ancestors came to this country," Matilda began her narrative, "we brought our own ways with us. We looked for a place as much like home as we could find. These mountains made us homesick, so we set about creatin' a new home here that was as much like the Old Country as we could make it. Very little changed about our way of life.

"The one thing that never did change was our belief in pooks, or pookas. We'd grown up on tales of bein' home before dark and if we had to be out after dark to stay away from pooks. No matter how far we needed to go to find shelter, we were not to stop but keep on goin'. Darkness could be evil, and there were things in it that would right out kill you or, worse, take your very soul and leave you to walk this earth neither dead nor alive.

"We didn't see no pooks for a long while. Horses were scarce. Oxen were better for movin' about these mountains. Most people walked everywhere. It was slow-movin', but it got us where we needed to go.

"One dark night of the new moon, a young man overstayed his time with the girl he was courtin'. It was about this time of year, and the nights could get real cold. The young man realized it was gettin' late when the girl's mother asked him if he had mornin' chores to do. When he said he did, she told him he better get 'em done afore breakfast. It was her way of tellin' him to go home so she could go to bed. The young man hoped he would be allowed to sleep before the fireplace and head home at daylight. He was greatly disappointed when the girl's father laughed to himself and shook his head as he took himself off to bed.

"The girl's mother instructed her to get on to bed herself. The girl climbed the ladder to her loft bedroom, glancing once apologetically at her beau. The older woman remained seated in her straight-backed chair, stiffly watchin' the fire burn down. In the uncomfortable silence that followed, he realized he would have to brave the cold night and whatever lurked in its darkness. He bid the woman a good night and stepped into his fear. He heard the latch fall on the door behind him.

"So he set off down the road, stumblin' in the dark as his eyes couldn't quite adjust enough for him to make out where he was goin'. He couldn't use the stars to guide him home because the clouds had bedded down between the earth and the heavens, blocking that luxury from his eyes.

"The path was narrow, and it was easy to get offtrack. Many times, he had to pull himself from a ditch where he'd fallen or stop to try and figure out where he was. He made slow progress, and time seemed to slow down even more. He didn't know how far from home he was or even if he was travelin' in the right direction. His fear was risin' with each step.

"So scared he was that he didn't even notice the woods around him had gone silent. It was only when that silence was broken by a steady clip-clop comin' toward him that he realized the woods were as silent as the night was dark. He stood frozen to the spot as the clopping noise came closer to him. He imagined every terror he could as he prepared for his death.

"To his surprise, a gray dappled horse lumbered into view, more defined than anything else around him. The beast stopped in front of the young man and dipped its head once in greeting. The young man nodded in return. Then. To his amazement, the horse bowed down, one leg extended forward, the other bent to hold itself steady. There was no saddle, bridle, reins, or rope on the animal. The young man knew every horse on the mountain, but none like this one.

"He was so desperate to get home out of the cold and evil darkness he approached the horse cautiously, talkin' to it in a soft voice. To his surprise, the horse remained in the bowed position until he had mounted it fully. It rose back up and began its slow plod forward as if it knew the destination.

"The young man began to relax his fear in the security of knowin' he would soon be home in his own bed, safe and sound. He even began to feel drowsy. When at last the horse passed by the barn that marked his family home, he sat up, glad to be there. He tried to stop the horse so he could get off, but having no reins, he could only cry out for the horse to whoa. The horse plodded on. He tried to turn and slide off the animal, but his lower half wouldn't work. His fear grew rapidly into stark terror as the house disappeared behind him. He remembered the childhood stories of the ghost horses of the Old Country. How they would show up when you were in need to get somewhere quickly during the night. How those who took the ride offered were never heard of again as they were carried off by the pooks to an everlasting life no one could imagine.

"After that, people spoke of seein' pooks in the night. Some foolishly rode off into eternity. Some managed to make their own way home, the horse followin' them near their doorstep before disappearin' back into the dark. 'Be ye fool or be ye wise, beware the pook when the moon doth rise.'"

The trio had been so engrossed in Matilda's story they had failed to notice that three of the horses had broken away from the grazing herd and approached the two-legged mortals. They had stopped a short distance from them and were bowing in invitation.

"You can wake up from a nightmare," droned Matilda, "but a pook runs forever."

Topic: The Puca (Pooka) in Irish Folklore

Source: www.YourIrish.com
Author: Serena
Date: Updated December 9, 2022

Summary

Puca means "goblin."

Other forms of the name are Puca, Plica, Phuca, Pwwka, Puka, and Pookah.

It may come from the Scandinavian work *pook* or *puke*, meaning "nature spirit."

A pooka is a mischievous spirit that can take on the form of an animal, such as a rabbit or horse, known for playing tricks on humans.

It may be benign but mischievous or malevolent with the ability to harm those who cross its path; associated with the Otherworld, a realm of magic and mystery in Irish mythology.

They have the power of human speech and, when inclined, make great sport of those who like to embellish the truth.

In Ireland, puca is the most feared faerie as it appears only at night and enjoys creating havoc and mischief; there is no record of a pooka actually causing any human any harm.

It is found in any rural location but especially likes open mountainous areas so that it can run free while in horse form.

Small mountainous lakes and springs in Ireland are called "Pooka Pools" or "Pollaphuca," Pooka or Demon Hole, renamed as St. Patrick's Wells during the Christianization of Ireland.

Superstitions and Irish Customs

- Drunken horse ride home—rider has had too much to drink and is on his way home from the pub; pooka terrifies rider by jumping over hedges and rocks and making death-defying leaps, throwing the rider from its back at dawn to find his way back home on his own.
- A conversation with a pooka—will stop to chat, give great advice, and make exceptional prophecies; a house with bench on the right side of the door and a gate post on the right will be smooth. On the left will be a rockery or some sort of uncomfortable mound. A good pook will always sit on the right, and a mischievous one on the left, usually opens with, "You are new here I think. Many years ago, I used to live in this house." It frequently talks about how the family lost its fortune or was swindled out of their money and lands, suddenly disappears, never says goodbye, and leaves no sign of its presence behind.
- Pooka's share—associated with Samhain (October 31), with November 1 being Pooka's Day; it coincides with the harvest. Traditionally, harvesters leave behind some stalks for the pooks so as not to incur their wrath.
- When rain falls on a sunny day, the puca will definitely make an appearance that night.
- Berries that have been killed by a frost overnight should not be eaten as they have pooka's spit on them and are now poisonous.

Pooka in Modern Culture

- *Harvey*, the six-foot white rabbit from the play by Mary Chase, was immortalized in film by Jimmy Stewart.

- *Darby O'Gill and the Little People* has a scene in which a pooka scares Darby into falling down the well where he meets King Brian of the Leprechauns.
- *Donnie Darko*, 2001—a pooka rabbit encourages Donnie to do malicious acts which have positive and negative results on the people around him.

Topic: Pookas: Digging into the Secrets of This Mischievous Irish Mythical Creature

Source: www.connollycove.com
Date: Updated December 12, 2022

Summary

Pooka is Irish for "goblin," "spirit," or "sprite."

It is believed to belong to the fey race, creatures who are known for their supernatural powers and ability to connect with nature.

They are commonly described as mischievous but benign creatures able to change their form, originated in Scotland and Ireland.

Cornish—called bucca, a water spirit or goblin, or merman who lived in mines and coastal areas during storms.

Welsh—called pwca.

Channel Islands—called poque, believed they were fairies who inhabited the areas around the ancient remnants.

They are rumored to be found in rural communities or marine areas and linked to the natural world.

In modern Irish, the word *Puca* is used to designate a ghost.

Some claim Pooka was a god in Europe, with the name "Boga," a nature god similar to the Greek god of nature, Pan, who was also god of flocks, the wild, and shepherds. Some argue *Bog*, the Slavic word meaning omnipotent or "God," derives from *Boga*.

Some myths say pookas are descendants of the Tuatha De Danann, the tribe of Danu, the ancient Celtic gods and goddesses of Ireland who were driven underground during the rise of Christianity in Ireland. They had their own Irish festivals and became the fairies that feature in much of Irish mythology.

Fairy—an umbrella term used to describe many different supernatural creatures including banshee, leprechaun, and some mythical Irish monsters.

Les Trois Freres Cave paintings in Pyrenees Mountains of southwestern Europe, specifically in southwest France, depict a man wearing the skin of a horse or a wolf with deer antlers upon its head. Some interpret this as a reference to pooka, called the sorcerer. Some interpret it as a depiction of a shaman or a horned god like Cerrunos, the Celtic god of the hunt and forest. Interpretation ironically mirrors the confusion and mischief created by the pooka of mythology.

Shamans—shamanism used to communicate with spirits in other worlds, a religious belief and a religious person regarded as having access to powers to interact with the world of good and mischievous spirits. Shaman's spirit can depart from their bodies and travel to other worlds to get visions or dreams and can reveal certain messages from the worlds of spirits; spirits manage to guide the shaman through their journey in the spirit world. Through spiritual rituals, a shaman enters a state of being in which they can reach a curative and soothsaying state during which they can cure any sickness caused by evil spirits.

What can we learn from the ambiguous origin of pooka? There are some claims of pooka worship in ancient Egypt, but there is no strong evidence to support that. All indications say that legends of pooka have both Irish and Scottish origins and that the word *pooka* itself is originally Irish.

Humanity evolved historically, as represented in art and mythology; animals always played a big part in mythology for their roles in people's daily lives. Most logical explanation is that pooka originated from an amalgamation of these concepts as legends are constantly changing and people built different stories around them and there have been some rituals; at some point, these stories have become a part of people's traditions and beliefs before ultimately fading into mythology.

Similar Shape-Shifting Mythological Creatures

Kelpies

Pixie horse, Scottish origins

The Lowland name of a demon in the shape of a horse.

Kelpies are horses that escaped from the faeries' master and went to hide in the water; theyhave the abilities of water creatures to swim and breathe underwater. They are so strong they can pull a huge boat on their own and will sometimes take a person on their backs but will try to take them back underwater. They take on a human form, just like a pooka, to catch prey, seduce, or trick a lone traveler. They vary in color from white to dark black and sometimes have a pale-grassy-green color.

Pookas and kelpies belong to the goblin's race in some cultures and are associated with marine locations, but a kelpie is always fiercer than a pooka.

Each-uisge

Scottish origin (*aughisky* or *echushkya*), a water spirit, literal meaning is "water-horse" and is very close to the kelpie but even more evil. Kelpies live in rivers; each-uisge lives in the sea, or lakes. Aushisky has the ability to shapeshift into ponies, horses, and big birds; euskya are able to take on the shape of a human. If a man is riding on its back, he's safe from danger as long as they're not close to water because they take their victim to the deepest point underwater.

The legend of pooka—takes any form that pleases them; they are benign yet mischievous creatures in the history of Irish folklore. They are mainly connected to mischief, black magic, damage, and sickness; however, they can bring fortune as well as misfortune to humans.

Pookas in different regions—they are respected or feared; people may have no belief in pookas but use them to keep children from misbehaving. They show up especially in November to give advice or warn about unpleasant news that might happen to them (November was the beginning of Celtic year, so pooka would especially advise people on the year to come).

Characteristics vary from one place to another, but three characteristics are common—they have red or sparkling eyes, dark-black fur or hair, and have the ability to speak, preferably taking human forms to trick people, chat with them, give advice, or even give forecasts for the upcoming year.

The only person ever recorded to have ridden a pooka was Brian Boru, high king of Ireland, 941–1014, known for his battles against Vikings. He had the guts to stay on the pooka's back long enough to force it to surrender to him. Pooka made to agree on two things—all pookas had to agree to never hurt Christians or mess with their properties and never assault an Irishman except for those with wicked intentions and drunk Irishmen. The pookas agreed but have forgotten their promises over the years.

Pooka's Day—mainly related to Samhain; year-end celebration, part of Gaels (ethnolinguistic group based in northwestern Europe and part of the Celtic language that comprehends Irish, Manx, and Scottish Gaelic; November 1 is Pooka's Day. Harvesters leave stalks behind to reconcile the pookas. "Pooka's share" cannot be eaten because no one wanted to infuriate a pooka.

If a pooka spits on some fruits (especially when frost kills berries), usually happens as November begins, it means they poisoned the fruits, and no one will be able to eat them.

If rain falls on a sunny day, it is an indication that pookas go out on this specific night.

Pookas in Pop Culture

1950, *Harvey*—James Stewart (inspired by the play of the same name; about a pooka with the name Harvey in the shape of a six-foot, three-and-a-half-inch-tall rabbit, who becomes best friends with Elwood P. Dowd and starts playing tricky games with people around him. He won an Oscar in 1951—Josephine Hull, best supporting actress; James Stewart nominated for best leading actor.

Shakespeare's *A Midsummer Night's Dream*—Robin Goodfellow, called Sweet Puck in direct reference to pooka; the character was a prankster.

Cheshire Cat from *Alice in Wonderland*—a trickster with supernatural powers and can disappear at will but is ultimately benign.

Pooka represented in many other forms—young adult fiction Merry Gentry, anime show Sword Art Online, digital game cabals: Magic & Battle Cards.

Artists tend to draw pooka as a wicked creature taking the form of an animal, usually a rabbit; "Knightmare" children's program from 1980s to 1990s, creators represented pookas as crazy creatures.

2001, "Donnie Darko"—psychological sci-fi thriller which portrays a scarier version of the creature similar to a horror movie version of Harvey.

Some artists design character of pooka as a weird but harmless creature, as seen in *The Spiderwick Chronicles*.

A hurling club in Pittsburgh calls itself the pucas and depicts an interpretation of the creature on their team crest.

There are some theories that both the Easter Bunny and the Boogeyman were inspired by pooka to varying degrees—more likely just one of countless interpretations of these figures as so many cultures have their own versions of the beings.

Pookas started to vanish when Christianity began to spread across the island of Ireland, where beliefs in animal worshipping, including the idea of pookas being gods.

Myth of pooka (like many other supernatural pagan beings) was unacceptable to the new faith of Christianity and was subsequently vilified or forgotten over time.

Pookas never say goodbye. If you have Celtic blood, pookas will always be watching over you; they'll try to trick you when they can, stare, smile, and chat with you. Their presence is annoying but rarely harmful.

Moving into a new house may cause a pooka to appear to tell stories of the people who lived there before you and will know everyone that once held the property, who lost their land in the area, and who lost his fortune or money. It may reveal their love of trickery and mischief, giving up the element of surprise but igniting a sense of dread in the person who has crossed their paths, as they now know what is to come.

During a conversation with a pooka, it is not uncommon to lose track of time, leaving you wondering if the conversation even happened.

Appendix A

An Apologetical Statement from Lurlene Joy McCoy

I don't believe in past lives. I believe we only live once but can be greatly influenced by those who have come before us. We are finite beings and have only a finite set of characteristics which we share. Sometimes our characteristics are combined in such a way that we resemble someone who has come before us. The odds of that are not staggering. What is staggering is the odds of us not only sharing those characteristics with someone from the past but also sharing similar experiences or passions that bring us onto the same path, albeit at different times, for similar purposes. That being said, I find myself aligned with theologian and author John Bunyan, whose work I did not become familiar with until young adulthood. I truly believed *The Pilgrim's Progress* to be his only, and greatest work, although it stood to reason that other works were available to those who sought them out. After reading *The Pilgrim's Progress*, and its companion *Christiana's Journey*, the story of Christian's wife and her pursuit to join her husband in the Celestial City, it became a recurring theme for my life, a road map for redemption, and a model for sharing the gospel. But I believe *Journey to Hell* is the story the world needs to hear most in our modern times. Though penned in the late seventeenth century, the message remains the same. It was originally published under the title *The Life and Death of Mr. Badman.*

In John Bunyan's own words from the preface to this book, you can see my modern pleas within this text:

> Reader, if you are of the race, lineage, stock, or brotherhood of Mr. Badman. I tell you, before you read this book, you will neither tolerate the author nor what he has written about Mr. Badman. For he who condemns the wicked who die also passes sentence upon the wicked who live; therefore, I expect neither credit nor approval from you for this narration of your kinsman's life. For your old love for your friend, his ways, and his actions will stir up in you enmity in your hearts against me. I imagine that you will tear up, burn, or throw away the book in contempt. You may even wish that for writing so notorious a truth, some harm may come my way. I expect that you may malign and slander me, saying I am a defamer of honest men's lives and deaths. For Mr. Badman, when he was alive, could not stand to be called a villain, although his actions told everyone that indeed he was one. How then should his friends who survive him, and follow in his very steps, approve of the sentence that by this book is pronounced against him? Will they not rail at me for condemning him and imitate Korah, Dathan. And Abiram's friends who falsely accused Moses of wrongdoing? (See Numbers 16: 1–33.)
>
> I know it is dangerous to "*put* [your] *hand on the cockatrice's* [viper's] *den*" (Isaiah 11:8) and hazardous to hunt for wild boar. Likewise, the man who writes about Mr. Badman's life needs to be protected with a coat of armor and with the shaft of a spear so that Mr. Badman's surviving friends will be less able to harm the writer; but

> I ventured to tell his story and to play, at this time, at the hole of these asps. If they bite, they bite; if they sting, they sting. Christ sends His lambs "*in the midst of wolves*" (Matthew 10:16), not to do like them, but to suffer by them for bearing plain testimony against their bad deeds. But does one not need to walk with a guard and to have a sentinel stand at one's door for protection? Verily, the flesh would be glad for such help, just as Paul was when the Jews conspired to kill him, and the commander circumvented their plot. (See Acts 23.) But I am stripped naked of support, yet I am commanded to be faithful in my service for Christ. Well, then, I have spoken what I have spoken, and now "*come on me what will!*" (Job 13:13). True, the Scripture says, "*He that reproveth a scorner getteth himself shame: and he that rebuketh a wicked man getteth himself a blot. Reprove not a scorner, lest he hate thee*" (Proverbs 9:7–8). But what then? "*Open rebuke is better than secret love*" (Proverbs 27:5), and he who receives it will find it so afterward."

This has been my exact message throughout this lengthy dialogue. I have been personally attacked by both scoffers and alleged believers. *How can you write such terrible stories that glorify evil?* they ask. For a long time, I pondered that very question. Why would God give me these stories if they were not to be used for His kingdom and glory? Why collect them and compile them in a format presentable to a secular audience? Only through the Holy Spirit's instruction in that delicate veil between heaven and earth could the answers be found. God foreordained me to be a collector of stories, a seeker of knowledge and understanding. Throughout my life, I have been tested and refined for just such a purpose. I have stridden the outskirts of hell and heard the angels sing outside the gates of heaven. Given the choice, I chose God. He has put me through boot camp and placed me on the front lines of this battle between good and evil. I have proven myself an obedient and faithful foot soldier. I am being promoted to a leadership role I have been in training for my whole life. Consider me a spiritual drill instructor. As your SDI, it is my job to train and correct those who are given into my care to create the next generation of foot soldiers who will one day be promoted to loftier positions in God's kingdom as He has foreordained. I will be gentle with you but unafraid to be blunt and confrontational when needed. I will not give up on you. Do not give up on me. Pray for me as I pray for you.

These stories are for you, the seeker, the one who walks in darkness but desires to find the light. May you find within these pages the path you seek.

These stories are for you, the believer. May you be strengthened by what you read. May you grow as you pass through this dark valley. May you become the light that leads a seeker along the way.

These stories are for you, the skeptic, the denier of truth. Consider these stories not as rebuke or reproof but as a reflection of what already lies within you. Just we are created in the image of God, we are free to redefine that image in the form of the god we choose. We can become one with our Creator, or we can create an image of self as god. Every image has a positive and a negative. The positive is the ideal, the truth; the negative is its reflection, a reversal of that truth. The image we produce is a combination of those two factors. Will you become the image of truth or a reflection of that truth in reverse. It is your responsibility to make that decision. My words are merely buzzing mosquitoes in your ears.

Like John Bunyan, I have faced those who scoff and won. I have also faced believers who question my interest in the things of the supernatural. I have been accused of chasing the darkness. I do not deny that I have courted the enemy. I have flirted with darkness, not to become one with it but to understand it. In my naivete, I once believed there could be a happy medium in which good and evil could be combined. (People speak of white witches and the goodness they do in opposition to black witches who seek only to harm others. Shouldn't *Bewitched* have dispelled that thinking in us?) New

Age teachings purport to do just this as we use the cosmic forces around us to become our own god. I wanted to *know* and *understand* the reality of these claims. Academic curiosity satisfied much of my curiosity, but field experience resolved it. God is the Ultimate Supernatural Being. All He does is supernatural. Being finite and fully natural, mankind cannot create anything on its own. It is by the grace of God that the knowledge we have been given is slowly being unveiled to us. Theologically speaking, the fallen angels who have inhabited this earth since their exile brought great knowledge with them and have been spoon-feeding us that knowledge ever since. They intentionally include knowledge of things that can be used against us, to appeal to the lusts of our eyes and the lusts of our flesh and fuel the pride of life they have cultivated in us throughout the millennia. They have groomed us with offering forbidden knowledge of evil things. They have enslaved us to their desire to retaliate against their Creator whom they once served. They have never been mortal. They were created as supernatural beings. They do have power in and of themselves. They offer that power to humanity which attempts to use that power for their own benefit. Don't be deceived by those who seek to harness the powers of the supernatural and being enslaved to those beings they seek to control. We are weak. They are strong. God is stronger and can break those unholy bonds. No matter the promises made, these forces will turn on you and drag you into the darkness they now hide in and will ultimately drag you into the lake of fire that has been prepared for them. It is not intended for humanity, but humanity is free to follow that path if it so chooses.

I hope my message is clear. *Hell is for the rebellious angels! It is their destiny! It is not yours!* They have made it their goal to destroy the upstart race that took their place in the eyes of God, and that means destroying the relationship with God we were created for. It began long ago in a Paradise Garden and has been passed down through the ages, creating an increasingly perverse humanity. The time of reckoning is soon coming. This may be your last opportunity to return to a relationship with the Father who made you carefully and precisely in His image and placed you right where He needed you to be. He has never left you, though you may have walked away from Him.

Return before the silver cord that is your lifeline is severed and that opportunity lost for eternity.

In the words of John Bunyan, "So then, whether Mr. Badman's friends will rage or laugh at what I have written, I know that the victory is mine. My endeavor is to stop a hellish course of life and to '*save a soul from death*' [James 5:20]. And if for doing so I meet with malice from them, from whom reasonably I should receive thanks, I must remember the man in the dream who cut his way through his armed enemies and thus entered the beautiful place [a reference to *The Pilgrim's Progress*]; I must, I say, remember him and do the same myself."

Appendix B

Lurlene Joy's Theory of the Tri-Universe

First, there is God:

- Good (Matthew 19:16)
- Heaven
- Creator/Savior (Genesis 1:1, 2)
- Love (Deuteronomy 6:4, 5; 1 John 4:8)
- Promotes selflessness—focus on others.
- Motto: "Do all for the glory of God's kingdom" (1 Corinthians 10:31)
- Triune—Father, Son, Holy Spirit (Genesis 1:1, 2, 26; Matthew 3:16, 17; Mark 1:9–11; 1 Thessalonians 1:9)
- Worshipped by Judeo-Christian faiths
- Agents—angels
- Promotes morality
- Righteous
- Pure
- Spirit
- Incorruptible
- Light
- Just (Deuteronomy 32:4)
- Requires personal accountability
- Requires personal salvation for personal relationship (Romans 8:24; 5:9–10; 13:11; Ephesians 2:5, 8; 1 Corinthians 1:18; 5:5; 15:2; 2 Corinthians 2:15;

Philippians 1:5–6; 2:12; 1 Thessalonians 5:8; Hebrews 1:14; 9:28; 1 Peter 1:9; 2:2; 3:21

- Complete harmony
- Created man in His own image, from the dust of the earth
- Holy Text: Bible
- Nature is evidence of God (Psalm 19:1–4).
- Truth will set you free.
- Promotes absolute truth
- One sacrifice made for all; belief required through faith in order to receive the free gift.
- Absolute light
- Requires faith and absolute trust in the unseen.
- Definite hierarchy with God as head, followed by angels, humanity, animals (Jeremiah 23:18–22)
- All outside of a relationship with God are called sinners on need of redemption.

God

Created angels
Loyal
Disloyal (Became the fallen, with Lucifer as head)
Created mankind
Created animals and plants

In a discussion of the hierarchy of heaven, the Bible speaks of a council that God has established as a means of acting as liaison between the angels and Himself. This council is described in Psalm 82. The original Hebrew uses the word *Elohim* to describe God Almighty, Yahweh. The spiritual beings Yahweh created as his servants are referred to as elohim. Where Elohim represents the concept of God the Creator, the word *elohim* refers to the spiritual creatures that were created and is translated as "gods" or "sons of God"). These spirits are said to inhabit the spiritual world and have specific attributes that separate them into six different entity types. Beneath this council is the contingent of beings known collectively as angels, which have specific tasks for which they were created. Verse 6 states, I have said, "You are gods, and sons of the Most High, all of you." The Psalm then goes on to describe how some of these council spirits rebelled and left God's glory. As second-in-command, Lucifer was likely the head of this council; hence, the number of angels that fell with him were influenced by these council spirits. These spirits are now under judgment and cannot be in the presence of the Trinity or bear the name of God. They are condemned to die as mortals do. These spirits had been given some sort of authority over the earth as a part of their responsibilities. In the description of the spiritual forces we are up against, Paul describes them as being principalities, powers, rulers of this age, and spiritual hosts of wickedness in the heavenly places (Ephesians 6), likely reflecting the positions once held in the High Council. Michael S. Heiser discusses both angels and demons in his books on those subjects, including the Hebrew and Greek interpretations of the concepts commonly held by Christian scholars. Nowhere in the Bible is this council identified as being comprised of humanity. In Job 1:6 and 2:1, they open up the heavens to reveal this council in session, and Satan is allowed to enter this session and is called to account for himself and his actions.

Second, there is Satan:

- Evil
- Hell
- Deceiver
- Associated with hate
- Promotes selfishness—focus on self
- Motto—"Do what you will."
- Definite hierarchy with Lucifer as head (each demonic "prince" is linked to a specific type of sin and has a "saint" which can be called upon to combat it; sins identified parallel the "7 Deadly Sins" and can be classified as lust of the flesh, lust of the eyes, or the pride of life in nature)
- Satanism—direct worshippers of Satan as god (can be in the form of worship of gods that are demonic in nature

or in a contrary and authoritarian belief based on biblical principles in which a religious leader has full authority over his/her followers and must be pleased in order for the followers to be accommodated—cults that place God as equal to or submissive to one person's authority)

- Agents—demons
- Promotes immorality
- Unrighteous
- Impure
- Carnal
- Corruptible
- Darkness
- Allows for blame and shifting of responsibility through rationalization and reasoning
- Is considered a "relationship" only in that an individual is not focusing on God
- Complete confusion
- Encourages recreating God in man's image, though he himself is a creation of God
- Satanic Bible (as written by Anton LeVey); other texts of specific intent and direction
- Suffering is evidence of his presence.
- Stretched truth and lies promote doubt.
- Truth is relative.
- Requires some sort of sacrifice in exchange for responses to petitions.
- Shades of gray that fade into darkness.
- Faith is based on quid pro quo.

As previously discussed, Satan has access to the High Council of God. This means he is a creation of God. While he has specific attributes bestowed upon him by God, he cannot be God. He is not omniscient (all-knowing), omnipresent (present in all space at once), or omnipotent (all-powerful). He is limited in what he can do and is accountable to his Creator. Deuteronomy 3:24 expresses this: what god is there in heaven or on earth who can do your works and according to your mighty deeds? This is repeated in 1 Kings 8:23 and Psalm 97:9. Nehemiah 9:6 makes it clear there is only One Yahweh; He is unique. All other beings are spirits (1 Kings 22:19–22; John 4:24; Hebrews 1:14; Revelation 1:4). Deuteronomy 32:17 describes the false gods worshipped by Israelites who had been seduced away from worship of God as "demons" or "gods." The word translated as *demon* comes from the Akkadian word *shedu*. The term *demon* is used to speak of a good or malevolent being interchangeably. The shedu are cast as guardians or protective entities, a term also used to describe the life force of a person. The context of Deuteronomy 32:17 refers to shedim as being elohim, spirit beings guarding foreign territory, who must *not* be worshipped. Israel was to worship only their own God as they had been set apart to do. These were not beings of wood or stone but actual spirits. First Corinthians 10:20 warns us to not fellowship with demons in any form. Here Paul uses the Greek *daimonion*, meaning evil spiritual beings, in comparative translation of *shedim* in Deuteronomy.

Ancient idol worshippers believed the objects they made for worship were actually inhabited by their gods. They performed ceremonies to open the "mouth" of the idol, which allowed the spirit of the deity to move in and occupy the object, to be "breathed" into existence. At that point, the deity was localized for worship and bargaining of the followers. When an idol was no longer usable for any reason, the physical object was destroyed, and a new vessel provided to house the spirit. Paul describes this process in contrast to the worship of God in 1 Corinthians 10:18–20. An idol has no real power in and of itself (1 Corinthians 8:4). Sacrifices made to idols were, indeed, sacrifice to demons.

Identifying the spirit beings created by God to inhabit the spiritual realm as "sons of God" clarifies, to some degree, the bothersome passage in Genesis 6:1–2, which describes how these spiritual beings came to intermingle with humanity and give rise to the race of giants referred to as Nephilim. This crossbreeding of humanity and spirits was not pleasing to God, resulting in a spread of rebellion in humanity that led God to cleanse the earth of all but eight humans in a worldwide flood. It also led to the establishment of the human life span to be no more than 120 years. Prior to that time, man lived for hundreds of years, with Methuselah capping it at nearly 1,000 years. A discussion of these "sons of god" based solely on the Old Testament scriptures is woefully inadequate to bring understanding or agreement. Extra-biblical sources and cultural records of other civilizations can shed some interesting light on the subject but bring no real consensus. For example, the origin of the word translated as Nephilim varies from "fall," "lie," "to fall," or "be cast down." The Aramaic culture uses the term to refer to the constellation Orion, implying that the Nephilim giants were the semi-divine ancestors of the hunter Orion. The Greek Septuagint translates the word as *gegenes*, meaning "earth born," indicating these beings were born to an earthly plane versus a heavenly plane. All definitions imply the spirit beings to be elohim. The epistle of Jude refers to these beings specifically as being rebellious angels as having a specific dwelling place that was violated, and they are now being punished for their indiscretions. The Greco-Roman traditions of the Titans greatly parallel this theory. The book of Enoch was banned from the biblical canon because its treatment of this subject was deemed heretical.

Third, are the fractals.

- Neither good nor evil, truly neutral and apathetic to all else
- Void (possibly the veil between heaven and earth? The cosmos?)
- Destroyers
- Apathetic
- Show no partiality and are all-encompassing
- Vacuous nature—all is equal.
- Demonstrates neither leadership nor follower mentality
- Paganism/nature worship, excluding agents of good or evil as opposing forces.
- Dual nature
    - Promotes individual self as a means of becoming a god; transcend nature and reasoning.

    - Promotes recognition of "overlords" who "seeded" earth and are uninterested in its development, gods from the stars, ancient aliens, etc.
- Often described in the works of H. P. Lovecraft and Manly Wade Wellman

Mathematics

- Mandelbrot—"A Fractal isa shape made up of parts similar to the whole in some way."
- Geometry
- Fractal art—geometric patterns created by computers, using mathematical algorithms, often kaleidoscopic, splitting and spiraling in symmetrical patterns
- Appears to have a surface but is strictly one-dimensional
- In art, may take on two-dimensional forms, as seen in the structure of Sumerian temples

H. P. Lovecraft describes his antagonistic Old Ones as follows (from "The Call of Cthulu"):

> Old Castro remembered bits of hideous Legend that paled the speculations of theosophists and made man and the world seem recent and transient indeed. There had been aeons when other Things ruled on the earth, and They had had great cities. Remains of Them, he said the deathless Chinaman had told him, were still to be found as Cyclopean stones on islands in the Pacific. They all died vast epochs of time before man came, but there were arts which could revive Them when the stars had come round again to the right positions in the cycle of eternity. They had, indeed, come Themselves from the stars, and brought Their images with Them.

These Great Old Ones, Castro continued, were not composed altogether of flesh and blood. They had shape – for did not all this star-fashioned image prove it? – but that shape was not made of matter. When the stars were right, They could plunge from world to world through the sky, but when the stars were wrong, They could not live. But although They no longer lived, They would never really die. They all lay in stone houses in their great city of Riley, preserved by the spells of mighty Cthulu for a glorious surrection when the stars and the earth might once more be ready for Them. But at that time some force from outside must serve to liberate Their bodies. The spells that preserved Them intact likewise prevented Them from making an initial move and They could only lie awake in the dark and think whilst uncounted millions of years rolled by. They knew all that was occurring in the universe for their mode of speech was transmitted thought. Even now They talked in Their tombs. When, after infinities of chaos, the first men came, the Great Old Ones spoke to the sensitive among them by moulding their dreams; for only thus could Their language reach the fleshly minds of mammals.

Then, whispered Castro, those first men formed the cult around tall idols which the Great Ones shewed them; idols brought in dim areas from dark stars. That cult will never die till the stars came right again, and the secret priests would take great Cthulu from His tomb to revive His subjects and resume His rule of earth. The time would be easy to know, for then mankind would have become as the Great Old Ones; free and wild and beyond good and evil, with laws

> and morals thrown aside and all men shouting and killing and reveling in joy. Then the liberated Old Ones would teach them new ways to shout and kill and revel and enjoy themselves and all the earth would flame with a huge holocaust of ecstasy and freedom. Meanwhile, the cult, by appropriate rites, must keep alive the memory of those ancient ways and shadow forth the prophecy of their return.

The irony of this is that I knew of the demon in the rock at Rock City long before I ever read these words. My training in things of spiritual warfare has all been against the accuser, Lucifer. These creatures I have dubbed fractals are far more dangerous that Satan as their goal appears to erase all creation as it has been made and recreate it in their own image, with themselves as teachers of mankind. This shadows Genesis in a terrifying parallel. When wickedness of mankind is first described in Genesis 6, the Sons of God took wives of the daughters of man without control. In verse 5 of chapter 6, it is described as being "every intent of the thoughts of his [mankind's] heart was only evil continually." This sounds like a summary of the condition of mankind described under the tutelage of Cthulhu and his Old Ones. The world would be remade in a form of holocaust in which humanity would be the ultimate sacrifice to these beings. If the book of Revelation was not so clear on the fact that the world would be remade as the new heaven and the new earth, I would faint with the prospect of becoming like these Great Ones. It would be utter devastation of humanity. We would become little more than animals locked in eternal survival of the fittest mode until we had utterly decimated ourselves as a species. Looking at the current trends in the news around the world, I am becoming convinced that more of these fractals are on the verge of being freed from their tombs. In his book *Worldview of the Christian Faith: Standing for God's Truth*, Joseph Charles Beach expresses his own concerns of the changes taking place in our world around us as we begin to redefine truth and tolerance as it would apply to a single body of beliefs in which everyone must agree or be eliminated from society in one way or another. The facts are that statistically, our world is becoming more responsive in violence to self and others in the name of compliance to a set of beliefs being imposed upon us in which what has traditionally been perceived as perverse or against the law of man or God has now become the "norm" and expected to receive recognition as being valid, while those who cling to the traditional beliefs are deemed haters and in need of reeducation. This has gone as far as rewriting the Bible to reflect those new beliefs with God as being gender-neutral and eliminating "offensive" passages that "God didn't really mean."

While H. P. Lovecraft allegedly practiced a form of worship with heavy occult overtones with such creatures as these at the center, his stories not only reflect the calling and worship of these creatures but also the crossbreeding of humanity with them and the devastating result and destruction caused by these creatures. His stories speak of familial responsibilities, passed down from generation to generation to not only monitor the presence of these creatures but also entomb them once more when they do appear. Much secrecy and conjecture about the truth of H. P. Lovecraft's practices remain unanswered as he took them to his grave.

Having read this description, I must add to the list of characteristics of the fractal:

- Hedonism
- Indifference
- Immaterial (as we understand matter)
- Vacuous antimatter
- Representative of universal night
- Promotes absolute freedom without law or accountability
- No visible focus on self or others; pure instinctive impulsivity
- No relationship—all for self, self for none
- Complete chaos
- Uninfluenced by man's perceptions, interpretations, or manipulations
- Isolated and secretive—oral tradition, myth, legend

- Sociopolitical patterns of a society give evidence of influence
- No truth or untruth—promotes absence of truth
- Animalistic slaughter, a form of worship
- Absolute absence of life in a system or hierarchy of life
- Faith not a concern as simple instinct rules

Their Hierarchy

- ❖ Overlords—became the old gods
  - ○ Took on humanoid/animal hybrid forms as evidenced by similar beings across cultures, some even with similar names
  - ○ Similarities in advanced technological applications, as evidenced by archaeology and inability to be replicated using modern technological techniques
    - ▪ Giant, monolithic stones and statues were said to fly, float in the air, or walk to their current positions.
    - ▪ Science has discovered that certain sound waves can move multiton objects short distances in laboratory experiments.
    - ▪ Stonehenge has acoustics that amplify softer sounds; rhythmic vibrations can induce a form of hypnotic state.
- ❖ Territorial sub lords—became regionally worshipped gods as evidenced by the similarities found in the Mesopotamian cultures, the Greco-Roman cultures, and the Asian cultures
  - ○ Took on humanoid shapes in general but may also feature animalistic characteristics
  - ○ Displayed similar personality traits as humanity—needing to be worshipped and pleased or disaster would befall the people or individual.
  - ○ Often portrayed in the form of giants
- ❖ Manifestations of humanoid liaisons—often portrayed in literary form as some form of "little people," fairies, gnomes, elementals, trolls, etc.

    - May appear benevolent in order to draw humans into their worldly dimensions but may also be portrayed as mischievous or malevolent, becoming vengeful if wronged.
    - Demonstrated in at least two cases in Appalachia where coal mine disasters have occurred and children who have reported seeing humanoid/dinosaur people their size
- Animalistic/hybrid creatures of a possible mystic or spiritual nature
    - Chupacabra
    - Dwayyo
    - Bigfoot/Sasquatch
    - Wendigo
    - Hellhounds/hound-like spirits
    - Werewolves
    - Vampires
- Base destroyers
    - Sentient only to instinct level, with the ultimate purpose of environmental destruction, including the human inhabitants

Fractals were created by the vacuum produced by the creation of the universe. Mathematics, such as sacred geometry, is the language of the universe. Fractals are the "shadows" or "reflections" of the universe of its previous state as void.

Evidence of the old gods can be seen in the Titans of Greco-Roman mythology, associated with the elements and elementals, for example Chronos (time) and Gaia (earth). The developmental pantheon of the Greco-Roman gods from Titans to humanlike gods is explained as Zeus murdering his father Chronos and imprisoning the Titans. Atlas, for example, is forced to hold the world on his shoulders.

The concept of the underworld evolved with Hades, brother of Zeus, as its head.

- Elysian Fields—realm of heroes and those judged as being "good"
- Netherworld—realm of those who are not good enough for the Elysian fields and must wander endlessly
- Sheol/underworld—land of the truly evil, with rings of punishment dependent upon the depth of depravity of the dead
- Must cross the River Styx in order to enter the underworld. Escorted by the boatman Charon, who is bribed with two coins placed on the eyes of the deceased prior to burial; no coins, no crossing; it is a one-way trip with no return of the dead to the land of the living

Also evidenced by the Egyptian gods with half animal-half human features:

- The underworld is only accessible after a series of trials, ending in a weighing of the soul; only those whose good deeds outweigh the bad are admitted.
- Egyptian tombs evidence both animal and human sacrifice in the tombs of the noble and royal social classes with the presence of "wives," servants, and pets for use by the deceased in the afterlife.

Both Greco-Roman and Egyptians reflect animal-human hybrids in their pantheons. Greco-Roman, Assyrian, Babylonian, Etruscan, and other cultures of the Fertile Crescent region depict animal-animal hybrids such as chimera, griffins, winged bulls, sphinx, and minotaur.

Central American cultures also depict animal-animal and animal-human hybrids, alongside depictions of what modern science recognizes as dinosaurs.

Pyramids are found all around the world, even under the ocean, alongside structures that cannot be explained to the satisfaction of modern engineering. They demonstrate a level of technology we cannot recreate with equipment, machinery, and techniques that are ever-evolving today.

The Nazca lines portray animals and humanoid creatures that are carved deeply into the ground and are so geometrically perfect that their size cannot explain them. They are linked to one another and can only be seen from the sky.

Native Americans, East Indian, Middle Eastern, Asian, and other cultures have constructed structures, series of structures, and cultural pattern designs that align perfectly with Orion's Belt, and the Pleiades in particular, with others indicating Sirius, Altara, and other very specific stars. Folklore and religious texts and traditions relate the cultural origins of the people and/or their gods as coming from those stars/constellations. Constellation patterns, names, and origin stories are eerily similar among those cultures.

Judeo-Christian Old Testament scriptures refer to the Pleiades and Orion, as well as the dog star, Sirius, all in reference to the Creation of the universe and their place in announcing the presence of a Creator God, as they "sing" out His praises (Psalm 19:1–4; Job 9:9; 38:31; Amos 5:8).

Modern astronomy has discovered that the planets and stars in our galaxy all emit a low-pitched vibrational pattern resembling a song in nature. This could explain how sound vibrations can move monolithic-sized stones or statues.

My studies have given me to believe that mathematics is the language of the universe, and music is its expression.

Bigfoot/Sasquatch/Yeti as Evidence

- Lorraine Warren claimed to have once "communicated" with telepathically with a wounded creature in an Appalachian mountain community; it revealed a humanlike sensitivity and compassion, claiming it had been attempting to touch a two-year-old child in order to communicate with it in its yet unbiased innocence. The creature had injured its foot in an attempt to escape those who were hunting it; it projected a cliff-like area near a river, with a cave where its mate and offspring were waiting. Lorraine tried to project attempts to treat the injured foot to the creature but lost all contact with it when she exited the woods and discovered the very cliffs and river that had been projected to her. No further contact could be made. It was if the creature had simply disappeared.

- Other modern reports of Bigfoot sightings in North America have recorded that the creatures simply seemed to disappear into thin air, opening the discussion that it could be an interdimensional traveler.
- Bigfoot appearances and disappearances have also been correlated with alleged UFO sightings, fueling the argument that they are extraterrestrial.
- In cases where Bigfoot was heard but not seen, observers state tree-knocking, strange grumble-growls, and strange howling.
- "Nests" and other structures constructed of unused and twisted-apart trees have been identified.
- "Gifting" observed in some instances—offerings of fruit not known to be eaten by local fauna are removed, and other items—stones, pine cones, marbles, etc.—are left in return.
- Reports of aggression seem territorial in nature; deliberate attacks on humans are preceded by tree-knocking, howling, a sense of being closed in or herded in a particular direction, stones and branches being thrown in the direction of the intruders—prewarning of territorial infringement.
- Do not appear to be eaters of human flesh and direct human contact is nearly unheard of.
- Fractals can be destructive. Bigfoot appears to prefer peaceful coexistence separate from humanity.
- Yetis are known for their aggression and destructive capabilities; resemble Bigfoot but tend to be larger, per eyewitness descriptions; many deaths and disappearances linked to Yeti folklore and superstitions.

Ley Lines, Monoliths and UFO Sightings as Evidence

- Sacred circles, or hinges, can be found around the world, all of which can be directly connected along earth's magnetic grid that is found geometrically around the world, known as ley lines.
- UFO sightings may coincide with certain ley line conjunctions.
- Ley line conjunctions center around "magic," "astral projection," ESP, and other occult phenomena as these abilities appear to increase or be more potent at these areas, and they may become meccas for practitioners of these arts.
- Ancient gods, old ones, often depicted as dwelling or being imprisoned at or near ley line conjunctions.
- The lines of a pentagram are used in occult practices to form a sort of "magical" ley line representation designed to mimic natural ley lines; hence, they are critical to practitioners for the protection from and control of the conjured beings, Dudleytown as evidence: Ed and Lorraine Warren.
- Dudleytown no longer exists in its original form, but its remains are located outside of Cornwall, Connecticut.
- Lorraine Warren grew up in the area and heard rumors and gossip connected to it all her life.
- History of Dudleytown
    - 1500s England—Edmund Dudley was minister to King Henry VII and served as president of the King's Council, considered powerful and greedy, accused of embezzling from the king's treasury and was beheaded August 18, 1510. His remaining family made its way to the New World.
    - Thomas Dudley became governor of the Massachusetts Bay Company, described as having a penchant for power and conniving. As a Puritan, he opposed the Quakers and tried them for various crimes and executed them in nasty ways. He came to be described as a madman and out of control. One man executed

by Dudley cursed Dudley and the entire Dudleytown area. He served four full terms as full governor before being hacked to death in the area that later became the Dudleytown settlement. His killer was never found.

- Four of Dudley's brothers, nephews of Thomas, were drawn to an area of wild land after returning from the French and Indian Wars—founded the village of Dudleytown in 1632.
- General Herman Swift, adviser to George Washington, lived in Dudleytown. While away on business, his wife was struck by a bolt of lightning and killed. General Swift went insane and was put away.
- Dr. William Clark watched his wife lose her mind as she believed she was being besieged by ghosts and terrible creatures that seemed to be half-man, half-beasts.
- Mary Cheney, wife of Horace Greeley, found her upbringing in Dudleytown to be frightening.
- Over the years, men, women, and children were mysteriously killed or died in tragic ways—drowning, burned, clawed, poisoned, suffocated, bludgeoned, every violent kind of death imaginable.
- Throughout the 1800s, the people began leaving Dudleytown.
- In 1901, sightings of ghosts, half-man, half-beasts continued until only the Brophy family remained. John Patrick Brophy scoffed at the concept of the land being cursed and was determined to stay. His wife died in a fall or sudden illness, his children vanished into the surrounding woods after his wife's funeral, and his house burned to the ground. Brophy stumbled to an inn in a neighboring township declaring madly about creatures with cloven hooves.
- That was the end of the occupation of Dudleytown.
- H. P. Lovecraft, who lived his entire life in Providence, Rhode Island, describes a similar situation in "The Dunwich Horror," in which a community is ravaged

by an otherworldly creature. His description of the land included dead crops, naked trees, diseased foliage, covered with a strange mist. Similar stories arose out of Dudleytown.

- In 1884, a traveling poet came upon the Dudleytown remains and described the land as being "very much like a moonscape as present-day science imagines such." He found little evidence of natural life anywhere. The grass grew a pale green, and tree limbs sprouted small buds, but for sound, there was only the lonely wind and for sight only the arc of a lone blackbird flying high, as if afraid to touch down anywhere in this valley. From a rocky crag, there was evidence of a once-prosperous village with houses, outbuildings, and a mill now in disrepair and empty. Moss and lichen covered most of the rough timber; he reported that he heard dark laughter, louder than any sound made by once-festive villages, a whisper of secrets known only to the elder pagan gods whose power extends throughout the cosmos. In the poet's vision, he saw babies die as they suckled and husbands die as they loved their wives, and innocent deer were rendered by unseen forces. Men were also flayed by unseen forces. Vengeance of the old gods on the Christian presence in the village brought on by the Dudley curse is blamed. He reported a faint smell of death and a remarkable chill.
- In the late 1930s, just before onset of WWII, Dudleytown became a popular make-out spot for teenagers, on the highest hill in Dudleytown. Hundreds of stories have been recorded of snout-faced creatures that materialized in a swirl of mist, ear-deafening shrieks that were not quite human, inhumanly cold hands that suddenly touched girls in their most secret places. One seventeen-year-old boy fought with some kind of monster deep in a ravine where he had gone to relieve himself. The beast had eyes the color of blood

and breath so foul the boy had to hold his own breath for much of the struggle; huge hands clawed the boy across his face, leaving deep gashes. He heard heavy footsteps rumbling away through the thick, shadowy underbrush. The boy later moved away, leaving no forwarding address.

- In 1983, a local television station decided to do a late-night report from Dudleytown. The crew treated it as a joke, making comments about Dracula, Frankenstein, and making werewolf calls. The female reporter sensed a chill in the air; the darkness seemed to have a different texture—darker, inexplicable odors—and she became violently ill, unable to tape the story. It is reported that most of the equipment brought to the location would not work at the location.
- Modern descendants of the Dudleys in America find no link in genealogy to Edmund Dudley. A portion of the original curse on Edmund Dudley was that the curse would fall upon every descendant, plagued with unrelenting horrors and death, until every last one the Dudley in that descent were wiped from the earth.
- Edmund's son, John, tried to get control of the British throne by having his son, Guileford, marry Lady Jane Grey for the crown. The plan failed, and all conspirators were executed. Guileford's brother returned from France after a stint in the military and brought with him a vicious plague that killed his officers and troops before spreading throughout the country, killing thousands. John's third son, Robert, earl of Leicester, decided to leave England and travel to the New World. Robert's descendant, William, settled in Guilford, Connecticut. Abiel, Barzillai, and Gideon, descendants of William, bought land that became Dudleytown in the middle of three large hills which looked dark even at noon. There they discovered iron ore, which led to prosperity, though goods such as food, cloth, tools,

etc. had to be purchased from towns down the mountain. Dudleytown never had any schools, churches, or a cemetery. The area is also known for its timber that was used to make wood coal for Leitchfield County Iron furnaces in Cornwall and other towns. There were strange deaths and bizarre occurrences from the beginning, including an unusually high number of people reported to have become insane and quite a few people who simply vanished and were never seen again.

- Abiel Dudley lost his fortune and his mind and was made a ward of the town. He wandered around aimlessly in his final years, mumbling about "strange creatures in the woods" and was unable to care for himself. He died at the age of ninety in 1799.
- William Tanner, Abiel's closest neighbor, is also said to have gone insane. He lived to the age of 104 and also spoke of "strange creatures" that come out of the woods at night.
- From the records of Dudleytown still in existence are reports of strange illnesses, numerous cases of people going insane, reports of strange creatures roaming the area at night (mostly from the insane folks).
- After the Civil War, the town began to die, and the families that remained packed up and moved away.
- In the 1940s, visitors to the old ruins reported seeing strange things.
- Modern reports include photographs of spooky mists that seem to show creepy faces that provoke feelings of terror, seeing mysterious lights, sights, and hearing creepy sounds.
- The land currently is in the private hands of the Dark Entry Forest Association. There is no public access, and access is denied to inquirers.

An interesting point must be inserted here. If Cornwall, Connecticut, is entered into a map quest of the Appalachian Trail, it should be noted that the two do form a conjunction. The city of Providence, Rhode Island, home of H. P. Lovecraft, is due east of Cornwall in a near-perfect geographical line.

Ancient alien proponents are now proposing a new facet of their theory regarding the increase in UFO sightings around the world in recent years.

Buried statues from ancient cultures of prehistory in otherwise known cultures have been uncovered and reerected, complete with their severed heads being replaced. Ancient alien theorists claim that these statues had been erected as a representation of the extraterrestrial gods that had been beheaded, pulled down, and buried as a means of severing contact with those gods. By reerecting them in modern times, we are reestablishing that connection and reopening portals that allow for interdimensional travel, thereby drawing these ancient gods/ancestors back to earth.

H. P. Lovecraft warned of opening interdimensional portals as they brought forth alien forces of destruction that were of a perverse nature. Cthulhu is only one such example, as referred to in "The Dunwich Horror." The human alien described grew infinitesimally fast to adulthood, passing as somewhat human until the chimeric physicality was revealed in the end. This hybrid's "twin," having been born at the same time to a human mother who had incubated both, was fully alien in nature and was released on the same day as its brother's death.

Examining the messages left behind by these truly ancient cultures gives rise to many questions as to there being so many carvings that depict the humanoid aliens communicating with the people of that time. Ant People, from the center of the earth, strange tentacle-headed humanoids, animal-headed gods—some perverse in appearance, many bloodthirsty, all cryptic and open to interpretation by modern man.

Could these multiton statues have been representations or prisons of the old gods—galactic fractals become earth-bound? Could these ancient cultures have become "enlightened" of the true nature of these gods and thus the statues were beheaded and buried to sever contact with their destructive perversity?

If so, by uncovering and reerecting these statues, we could inadvertently be reopening those interdimensional portals that draw those with paganistic temperaments to renew their efforts to reconnect with these forces? Being cosmic in nature, fractals are shaped by the environment in which they have been trapped. On earth, they are humanoid, with animalistic characteristics. In other dimensions, such as those described by Lovecraft, they take on mindless and monstrous forms, hell-bent on the destruction of our planet. The aliens of modern description, the grays, for example, could be the construct of fractals from other planets or galaxies. Rarely are aliens described as being friendly and beneficent in their contact with humans, The documentation of abductees describes horrors of medical-type probing and examinations. They have been introduced to alien-human hybrid children that were allegedly formed from their own DNA, combined with that of their abductors. What is the purpose of this?

Are sentient fractals contaminating other galactic races in an attempt to retake the universe and bring it back to its neutral void ante creation?

Are they angry that they were separated from the void of their natural formation?

Evidence from Appalachia

- Roan Mountain, on the border between Tennessee and North Carolina—6,285 feet above sea level and eternally cloud-capped, located in an untouched dense wilderness in the Cherokee National Forest and Roan Mountain State Park along the Appalachian Trail. It has the largest grassy highland, known as a grassy bald, in the entire Appalachian range. One of the most well-known and reported phenomena is a ghostly choir of disembodied voices that are said to roam about the highest of the peaks and passes. One report dated to the early 1800s tells of settlers and explorers who heard mysterious music and singing voices floating through the wind. The quality of this unexplained music and the voices seemed to change depended on the one who heard them, with some saying they were "beautiful and angelic, accompanied by the sound of ethereal harps" and others reporting them to be more "sinister and sounding like chaotic screeching and the horrific wailing and screaming of the damned in the symphony of hellish noise." Other reports identified the music and singing as belonging to faeries or Cherokee and Catawba spirits. A few claimed it was the mountain itself speaking to them. Great fear is a common response. Reports escalated with the rise of tourism that began with the building of the Cloudland Hotel in 1878. One guest reportedly heard the singing and went looking for its source. He was caught in a fierce thunderstorm and took shelter in a cave he claimed was a portal that had opened up in the rock and spewed out a procession of singing ghosts that looked like zombies, complete with rotting skin and jagged teeth. As he watched, their singing became wails of pain. He fainted. When he awoke, his clothes were torn. Another guest heard a sound like the "humming of a thousand bees." Being a geologist, he concluded the sound was the result of electricity generated by friction.

- There is a decrepit cemetery along Dark Hollow Road, right up against Roan Mountain. It is small and unkempt with the majority of overgrown, unmarked, and occupied by the unknown bodies of the forgotten. One grave, however, belongs to a man named Jankins who died sometime around the turn of the twentieth century. It is said that this man was having an affair with a woman named Delinda, a local woman of ill repute. Jankins was shot, possibly by his wife. Stories say that the women of the community were seen outside the church where Jankins's body was laying for burial the following day. They were seen in conversation with Delinda. At the funeral, everyone expected the grieved other woman to put in an appearance. She didn't appear that day or on any other as she seemingly disappeared from the area. It is said that Jankins's coffin seemed heavier than it should have been at the time of burial. While unproven, it was whispered that Delinda was entombed with Jankins that day. To this day, cars that drive by or park at the cemetery at night will have their car unexpectedly rocked or bumped by an unseen force believed to be Delinda trying to get away from the cemetery.

- During the early pioneering days, a wealthy rancher known only as the Baron brought in a large herd of cattle that took over the best grazing land. He had an enormous and very aggressive bull that would ferociously chase anyone away, sometimes causing injury or death. Fellow ranchers believed the purchase of this aggressive bull was intentional and intended to keep other ranchers from the prime grazing lands, which threatened to put them out of business. Someone shot and killed the bull near the top of Roan Mountain. The Baron left the carcass there to rot. To this day, there can be heard the sound of an enraged bull in that area, sometimes accompanied by the apparition of a spectral bull which charges at intruders before disappearing just before it makes an impact.
- Ghost lights have also been reported. One camper noted that they appeared just as it got dark. It began with the sound of footsteps along a side trail near the campsite, leaves crunching, and twigs snapping under the weight of a body in motion. Then the woods become quiet—no sound at all. The light appears to sway back and forth along the main trail—a glowing ball without any radiance. It bobbed back and forth, went into the woods, circled back to the campsite, and then trailed off back into the woods. It moved like someone was carrying it, like a lantern, or wearing a headlamp, if the person were short. The camp-

ers looked for the person in the pitch-black night but found no one. They packed up and left that night.

- The Appalachian Mountains were formed over 480 million years ago, according to modern dating methods, and are among the oldest in North America. They are believed to have once rivaled the Rock Mountains of Western North America. Because of their vast age, there are many stories of ancient life that may or may not continue to exist there.
  - One is the Appalachian Black Panther, which has been reportedly seen as far back as the early settlers of the Appalachians and the Ozarks. These sightings continue today. My neighbors have reported seeing one within the past year, less than half a mile from my home. I have heard cries of a large cat periodically since my youth. The state Wildlife Services claim there are no panthers in Kentucky as they were all hunted out in the 1800s. The bobcat, a smaller wildcat, is just now being reintroduced to the area and is being tracked by Wildlife Services.

    Historically, however, dead specimens have turned up from time to time. In the 1800s, a settler named Emily Settler shot one of the black species with a musket through her closed cabin door when it tried to savagely enter her home. Sir William Jardine, a naturalist, described two specimens of "black cougar" supposedly killed in America and placed in London during the 1700s. He assigned them the name Felis Nigra the Black Puma, although the exact species of cat can no longer be determined as the original displays are now gone. Cougars are not known to exhibit a melanistic or black phase. Jaguars and leopards are the only two species of large cats known to have a black color phase, which leads to the name "black panther." The panther in question has been considered extinct in America for over a century. American settlers in the 1500s reportedly hunted them down;

promoted deforestation led to habitat loss until the species was declared extinct in the nineteenth century. Yet sightings continue to this day. It is speculated that black jaguars may have migrated to this region. They once roamed the Southwestern United States and are known to have a melanistic phase. Cherokee legends have portrayed the black panther as a guardian spirit.

- Bigfoot, also called Yahoo for its booming vocalizations—brown in color and somewhat smaller than a typical sasquatch, standing between six and eight feet tall. They are known for being quite aggressive, highly territorial, and dangerous. There are many active Bigfoot hunter groups in this region, and their activity is mapped and studied.
- Dwayyo—this is a seven- to nine-foot-tall creature described as being a bipedal wolf, complete with a bushy tail. It emits an eerie, piercing howl which echoes through the night. It is reported to have a nasty disposition and has been associated with cattle mutilations. It has been known to attack and mutilate dogs without hesitation. It has been reported to lunge at passing cars from the woods and has been reported to have attacked people. One report is of a farmer who went out to investigate what was upsetting his dogs. He encountered a monster which snarled and leaped at the farmer in a rage. The farmer was barely able to escape the creature's slashing claws before locking himself inside his home. The creature continued pacing outside for a time before returning to the surrounding wilderness.
- Snarley Yow, Black Dog, or Dog Fiend—an enormous black dog with a frighteningly large red mouth and jagged fangs. It is said to maraud through the countryside near South Mountain, Maryland. The reports of this creature mostly revolve around a pass where the Old National Road cuts across a brook and a can-

yon. Accounts suggest it is more phantom or spectral in nature, with the purported ability to change colors from black to white, as well as the ability to grow or shrink in size at will. It is also reported to be able to pass through walls or trees. Hunters who have shot at the creature report that their bullets passed through the creature without effect. The Snarly Yow has a long history of causing mischief and mayhem. During colonial times, it would appear just long enough to terrify horses into throwing their riders before vanishing. This behavior has carried over into modern times and applied to modern modes of transportation. It has been reported to lunge in front of cars, causing the drivers to swerve and crash to try and avoid hitting what appears to be a dog in the road. Upon getting out of the car, the driver sees the fierce creature, which growls and bares its fangs at them before disappearing into thin air. While it seems to enjoy chasing cars, it has also been known to appear to hikers, blocking their path and refusing to move, forcing them to find an alternate trail. It has never reportedly actually attacked people. The threat seems to be enough.

- Snarlygaster—a monstrous abomination said to be some sort of cross between a reptile and a bird, with an alligator-like head with a fang-filled beak, sharp, formidable talons, and a 25-foot wingspan. In some reports, the creature also had tentacles and poisonous breath. Appearances of the creature can be traced back to the 1730s when German settlers claimed to have been terrorized by a flying reptilian monster they called Scneller Geist, "quick spirit," in reference to its ability to silently descend upon prey with a breathtaking speed, after which it would supposedly suck the blood from its victim. Sightings continued and were given a great deal of coverage in February and March of 1909 when several news publications printed stories of encounters by locals which described a terrifying winged beast with "claws like steel hooks, and an eye in the center of its forehead" as well as a screech that sounded like a locomotive whistle. The Smithsonian Institution became intrigued with the amount of publicity this creature was receiving and offered a reward for the monster's skin. Then United States president Theodore Roosevelt allegedly considered postponing an already planned African safari to go after the beast himself. The Snarlygaster is said to have supernatural abilities, so a five-pointed star would keep it at bay. This belief became so prominent that some Old Country houses and barns in the region still sport images of five-pointed stars to this day. Snarlygaster and the Dwayyo are believed to be mortal enemies, and occasionally there have been reports of these two creatures engaged in vicious, epic fights.

- Enigmatic humanoids are believed to originate in deep, dark coal mines, quarries, and caves in the Appalachian region. On December 26, 1945, there was a spectacular mine explosion at the Belva Mine in Kentucky. Survivors of the explosion reported that some of the trapped miners had seen a mysterious door suddenly open in the sheer rock wall of the mine. A mysterious figure that looked somewhat like "a lumberjack" stepped out from a well-lit room beyond the door. The weird entity assured the miners they would be all right, then returned to the secret room, which then closed back up as if it had never really existed.
  - This is not an isolated case as a mine disaster in Shipton, Pennsylvania, has a similar response as told by the only two men who survived the disaster. They told of being rescued by strange men in odd clothes, who had guided them with a mysterious blue glow. Whenever the figures touched the sides of the mine, the walls flickered to life with a

shifting array of psychedelic, holographic images. After the miners had been taken to a safe area to wait for rescue, the strange men who had rescued them seemed to creep back into the darkness they had come from, with the blue glow becoming fainter as they went until it was out of sight. Both survivors were interrogated separately but gave identical responses. They insisted they had not seen hallucinations and were not delusional.

- In the March 5, 1981, edition of *The Valley News Dispatch*, there was a report of a group of children that had come across a four-foot-tall creature crawling from a sewer in New Kinsington that looked like a cross between a human and a dinosaur. The children chased the creature, nearly managing to grab its tail, before it scrambled back into the sewer tunnel. This report appears to tie in with other numerous sightings of small reptilian creatures said to be around the size of a child that have been spotted around the Appalachians.
- A 1944 report of a mining disaster that killed fifteen men described the disaster to have been caused by subterranean humanoids that had the power to manipulate the earth. One miner reported having seen one of these "vicious" humanoids after the miners had broken through into a previously unknown and untouched passage. The creature had allegedly used some sort of supernatural ability to cause a partial cave-in to block their escape. It then began to mercilessly attack the miners until it was frightened off by the arriving rescuers. The mine inspector reported that none of the dead men exhibited injuries from falling rocks but had grievous slashes across their bodies that seemed to have been made by large

claws. Some of the miners trapped in the disaster were never found.

- Two boys reported finding a hole that was perfectly smooth as if it had been melted straight into the earth. The hole was found after the earth had been removed by an excavator in preparation for the building of a road. The shaft was about four feet across and sloped downward at a slight angle. The boy's dog ran down the shaft. They heard the dog barking, followed by a low rumble from the darkness. The dog scurried back to the surface in a desperate and terrified panic. The hole was subsequently covered by the road construction with no further reported incidences. There are many other reports of strange shafts and hidden doors across the entire region.
- In 1690, French traders slogging through the wilderness of Southern Appalachia reportedly came across an odd sight. They hacked their way through thick, impenetrable underbrush and emerged into a clearing that had a town of neatly lined-up log cabins populated by olive-skinned people who had European features, beards, light-colored eyes, and fair hair. These people spoke a form of broken Elizabethan English. The French explorers were convinced they had found a group of displaced Moors who had colonized the New World, but their discovery was dismissed and forgotten over time. Further reports of these mysterious people came from the natives living in that region. These were considered to be nothing more than folklore or superstition. Nearly a century passed before John Xavier, a Frenchman, made a discovery in Newman's Ridge in upper East Tennessee. He found there a village of people with distinctly European features who called

themselves the "Porty-aghee," "Melungeon," and referred to one another with Anglo surnames. These people were either unwilling or unable to describe their origins in the wilderness. They had no written records and a general aversion to discussing their history. These Melungeons reportedly got along well with the native tribes of the area and were perceived to be primarily a curiosity. There have been many theories as to the origin of these people, ranging from being the Lost Tribe of Israel to being shipwrecked explorers or the lost colony of Roanoke. These people experienced great discrimination from the time of their discovery and were segregated as being "free people of color." The political system of the nineteenth century barred them from owning land, getting a public education, and voting. Many of these people began to migrate to other areas, and by the twentieth century, only a scattered few still remained in very remote corners of East Tennessee and Western Virginia. Much of their earlier culture has disappeared. They claimed no identity with the Native Americans but a separate and distinct group identity. The Melungeons are considered one of America's greatest anthropological mysteries. Their descendants continue to be found in remote and poverty-stricken areas of the Southern Appalachian region. They are believed to be of a triracial isolate group—a mix of European, African, and Native American ancestry—with some DNA link to Mediterranean peoples. Genetic testing is inconclusive, however, and leads only to more questions than answers. In his moving novel *Daughter of the Legend*, Appalachian author Jesse Stuart describes an unconventional romance with a Melungeon girl and a Town boy raised to be prejudiced against these fellow citizens.

- The wog of Winder, Georgia—In a boggy pond called Nodoroc by the Creek Indians is a small volcano that seethes and bubbles, spewing out smoke that gives the entire area a hellish appearance. Nodoroc means "gateway to hell." During the 1800s, the Creeks built a stone altar where they executed prisoners and tossed their bodies into the water where the soul would suffer in hell for all eternity. This area is said to be protected by the wog, a creature the size of a small horse, covered in long black fur, with legs that are longer in the front than those at its rear. A 1914 historian for *The Early History of Jackson County, Georgia*, described a creature with the head of a bear, a long tail tipped with a white puff that extends almost three feet and is used to sweep those who have sought forgiveness under the water to start their journey in hell forever. It had glowing red eyes and a pink, forked tongue it used to taste the air between its tusked maw.
- The Tennessee Wildman of McNairy County, Tennessee—first recorded in the 1800s, this manlike creature covered in either ginger or gray fur stands about seven to nine feet tall and reportedly stalks hikers in the woods. Though it is sometimes referred to as the sasquatch based on similarities, it has other qualities that differ. It resembles a man more than the legendary Bigfoot, is considered incredibly aggressive, and may be fighting sasquatch for its territory. One legend states that a circus showman once captured the beast to put him on display. The beast's immense strength allowed it to break free from its confines and return to its natural habitat. The last documented sighting was in the late 1900s by two hikers exploring a trail in the town of Elizabethton. They reported smelling something like a dead animal, crippled by a loud piercing

scream and a massive thumping of something jumping through the trees. During peak sightings in the 1800s, dogs and women seemed to be the preferred targets.

- The Hopkinsville Goblins of Hopkinsville, Kentucky—in 1955, a Kelly Community family reported that they had seen a weird flying aircraft during a small family reunion. One witness described it as being round with rainbow streaks behind it. He was laughed at as being a prankster. However, the entire family went out to see for themselves and discovered a short glowing figure that was humanlike, with two large eyes. It seemed to float, more than walk, toward them, arms raised as if in surrender. Two of the witnesses got gums and shot at the three-foot-tall creature. As the initial witness stepped out from the porch to examine the creature, a clawed hand reached down from the roof and grazed his head. The man's wife pulled him back into the house. The brother who had shot the creature on the roof heard it whine and roll off the roof to the ground, apparently uninjured. Later that night, another family member spotted bright eyes rise behind two clawed hands in a window. It was shot at again. Other "little men" were spotted in trees and peeking around the house. They were shot at. The bullets reportedly sounded like they hit metal. The creatures floated away. The family turned on or lit up all light-producing items in the house in the hope that the light would harm the creature's large eyes. The family escaped and made their report to the local police. In the aftermath of the widespread headlines, Steven Spielberg was inspired to create *E.T.* and mastermind *Close Encounters of the Third Kind.*
- Raystown Ray of Raystown Lake, Huntington County, Pennsylvania—in 1962, something was spotted swimming in the Raystown Dam. In 1971, the dam was destroyed by the US Army Corps of Engineers to

create Raystown Lake, with a depth of 185 feet. The Raystown Ski Club organizers nearly canceled an event when there were reports of seeing some large dark creature, akin to the Loch Ness monster, looming just beneath the surface. It was described as serpentlike, fifty to sixty feet in length, but no one knows just how large the creature is because only a large reptilian head has ever been seen above water. Local gift shops carry Raystown Ray merchandise. Sparse reports of the creature carried over into 2008. In 2010, *Fact or Faked: Paranormal Files*, a production of the SYFY Channel, made a trip to search the lake but turned up nothing.

- Mothman of Point Pleasant, West Virginia—on November 12, 1966, five men were in a cemetery preparing a burial plot when they reported seeing a figure in the distance. It looked like a man but had large furry wings and swooped over the men's heads. The sightings continued, with two married couples who were driving past an abandoned TNT plant near Point Pleasant when they saw two large eyes, glowing red, on a six- to seven-foot-tall figure with a large wingspan that disappeared into the TNT plant. That same night, a local contractor about ninety miles away in Newell Partridge became confused by strange whining sounds like "a machine starting up." He spotted two red eyes watching him. On December 15, 1967, the bridge at Point Pleasant collapsed in a devastating tragedy. Mothman had been reportedly seen just prior to the event.
- Goatman of Maryland, Virginia—this creature is said to have brutally murdered young couples who parked their cars in discrete places for an opportunity to be alone. It has been known to kill family pets or break into homes and spread his seed with the house residents, regardless of gender. Some legends say the goatman began as a simple farmer who became angered

when a group of teens killed his flock of sheep, and he vowed to take revenge on teenagers forever. Another legend says that a scientist was experimenting on a goat when there was an explosion that turned him into a humanoid goat with a thirst for blood. Legends of a goatman are typically found in Louisiana and Texas. The goatman is an alleged cousin of the New Orleans evil Grunch and the New Jersey Jersey Devil.

- The Beast of Bladenboro, North Carolina—in December 1953, a woman reported hearing cries and whimpers from her neighbor's dogs. When investigating, she saw a large catlike creature return to the darkness once the dogs were silenced. On New Year's Eve, 1953, police chief Roy Fores answered a call from the farm of Woody Storm who had found both of his dogs on his back porch drained of blood. That night, another man reported watching a huge cat creature attack his dogs and go into the woods. Other reports described the creature as three feet long with a long tail and a catlike face that produced a scream like a woman stabbed in the back. In January 1954, two more dogs were reported having been drained of blood. Professional hunters were brought in, and four days later, the beast attacked a human for the first time. A woman had heard the cry of her dogs and had gone outside to check on them. The beast charged her, and she screamed. Her husband exited the house in time to see the creature run back into the woods. The hunt for the creature was called off on January 13, 1954, with the plan of killing the largest bobcat they could locate and hanging it from the flagpole as the Beast of Blandenboro. The creature has not been seen since.
- The Moon-Eyed People—this Cherokee legend describes a small race of people that lived in Appalachia before the Indians came. They are described as being very pale, with blond hair and blue eyes which appear

too big for their heads. They were never seen in the daytime and moved about only at night. It was believed that these people lived underground. They reportedly built the 850-foot-long, twelve-feet-thick, seven-foot-high wall known as Fort Mountain, possibly around AD 400–500. One legend says that the Cherokee defeated the Moon-Eyed people during a full moon and drove them away. Another legend declares that the Cherokee chased the Moon-Eyed people from their home at Hiwassee, a village now known as Murphy, North Carolina. In the 1840s, the land was being cleared at Murphy when an ancient soapstone depicting two three-foot-tall creatures conjoined like Siamese twins was uncovered. It is now on display at the Cherokee Historical Museum.

- The Appalachian Trail is 2,200 miles long and is the longest hiking-only trail in the world. It passes through fourteen states, with the International Appalachian Trail crossing from Maine into Canada, to Newfoundland, with sections that continue into Greenland, Europe, and Morocco.
    - In the summer of 2011, a hiker named Brad Lane was camped about fifteen miles from New Castle, Virginia, when he was reportedly awakened on several occasions by what sounded like footsteps crunching around his tent, accompanied by a "grumble" of a voice talking to itself. One night, he clearly saw a man reaching down with a scorched hand for firewood. The man wore plaid with large black burns tearing at the trim. His red ashy beard smoldered at his face. His eyes were vacant and white when he made eye contact with Brad. The man scrunched up his nose, then left. Brad packed up and moved on until dawn. Three hours after settling into the new camp, he was awakened by a funny smell. He

then discovered his tent had melted down around its tent poles. Brad ran until he reached a gravel road and found a sheriff's patrol car parked just outside the remains of a charred house. Nothing remained but the mailbox out front. Brad did not tell the officer what had happened to him but did ask about the house fire. Four days previously, the day Brad had begun his trip, the house had burned down, possibly by arson. A man and woman and their two daughters had all perished.

- In mid-December 1980, a witness at an Appalachian Trail shelter in Amherst County, Virginia, along with his son and dog, Ginger, reported seeing a figure come out of the wilderness to within a hundred feet of the shelter. The figure was tall and wore a dark brown "fur" coat. The dog responded to the presence with a bark its owner had never heard before. The witness called to the figure to come over and share a hot drink. The creature looked human in shape but not appearance. The dog responded with quivering hind legs and gurgling sounds of great pain. The creature turned and reentered the forest; the dog resumed its unusual bark. The witness later learned that in the fall and winter, there are many reports of dogs making a lot of noise, with a great number going missing. One man who had cattle that went missing spoke of a Brown Man his grandfather had told him about, though he was personally skeptical. He said he had seen nothing at the time his cattle went missing, but his neighbor had.
- In Pennsylvania, a ten-year-old witness was back-country camping with her parents. At the campsite, the girl became uneasy, causing her mother to grow pale and ask to move their camp elsewhere. The father refused. Early in the morn-

ing, the girl and her mother went for a walk. They reported seeing a hazy image of a man leaning against a birch tree twenty feet away. The figure was not threatening but calm and solemn. The figure disappeared as they watched.

- A man backpacking with friends awoke one morning to the sound of children's laughter all around their otherwise isolated site. A procession of kids walked around, asking them what they were doing there. The men responded that they were hiking the Appalachian Trail. The children responded that the men weren't on the Appalachian Trail. The kids then wandered out of sight but could still be heard, taunting them from the trees and underbrush for the duration of their hike.
- May 1972—a lone hiker noticed a thick fog gathering around him. Ahead of him, he noticed a tall, black figure wearing a heavy coat and a wide-brimmed hat. The stranger seemed to be confused and was looking around him as if he had lost something. He nearly collided with the hiker. When they made eye contact, the stranger had icy-blue eyes that generated a swell of dread in the hiker. He also realized the stranger was wearing out-of-date period clothing from another time. When the hiker tried to greet the man, the man ignored him and vanished.
- A lone hiker camping near Pierce Pond in Maine, during June, reported seeing flames of light that danced around him. Within those flames, he saw the spectral form of a woodsy, outdoorsman type with a small backpack and what appeared to be fishing equipment. As he watched, the vision faded into the night. The next night, the same figure reappeared and made eye contact with the hiker, causing the hiker to run away from

his lean-to. He returned for his equipment the following morning. He was told that that same vision had been haunting a wide area of Maine but had not been connected with any trouble.

- At Greenleaf Hut, White Mountains, Bluff Mountain, Virginia, there is a marker that tells of four-year-old Ottie Cline who died there more than one hundred years ago after going hunting for kindling wood. There have been numerous reports of a ghostly child stalking the wilderness and wandering about as if looking for something.
- Sarver Cabin in Virginia was built in the 1850s and is well off the beaten path along the trail and is surrounded by feral wilderness. Its crumpled ruins are said to be haunted by an unidentified boy dubbed George who makes his presence known to all who pass through.
- In the Big Ridge Park of Tennessee can be found the ruins of the Hutchinson family home, a nineteenth-century home. One girl fell ill. When the neighbors came to help, they reported a dog running through the forest toward them. They saw no dog, only heard it. It was later confirmed that the girl passed away at precisely the same time the neighbors had heard the spectral dog.
- Compton's and Fox's Gap at Spook Hill was the location for fierce battles of the American Civil War in 1862. It was a place of absolute carnage and mayhem that left the area soaked in blood and littered with dead bodies, many of which were not properly buried. Intense paranormal activity has been reported in that area ever since. There have been many reports of Civil War era soldiers, and one location at Spook Hill has a reputation of spectral handprints appearing on parked vehicles that appear to be pushed up an incline.

Moloch

Moloch worship is condemned specifically in the Bible as it appears to have condoned the sacrifice of children in worship.

It is traditionally understood to be a Canaanite god.

A 1935 debate of scholars occurred in question of whether the term refers to the type of sacrifice or the god itself as there is a similarity with the term *mlk*, which means "sacrifice" in the Punic language. Other forms of the Punic word are *molk* or *mulk*.

There continues to be debate as to whether these sacrifices were offered to Yahweh or another deity and whether the practice originated with the Israelites or was adopted with the influence of Phoenician practices.

During the Medieval period, Moloch was portrayed as a bull-headed idol with outstretched hands over a fire. This description combines biblical depictions and other sources, including ancient accounts of Carthaginian child sacrifice and the legend of the minotaur.

The term is used figuratively in reference to a person or a thing which demands or requires a very costly sacrifice.

Moloch appears in literary works such as John Milton's *Paradise Lost*, Gustave Flaubert's *Salammbo*, and Allen Ginsberg's "Howl."

The use of the word in Hebrews 11:7 has led some to suggest that it was likely intended as a reference to the Ammonite god Milcom and not to Moloch.

The books of Leviticus, 2 Kings, and Jeremiah all condemn Israelites who engaged in practices associated with Moloch, who called for the use of children as sacrifices. Other passages refer to the practice of having children "to pass over the fire" without ever referencing Moloch or any other god (Deuteronomy 12:31; 18:10; 2 Kings 16:3; 17:17; 21:6; 2 Chronicles 28:3; 33:6; Jeremiah 7:31; 19:5; and Ezekiel 16:21; 20:26, 31; 23:37).

Leviticus repeatedly and specifically forbids the practice of offering children to Moloch: "And thou shalt not give any of thy seed to set them apart to Molech, neither shalt thou profane the name of thy God: I am the Lord" (18:21).

"Moreover, thou shalt say to the children of Israel: whosoever he be of the children of Isarael, or of the strangers that sojourn in Israel, that giveth of his seed unto Molech, he shall surely be put to death; the people of the land shall stone him with stones. I also will set my face against that man, and will cut him off from among his people, because he hath given of his seed unto Moloch, to defile My sanctuary, and to profane My holy name. And if the people of the land do it all hide their eyes from that man, when he giveth of his seed unto Molech, and put him not to death; then I will set My face against that man, and will cut him off, and all that go astray after Molech, from among their people" (20:2–5).

Jeremiah equates practices associated with Moloch worship with infidelity to Yahweh (32:35).

The word *Moloch* bears a similarity to the Hebrew word *Melek*, meaning "king." While this term is used throughout the Bible, scholars agree upon only a single incidence in which this confusion possibly occurs (Isaiah 30:33).

The Greek Septuagint translates "Molech" in Leviticus as meaning "ruler" and as "king" in 1 Kings 11:7. It refers to Molech in 2 Kings 23:10 and Jeremiah 30:35. However, it also uses the name Moloch in Amos 5:26, which is not present in the Masoretic text. The Greek New Testament refers to Moloch only once (Acts 7:43).

Before 1935, Moloch was held to be a pagan god by scholars, based on the recorded child sacrifice offered at the Jerusalem Tophet (2 Kings).

Challenges to the Concept of Moloch as a Specific God

Molech is rarely mentioned in the Bible and is not mentioned at all outside of it, and connections to other deities with similar names are uncertain.

It is possible that some of the proposed deities named Mlk are epithets for another god, given that Mlk can also mean "king."

The Israelite practice conforms to the Mlk rite in that both involved the sacrifice of children.

None of the proposed gods identified as Moloch is associated with human child sacrifice; the god Mlk of Ugarit appears to have only received animal sacrifices, and the Mlk sacrifice is never offered to a god named Mlk but rather to another deity.

Moloch as a Form of Sacrifice

In 1935, Otto Eissfeldt based this theory on the basis of Punic inscriptions. These inscriptions commonly associate mlk with other words: *mr* (lamb), *b'l* (citizen), and *'dm* (human being). The last two are used interchangeably and never occur in the same description. Another word that sometimes occurs is *bsr* (flesh). When combined with *mlk*, it indicates a "mlk sacrifice consisting of..." Therefore, the biblical term *lammolech* would not be translated as "to Molech" but as "a mlk-sacrifice," a meaning consistent with the Hebrew preposition.

Bennie Reynolds argues that Jeremiah's use of Moloch in connection with Baal (Jeremiah 32:25) is parallel with the use of "burnt offering," as presented in Jeremiah 19:4–5.

In the 1980s, scholars Day and Heider argued that Leviticus 20:55, which mentions "whoring after Moloch," implied an actual god but that the Punic use of a sacrifice resulted as an import to Phoenicia through the Punic diaspora.

Many other arguments for mistranslation appear in academia and will not likely be resolved.

Moloch as a Rite of Passage

Primarily Punic scholars argue that the term refers to nonlethal ceremonies practiced by these cultures. This is partially supported by commentary in the Talmud and early Jewish commentators on the Bible.

One website (www.amonrasit.wordpress.com) offers one person's opinion of Yahweh as the impostor god. He makes reference to texts from other traditions as evidence that the Bible and Yahweh worship was in fact stolen from the traditions of the cultures that surrounded the Israelite nation of the Old Testament period. While in the form of an angry rant, fueled by information from www.joyofSatan.net, he does present a case for the possible confusion and misinterpretations found in modern academia in terms of interpretation and confirmation of the Bible as historical text.

Having examined this wide and varied evidence, I have began to formulate a possible hierarchy for the fractal faction.

At the top of this dark food chain are the overlords:

- These are the old gods.
- Possibly the fallen angels of God's High Council.
- Often reported as having come from the stars.
- Possible Prometheus effect in that they brought otherwise forbidden, at that time, knowledge and technology to the people of earth.
- Cthulhu?
- Statues/images of these gods may also be prisons for these overlords. If an image had to be "opened" to be indwelled by the deity and another ceremony completed to release the deity from a broken or worn idol before it was destroyed and replaced by a newer one, the old deity could have remained trapped within the idol by those who once worshipped it but were no longer a believer or follower of that god. Reerecting them or disturbing their resting places could "awaken" them in some way and reintroduce them to modern society by inducing an unnatural longing or compulsion for worshipping them in one form or another.

The next group would be the territorial lords:

- They would appear as humanoid, such as Bigfoot or sasquatch.
- Sentient.

- They are reported to disappear into thin air, have been described as entering UFOs, and have been linked to possible interdimensional travel.
- They build nests and other odd structures.
- May interact with human beings, as demonstrated through gifting.
- Are aggressive at times but no actual attacks on or killing of human beings have been reported.
- They communicate with tree knocks, howling, growling, throwing of rocks, and other items of large size.
- Generally described as being shy.
- Yeti share characteristics with Bigfoot but are larger and much more aggressive; human mutilation has been reported.

The next level involves the spirits that act as the low-level instigators of their overlords.

- Include spirits/ghosts.
- May take on forms of historical significance to an area.
- May appear to be benevolent or act maliciously.
- Differentiate from demonic forces—identified as elementals and interdimensional beings.
- Very territorial.
- Dangerous to humans—capable of physical harm, unexplained medical conditions, and death; can encourage the development of mental illnesses.
- Obsessed with specific targets for control of individuals.
- Able to influence an individual's thinking and cognitive ability.
- Shadow people.
- Interact as "intelligent" hauntings.
- May produce "residual" behaviors that appear redundant and project complacency or curiosity in the fearful observers.

- May lead to an unhealthy obsession with the supernatural and the paranormal, occult activity.
- Feigns "mediumistic" behavior in those who desire these "gifts," manifest as spirit guides.
- May not respond to exorcism as they are not demonic in nature. They are not of the same created spirit of demons, having resulted from the shattering of the void.
- They cannot be driven from a location but can be contained or imprisoned to limit their ability to move about or influence humanity. As a result, there may be areas of "dead" ground where nothing grows or grows only outside of expected genetic patterns, resulting in twisted or black trees, unfruitful plants, failure to produce leaves, etc.

The next subgroup is comprised of hybrids.

- Many of these are reflected in the ancient gods of Mesopotamian and Egyptian cultures, indicating that they hold no single tier in the hierarchy but may flow throughout the tiers as their designated purpose dictates.
- Also seen in Central American pyramid cultures, and among the Southwest American Indians, which describes the Ant People who live within the earth.
- Often described as living in communities or cities rather than being individuals.
- Reportedly interdimensional and often indescribable in their alienness when encountered in places with no known cultural connections to such beings.

Another subgroup, elementals, appears to exist, primarily in the upper levels of the hierarchy but can be found in the lower levels as servants or slaves, such as the djinn of the Middle East.

- Titans of Greco-Roman mythology
- Often described by Amy Allen in her "walks" (Amy appears in "The Dead Files" on the Travel Channel; she works with

her partner, former New York city cop Steve DiSchiavi, to uncover past activities, both criminal and tragic, that have led to devastating hauntings.)

- Four elements are recognized—fire, water, air, and earth—which are used as components in rituals and spells by pagans and satanists. They are also accepted as common in Christianized cultures such as voodoo.
- Native Americans speak of these elements as spirits and seek to use them compatibly.
- A fifth element—spirit or soul—has been identified but does not appear to have been assigned a specific being to represent it; it occurs in common popular culture as "manna" or "soul manna" in video games and is considered to be a critical and often magical life force.
- Popular fantasy writers such as Robert Jordan (The Wheel of Time Series) and Terry Goodkind (The Sword of Truth series) have adopted elemental control magic into their worlds. In these fantasy realms, it is women who are able to control these elements. Any man who attempts to manipulate them is driven mad or dies in the attempt. Soul bonding between a woman and a man is another concept made popular by these writers—a woman can forcibly bond a man or bond one who has chosen to be bonded to herself through the use of these powers. Does this make spirit the strongest of all elements? If so, it is a strong argument for the Christian concept of an indwelled Holy Spirit, a part of the Holy Trinity, the ultimate force of Creation.
- The soul is strictly used in relation to a human being. There is no being of a nonmortal nature that is identified as having a soul. Any soul exchange with a supernatural creature appears to only occur with the crossbreeding required with a human.

That brings us to the base destroyers as described by H. P. Lovecraft. They appear to be fully mindless and destructive. The fact that that they are described as being found in isolated areas rich with limestone mountains and iron ore, as described by the history of Dudleytown, indicates their base elemental nature, and their apparent vacuous appetite speaks of their connection to the void.

In a side note, King Tut was buried with a dagger created from cosmic materials of an unknown source. While meteors are the first resource to come to mind, the materials do not match any known meteoric materials discovered on earth to this point. This fuels ancient astronaut theories.

It also supports the theory of fractals. Fractals are cosmic dust, influenced by the materials found in the environment in which they came to rest, forming the creatures of nightmares and fairy tales the peoples of the earth required for their cultural development. Thus, there are similarities between cultures that allegedly had no contact with one another. The ancient alien gods portrayed in these otherwise unconnected cultures depict individuals in modern astronaut-like suits. These could be fractals from other dimensions or galaxies or even planets within our solar system that developed from elements that differ from those on earth and, therefore, require life support or to be safely hidden away from the eyes of mortal men who find them so terrifyingly different.

These alien fractals brought their metallurgical, mathematic, and engineering knowledge from the void, and they were given to the primitive, by comparison, peoples of earth, introducing them to technology beyond their developmental understanding, which explains why there are no records of these civilizations that exist today, except for the enigmatic remains they left behind.

In Hebrews 1:1–4, God, who at various times and in various ways spoke in time past to the prophets, has in these last days spoken to us by His Son, whom he has appointed heir of all things, through whom also He made the worlds, who is the brightest of His glory and the express image of His person and upholding all things by the word of His power, when He had by Himself purged our sins, sat down at the right hand of Majesty on high, having become so much better than the angels, as He has by inheritance obtained a more excellent name than they.

In Job 33:4, the spirit of God has made me. And the breath of the Almighty gives me life.

In a discussion on the origin of life in *The Evidence Bible*, several renowned scientists are discussed and quoted. Here are a few:

- Louis Pasteur: Discovered the law of biogenesis and concluded that "spontaneous generation" is impossible; life can only arise from other life.
- Sir Frederick Hoyle: astronomer and mathematician; calculated the probability of the spontaneous generation of life:
    - "No matter how large the environment one considers, life cannot have a random beginning. Troops of monkeys thundering away at random on typewriters could not produce the words of Shakespeare, for the practical reason that the whole observable universe is not large enough to contain the necessary monkey hordes, the necessary typewriters, and certainly not the wastepaper basket required for the deposition of wrong attempts. The same is true for living material…

      "The likelihood of the spontaneous formation of life from inanimate matter is one to a number with 40,000 noughts after it…it is big enough to bury Darwin and the whole theory of evolution. There was no primeval soup, neither on this planet nor on any other, and if the beginnings of life were not random, they must therefore have been the product of purposeful intelligence."
- In Darwin's time, it was assumed that "simple" cells were just primitive blobs of protoplasm, so it wasn't hard for scientists to envision them assembling by random chance. Because cells cannot be seen with the naked eye, scientists mistakenly thought the chemistry of life was simple. But with today's sophisticated microscopes, molecular biology has shown how vastly complex even a simple cell actually is.

- Michael Denton, molecular biologist and evolutionist
    - Although the tiniest bacterial cells are incredibly small, weighing less than 10^{12} grams, each is in effect a veritable microminiaturized factory containing thousands of exquisitely designed pieces of intricate molecular machinery, made up altogether of one hundred thousand million atoms, far more complicated than any machinery built by man and absolutely without parallel in the nonliving world.
- Jeffrey Bada, geochemist from the San Diego Scripps Institute—"the evolutionists ongoing dilemma":
    - Today as we leave the twentieth century, we still face the biggest unsolved problem that we had when we entered the twentieth century. How did life originate on earth?
- In 2001, PBS airs "Evolution" series, in which they put together all the best information they could find to demonstrate the case for evolution.
    - *The Washington Post* online forum—producer Richard Hutton responded to the question, "What are some of the larger questions which are still unanswered by evolutionary theory?" Among his responses, he stated, "The origin of life. There is no consensus at all here—lots of theories, little science. That's one of the reasons we didn't cover it in the series. The evidence wasn't very good."
- "There is not a shred of evidence to support the hypothesis that life began in an organic soup here on this earth ... so why do biologists indulge in unsubstantiated fantasies in order to deny what is so patently obvious, that the 200,000 amino acid chains, and hence life, did not appear by chance?" (Frederick Hoyle).

On the origin of the universe, *The Evidence Bible* has this to say: "For thus says the Lord, Who created the heavens, Who is God, Who formed the earth and made it, Who has established it, Who did not create it in vain, Who formed it to be inhabited: "I **am** the Lord, and there is no other" (Isaiah 45:18).

"Old" thinking: eternal universe = eternal God

The beginning of the universe? = cause and effect (catalyst)

The big bang = "nothing" suddenly became time, space, matter, and energy, forming a vast, complex orderly universe composed of over 100 million galaxies and containing an estimated trillion, trillion, trillion, trillion tons of matter. Where did that matter come from? How could something come from out of nowhere by itself? What caused it to go bang? What was the catalyst that sent the particles flying?

- Andre Linde, cosmologist, professor of physics, Stanford University, stated, "The first, and main, problem is the very existence of the big bang. One may wonder, what came before? If space-time did not exist then, how could everything appear from nothing? What arose first? The universe or the Laws determining its evolution? Explaining this initial dust particles in space modern cosmology."
- Ciska Marwick-Kemper, University of Manchester, England, stated, "In the end, everything comes from space dust…dust that was belched from dying stars [about 8 billion light years from here]."
- Dr. Michael Barlow said, "Dust particles in space are the building blocks of comets, planets, and life, yet our knowledge of where the dust was made is still incomplete."
- First cause—the unavoidable question
    - Agrees with logic, reason, and scientific laws.
        - Something being created from nothing is contrary to all known science. Even Darwin admitted that logically the universe could not have created itself.
        - The impossibility of conceiving that this grand and wonderous universe, with our conscious selves, arose through chance seems to me the chief argument for the existence of God. I am

aware that if we admit a first cause, the mind still craves to know whence it came and how it arose.

- Stepen Hawking said, "The universe and the laws of physics seem to have been specifically designed for us. If any one of about 40 physical qualities had more than slightly different values, life as we know it could not exist. Either atoms would not be stable, or they wouldn't combine into molecules, or the stars wouldn't form the heavier elements, or the universe would collapse before life could collapse before life could develop, and so on."
- The evolutionary view cannot offer a logical, scientific explanation for either the origin of the complexity of the universe. There are only two choices: (1) no one created everything out of nothing or (2) someone—an intelligent, omnipotent, eternal first cause—created everything out of nothing.
- Sir Frederick Hoyle said, "A common sense interpretation of the facts suggests that a superintellect has monkeyed with physics, as well as with Chemistry and biology and that there are no blind forces worth speaking about in nature. The numbers one calculates from the facts seem to me so overwhelming as to put this conclusion almost beyond question."

God in His great goodness created a vast universe to express the width and breadth of His creativity, a gallery of the many facets of His image. The cosmic dust released by this big bang scattered throughout this newly created diversity. A shard of this dust, minute and unseen, struck Lucifer, the most beautiful of God's heavenly servants. Whether it is aimed at God Himself or randomly seeded is not revealed as yet. This foreign matter grew within the perfection of Lucifer and created a sense of free will beyond the desire to serve his Creator. As he began exploring this new train of thought, he realizes all creations seems to be made up of opposites—light and darkness, sky and earth, hot and cold. He is unable to establish a correlative opposite to His Creator, however, and comes to believe that the ultimate perfection of God the Father, Son, and Holy Spirit had no opposite. He came to desire that level of perfection and power, now marked by foreign matter. He began to question Creation, the nature of the Trinity, and his own origin and purpose. This new chaos of thought confused him. Eventually, he began to rationalize and intellectualize this new thought and formulated his own beliefs that separated him from servant to the Most High God to an individual of celestial origin that now understands that he could create his greatest desire—a kingdom of his own, a newborn planet called earth. He became the Prince of the Air, the Lord of Lies, and had loyal nobles who had followed him in the fall to act as his liege lords. Lucifer found his kingdom void of sentient life he could manipulate into worshipful subjects. The creatures he found were base in nature and uninterested in domination.

Lucifer discovered a little pocket of heaven within his vast (yet quite tiny) realm. Two new creatures, so like angels in form, yet so primitive in being, living, and thriving in a garden reflective of that God had designed in heaven. These creatures were alike but different—one male and one female; one born of the earth, the other born of the first, thus in lower position, with the firstborn as head. He observed these two as they went about their tasks as tenders of this garden. He watched enviously as they walked with the Most High as he had once walked. These creatures were weaker and much more fragile than their angelic brothers. He sought out their weaknesses. He had been ejected from the presence of God; he would see that these creatures were also separated from God. He felt as if God were trying to replace him as His second-in-command. No one, especially not these vessels of clay and flesh, would take his former place!

He found a way into the garden and waited where he could do the most harm, the Tree of the Knowledge of Good and Evil. If these creatures ate of the tree, they were told they would die. Only Lucifer knew they would not cease to exist. They were created as immortal as the angels themselves. Locked away in their bubble of heaven, they were incorruptible, if he could convince them that they had a choice to remain in ignorance, serving selflessly without understanding, or to know that they could choose to serve on their own terms—receiving the rewards they desire instead of blindingly accepting the morsels they were given from their Master's table. Using the very words of God, "Thou shalt not eat of the Tree of the Knowledge of Good and Evil lest you die," he added his own twist by explaining to the one called Eve that she wouldn't die. In fact, there was no such thing as death. Weren't all things eternal? Having no concept of death, the woman, in her lack of experience in the cessation of life, ate of the fruit. In that moment, a shadow of the fractal within Lucifer fell over her, clouding her eyes to what she had once known. Suddenly, her world wasn't as vivid; shadows appeared, and shades of gray created illusions of deception. Her world was not as clear as it once was. Her "eyes were opened" to the concept of free will that was already within her but previously focused only on the object of her greatest love—her Creator. Frightened, she went to her husband and tried to tell him how her perception had changed. Still being that pure creature he had been created to be, he could not understand. She offered him the fruit to eat as well. His eyes were also opened to this new sense of self in relation to all. They recognized their individuality as expressed as a united one in service to the Almighty. They had been of one heart and one mind in their service. All creation was for the service of God. There was no other, no species, no organic and inorganic, no separation of purpose. Now man saw that he truly had dominion over the things of the earth. He could experiment and develop different reactions by altering the use of plants, breaking down earth materials, and building them up again in new ways. Animals were no longer a gentle source of joy but could be slaughtered for food, and their skins preserved as a covering. They were in awe of all this new knowledge and eager to put new ideas to use. By doing so, they were becoming independent of the One who had provided their every need. They became more aware of their own capabilities and less dependent on God's providence and wisdom. They had, in effect, died to their previous perfection and were now corruptible flesh that would age and then cease to be, returning to the earth from whence they came.

Shame rose with this new knowledge. Their nakedness was not shameful in itself; it was their new understanding of individual mortality they had traded for the perfect relationship of Father and child they had previously experienced. The earth had given birth. From the Utopia of the Womb of Eden to the harsh realities of the other side of free will, these children of earth cried out at the separation from their Life Giver. They were now helpless, struggling to figure out how to survive in this new place. Their shame came from recognition that they had blatantly pulled away from a loving Parent to run out into the unsafe traffic of life without Him. They tried to hide their naked guilt but were found out. The sad but still loving Parent slew a harmless beast to not only cover the differences in their physical bodies but to mark them as having been born into a broken relationship with their Creator.

Lucifer rejoiced as he watched his new subjects struggle to repair this broken relationship. He actively plotted against them, to misinform them, to destroy their efforts to return to Eden. They were so very corruptible. When the first two sons of man came forth from their mother's womb, they, too, had to struggle to become individuals, separate from their parents and from each other. Having never known the relationship with the Creator Father their parents had once known, they could never please the One they were to make sacrifices to as their parents had taught them. Their attempts at reconciliation were feeble at best—Cain, who brought vegetables and fruit he had cultivated himself, and Abel, who had only a lamb from the flocks he tended to from boyhood. God saw these sacrifices and weighed them against His plan for real redemption to come. In the garden, herbs of the field were consumed by all creatures. It was God's provision. Cain had cultivated vegetation just as his parents had cultivated in the garden. Yes, he had planted and labored, but his labor required no sacrifice as it simply provided expected sustenance. Abel tended to the creatures of Eden. The sacrifice of Abel's labor came in the taking of the life of one of his flocks, not for the purpose of sustenance but for the consumption of a God he only knew through his parents' stories. This was acceptable to God as one life was exchanged for another, selflessly. A tiny speck of jealousy provided by cosmic dust blown at Abel by Lucifer's laughter at the rejection of vegetation, blotted the heart of Cain, marking him as being further separated from the one Who Loved Him Best. With whispers of suggestion, Cain rose up against his brother, taking Abel's life. Eating from the Tree of the Knowledge of Good and Evil had finally introduced true death to what was once immortal. Doubtlessly, Adam and Eve mourned for the loss of both their children, one whose life was taken from them and one whose life was tainted with the guilt of jealousy and murder. What Adam and Eve had done could not compare with what Cain had done. The parents were guilty of questioning their relationship with God. Cain had defied relationship with God by willingly separating his brother from life. He had not only questioned God but had defied Him and refused to accept consequences of his choice. Cain was forced to leave all he had ever known to enter a godless country, filled with Lucifer and his warlords, first subject to this fallen prince who would be king.

There lies the mark of Cain.

It is not a physical mark. It cannot be seen by the human eye.

The mark of Cain is defiance and denial—in the full knowledge of the divinity of God, the unpardonable sin, knowing God is real and choosing to be against Him in all things.

An atheist cannot claim to be unforgivable. How can you be held accountable for what you do not believe?

A satanist cannot claim to be unforgivable simply because he recognizes God and Satan and has chosen to be accountable to Satan rather than God in his time on earth.

Agnostics are not to claim the label of unforgivable because they aren't sure about the existence of a very real God. They are seekers.

Practitioners of religions outside the realm of monotheism cannot be said to be unforgivable because they see the universe in terms of earthly prophets or philosophers who explain how their gods can be reached and that we can become gods if we follow the precepts laid out for us.

All these things require a belief in what is understood from upbringing or experience. It can be called faith.

Faith is hope in things not seen.

Having faith one can retire a multimillionaire at age forty is contingent on far too many factors to be realistic, yet we all continue to dream.

Yet faith is required for hope to prevail.

No, the true unpardonable sin comes from the rejection of faith in a Creator whom one acknowledges to exist but chooses to defy and question until death steals their final breath.

What Lucifer began in Cain has been reinforced through countless generations of separation from the Edenic Father who expected nothing from His creations in turn but unconditional recognition of His love for them. Service and obedience come not through duty but in response to love.

Cain had neither love nor fear of God, though God spoke with him directly. Resentment, not hatred, separated Cain from salvation.

Cain went into exile in a strange land inhabited by giants, whose presence has never been identified to the satisfaction of scholars.

Could these have been fractals, attempting to create their own brand of the universe?

We are told that fallen angels, the "Sons of God," coupled with earthly women to create Nephilim, which are historically tolerated as hybrid monstrosities.

Could the fractal dust that inflicted Lucifer and his followers have evolved into these giants when they fell?

Only God knows.

It is only agreed upon that the city to which Cain went with his wife became a center of paganistic worship. These were the old gods of prehistory, present before Lucifer's fall, the true lords of this earth, with Lucifer in their thrall.

Lucifer, once good and perfect, now twisted and considered evil, works only to that end—anti-God. All things turned from their natural design to Satan's use.

Fractals are hell-bent on destroying creation and returning it to the void from which it was created, their place of safety.

Lucifer has been given the tools of destruction to use against the forces of light. He works in the darkness and is darker than dark, but he still fears a pinprick of the light from which he was created.

Fractals are absolute darkness. Where God is light and life, they are darkness and death, though they may become sentient and masterful in their methods of destruction, they may also be mindless and simply hungry, consuming everything in their path.

Modern science has identified universe-consuming vacuous voids they have called black holes. These phenomena appear to have a gravitational pull that overwhelms all matter in their path, drawing it into its vast maw to an unknown destiny. The matter is believed to be destroyed and/or consumed by the black holes and to no longer exist in their original forms.

That which does not create destroys. Opposites: creator and destroyer, with only a middleman to tip the scales as mankind allows.

If Satan is not true evil, then what of hell?

Scriptures tell us that hell has been created as a prison for the devil and his angels when their reign upon earth is complete. They will be imprisoned for eternity at that time. They lived in light for a portion of eternity, dwelt in the shadows of earth as rulers of mankind for the blink of an eye and will spend the remainder of eternity being punished for their disobedience.

Obedience is a choice.

Disobedience is a choice.

Lucifer is simply the catalyst to present the options available, with a heavily biased emphasis on the immediate rewards of disobedience and downplaying the rewards and eternal peace of obedience.

He is a liar, a deceiver, a twister of truth.

He is also only a shadow of the true evil of a fractal; fractals want to undo Creation itself.

Lucifer discovered free will and exploits it. Humanity can be redeemed if it chooses. If redemption is offered and rejected, true evil draws the individual into an eternity of destruction. Even Lucifer will scream in torment beside them.

Following Cain to demonstrate theoretical connections to fractal, we discover the city where he dwelt to be much further advanced than the primitive agriculture-based community of his parents.

How can this be? A technologically advanced and organized city parallel to what would otherwise be classified as a Stone Age settlement comprised of one man and his wife?

Here is where the old gods and fractal theory converge with traditional Judeo-Christian tradition.

Cain himself is great-great-grandfather to two men of note historically and scripturally.

Jubal (from whose name the word *jubilee* is derived) was given knowledge of musical development and design of instruments to produce that music. A natural gift to be bestowed if sacred mathematics is the true language of the universe and music is its expression.

Our bodies are designed to respond to rhythm. Our heartbeat, for example—it is a regular lubb-dupp unless there is some cause for interference that causes it to accelerate, decelerate, or become irregular (atrial fibrillation or a-fib). When accelerated, we can influence it to return to a normal rhythm by exposing it to other rhythms that are both soothing and provide a rhythmic pattern more in keeping with the normal pace of the body. The purring of a cat produces such a rhythm. Watching a sleeping baby produces a more relaxed heart rate. Petting a dog provides a rhythmic pattern that allows our heart rate to calm down. Classical music uses notational mathematics to mimic a relaxed heart rate and produces a calmer nature in listeners.

None of this is an accident.

Though Cain was cursed, Jubal was blessed with knowledge of the heartbeat of the universe. Through this knowledge of God's goodness in creation, we learned to worship our Creator in His own language.

Cain's other great-great-grandson, Tubal-Cain, was given the gift of understanding the raw materials of the earth itself. Through this gift, mankind was instructed in the higher knowledge of Creation known as metallurgy. Tubal-Cain could refine metals and blend them together to create tools and weapons. These tools allowed mankind to explore the gifts of engineering and the progress toward modern advancement began.

Simultaneously, we had a Stone Age community consisting of Adam, Eve, and the children born to them after the death of Abel and the exile of Cain. Those individuals developed their own civilization at a much slower pace but eventually converged with the more developed city dwellers.

Sentient fractals could have used their knowledge of the structure of the cosmos, from whence they came, to attempt to reconstruct their own culture from that memory, with the limited resources of earth.

Following this line of thought, prehistoric, highly advanced civilizations could have existed at the fall of mankind and the expulsion from Eden.

Adam and Eve were likely ignorant of these neighbors. God intentionally left them in a position where they had to discover how to use their limited resources themselves. They would only accomplish what they could do on their own under God's guidance. Unless they reconnected to God in full trust, they would be required to struggle in their labors, under His loving watch.

They truly had the knowledge of good and evil. They had experienced both sides of that coin. Their new task was to create a world in which knowledge would be used for the good of God's kingdom. Trial and error would determine good and bad results. The morality of these decisions became blurred when progress forced early man to determine whether an idea was beneficial to humanity (on the surface) or to the development of God's kingdom of humanity on earth. Being fallen, with finicky free wills, and dark whispers from Satan and his minions, self-satisfaction overcame God-satisfaction, and mankind became competitive intellectually, replacing reason for truth and faith and trust in the Provider.

The Tower of Babel is an example of this higher technology and its influence on the selfishness of mankind. The tower was built in an effort to reach God. Was their purpose to attempt a takeover (no doubt influenced by Lucifer) or an attempt to become gods (as influenced by fractals)?

If cosmic fractals were behind it, no doubt it was the latter. By attempting to become gods at the urgings of those they worshipped as gods, the human interloper would either self-destruct or be destroyed by the God who created them, leaving them to redevelop their own vacuous kingdom apart from the rest of creation. Examining the possible style of this tower, in comparison with the architectural ruins of later civilizations in that area, there is a definite symmetrical pattern that is reflective of the mathematical fractal and convincingly kaleidoscopic if viewed from an aerial position. Archaeology has discovered these symmetrical patterns used consistently in cultures around the world—the labyrinth of Crete, swastika-like crosses and patterns, swirls, acorn shapes, and textured roofs. Even the layout of ancient cities all reflect an artistic symmetry exhibiting a form of sacred geometry. They had no computers to create the algorithms or artwork from which they found inspiration. Inspiration came from nature itself but required an understanding that is found by very few in our modern world. We all see it and appreciate it on some level but walk away without understanding as to how it was produced, simply referring to its creator as a genius.

God had other ideas. He separated the people by endowing them with languages that would bring together those who could understand one another and separate them from those who could not understand them. They were to scatter across the planet and populate it accordingly.

Interference by darker forces encouraged persistence in these groups and managed to keep them separated from God, no doubt blaming the Creator for their predicament.

Though it is believed that the Nephilim and other bothersome characters were destroyed in the flood that gave rise to the three "races" known to humanity, fractals as the old gods continued to be an influence on humanity, rising as the false gods of the Old Testament narrative. It is God's attempt at guiding humanity to destroy all contact with these fractals and their worship that gives rise to the "evil" God of the Old Testament that frequently called for the genocide of entire populations. God has never been and never will be evil. He is goodness. In his love for His creation, He raised up a people for Himself and provided them with a homeland that would allow for them to return to a form of worship with God as Provider and all other influences eliminated, or at least curtailed, from influencing the people back to a form of rebellious rejection of God that would sever them from the presence of God for eternity.

If we do not remove ourselves from the influence of evil, we will be led by temptation into its gaping maw to never be redeemed. God's efforts to teach us this lesson is chronicled in the Old Testament. The response of those cultures around the chosen people of God reflects the continued influence of the fractal old gods as chronicled by the Egyptians, Chinese, East Indian, and Central and South American cultures through their god-kings.

After the Exodus from Egypt, Moses received laws and commandments that were to separate the Hebrew people from the pagan cultures around them. Some of these cultures had methods of worship and sacrifice that were in direct opposition to or were a perverse twisting of God's expectations. These were dangerous cults for these new God worshippers. They were already ancient in comparison to this new monotheism of One God as Creator. That is why the purity of this new "race" was essential. They were an opportunity to develop the form of relationship with their God as was intended in the Garden of Eden, prior to the fall that introduced fractals to humanity.

Lucifer is mentioned nowhere else in the Pentateuch after the temptation in Eden. These old gods are the focus of man's downfall. He then makes a cameo appearance in Job and described in literary terms in the remainder of the Old Testament. He is in the back seat. He is not the driving force of the Old Testament conflict. That does not occur until he becomes the poster child for evil at the temptation of Christ in the New Testament.

The Baals of the Old Testament, Asherah, and Moloch cults predominated. The earlier civilizations developed by these cosmic fractals were washed away and buried during the flood. The fractals remained, however, and redeveloped their worship while God was busy developing His troops.

Cycles of obedience followed by disobedience spiral throughout the Old Testament, culminating in the final fall of Jerusalem to captivity in Babylon, a pagan culture. Only Daniel and his three companions had the stamina to stand up to these old ones and promote the truth of a Creator God.

This was the beginning of the end of popular pagan worship. Paganism took on new forms as social changes toward monotheism began—witchcraft, shamanism, divination, occult practices—and shifted from the old gods to the polytheistic cultures in which multiple gods were worshipped in a related pantheon, with regional "favorites" dependent upon industrial focus or social function of the communities. This is when we begin to see the rise of satanic forces and demons as primary forces of evil, as demonstrated by the references to demons and their influences in the New Testament. The fractals backed down and sent in their ace in the hole, Lucifer, to deceive and draw people away from the worship of the Messiah, the part of the Godhead known as the Son.

Christianity began to first overcome Judaism by connecting the Old Testament and its prophecies to a man who was proclaimed to be the Son of God incarnate, the Messiah Jesus Christ. God Himself come to oversee Creation and offer reconciliation and redemption to a relationship heretofore only experienced by Adam and Eve.

After the ascension of Jesus, His apostles were given the task of creating a new army against evil by proclaiming a redemptive salvation with God through the sacrifice and blood of Jesus Christ. Paul even presents an "armor" of beliefs and behaviors a Christian is to don daily. Spiritual warfare became the language of Christian households.

The old gods had been effectively "put down" and lay in wait in stony graves for their opportunity to be resurrected into the power they claim.

Satan, being a spiritual being, moved from catalyst to prime suspect in the disobedience of mankind. Demons gained powers over humanity to influence, harm, and kill them as they chose. Jesus commanded them to depart from the inflicted, and they had to obey One greater than themselves.

Pagan cults continued to exist but were considered extreme forms of witchcraft and satanism, though Satan was never directly connected with any of them.

The Roman Empire, in its effort to bring their version of Christianity to the world by force, encountered druids and other pagan groups that believed in magic acquired from their gods and had beliefs in creatures of spirit and magic they could call upon to torment this new enemy. These beliefs came down through the Middle Ages and were recorded with the coming of the printing press as fairy tales that were terrifying warnings against the things not of God. They were retold with variation until we find ourselves with the sugarcoated Disney stories popular with kids today. The rise of fantasy as a literary genre began as an attempt at recreating the Dark Ages world of paganism and Christianity at war.

Fantasy of a dark nature gave rise to the modern gothic and horror genres.

A renewed interest in the things of darkness sheds light on the Reformation era of the church as it split from corrupted Catholicism.

The Salem witch trials are an example of the type of hysteria that arises from spiritual and scriptural ignorance and illiteracy.

A narrow-minded, hypercritical religious system gave way to enlightenment as academia and the advancement of educational opportunities came to all people and not just certain chosen individuals.

Westward expansion in what is now the United States of America not only allowed for expansion of population but allowed for isolated communities to settle away from the paths being taken by those who wished to go farther west.

Case in point are the Appalachian Mountain communities of primarily Scotts-Irish-German immigrants. Lutheranism and Methodism was carried in by Germanic traditions. Scotts and Irish carried in forms of Catholicism that grew up with the British occupation of their isolated island locales and forbade all old ways and languages. Protestantism was beginning to arise and compete with the Catholicism of England as well, bringing in the influences of escaping Anabaptists. These influences gave rise to the faith practices found in these regions today.

The isolation of communities, lack of leadership for consistent church development due to strict regulations imposed by early colonial governments, and widespread prejudices regarding Catholicism united these peoples and led to the development of new denominations such as the Old Regular and Enterprise Baptists, which became fully organized in the late nineteenth and early twentieth centuries. Itinerant ministers were appointed to ride a general circuit of communities that allowed for a single, organized minister-led church service once a month, which generally lasted all day, with a dinner served around midday.

These groups combined doctrines most could agree on with traditions from their countries of origin to create a generally eclectic belief system that can still be seen in Appalachian communities today. They can range from modern buildings with musical instruments and syncopated rhythms to very primitive settings that depend on snake-handling as a means of demonstrating their faith. The majority still in operation of these denominational headings have modernized. There are some that continue to have gender separation in the sanctuary, no form of Sunday school, distinct gender roles and duties within the church, and multiple preachers who are allowed to speak simply because they attended church that day. Every preacher who comes is given opportunity to speak. Variations in interpretation are often "called out" by subsequent preachers. Attending one of these older order services can be entertaining for those who study doctrinal differences or want to understand a community better. As a child, I always enjoyed observing the service and doing comparative analysis of the more organized church our family attended on a regular basis. The food was an incentive to sit through the long services in an unairconditioned building with electricity but no indoor plumbing.

Their basic doctrines have not, however, evolved and demonstrate almost closed-community settings, not practicing evangelism, limiting educational opportunities for youth (Sunday school, vacation Bible school, youth groups, etc.), establishing strict guidelines for members, dress, and behavior that are not much beyond Puritanism.

At the other end of the spectrum are the liberal churches that teach such doctrine as all are already saved because Jesus died for all, homosexuality is acceptable, tolerance of all regardless of morality, and religious beliefs that may be perceived as being contradictory to Christian scripture.

In between these Christian examples are a wide range of denominations, each with their own interpretation and expectations for church membership. Some are classified as fully cultic, cultlike, ultraconservative, moderate, or liberal as identifiers. There are churches that identify as Democrat or Republican, believe in female leadership or confine women to learning only from men, and leadership is limited to certain groups of individuals only or open to all comers.

Ritualism, pagan-like worship rites and techniques, idolatry, and questionable morality of leadership can be claimed as criticisms across these denominations and independent factions.

No single church is perfect as man-led leadership tends to overshadow God-led leadership. Certain individuals and family groups tend to dominate the church decision-making process, and man-determined interpretations and limitations tend to be imposed on the congregations. Members of the congregation are guilty of allowing the church to operate under these conditions as they do not want to make ripples or take on these responsibilities for themselves.

What the New Testament laid out as God's church, the people and their obedience, was organized into a church (building) that established itself as a form of earthly government, complete with a judicial system.

History repeats itself when we fail to use knowledge for the good of God's kingdom and allow evil knowledge to overrule us in our fragile faith in a benevolent God, Father, Creator, Savior.

We are currently cycling back into social paganism where all is acceptable as long as "I" approve. There is no black or white, right or wrong; truth is relative.

As Revelation is being unveiled to our world, the fractals are preparing to burst from their stone prisons, and cosmic destruction of our planet will begin.

Perhaps those who follow us will learn from our archives and create God's kingdom here on earth, trapping the fractals in eternal prison bars.

May all that is deceptive and evil be dispersed by the light of truth at the center of thc universal creation, single or multidimensional it may be.

Appendix C

Books for the Curious

Alighiere, Dante. *The Divine Comedy.* London, United Kingdom: Penguin Press, 2014.

Arthur, Kay. *Lord, Is It Warfare? Teach Me to Stand.* Waterbrook, 2000.

Baldwin, Juanitta, and Grubb, Ester. *Unsolved Disappearances in the Great Smoky Mountains: True Mysteries of Persons Who Vanished Without a Trace, and Other Disappearances.* Kodak, Tennessee: Suntop Press, 2009.

Baxter, Mary K. *A Divine Revelation of Hell.* New Kensington, Pennsylvania: Whitaker House, 1993.

Beach, Joseph Charles. *Worldview of the Christian Faith: Standing for God's Truth.* Bloomington, Indiana, Westbow Press, 2022.

Bouma, J. A. Group X Series: *Not of This World* (2022); *The Darkest Valley* (2022), and the Order of Thaddaeus Series, *Holy Shroud (2018).* Emmaeus Way Press.

Bullinger, E. W. *Number in Scripture: It's Supernatural Design and Spiritual Significance.* Scotts Valley, California: CreateSpace Independent Publishing Platform, 2014.

Bunyan, John. *The Pilgrim's Progress; Christiana's Journey; The Life and Death of Mr. Badman.* Brown Chair Books, 2023. [Note: *The Life and Death of Mr. Badman* is the original title of the newer release *Journey to Hell.*]

Church, Philip Kent. *Appalachian Lore: Haints, Hexes, Hoo-Doos and Such.* Blacksburg, Virginia: Spirit Hollow Publishing, 2016.

Cook, William F., III, and Lawless, Chuck. *Spiritual Warfare in the Storyline of Scripture.* Nashville, Tennessee: B & H Academic, 2019.

Glaze, Bryan H. *A Message from Hell to You from the Fire of Hell Past Redemption Point.*

Heiser, Michael S. *Angels: What the Bible Really Says about God's Heavenly Host*. Bellingham, Washington: Lexham Press, 2018.

Heiser, Michael S. *Demons: What the Bible Really Says about the Powers of Darkness*. Bellingham, Washington: Lexham Press, 2020.

Heiser, Michael S. *The Unseen Realm: Recovering the Supernatural Worldview of the Bible*. Bellingham, Washington: Lexham Press, 2015.

Hoag, Zach. *The Light Is Winning: Why Religion Just Might Bring Us Back to Life.* Grand Rapids, Michigan: Zondervan, 2017.

Horton, David. *The Portable Seminary.* Bloomington, Minnesotta: Bethany House, 2006.

Jackson, Shirley. *The Haunting of Hill House.* London, United Kingdom: Penguin Classics, 2006.

James, Aiden. The Cades Cove Series: *The Curse of Allie Mae (2010); Raven Mocker (2010); Devil Mountain (2015); The Obsidian Curse (2021).* CreateSpace Independent Publishing Platform.

Jeffries, Robert. *Invincible.* Grand Rapids, Michigan: Baker Books, 2021.

Lewis, C. S. *The Chronicles of Narnia.*

Little, Bentley. *The Burning.* Cemetery Dance Publications, 2017.

Lovecraft, H. P. *The Call of Cthulhu and Other Weird Stories.* New York, New York: Penguin, 1999.

McDowell, Josh, and McDowell, Sean. *Evidence That Demands a Verdict: Life-Changing Truth for a Skeptical World.* Nashville, Tennessee: Thomas Nelson, 2017.

Meechan, Patrick. *Nightmare in Holmes County.* Beyond the Fray Publishing, 2021.

Milligan, Ira. *Understanding the Dreams You Dream.* Shippensburg, Pennsylvania: Destiny Image Printers Inc., 1997.

Mooney, James. *Myths of the Cherokee.* Mineola, New York: Dover Publishing, 1996.

Morris, Henry. *The Biblical Basis for Modern Science.* Green Forest, Arizona: Master Books, 2020.

Rubart, James L. The Well Spring Trilogy: *Soul's Gate* (2012), *Memory's Door (2013), Spirit Bridge* (2014). Nashville, Tennessee: Thomas Nelson.

———. *Book of Days.* 2011.

———. *The Five Times I Met Myself.* 2015.

Russell, Randy, and Barnett, Janet. *The Granny Curse and Other and Legends from East Tennessee.* Winston-Salem, North Carolina: John F. Blair, 2006.

Savage, Robert C. *Pocket Wisdom.* Minneapolis, Minnesota: Tyndale House, 1984.

Schwartz, Howard. *Tree of Souls: The Mythology of Judaism.* Oxford, New York: Oxford University Press, 2004.

Shaver, Jim. The Evans Grove Series, *Exit Wonderland* (2020), *Darkside of the Looking Glass* (2021), *Chasing White Rabbits* (2021), *Rise of the Red Queen* (2022), *The Legacy of the Mad Hatter* (2023).

Snyder, James L. "*The Quotable Tozer.*" Bloomington, Minnesota: Bethany House, 2018.

Stanley, Charles F. *When the Enemy Strikes.* Nashville, Tennessee: Nelson Books, 2004.

Stuart, Jesse. *Daughter of the Legend.* Ashland, Kentucky: Jesse Stuart Foundation, 1994

Szumsky, Benjamin. *Fantasy, Horror and the Truth: A Christian Insider's Story.* Aneko Press, 2021.

Tongs, Taichuan. *Numbers and Roots of Numbers in the Bible.* Scotts Valley, California: CreateSpace Independent Publishing Platform, 2013.

Van Dorn, Douglas. *The Unseen Realm: Q and A Companion.* Bellingham, Washington: Lexham Press, 2016.

Warren, Ed and Lorraine. *Ghost Hunters.* Graymalkin Media, 2014.

Wellman, Manly Wade.

Silver John Collection:

Who Fears the Devil? (1963, Arkham Press)
John the Balladeer (1988)
Owls hoot in the daytime and other Omens (2003, Nightshade Press)
The Old Gods Waken (1984)
After Dark (1980)
The Lost and the Lurking (1981)
The Hanging Stones (1982)
The Voice of the Mountain (1984)

John Thunstone Collection:

Lonely Vigils (1981)
What Dreams May Come (1983)
The School of Darkness (1985)
The Complete John Thunstone (2012)

Wiese, Bill. *23 Minutes in Hell.* Lake Mary, Florida: Charisma House, 2017.

Wilson, Neil, and Taylor, Nancy Ryken. *The A to Z Guide to Bible Signs and Symbols: Their Meaning and Significance.* Grand Rapids, Michigan: Baker Books, 2015.

Bibles Used as References

The Jeremiah Study Bible. Commentary and notes by Dr. David Jeremiah, NKJV.

Life Application Study Bible. Zondervan Publishing.

Cultural Background Bible. Zondervan Publishing.

Complete Jewish Bible. David H. Stem. Messianic Jewish Publishers, 2017.

The Evidence Bible. Ray Comfort. Bridge-Logos Publishing, Newberry, Florida.

Appendix D

Websites of Interest

Cave Art

https://tennesseeencyclopedia.net

Simek, Jan F. "Prehistoric Cave Art." *Tennessee Encyclopedia*. June 13, 2013. www.cnn.com.

Smith, Matt. "Ancient Tennessee Cave Paintings Show Deep Thinking by Natives." CNN. June 23, 2013. www.bradshaw-foundation.com.

"Cumberland Plateau Rock Art Provides Insights into Native American Societies." June 14, 2013.

Indian Head Rock. https://www.en.wikipedia.org.

Judaculla Rock. www.Appalachianhistory.net.

Dreams and Dream Interpretation

www.dreamingandsleeping.com

www.alodroeams.com

Lucid Dreams

https://www.en.wikiperdia.org

Elementals

https://www.en.wikipedia.org

Hierarchy of Demons

www.hierarchystructure.com

Ley Lines

www.livescience.com
www.learnreligions.com

New Madrid Seismic Zone

https://www.en.wikipedia.org

Pleiades and Orion in the Bible

www.biblescienceforum.com
www.creationscience4kids.com

Seven Deadly Sins

www.learnreligions.com

Witchcraft

www.thegypsythread.org

Witchcraft in the Bible

www.Biblestudytools.com

Appendix E

Articles to Consider

"Ancient Gods: Exposing the Old Testament." www.amonrasit.wordpress.com.

Associated Press. "Spacewalking Astronaut Loses Mirror, Newest Space Junk." June 26, 2020.

Bohlin, Sue. "What's a Biblical Definition of Witchcraft?" Probe Ministries, May 27, 2005. www.probe.org.

"Can an Object Become Haunted?" Living Life in Full Spectrum. November 6, 2017. www.llifs.com.

Cursi, Art Li. "The Process of Temptation," Part 2 of 10, Casting Down Imaginations Series. www.artlicursi.com.

"Demons in the Bible: Different Types and How They Attack." www.biblesprout.com.

"Familiar Spirits *Can* and *Do* Plague Christians." www.shoutingfromtherooftop.com.

Hunnemann, Reverend Mark A. "Christianity versus Paganism." December 7, 2017. www.eyeontheparanormal.blogspot.com.

Hunnemann, Reverend Mark A. "12 Points Regarding the True Identity of Ghosts." www.spiritualrealities.org.

Imes, Carmen Joy. "Eve: The Mother of the Living." *Christianity Today.* May/June 2023. 34–39.

LeClaire, Jennifer. "Why Are So Many Christians Practicing Witchcraft?" August 27, 2013. www.charismanews.com.

"Mountain Mysteries: Appalachian Creatures." www.appalachianmyhtology.worldpress.com.

"Mysteries of Dudleytown, Abandoned Town in Connecticut." www.anomalien.com.
"Mystery of the Moon-Eyed People." www.creeksidemusings.com.
"Pookas: Digging into the Secrets of This Mischievous Irish Mythical Creature." December 12, 2022, updated. www.connollycove.com.
Purdy, Alicia. "Get Back, Satan! 5 Tips for Using Scripture as Defense." August 8, 2019. www.crosswalk.com.
Rice, Jacob. "Haunted Objects and How to Break Attachments." January 9, 2014. www.ghostlyactivities.com.
Riolanno, Victoria. "6 Things Satan Wants More Than Anything Else." May 13, 2022. www.crosswalk.com.
Serena. "Puca [Pooka] in Irish Folklore." December 9, 2022, updated. www.YourIrish.com.
Swancer, Brent. "A Haunted Mountain in Appalachia." April 11, 2019. www.mysteriousuniverse.org.
Swancer, Brent. "Paranormal Encounters Along the Appalachian Trail." January 15, 2019. www.mysteriousuniverse.org.
Swancer, Brent. "Strange Mysteries of the Appalachian Mountains." June 5, 2015. www.mysteriousuniverse.org.
"The Nephilim Giants." www.israel-a-history-of.com.
"What Does the Bible Say about Lust?" www.gotquestions.org.
"What Does the Bible Say about Witchcraft/Witches?" www.gotquestions.org.
"What Is Paranoia?" www.healthline.com.
Wilson, Larry W. "Demonic Possession: How Demons Take Control" Part 2. Wake Up America Seminars, August 2017 (updated August 3, 2018). www.wake-up.org.
Zavada, Jack. "Major False Gods of the Old Testament." www.learnreligions.com.

About the Author

Since the first story she wrote at age six, Kim has wanted to share her stories with the world. She has perused both fiction and nonfiction to develop a flow of writing that utilizes both in an entertaining and informative manner that captures her audience and takes them through thought-provoking discussions that connect our reality with our chosen fictional perspectives. Her passion for folklore and things of the supernatural come honestly through her heritage deep in the Appalachians of Eastern Kentucky and go back to her roots in Western Europe. Her faith in Jesus Christ also comes from her rich heritage and has challenged her to explore the supernatural aspects of Christianity as it applies to our modern world.

Printed in the USA
CPSIA information can be obtained
at www.ICGtesting.com
CBHW031555300724
12433CB00001B/12